# HARTISBORNE

Stephanie Norgate

Copyright © 2025 Stephanie Norgate

All rights reserved

The right of Stephanie Norgate to be identified as author of this work has been asserted in accordance with Section 77 of the Copyright, Designs and Patents Act 1988.

This book is a work of fiction. Any references to historical events, real people, or real places are used fictitiously. Other names, characters, places, and events are products of the author's imagination, and any resemblances to actual events for places or persons, living or dead, is entirely coincidental.

You may not copy, store, distribute, transmit, reproduce or otherwise make available this
publication (or any part of it) in any form, or by any means (electronic, digital, optical,
mechanical, photocopying, recording or otherwise) including, but not limited to, for the purposes of training generative AI technologies.

Cover Design: Giorgia Chiarion ©
Swallows by NatashaKun ©
Background image by explorich ©

ISBN 9798 830 8206842

# CONTENTS

Title Page
Copyright
Dedication
Epigraph
Chapter 1 — 1
Chapter 2 — 18
Chapter 3 — 46
Chapter 4 — 67
Chapter 5 — 90
Chapter 6 — 108
Chapter 7 — 132
Chapter 8 — 164
Chapter 9 — 187
Chapter 10 — 204
Chapter 11 — 226
Chapter 12 — 244
Chapter 13 — 259
Chapter 14 — 271
Chapter 15 — 292

| | |
|---|---|
| Chapter 16 | 311 |
| Chapter 17 | 324 |
| Chapter 18 | 336 |
| Chapter 19 | 348 |
| Chapter 20 | 359 |
| Chapter 21 | 372 |
| Chapter 22 | 380 |
| Acknowledgements | 393 |
| About The Author | 397 |

*in memory of my grandmothers,
Hilda and Norah*

*Sweet is the splendor of the morning sun;*
*And sweet to see the gently heaving main;*
*Sweet is the vernal face of hill or dale;*
*And sweet th'effect of fertilizing stream:*
*But far more cheering, far more lovely scene*
*Is to the childless man, wrung with desire,*
*The sight of new-born children in his house.*

FROM THE DANAE OF EURIPIDES,
TRANSLATED BY GILBERT WHITE
(1720-1793)

# CHAPTER 1

*A figure in the lane, as if my longing had taken shape. At other times, in the street, in the garden, the seat by the wall? Was it a phantasy? Or my longing?* Then, nothing more.

In David's experience, the naturalist wrote clearly in straight lines and was thrifty with paper, but he has scrawled these words across the page, wasting expensive space, leaving his thought unfinished. The word *longing* is uncharacteristic too. In the naturalist's journals, a brief precision is more the style: *Set two hundred cucumber seeds under glass. Rooks mighty loud at dusk. Miss Butter came at seven. We ate a pair of grouse with three carrots apiece.*

Maybe historical discoveries are simply scraps caught behind drawers. Centuries later, someone finds them. And on this day of ice and freezing fog, when he can barely move his fingers and his body is swathed in as many layers as an Egyptian mummy, the finder is David, the naturalist's would-be biographer.

Attempting to be scholarly, David writes 'Found 3rd January 1963, stuck behind bottom drawer of G's desk' on a yellowing index card, which he attaches to the precious scrap with a paper clip.

Two hundred years ago, in the eighteenth century, Wakeling House was Gil's beloved home. No doubt, Gil would have laughed if anyone from the nineteen sixties had informed him his house would become a museum or that a muddler like David would be appointed to curate his legacy and would meddle with the study in which Gil wrote the world-famous *Natural History of Hartisborne*.

*Longing* suggests an affection beyond birds and bees. Gil's passionate style flares only when he writes about a great crested newt or a swallow, but this mysterious scrawl is written with emotion, love or even lust. David's unwritten book flies into his mind, its dust jacket floating with puffs about a fascinating discovery. He fantasises a review which begins, 'David Daunt's remarkable biography gives startling insights into the enigmatic curate and eighteenth-century natural history writer, now known as the father of ecology.'

Leaning on the hallowed desk, David returns to his list of missing evidence and the chapter plan which always stalls him, a ladder descending to nowhere. But here is something new to energise his progress. The ice cracks and melts. His book flows through his mind, as he reads and rereads this uncatalogued note suggesting Gil's wilder side. He can almost hear the story running on, without obstacles like a stream of clear water.

Optimism flickers once more like a candle flame in a power cut, until the pipes above the ceiling burst, water drips into the study, and all David can think of is racing downstairs with drawerfuls of documents to save them from the deluge. He fears losing this job which his former tutor at Oxford organised for him. The fabric of the building and its artefacts are his responsibility, and he'd bluffed the questions about upkeep at his interview. He fears being revealed as the total ninny his stepfather always says he is, and yet through it all, the scrawled note comforts him, a sign that Gil has chosen David to uncover his secret passion. 'Thank you,' he murmurs as the light flicks on again.

Gil's niece and nephew want a last whirl in the barrel. They want the meadows, woods and ha-ha to circle them dizzily, saying 'stay, stay.' Gil understands why the children are crying, as his sister-in-law drags them away.

Years ago, whenever it was time to travel to school and later to Oxford, Gil had felt that same reluctance to leave. He would climb the meadow's mound and step through the doorless arch of the upright barrel. Sitting inside, he'd grab the stick poking through the coopered timber and push it against the ground, until the barrel's narrow merry-go-round revolved on its under-wheel of its own volition.

Yellowing trees swooped across his vision. Fields spun around him. Sometimes it seemed the village moved while the barrel remained still. Wood pigeons cooed, 'don't go, don't go'. Grasses whispered village gossip, enticing him to stay. When time was running out, he dragged the stick groundward, braking, until the barrel slowed, then stopped, allowing his giddy release.

He understands the children's fear that Hartisborne will vanish in their absence. When he was younger, he too prayed the village would still be here when he returned. For how could it exist without him?

When he waves them off in the chaise, little Fanny and little Ben weep so heartily that he weeps too. He is glad to be an uncle. Yet even in Hartisborne, years pass. People age. Is he never to be married? Never to be a father himself?

Last week, a young lady visiting from London, squealed with delight when he brushed her hair till it crackled with static. She screamed with happiness when he weighed her, taking her turn after the tortoise who, for his part, exhibited no reptilian excitement whatsoever. She raced the children up the newly cut zigzag path to the marquee, exultant to reach the hanger's summit before the other guests. How ever many witty questions she posed for the hermit to answer, however loudly she shrieked with laughter when the hermit was revealed as Gil's brother in a false beard, and however tunefully she played the harpsichord lit by candles that cast her with their glamour, he knows in his heart that she will not, cannot fit.

Her ecstasies were bountiful, perhaps a little tiring. She has already sent him a poem on 'pastoral lovers of the happy vale', a hint that she could be tempted, but Gil will never be so unkind as to make an offer of marriage. How could such an enthusiast for drawing rooms, balls and soirées, such a lover of the world's business - and its choicest muslins - ever live here in the bosky shade, her escape from Hartisborne blocked by erupting springs, falling flints or the deepest snow? The ease of summer over, her nature could not survive the tenancy of this quietness. And Hartisborne must not be allowed to extinguish her flame.

The harpsichord, where her dancing fingers played so sonorously, is silent. The toy swords, false beards, fancy caps, whistles and wooden birds rest again in their chest. *I have put away childish things*, he thinks sadly. I know the village cannot swing around or fly into the heavens. Only people leave, while Hartisborne stays. And I stay too.

He should have reassured the children, should have told them that Hartisborne is the parish of everyone's soul, and, once found, it can never be lost.

Now all is silent, but for the birds conversing before their evening roost. The empty house should be welcome, a blessing on his work. He must brush the children's chatter from the walls. All through their visit, he fretted about his writing. His fingers itched to take up the pen, but, in this new emptiness, he longs to hear their voices again.

Eventually, Gil takes his candle upstairs to his study. He will settle to his observations and make something of this quiet evening. A *Natural History* will not write itself. He sharpens his pen and then dips it in ink.

Outside, a couple of owls call to one another through the night air. A leveret screams. The owlets will eat well tonight when a parent returns to the nest with prey. He notes the sounds in his journal and then goes to his lonely bed.


Georgie leaves for work early to avoid breakfast with Uncle Trevor. Evenings with him exhaust her. During power cuts, her uncle controls the camping Gaz light and the candles. Georgie fears the dark and must choose between spending time with him or braving her bedroom alone without even the streetlight leaking through the curtain. Last night, Trevor harangued her for two long hours until she pleaded for an early night, because Marco wanted her at the shop at seven, though there was little urgency in the book trade especially during this cold weather. Marco probably wouldn't be in till eleven. Still, Uncle Trevor swallowed it. And now she's leaving the house at six, relieved not to share a bad-tempered breakfast. She closes the door quietly and climbs carefully down the icy steps.

Lights glimmer from early windows. A postman shines his torch for her. The sniff of coal dust and ice in her nose is comforting. Even the dangerous pavement is her friend.

She slithers her way from Bermondsey to the Charing Cross Road. Outside Bracco & March, she retrieves her thermos from her bag, unscrews the lid and tips hot water carefully into the lock to melt the ice. With a little rattling and more hot water, the lock gives way to the key. The safe part of the day can begin.

Georgie lights the paraffin stove. Then, she hurries down to the basement to boil the kettle while the electricity still works. She tops up the thermos. Even if the power is out, she'll be able to make a hot drink for Marco later. She slips on Marco's fur coat. He rescued it from a house clearance. Because of the *big freeze* as they call it on the news, he leaves the coat on the hook for general use. The coat stinks. The fur is matted, but yesterday, Marco draped the coat round her, worried that she was cold.

The bookshop should be a refuge, but even here with the promise of seeing Marco and the soothing task of pricing tattered paperbacks, Uncle Trevor's crude tones hammer in her head. *Antiquarian? - second-hand tat not worth wiping your arse on - posh bit Celia bloody March - underwriting that greasy yob - sod that for a game of soldiers - Bracco and sodding March - fancy getting tucked up with the likes of them - effing Eye-tie - fought them in the war, thought numb, thought numb.*

In Trevor's bitter voice, *effing* sounds far worse than the word he avoids in deference, she supposes, to her womanhood. Just say it, she wants to yell at him. You might as well. She doesn't know why she hears 'thought numb' when Trevor says, 'fought them'. Her head scrambles his talk. As water wears away a stone, Trevor wears away her sanity. *Sanity, vanity, effing tart.* Her ear for voices is a curse.

To calm herself, Georgie opens *The Natural History of Hartisborne*, though she knows it almost by heart. She is relieved there is no love plot to stoke her feelings, though sex and generation (don't tell Trevor) are plentiful among the animals and birds. Since childhood, the naturalist has changed shape in Georgie's mind. He was once a boy she liked at school, her first crush, and now, although the naturalist was short and fair, he has grown tall like Marco, with dark hair and Italian eyes.

To touch the well-thumbed pages is to slip into the entrance of a lane, where woody roots cling to limestone banks that might otherwise fall, for trees and stones support each other in Hartisborne. In summer, swifts and swallows dart and dip across the fields. House martins build in the eaves of the naturalist's house. Bees nest in a giant shell hung from a nail in the brickwork.

The naturalist digs the tortoise from its earthen den and weighs it. The melons grow round in hot beds, so liberally stoked with dung that steam rises from the straw bales supporting the glass frames. In autumn, gossamer falls from frosty heavens, and, in May, willow seeds float over green meadows. Earth and sky, sky and earth, harmonise in Hartisborne, where the air is scented by the orchard's blossom.

The naturalist seldom mentions villagers, except when he needs a man to dig out a bank in search of hedge-crickets, to measure the depth of the stream or to cut a zigzag path up the hill. The farmer's man, the weeding-woman, the bee-boy, uncomplicated souls, exist only to serve his study of nature, while happy children twirl in the upright barrel on the meadow's mound.

In a winter like this, two centuries ago, the naturalist, wakes to ice crystals frozen on his bedroom wall. He observes the smallest phenomenon so vividly that Georgie, half-dozing now, accompanies him along a snow-laden hedge to save a bird stunned by cold.

Sitting by his hearth, she holds the bird gently,

aware of its frightened heartbeat, while the naturalist spoons syrup down its gullet and then smiles Marco's lop-sided smile.

In the naturalist's journal, even a day of stormy rain is noted as a *sweet day*, should the sun appear but once. The naturalist is in love, not with a person, but with Hartisborne and all that grows there. He expresses no grievances, no grudges, no enmity, and, when at last the naturalist's gentle rhythms have replaced the violence of Trevor's tirade, Georgie closes the precious book and caresses its damaged cover.

Surely, this gash was caused by a bullet fired at her father in the Great War? The memory of the story is hazy, words floating in the breath of a boiling kettle. If this book hadn't stopped a bullet, her father wouldn't have survived the trenches. He would never have met her mother, and Georgie would never have been born.

She can't remember her mother or the night she left *The Natural History of Hartisborne* on Georgie's bed. Georgie was only three. It was some time before she could read the precious book, her only inheritance, or understand that she was an evacuee child, and later an orphan, and that Cornwall was not her home.

The naturalist has been her comfort, her first love and ideal man. The village of Hartisborne, his birthplace, habitat and subject of ecological study, is Georgie's idyll, her longed-for home, though she has never been there in reality.

She was shocked when Marco's friend Tom Swallow told her he was illustrating a new edition of *The Natural History* and staying in Hartisborne half the week. It never occurred to her that Hartisborne existed beyond the naturalist's book and the eighteenth century. But, of course, a village, unlike relatives, doesn't die or disappear.

In her first days at Bracco & March, Tom flustered Georgie, rushing in with books to sell, pressurising her to give him cash so he could take a girlfriend out to dinner. No one could care less than Tom about his looks. His lazy eye roams. His glasses are always splashed with paint. His hair is a stiff fuzz. Yet, he exudes sex appeal. According to Celia and Marco's gossip, his magnetism is the reason for his two divorces.

Georgie enjoys their talks about the naturalist and the village. And yesterday, just before he cadged a fiver from Marco, Tom handed her a pile of Hartisborne parish magazines, saying, 'Here, have a read.'

Looking back through the magazine, she's almost disappointed to learn of parish council and Women's Institute meetings. There's an obituary for a Winifred 'Winnie' Meadows. A car knocked her over on the iced-up road, killed her and then drove away into the night. In the letters section, parishioners debate the lack of street lighting, with some correspondents blaming the darkness for Winnie Meadows' death.

Georgie looks back through the magazine for something more hopeful and she finds it. Gil's home, Wakeling House Museum, where he wrote *The Natural History of Hartisborne,* is advertising for an assistant to the curator with 'an affinity for the naturalist's oeuvre and experience of working with the public.'

Trevor is no more than an in-law uncle. She owes him nothing. Even so, she will not be brave enough to leave him alone in his misery. Yet, here, by some miracle, is work she could do in her longed-for Hartisborne.

She daydreams about her job application, which makes a change from daydreaming about Marco or guiltily fantasising about Celia divorcing him. She can see him now struggling along the icy street with a pile of empty cardboard boxes. She rushes to open the door, and Hartisborne fades away.

Gil pulls back his bed curtains. Particles of ice have formed on his walls. The daub exhales moisture that freezes. How the room glitters! The slit of light between the shutters glows white, suggesting the weight of snow on the wooded hanger.

He rises from the bed to investigate. Interesting. The piss has frozen in his pot. The wine bottles he warms in the cupboard over the fire retain no heat. Their glass is cold on his palm. He opens the shutters. A patina of frost flowers along the window's edge. In the meadow, the barrel's hat of thatch is heavy with icicles which, even from this distance, glint dangerously.

Down in the garden, despite the earliness of the hour, his weeding-woman, in her red cloak, is knocking snow off the laurels with a broom

The water in the wash bowl is frozen. He'd like to wash his face before seeing Mary, but he flings on his clothes, his wig - for warmth not ceremony - and his hat and runs downstairs.

Thomas has a fire spitting to life in the little parlour. Gil warms his hands over the uncertain flames.

'The mercury fell below zero yet again, Mr Gil,' Thomas informs him, passing him some fingerless mittens.

'Yet Mary has walked ten miles from her mother's house to be here. What is the girl thinking of? Freezing to death? She must have risen in the dark.'

In the boot room, Gil puts on his heaviest cape and stoutest boots. He leaves the house and hastens across the snow. His feet sink in its depths.

The sun has barely risen. The hanger - a hillside hung with trees – how he loves the country words - huddles in the cold, a mound of white muffling the trees. Snow falls, whispers from twigs.

'Mary, Mary, what are you doing? Why are you here? Walking so far on such a day?'

She turns to him with a smile. 'Kept thinking of these poor bushes, weighed down by snow. All the way from Portugal and burnt by the cold, Mr Gil.'

Gil takes her broom and sends a few shivering lumps of snow flying from the hedge. Edges of ice crack and slide from the laurel leaves. They shudder into shiny green.

'The truth is - I couldn't sleep for thinking how things change. So, I walked here to calm my mind.'

'Nature is in a constant state of flux.'

Mary turns away.

Forget your parson's voice, he tells himself, ashamed of his pomposity. The girl hints at a trouble, and I must not ignore it. He gives the row of laurels another nudge with the broom. 'What is it that has changed?'

He observes her narrowly. The girl is different. That bloom on her cheek. Her hair thicker. Her slender neck and wrists fleshier. He recognises the signs from observing his own mother when he was younger, and more lately his sisters and sisters-in-law. She is with child. 'Mary, go into the kitchen and take breakfast with Thomas.'

'Perhaps I shouldn't. I couldn't keep it down.'

'That means you need to eat. Go now.' He looks away so as not to embarrass her. He should let her know he knows. 'New life needs food, does it not?'

'You are not angry with me?'

'Yes, I'm fearfully, fearfully angry.' He forces a laugh. 'I'm never angry with what is only natural.' But perhaps he is.

'A single woman with child is always let go by her employer.'

'Is *sometimes* let go,' he corrects her, though *usually let go* would be more truthful.

'But you will not employ me now?'

'We can't neglect our garden plans, can we? Now go in and eat some bread and bacon.'

He watches her walk across the field, her red cloak flapping, as her feet sink in the snowy depths. She is treading where he trod, right in his footsteps. Her feet must ache with cold. It was moonlight last night to be sure, and maybe when she rose the morning moon lit her on her way.

Why doesn't she move here for the winter to protect the delicate plants she persuades him to buy? Nine months of the year, the girl is here, planning, sowing, gently asserting her garden ideas. But come winter, she moves home to that benighted parish of Binford. She'll walk here for a day or a night, staying sometimes with Goody Newton, sometimes with the Kemp family or even he suspects, on summer nights, sleeping in the woodland.

He has often asked her why she doesn't fulfil a twelvemonth in this parish and gain legal settlement – he'd willingly write her a contract for the requisite year, so that she can stay in Hartisborne. But she always shakes her head, saying, 'In the winter, I must look after my mother. In the short days, she's poorly, her mind somehow bruised, and I can't leave her.'

'Can you not move your mother here?' he has asked more than once.

'She cannot abide Hartisborne,' is all Mary will say.

This repeated conversation, his offer and her refusal, spark an angry local patriotism inside him. What mother would want their child to live in blighted Binford when she could make a home in Hartisborne?

In Binford, no one concerns themselves with health or welfare, because there is no order there, no example given by either gentry or clergy, no visiting of the poor, no doctor, no midwife, none of the working out of charity that every parish is required to administer. A toad doctoress, a simpler of past lore, is all that Binford can boast. He blames the absent vicar, a bon-vivant whose company he barely tolerates on the occasions they meet at his brother's house in London, where the bon-vivant flirts shamelessly with his brother's wife or any adjacent woman.

'Your mother is lucky to have you,' Gil says resentfully whenever the matter of Mary's dwelling place arises.

Now Mary will need to manage a child and a

mother. There must be a wedding, he supposes. He wonders about the father's identity. If the young man steps forward and if he is a settled villager in Hartisborne and is willing to marry Mary, there will be no objection to Mary's settlement here. She will no longer be considered a migrant. She can continue to work in his garden and bring her baby with her, even if she sometimes returns to her mother.

Or maybe the young man lives in her mother's village? Maybe they will both settle in Binford, and Gil will rarely see her except when he's the visiting curate to that disordered place. Maybe she has been secretly betrothed all along, all the time he's known her. But why feel so discomfited?

# CHAPTER 2

Priory Farmhouse on the outer edge of Hartisborne is a cold place at the best of times. Three days ago, Nick Luckin moved his father's bed into the kitchen. His dad is dying in the worst winter Hartisborne has known for years. Nick has lit a paraffin stove for extra heat. He's pulled the bed close to the Rayburn. Now, in a burst of duty, he telephones his mother in London.

'Would you like to see Dad before he goes?' he asks.

'The trains aren't running, and Dick' - her new man is called Dick, another Richard, an irony that irks Nick - 'doesn't think it's safe to drive. He says he wouldn't want you to lose both parents.'

Although he hates them visiting, and it is true the roads are lethal, Nick is angry with Dick for presuming to decide his mother's movements.

'Are you sure you won't have regrets?'

'Regrets won't melt away the snow. And look what happened to Winnie Meadows.'

Nick hates his mother's flippant tone. How dare she use Winnie's fatal accident as an excuse for her own neglect. Poor Winnie. His mother didn't even ask how Wilf the cowman was doing, after losing his wife.

Nick prepares his diatribe. *Typical! Putting your own safety above seeing the father of your child before he dies.* The phone goes dead. The bloody ice and snow have done their worst again. He can't even ring her back with his reproaches. *And how are you, Nick? How are you coping with nursing Dad in the worst winter for years? And living in this damp, haunted place?* His mother never asks.

She never treats him as a real person. If she had, she couldn't have left when he was eight, making only strategic visits since then. He tries the phone again. It could be out for hours or days now, like the electricity. It's the same story everywhere. But damn the bloody phone for cutting out. Even the weather is on his mother's side, though it wasn't on poor old Winnie's side, when a car slid across the ice and killed her in the unlit village street.

Nick returns to the kitchen. He checks the temperature of his father's feet under the blankets and pulls the eiderdown up to his neck. He regales the bloody useless phone call to his father and then feels ashamed of wasting their precious time together. But there's no one else to tell, and soon he won't even be able to tell Dad.

Someone knocks on the back door. It's Miss Bewley - Iris - as he is supposed to call her, though using her first name is awkward because she was his teacher at primary school before he left to board. Miss Bewley moves tentatively towards his father.

Nick offers her the chair next to the bed.

'Is your mother here?' Iris looks around warily as if Marilyn might be hiding behind the coats. 'She'll want to see Richard, won't she?'

'The trains are cancelled. And her bloke won't drive her. I'd make you a cup of coffee, but I've turned off the water to protect the pipes. We've used all the jugs we filled.'

'Richard should have hot drinks. There's always the snow. Maybe we should scoop some up and boil that?'

His father gestures to the floor. Nick understands.

Why not indulge him? Nick drags away the kitchen table. When he was a child, his mother had wanted the well permanently blocked up. She feared Nick might fall in and drown. But Richard couldn't bear *stoppering the past*, as he put it in one of their memorable rows. So, they kept the table over the well cover and moved it only occasionally to draw water if there was a drought or a problem with the pipes.

According to the BBC Home Service, pipes have frozen below ground in some places. This well is so deep that its water never freezes. The water that rains over the hanger's wooded hillside, flows into the village's two streams and sinks into the fields to bubble up again from spring holes, finds its way into that depth as it has for centuries.

'Watch out, Iris,' Nick says. 'Stand well back.'

He unbolts the cover and lifts it off, exposing the deep hole. He takes the coil of rope from the shelf, ties it round the bucket's handle and lowers the bucket till it hits the water and drowns. Then he pulls it up, hand over hand, slopping and heavy, the rope almost burning his skin. He grabs the handle with relief. A mist fills the kitchen as the cold of the water hits the warmer air.

Nick carries the bucket to the draining board. Dad nods with satisfaction. Nick bolts down the cover, before pulling the table back again. The drag of the legs on the floor jars him. In the neighbourhood of death, all sounds should be gentle.

Using the well unnerves Nick. As a rule, he ignores the legends of the dissolute monks. He tells himself the mist is nothing more than the clash of two temperatures, not two times. He scoops up some water from the bucket with a jug, pours it into the enamel kettle and sets it on the Rayburn.

Iris takes his father's hand again. He cannot label her his father's woman or mistress or any crude term the village might use. Maybe nothing physical ever happened between them, Nick thinks hopefully, though they stare at each other with such longing that he is forced to look away.

Richard tries to say something, but his mouth doesn't work.

'He's saying old Farmer Luckin from the naturalist's time used that well too,' Nick interprets.

Iris nods. She must have heard the family tales from his father.

The kettle is slow to boil. They make desultory conversation. Richard joins in with a tremendous yawn that turns into the word *tired*, taking both Nick and Iris by surprise. His father has never uttered the word *tired* even when worn out by calving or harvesting.

As Nick pours hot water into the coffee jug, someone hammers on the back door. No harm if it's old Sylvia, traipsing here after all, as he's been half-expecting. She's the only person he can tolerate today. He even wishes Iris away. Early this morning, he'd shovelled the bank of snow from the door, in case the doctor made it down the track. If only he hadn't cleared it, then the door would be blocked to visitors. He could throw the top bolt and call out that the door is stuck, but then Iris will think him mad.

The vicar hurries in, removes his snowy wellingtons and walks in his socked feet over to the Rayburn, his eyes on Richard.

'Good morning, Nick. I heard about your father. I wondered whether he'd like the last rites.'

Nick sighs. 'It's up to him.' He shakes the

vicar's cold hand, takes his coat and sits him down with the coffee he'd made for himself. 'Sugar?' he asks, compelled to make small talk even in the face of death.

The spoon in the sugar bowl is tarnished silver, shaped like a windmill. His parents bought it on their honeymoon in Holland. Its sails move as he shovels sugar into the vicar's cup. When his mother left his father, she'd wanted to take the spoon, but his father had yelled that it was part of Nick's childhood. Ever since, the spoon has filled Nick with sadness, a constant reminder of that day of shouting. She'd have taken everything if she could, his father told him. Even the jewellery that belonged to Richard's grandmother, the Luckin inheritance and nothing to do with her, but all to be passed on to Nick's future bride. 'We're in the nineteen sixties,' Nick had joked. 'I don't think today's women are interested in old family brooches.' 'Inheritance is inheritance,' Dad had said, a view which at least reassured Nick as to the farm.

Richard moves restlessly. Iris releases his hand in honour of the vicar.

'It's very nice of you to walk here on such a day,' the vicar says to Miss Bewley pointedly.

'No children turned up, so I closed the school.'

'The weather is thawing, I believe.'

The vicar thinks Iris should have heated the school and sat there doing nothing, in case an unlikely child braved it in, while the man she loves lies dying.

'I wanted to see Richard,' she says more boldly.

'And Dad is so glad you're here,' Nick says, adding untruthfully, 'and so am I.'

The vicar takes an embroidered cloth from his duffel bag and spreads it on the table. He adds a chalice, a box of holy wafers and a tartan-patterned thermos containing wine. He pours the wine into the chalice, blesses it and makes the sign of the cross over Richard.

'Are you sure you want this, Dad?' Nick asks. His father's eyes are bright with laughter.

'Your father was a church warden for several years. And whatever our differences lately, he grew up in the traditions of the Church of England.' The vicar intones the words of the Eucharist and offers Nick's father a wafer.

'He won't be able to eat that,' Nick says.

'Just the wine then,' the vicar agrees.

Nick sees the glint of his father's eyes, mischievous, mesmeric, saying *might as well have a drink*, but the vicar only manages to wet Richard's lips.

'We're obliged to drink it up once it's been blessed.' The vicar offers Nick the chalice. They take it in turns to finish the wine. It's rich and sweet, and makes Nick's head spin, as he has eaten nothing for a day and a night.

Outside, a blackbird sings a warning, which Nick chooses to ignore. Surely no one else will brave it down here today.

If Iris and the vicar weren't here, Nick could sit beside his father and talk with him, ask him advice about the farm, even if Dad couldn't answer. He could hold his hand again. If only they were alone, and if others had to be here, why couldn't it be someone useful?

As if on cue, old Sylvia lets herself in, bashes the snow off her boots on the mat, hangs up her coat, and takes the cups from the table.

'No other visitors?' she murmurs. 'Haven't Joan and Maisie visited Richard yet?'

'They came the day before yesterday.'

'I thought I saw a girl in a red coat walking ahead, with fair curly hair like Maisie's. Unless it's a migraine coming on. Always gives me flashes.'

Nick senses her moving round the room, putting things to rights without any bothersome talk. If his mother were here, she'd be deliberating aloud about every darned thing, where the cups go, whether the well water should be sieved, and who put that hefty bucket on the draining board. Just as well she's not here, isn't it? And yet, maybe he would like a mother here while his father is dying, but at least he has old Sylvia.

When Nick was a child – and Sylvia came to work here because of his mother leaving – she'd accidentally caught his finger in the drawer that stretches right through the Luckins' kitchen table. Eight year old Nick had screamed and screamed. Sylvia was distraught and had cried too because she thought she'd broken his finger.

Now Sylvia approaches the vicar. 'I wonder if you could say a prayer with me in the long hall. I'm bothered by the monks every time I clean. Nick, why don't you sit alongside Miss Bewley?' Sylvia moves a chair forward. 'Your dad needs you near.'

With one last look at Richard, his friend and antagonist, the vicar allows Sylvia to prod him into the long hall

Nick exchanges a look with his father. Sylvia knows the vicar is irritating him. 'She's still trying to make it up to me,' Nick whispers to Dad, thinking of the drawer and Sylvia wanting to protect him from pain. His father squeezes his fingers in agreement. The history of Nick's childhood in all its small intimacies stretches between them like an open hand that will soon close.

Richard jerks his other hand towards Nick, but then sinks into the pillow with the effort. His chest bubbles.

'This is it. I saw this with my brother.' Iris leans forward and kisses Richard on the cheek. She whispers something in his ear. He tries to answer.

Nick spoons some morphine from the bottle and offers it to Dad but it's too late.

Dad's breath rattles out. On and on and yet for no time that Nick can really count. Then, there's a quietness. The most vital man in the village – and he lies here without that vitality, without himself somehow and yet almost still here.

Iris starts to cry. She kisses Richard on the forehead over and over. Eventually she pulls herself together and reverts to her usual discretion. 'I'll leave you with him. You might like to be alone.' He hears her murmuring the news to the others as the door to the long hall swings slowly shut.

'Dad,' Nick says, leaning over his father, 'you were a great dad to me.' His father had been a terrible husband. Guiltily, he pushes away his mother's face creased up with jealousy, her voice screeching and ugly, and all because of his father's behaviour.

Alone with Dad at last, Nick lets himself weep. 'What a mess you always make.' He can't yet bring himself to cover Dad's face.

He must phone the doctor. Won't he need a death certificate? And the undertaker? But the phone still isn't working. Monksway, the track through the woods to the village, and the tarmacked lane high above it are both impassable to cars. 'What should I do? How will I get you out of here?'

'You could use the tractor.' Was Dad really speaking?

'I must tell Mum.'

'Watch out for the Luckin jewellery then,' Richard says. 'I always meant to tell you... woodpigeon's nest in the honeysuckle... heirlooms or so they said... relics... little finger... old, old words... ' Did he say 'words' or 'worlds'?

Nick's mind whirls through his father's stories and then back to the necessary tasks. If the vicarage phone is working, the vicar can phone the doctor and the undertaker. Sylvia can ask the village shop to put up a notice. And Nick will make a hot water bottle and go to bed. Though later there'll be the evening milking. And keeping the cows warm in the big barn. He'll need to do the cowman's jobs as well as his own. Wilf hasn't been fit for work since the shock of Winnie's death.

Nick will need to tell the artist Tom Swallow, who rents the barn-studio, in case he's suddenly down from London and blunders in on Dad's body. And the body - who is no longer Dad - aren't there things you should do? Physical procedures?

He hears voices in the long hall. Hartisborne is speaking. One of its own has gone. Someone, probably Sylvia, will lead Nick upstairs and tuck him into his bed. His father's voice says, 'The village will know what to do.'

Male voices murmur in the kitchen. Have the ghosts of the excommunicated monks returned to gather Richard into their number? Or is it the sound of his father's folk band, The Pipe Barrel, planning what to sing at the funeral? But none of this has happened yet. They don't even know Richard is dead.

In Nick's head, past, present and future merge in Priory Farmhouse where they say no women can live happily and even tough old Sylvia is troubled by ghosts and someone as alive as his father, his dear dad, Richard Luckin, with those eyes that, almost beyond his volition, mesmerised women and made them love him, has gone.


Snow pocks. Suburbs melt. Whiteness slips from ivy garlanding the trees. The train rumbles through the long-awaited thaw.

Everything hinges on this interview. If Georgie wins the job in the museum, she need never hear Uncle Trevor's rants again. She can escape this new self, *effing bit on the side*.

Please let me change, she prays to whatever power stalks the suburbs, the snowy fields, the hedges thawing into tangles. Let me be good again, she begs a flock of rooks rising from a garden. The rooks disperse leaving the sky bereft of energy, empty and grey, the way she will feel without Marco.

When Georgie alights from the train in the small market town, four miles from Hartisborne, the bus to the village won't start. Surely, the trustees will understand if she's late? The bus driver tries the choke again until finally the pre-war vehicle groans into life. Its door swings out into the road and bangs into place round each bend. Cold air blasts through. She's glad of Marco's coat, even though it stinks of damp, mothballs and wet fur.

The icy sludge makes for a slow ride. Double thoughts. If only she could stay with Marco. If only she could travel to the past and meet the naturalist. The sliding bus slows and quickens, eventually skidding to a stop in Hartisborne High Street and letting her out.

Georgie knocks on and then opens the museum's door. The naturalist rushed in and out of this doorway, never guessing how his book would comfort her on her first night in Connie and Trevor's box room. She knows Gil but he can never know her. Her parents knew her, but she can never know them. The passing of time is a lonely business.

In the museum hallway, Georgie takes off the fur coat. A woman jumps up to greet her, saying, 'You must be Miss Gardner. I'm Joan Hill. Colonel Camden says to make yourself comfortable.' She gestures to the seat beside her. Joan adds, 'Love your suit!' Georgie can't respond, as the suit is Celia's, lent her by Marco in Celia's absence. *Little thief – effing with that Eyetie.* Not now, Trevor, please.

Georgie takes some sharp breaths.

'Are you alright?' Joan asks.

'Bit nervous,' Georgie says.

'Oh, so am I!'

'You're being interviewed too?'

'Yes, apparently it's between you and me.'

Georgie takes her notes from her handbag and lets her hair fall over her face, a curtain between her and her rival.

Her eyes focus on the slubbed tweed. She's disguised as Marco's wife, yet classy Celia would know exactly what to say. She sniffs her sleeve surreptitiously. It smells of must and of Celia's favourite perfume, Tweed. *Tweed all over*, Marco had said, when he'd sprayed her neck with his wife's perfume. Her body tenses involuntarily. She hopes her rival doesn't notice.

'First come, first served,' a vicar says, ushering Joan into the little parlour.

Georgie hears snatches of muffled laughter from behind the door. To calm herself, she checks that all her certificates are in her bag. The minutes tick by. *They'll see through you, you little tart.*

When Joan leaves the interview, someone calls, 'Come back at half three! We'll have decided by then.'

'I will. Thank you. Must check on Maisie now – she's off school with tonsilitis.' She mouths, 'Good luck' at Georgie before leaving.

*Local woman – someone they can trust – not an effing floozy with her hands in the till - and her eyes on the boss.*

'Miss Gardner? Could you come through?' Colonel Camden is the chair of the trustees. He introduces her to the vicar, another trustee, and to David Daunt, the curator and her future colleague, should she be offered the position of his assistant.

'And this is Miss Bewley, the headteacher of our primary school.'

'Wasn't the school built in memory of the naturalist?'

'Yes, indeed.' The Colonel seems momentarily impressed by Georgie's knowledge.

Miss Bewley looks as though she has been crying for days. Her eyes are puffy through her glasses. Her jacket sleeves are dusted with chalk. She summons a smile, before delving in her pocket for a handkerchief. The Colonel pats her on the arm. The vicar sighs impatiently.

'Now Miss Gardner, can you tell us why you want to leave such a renowned bookshop in the heart of – what do young people call it now? – oh yes, *swinging* London?' Colonel Camden asks. 'Why leave *swinging* London to live in our tiny dull village where you'll be working with only one other person? Won't you find that monotonous? It can be fearfully bleak here in the winter, when the lanes fill up and nothing happens at all.'

'I've been reading *The Natural History of Hartisborne* all my life,' Georgie replies, dodging the question. She should focus on her office skills, but her mind flicks to the book in her bag, the pages ripped by the bullet, the last gift of her unknown parents. She clears her throat but nothing else comes out.

Colonel Camden fills the silence eventually, 'Well, my dear, that's the answer everyone gives. It's easy to be sentimental about Hartisborne, but we trustees, and Mr Daunt of course, need to be hard-headed.'

'Can you tell us a little more about your previous experience?' Miss Bewley asks. Her voice entrances Georgie. Rich, resonant, like water over stones.

'My first job, after secretarial college, was at Palliser's warehouse and involved invoicing, typing correspondence and taking the minutes of meetings.' Georgie took the position because Uncle Trevor forced her. He worked for Palliser's and wanted to keep tabs on her. He even caught the same bus home so she couldn't stray. 'I answered directly to Mr Palliser, the owner.'

'Sounds top notch,' Colonel Camden says.

'Why did you leave?' the vicar asks suspiciously.

She can't tell the vicar about the dirty comments. She should have given witty rejoinders to make the men respect her. But she couldn't summon wise cracks, only anger. Then, the men ribbed her, saying, 'It's got a temper on it as well as a big arse.' The men's eyes would follow her into the office where there wasn't even a plant to hide behind. Then one day, she glimpsed Uncle Trevor covering a smile as he checked off a box of paper on his clipboard. The pressure never to forget her body made her feel sick. But it was Trevor's secret smile that drove her to leave.

'No use working with men, if you don't have a sense of humour,' Aunt Connie said, when Georgie tearfully confided in her. Georgie's sense of humour grew so thin she thought she might stab someone with the paper knife.

Mr Palliser told unhappy workers, 'Get out of the kitchen, if it's too hot.' Well, she did get out, though the office certainly wasn't hot. It was cold, built from single skin breeze blocks, with no windows but a skylight, and not even a paraffin heater.

'Miss Gardner, are you alright?' Miss Bewley says quietly.

'Sorry. Must be nerves.'

'I was asking why you left your job with Palliser's?' the vicar prompts her.

'I've always had an interest in old books. I suppose, because I loved *The Natural History of Hartisborne* so much, and it was my first experience of powerful writing. So, I volunteered to help in Bracco and March one Saturday.' The shop was her Saturday refuge. She'd stand for hours reading books for free, until Marco and Celia made friends with her. 'Afterwards, Mr Bracco offered me a job. So, I'm used to dealing with the public. And my secretarial experience will help with filing and archiving.' Even to herself, Georgie sounds desperate, laying out her wares.

The vicar, Colonel Camden and David Daunt, are examining her from head to toe as if they have never met a woman of twenty-five before. Miss Bewley frowns at them.

'I have a PSC with Distinction, as you can see in my letter of application.'

'Yes, what is a PSC?' the vicar asks as if it's a disease. 'I didn't understand that.'

'A Private Secretary's Certificate.'

'Of course,' the vicar murmurs.

'I have RSA certificates in Pitman shorthand and typing.'

The vicar sighs at such boasting.

'You said that you've been reading *The Natural History* all your life,' David Daunt says. 'With all respect to Colonel Camden, *I'm* very interested in knowing why you've been reading it *all* your life?'

'Yes, do tell us,' Miss Bewley says.

Georgie leans forward. 'My mother gave me a copy of *The Natural History* when I was evacuated to Cornwall. I was too young to read then, but I liked the pictures, which I discovered later were the original Grimm engravings. When I was older and went back to live in London, I missed the countryside. *Hartisborne* became my substitute, I suppose.'

'Your mother must have been delighted you valued the book so much?' Miss Bewley says.

'Well, no, actually.'

'Why ever not?' the vicar snaps.

'She never knew. She died in the blitz.'

The three men look at their feet.

'I'm so very sorry,' Miss Bewley says, her voice breaking with pain. 'That must have been very hard.'

No one has said that to her since she left Cornwall. Connie and Trevor never once said they were sorry her parents died, even though Connie was her mother's sister.

'During my time at Bracco and March, I've been researching various editions of *Hartisborne* and its illustrators. We have several interested collectors.'

'Mr Bracco says you have an unusual approach to sales,' the vicar says distastefully. Surely Marco hadn't described her mimicking Celia on the phone to tempt a rich, flirtatious client into clinching the deal?

'Mr Bracco says here that you've become quite the expert on *Hartisborne*.' David waves Marco's reference in front of her.

Marco's stylish handwriting, though only glimpsed, unsettles Georgie. Why leave when she could stay? *Tucked up with that Eyetie – be on the effing streets next.*

'Yes, do tell us more about your expertise,' Miss Bewley says, nudging Georgie on.

Georgie shifts in her seat, hoping not to tear the lining of Celia's skirt. 'I suppose, every age needs new illustrations of *Hartisborne* because it's supposed to be the secret parish of everyone's soul. For instance, the Grimm engravings look rather too tidy now. Newer illustrations can be looser, more fragmented or dynamic. Every age looks at nature differently.' She runs out of steam. 'We post different editions to clients all over the world.' Not entirely relevant as a comment, but better than saying nothing at all. 'We restore some copies, before sending out. Mr Bracco has been teaching me bookbinding.' Fingers touching in the basement bindery. Marco's hand steadying her arm. Turning her face to his. *Saw you coming,* Trevor says.

'What do you personally find so compelling about *The Natural History of Hartisborne*?' David asks her.

'We must stick to the same questions with all applicants,' Colonel Camden murmurs, 'and that isn't one of them.'

'No, really – Mr Daunt's question is crucial,' Miss Bewley says. 'Please tell us, Miss Gardner.'

'The naturalist doesn't say much about people, but he observes animals with almost surreal detail. He uses words like 'browsing'. Some horses were browsing a yew hedge, for instance. Unfortunately, they all died of yew poisoning, but the word caught me. And then the story of the horse and the hen,' - *bloody nonsense* - she manages to override Trevor's voice, 'the swallows and the house martins…'

'Yes,' David says, gesturing outside, but not taking his eyes from Georgie. 'Every spring, the house martins nest in the eaves exactly where they nested in the naturalist's time. It's all icicles now but do have a look after the interview.'

'We mustn't give you more time than the other candidate,' Colonel Camden says after Georgie has proved she can answer nearly every question they throw at her about the naturalist. 'All's fair and so on. If you'd like to go through to the kitchen, Miss Gardner, Mrs Pearson will rustle up some tea and biscuits.'

'Do look round the garden. I expect you'd like to see all the rooms while you're here.' Miss Bewley's voice is full of invitation. 'I wonder whether you'll find it different to your imaginings. It really is a magical place, but in a much smaller way than readers of *The Natural History* ever conceive before they visit.'

'Probably far too small for someone who has worked in London,' Colonel Camden adds. 'All the young people, all the goings-on – it would be very hard for you to say goodbye to that, I expect.'

*See? They sodding hate you.*

'That was not at all what I meant,' Miss Bewley says.

'Well, Miss Gardner, we're going to make our decision and tell you and Maisie's mother later today. If you can hang around till three thirty, that would be grand. But if you need to go, we can always write to you. And if you've changed your mind about wanting the job,' he says eagerly, 'we won't be at all offended.'

'Three will be fine,' Georgie says. She needs to know today, or she'll go mad. If she misses the bus, she can stay at Tom Swallow's barn-cum-studio. He's drawn a map showing how to walk to Priory Farm but warned her not to mention him.

'Do get some tea, Miss Gardner.'

Georgie picks up the fur coat in the hall.

'What a monstrous coat!' Colonel Camden jokes, pointing the way.

In the naturalist's kitchen – how strange to find herself here - Georgie introduces herself to Mrs Pearson. Her husband, the caretaker and handyman, Nev Pearson gestures to Georgie to take a seat. He sits down and rests his boots on the table.

Without looking at him, his wife says, 'Captain Pearson, take those feet off the table please.' Then she pours Georgie a cup of stewed tea and resumes the washing up.

Without removing his feet, Captain Pearson lifts a plate of melting chocolate biscuits from the top of the stove and waves it at Georgie. If she takes one, she will drip chocolate on Celia's slubbed tweed skirt.

'No thanks,' she says.

'Go on, do have one.'

'I'm not hungry, thanks.' She has had no lunch, but clothes are sacred to Celia, and Georgie hopes to get the suit back unscathed before Celia returns from Oxford.

'No one thought a Londoner would travel down for the interview. Not in weather like this. It's a miracle you got here.'

Without raising her face from the washing up, Romilly Pearson adds, 'The job was only advertised in the parish magazine. How did *you* come to hear of it?'

A woman who addresses her own husband as 'Captain' won't approve of Tom Swallow. And Tom did advise her not to mention him. 'Someone brought a pile of Hartisborne parish magazines to the bookshop where I work.'

'Why would anyone stock our parish mag in a London bookshop?'

'Hartisborne is famous, I suppose.'

Nev Pearson removes his feet from the table. 'They'll want a local, I expect. Joan Hill has been waiting on this job for months.'

So, the result is pre-arranged. Yet David Daunt likes her, and so does Miss Bewley, even if the vicar doesn't. But the job is designed for Joan Hill. No wonder she was so smiley.

'Never take failure to heart. That's my advice. Anyone can be underestimated. Take Schubert. He was underestimated until forty years after his death. Little soirées for his friends, and only a few realising his genius. Die Winterreise sequence for example…'

Captain Pearson strings his pauses with 'ahs' and 'erms' and sudden guttural laughs which make interruption impossible. A stream of Schubertiads and Germanic names obstruct Georgie's exit to the longed-for garden. She can bear it no longer when Schubert is very ill but nevertheless composing and quite possibly visiting prostitutes.

'Do excuse me and thank you for the tea, Mrs Pearson. But I should go and see the naturalist's garden before the bus leaves.' She pushes her chair aside, pulls on the fur coat and slips out.

It's all over now. She'll see where the naturalist grew the melons, and then she'll return to Trevor's prison, and the guilt of loving Marco. She stares across the ha-ha to the meadow. The upright barrel must be a replica, she supposes.

When this thaw is over, the famed hanger will begin to leaf, for March is only posing as January. The birds are singing. The naturalist would call them songsters. She imagines him standing next to her, wearing his clerical black, his head on one side. A blackbird darts across the icy grass, listens for a worm and stabs through thin snow to find its prey.

If only she could live here forever and never again have to hear Trevor's voice. If only she could express herself like the naturalist, truthfully, elegantly, accurately, with no self-obsession. *Treacherous little bitch.*

'If you're sure?' Colonel Camden says. 'We did say

we'd give you the deciding vote, David.'

'She seems a bit of a popsy,' the vicar says, 'whereas Maisie's mother would lend a steady hand. She would know what to do if the pipes burst, for instance.' He eyes David antagonistically and gestures to the line of damp around the panelling.

'Miss Gardner has real enthusiasm for the naturalist's work,' Miss Bewley says. 'And apart from some longueurs due to her nervousness, I thought she answered very well. Also, she would get on with David.'

'Miss Gardner is exactly what we need,' David adds eagerly. 'She has the perfect qualities for the job. Exactly what the Pearsons don't have.'

'Please don't start on the Pearsons again, Mr Daunt,' the Colonel says. 'You forget Captain Pearson's distinguished war record. His situation is assured so long as I am one of the trustees. The Captain is... ' the Colonel struggles to find faint praise, 'an adequate handyman and Mrs Pearson is a competent worker. The gardener's cottage gives them a safe haven. And Pearson does appreciate history, otherwise why would he be so fascinated by the lives of the composers?'

'I have a theory about that,' David says rather too warmly. 'It's just a method of... '

'Miss Gardner is the matter in hand, and Captain Pearson is not,' the Colonel insists.

David sinks his desire to argue. After the burst pipe incident, when water soaked the naturalist's tricorne, damaged Miss Butter's famous fan and blurred some important letters, he'd doubted whether the committee would still employ him, let alone make good their promise of an assistant to give David more time for Gil's biography.

'What should we do now?' David asks pacifically.

'We check that Miss Gardner will take the job. Maisie's mother will be very disappointed. Unless of course Miss Gardner refuses,' the Colonel adds hopefully. 'Someone used to central London and the Charing Cross Road may find us very dull indeed, I expect.'

'It was Richard Luckin's dearest hope that Maisie's mother be given this job because he worried about Maisie.' The vicar scowls at Miss Bewley as if blaming her for thwarting a man's last wishes.

'I don't believe Joan was christened *Maisie's mother*,' Miss Bewley says.

The Colonel shuffles his papers, signalling the discussion's end. 'David, perhaps you should find Miss Gardner and deliver the good news.'


In the garden, David takes a few cold breaths to clear his head.

Soon, Miss Gardner will be here to help. He won't be alone with the Pearsons every live-long day. If only Nev hasn't put her off with his boring monologues.

He is aware of Miss Gardner, standing beyond the yew hedge in the garden of six quarters. Her heavy dark hair. Her freckled skin. Her gorgeous brown eyes which lit up every time she mentioned old Gil. Her eccentric dress sense – the suit that veered on Chanel and showed her figure off so well - and by contrast that tatty fur coat.

The snowdrops are flowering at last. And if the naturalist were here, he'd be noting their late blooming in his garden journal. How would he describe Georgina Gardner? Well, he wouldn't, meticulous as he was about others' privacy. He's never given a hint as to Miss Butter's looks or any clues as to the character of the weeding woman, a potentially interesting historical subject, who crops up now and again in the garden journal. If it weren't for that scrawled note he found during the burst pipes' fiasco, David wouldn't even think the naturalist interested in women.

Miss Gardner will be a colleague of his own generation, assuaging his loneliness. David dreads the empty evenings, fearing Richard's folk band The Pipe Barrel will disband now the farmer has died. Hard to believe he will never again sing with Richard in Priory Farmhouse's long hall, the best nights of his lonely life in Hartisborne.

Come on old Gil, David prays as he walks under the yew arch to find Miss Gardner, it's your house after all. Invite her in. Let her say yes. Or I may go bonkers trying to discover who the hell you really were on my own.

# CHAPTER 3

It is March, a sweet day, as Thomas so rightly remarks, and a special day, on which Gil has a special duty. Mary Trimmer, his weeding-woman, lovely Mary, is to marry Farmer Luckin's man, Eddy Kemp. As curate-in-charge, Gil will be officiating.

No need now for a meeting of parish officers to discuss Mary's right to stay in the village. No need for a bastardy examination either. Kemp is a Hartisborne man. Her marriage to him absolves the parish of expenses for Mary's child and prevents her from being passed back to Binford.

Mr Blundel is the parish overseer. He was elected last year and will be in post for another fortnight when, Gil prays, the next Easter Vestry meeting will release the poor from his pettiness. Blundel protects parish funds as he would his own income. He spent days chasing Eddy until the young man confessed rather woodenly to fathering Mary's child. Gil hopes that Eddy is the father because he is sweet on Mary. And why would the lad lie? And if he lies, isn't that a sign of his love for Mary, even though lying is a sin?

After breakfast, Gil consults the garden journal. On this day a twelve month ago, the wild white cherry blossom fell from a sky blue with gusts of wind. The flower fall was so thick that Mary set to with a besom and swept the petals into a pile.

Mary will not come so often to plan the garden with him once she is married to Eddy and lives at Priory Farm cottage on the edge of the parish. The garden there is dank, pinned tight to the chalk cliff and rife with ivy. No light gets in. Water greens the chalkface and drips into the walls. The ground is stony.

*I will still be your weeding woman, Mr Gil*, Mary said after she whispered news of her marriage with a blush. *I will still walk over and weed for you.*

Every day since her announcement, he has quelled his heart, never averring aloud that Mary is more than a weeding woman to him. She is a fellow gardener, a plantswoman in the making, that much he will admit. He has taught her the Latin names for different species. Mary can read and write and has a prodigious memory for both words and the ways of plants. Together, they have experimented with crossbreeding and pollinating with slender brushes.

How often he's seen Mary warm her hands above the steaming glass-covered beds. And once, without a thought, she took his hand in both of hers and rubbed the cold away. To her he was not a curate, not a landowner, not a scientist, nor a philosopher, not a poet – all the terms bestowed on him by his admiring friends and professional acquaintances - but just a man gardening outside for long hours with cold hands that needed warming. 'There, that's better,' she had said with satisfaction, as if he were a lad of the village, not a gentleman whose people would do all the planting for him if he'd let them.

When Mary snaps off a stem below the bud, and presses it into a bed with her thumb, the cutting is sure to grow. When she begs seeds from the cottagers, she notes the location of the parent plants, how the sun falls, the qualities of earth, so she can choose apt sowing grounds. She scatters coins of honesty and half-moons of marigold seeds over the basons. Her eye is quick, yet she has the patience of a scientist. Such a woman will be wasted at Priory Farm Cottage, that sunless spot where only ferns and ivy grow.

Gil does not credit ghosts and has refused Farmer Luckin's request for an exorcism at Priory Farmhouse. Nevertheless, with Mary soon to be working there, perhaps he should agree to bell, book and candle. What a fool he would appear to his correspondents in the Royal Society and to the Fellows of his college, he, a modern man, supping on superstition. Better to find Eddy Kemp new employ and a cottage in the village, so that Mary may return and set seed with Gil side by side in the glasshouse's silence, than to damn his scientific reputation in a battle against ghostly monks.

'I'm sure you have your marriage sermon ready, Mr Gil?' Thomas knows full well that Gil has written nothing.

'The words will come soon enough,' he says, troubled by a forbidden gospel he once read secretly at Oxford. A woman travels down a lane, that, in Gil's mind, has become Monksway, the track through the woods from Priory Farm. She is carrying a sack. As she walks, seeds fly out through a tear. Along the way, she senses not the flying seeds nor feels the sack's weight lighten. The text is glossed by no parable, no words of comfort or interpretation. He can't form a face from his imaginings, but he suspects that the woman crying into her empty sack, is Mary, his fellow seed collector.

A different seed has now been set, and Mary's belly grows. How round her face is, how lush her hair, how hungrily she eats a crust of bread, signs of generation, of life quick within her. Eddy's child - if Eddy is the father - will banish her to a stony garden and the breath of dead monks in her ear. But this is no matter for the happy sermon Gil must conjure.

'Shall we cut some boughs of blossom for the bride?' he asks Thomas, who nods with pleasure, always a generous fellow, a kinder man than Gil deserves. Thomas loves a wedding, especially when Gil officiates, and if there is dancing afterwards and a tankard of ale.

Mr Blundel, the overseer, has paid for the ring and the wedding dinner from parish funds, as is the custom when matrimony needs prompting. The ring and vittles are a bargain compared to the price of a bastard's upbringing.

Farmer Luckin offers his barn down at Priory for the occasion. The cherry boughs will be welcome on the old oak beams. The villagers will walk through the woods with their jars of cider and baskets of offerings. Already in his mind's eye, they tread the leaf mould in the dusk, some with burning torches, some with lanterns, some trusting their eyes to settle to the darkness. March is a cold month for a dance in a barn, but a bride must be celebrated with fiddles and jigs. Gil will stand stiffly by while the farming folk dance. Already he anticipates his return along Monksway, alone before midnight, his only comfort the sight of a swooping owl or the flitter of an early bat.

All morning in the glasshouse, Gil searches for words to bless the future of Mary and Eddy, but his head is empty. He pictures Mary at Goody Newton's tying her skirts over her new weight. Mary's mother vowed long ago never to set foot in Hartisborne, a place she considers dangerously spellbinding. Such foolish vows are made to be broken. He is sure she will attend her own daughter's wedding. And any woman who hates his beloved Hartisborne must be a harridan.

In the distance, he sees Thomas, on the stepladder with the pruning saw, reaching for the boughs of wild white cherry. Tom balances over the very spot, where last year Mary paused for a moment with her garden brush, delighting in her heap of flowers, before she shovelled them into the bushel basket.

The wind whipped her hair loose from her scarf. Mary was singing. Her voice made Gil shiver with pleasure, and he turned away lest she realise. To his surprise, she came over and placed her strong gardener's hand on his sleeve and pulled him under the cherry tree.

'Look Mr Gil,' she'd said. 'The flowers fall so thickly this year. We can discover the weight of their blossom!'

The weight of their blossom. Such seeking after knowledge. Such shared passion.

On impulse, he had snatched up the basket and tossed the blossoms over her. They caught in her hair and on her red cloak. Mary had laughed as if there weren't twenty-three years between them. He'd apologised and gently dashed the petals away. His hands remember the rough wool of her cloak, the softness of her hair.

Then, the wind lifted the cherry blossom and scattered it over the fields of Hartisborne, presaging a wedding, though a twelve month ago Gil had no idea it would be this one.

If only you could speak to your mummy on the phone, Auntie Julia, her foster auntie, would say whenever they went to the village shop. Though Georgie had no pennies for the telephone inside the silence cabinet, she'd make pretend calls, by putting her panda to the mouthpiece to growl, 'Mummy I love you' or 'Daddy, come home.' Uncle Tris and Auntie Julia helped her write letters to Mummy in London, but Mummy didn't reply.

From inside the silence cabinet, she could hear the shop door clang and the Cornish weather buffeting in. The silence cabinet lived up to its name in one respect. No one replied to her panda, except when a lady called the-operator-in-Penzance asked her to put down the receiver.

Georgie was good at her lessons. Soon, she put aside her panda and wrote to her parents without anyone's help. She decorated her letters with chickens and posted them in the post box in the farm wall.

When her parents didn't reply, Morwenna and Uncle Tris said, 'the post is difficult in war time.' It wasn't fair. Other evacuees got letters. So, the post did work.

'What's my mummy like?' Georgie wanted to know.

'She's a quiet woman,' Uncle Tris said, almost too quickly.

'She wanted to be sure we'd look after you,' Aunty Julia said. 'She must have trusted us, because she caught the train early the next morning without saying goodbye.'

Her mummy was a nice mystery, who had left *The Natural History of Hartisborne* on her bed with a wedding photograph tucked inside. Maybe her sister Aunty Connie will also be nice even though she has sent only one Christmas card in all Georgie's time as an evacuee.

A year after the war ended, Georgie was told by her teacher to be in the silence cabinet at four. Aunty Connie, her mother's sister, would be telephoning her.

The voice of Aunty Connie! Aunty Connie is getting married! It's at long last. Trevor will be Georgie's new uncle.

'Isn't that wonderful?'

'Aunty Connie, can I speak to Mummy?'

All she could hear was Connie's raspy breath. Finally, she replied. 'You were having such a lovely time at the seaside. Lucky girl.'

Georgie stared through the window of the silence cabinet. Her teacher was buying carrots. Mrs Trevis, the shopkeeper, was putting them in a bag. Georgie was good at voices. She could talk in Mrs Trevis' voice as well as in Morwenna's or her teacher's. She wondered what her mummy's voice sounded like.

'Can I speak to Mummy?'

'To be honest, shortly after you were

evacuated, your Mummy was - caught by an act of God. And she left us.'

'But she must be back by now?' Was it God whispering in the phone box with Auntie Connie? A gruff stabbing voice that she didn't like.

'I mean - she passed away. She died. It was a shock. You were so young. I couldn't bring myself to tell you. Thought I should let you grow up a bit first.'

Georgie understood shock.

Since her son drowned near Dunkirk, her foster auntie had taken to sitting in a darkened room. Auntie Julia felt safer in the dark, whereas Georgie felt frightened. When Georgie opened the curtains, Uncle Tris closed them again, murmuring, 'For some people it's hard work just to be, and that's all we can ask of her.' When his fisherman friend left Julia a couple of mackerel, Uncle Tris gutted them himself. He washed the fish under the yard pump and let the blood spatter over the ground. Julia couldn't face cooking or eating fish anymore. There it is, Uncle Tris said, holding the fish-slice in his scarred bony hands and serving the mackerel to Georgie and Morwenna.

'Georgina, are you still there?'

'Yes,' Georgie said, trying not to cry for the mother she couldn't remember.

'Now I'm married, you'll be coming home to live with us.' Connie trailed off.

'Has Daddy come home?' Georgie asked.

'Your father was posted to Burma. Soldiers get killed in wars, and I'm afraid your dad was one of them.'

Georgie didn't know where Burma was. All she knew was that she couldn't listen to Aunt Connie's monotonous voice anymore.

'Georgina must go now,' she said mimicking her teacher. 'She's got homework to do.'

'But I haven't finished,' Aunt Connie said. 'Can you put her back on?'

'I'm sorry Mrs Cousins. Georgina has to go. Please put your query in writing.' She'd heard her teacher say that once to a complaining parent.

Unfortunately, Connie did put her query in writing, though it was another six months before Georgie left the farm, because Connie and Trevor kept postponing.

On the train to London, a family befriended Georgie. They offered to take her to the restaurant car so long as she had her ration card, but she'd already eaten her egg sandwiches, packed by Morwenna in an old biscuit tin.

The upholstery irritated Georgie's skin. When the family had gone, she twisted round to see two red patches on the back of her legs, raised and crusty like the ringworm everyone feared at school. If it was ringworm, then Aunt Connie would find her disgusting. Georgie pulled her raincoat from the rack and sat on its silky lining to protect her skin.

She couldn't picture Aunt Connie, but she knew she was her mother's older sister. She must be one of the women in the wedding photograph that lived inside *The Natural History of Hartisborne*.

At Paddington, Georgie stretched her stiff legs, bundled her raincoat under her arm and pulled her suitcase onto the steamy platform. Porters offloaded cages of hens, crates of cream and buckets of budding gladioli. She wanted to cling to the gladioli as if they were the fields of home. But she was upcountry now and must make the most of it, as she had promised Morwenna and Uncle Tris. How would she recognise Aunt Connie?

Thrilled to see her own name, she heaved her case towards a woman, holding a sign with 'Georgina Gardner' written in uneven black capitals.

'I'm Georgie,' she said.

'Hello, Georgina. I'm your – I'm Constance. You can call me Aunty Connie, if you like.'

Aunty Connie was wearing a bobbly woollen skirt even though it was a warm afternoon in summer. Her blouse was a muddy pink. Her winged glasses suggested a surprised bird of prey. She smelt of disinfectant.

Georgie went to hug her Aunty, and after a moment Connie opened her arms. She put a vague hand on each of Georgie's shoulders and then quickly stood away from her.

'We're getting the bus home. This way.' Aunty Connie didn't take her suitcase. Georgie tied her raincoat round her waist and hurried to keep up.

On the bus, Connie told Georgie to put her suitcase in the luggage space, but Georgie wouldn't. Connie wrenched the case from her, saying, 'Don't hold everyone up.' She pulled Georgie further down the aisle, where she could only just see the edge of the suitcase holding the irreplaceable copy of *The Natural History of Hartisborne*, the only remnant of her parents. No one can replace your mum and dad, Morwenna had said when Georgie wept for her dead parents, but we will always be your friends.

'Don't worry,' Connie said. 'No one would touch that case with a bargepole.'

The irreplaceable suitcase was scratched, where Georgie pulled it over rocks to collect shells and sea glass washed up through barbed wire on the beach. When the wire hedges were pulled away, and the children had been able to run right down to the sea again, salt water had washed wavy white curves onto the leather.

In Connie's street, her aunt snatched up the case. 'Must be rather heavy for you.' She insisted on holding Georgie's hand all the way to the house. Then, she lingered on the step making a performance of unlocking the front door and waving at neighbours.

Georgie's bedroom was a boxroom. In Cornwall, she used to share with Morwenna, because she was frightened of the dark. And when she was older, they carried on sharing, because Wenna liked sharing too.

In Cornwall, her bed was under a wide windowsill, on which Morwenna placed a posy of wildflowers. At night, she put Georgie's glass of water on the wide uneven sill, and Georgie would add her copy of *The Natural History of Hartisborne*, so that it was always in reach.

Now the war was over, the lighthouse flashed across the bay again. The wind bent the trees into brushes. In the morning, Georgie flung open the window to smell the salt air, the damp rising from foxgloves and montbretia. Sparrows sang in the scrub, and, out at sea a marker buoy whistled. If it was fine, the Scilly Isles floated on the blue horizon.

The window in her London bedroom was a sash. The panes were grimy. There was no sill.

'How do I open the window?' she asked Connie.

'We've nailed it down to stop draughts. Here's your wardrobe and chest of drawers. And this is a desk we bought specially for your schoolwork.'

Everything was crammed together in a line against the brown papered wall. In Cornwall, Georgie sat at the kitchen table by the range and did her homework, while Morwenna cooked and chatted to her, and the cat dozed in an old grocery box.

Now Connie was staring at her, as if checking

off every feature on a list. The silence grew thick with expectation.

'Thank you,' Georgie said for something to say.

At last, Connie smiled. She snapped open Georgie's case and then wiped her hands hurriedly on her skirt.

For the first few days, Georgie saw little of Uncle Trevor. He rose early for work and, when he came home late, Connie sent her to her bedroom to be out of his way.

It was the summer holidays, yet neither Connie nor Trevor asked her what she was doing or gave her games or books. She read her mother's copy of *The Natural History of Hartisborne* over and over, looking up words in the dictionary, the only other book in her room. In her mind, she played with the baby hedgehogs of two hundred years ago and talked to the bee-boy, as he walked through Hartisborne, covered head to toe in bees.

'Can I help you with the garden?' Georgie asked Connie, as they pegged up the washing together. The yard was a strip of concrete and a coal store. In Cornwall, blackcurrants were ripening. The celery was ready to be cut. Tomatoes clustered along the warmest wall. If she were there instead of here, Uncle Tris would find jobs for her. Picking tomatoes. Watering beetroot. Taking caterpillars off the lettuce. 'Put out your foot,' Uncle Tris used to say, 'and the robin will land on it.'

'I don't have time for gardening,' Connie said.

Georgie chatted about Uncle Tris' garden. Connie's face sharpened. 'I don't want to hear about that lot,' she said decisively. 'They spoilt you and tried to keep you from us. And they sent you back with filthy toenails.'

Above the wall, a runner bean flaunted its scarlet as it searched the air for support. The neighbour's clematis tumbled over onto Connie's side.

'Gardening is all very well, but I don't want a mess *like her over there*,' Connie whispered.

When Connie went in, Georgie climbed on Trevor's stepladder to see the neighbour's yard. The ground was crammed with boxes of lettuces, lilies in pots and mint and rosemary growing in buckets. Passion flowers rambled across the wall. Runner beans tangled along strings nailed into the bricks. A child was watering pinks with a toy can and, as if in gratitude, the flowers released a clove-like scent. The child's mother waved at Georgie.

'Are you Mrs Cousins's niece?' she called. 'What's your name?'

'Georgie Gardner.'

The neighbour picked up her little girl and said, 'This is Cathy. She's only five, but would you like to play with her?'

Georgie ran in to see Connie. 'May I go and see Cathy next door?'

Connie's face tensed.

'Please, may I?' Georgie asked.

Connie lowered her voice. 'To be honest, they're a bit dirty, next door.'

'Just for a little while?'

'Someone to play with?' Connie frowned as if recalling something difficult. 'Maybe half an hour? So, I can get this carpet-sweeping done. Be back by eleven.'

Next door, Georgie sat at a small table under a mass of Russian vine and ate some lemon cake, while Cathy chattered away. Rosemary, Cathy's mother, told her the names of her climbers, saying 'If you can't grow out, you have to grow up.' She asked Georgie about her parents. What were their names? What did they do?

'I don't know,' Georgie said.

How sad that they'd died in the war – Rosemary had heard this from Connie.

After half an hour – her watch was a birthday present from Morwenna - Georgie made to leave. Rosemary was disappointed. 'Come again, won't you?' she said. 'Stay longer. Cathy likes you.'

In bed that night, Georgie revisited the funny things Cathy said. If something awful happened - but why would it - she could shout over the wall to Rosemary, Cathy's mother.

She went next door often. Connie preferred her out from under her feet, though sometimes she was as jealous of Rosemary and Cathy as she was of the Cornish family. Connie always said, 'We won't tell Trevor. He doesn't care for

Rosemary Morton. On her own with that child. And always wearing that garish bandana.'

Georgie had already learned to say nothing about Tris, Julia and Morwenna, though every day the farm flashed into her mind with its hens and hydrangeas.

At the weekend, Trevor hacked at the overhanging clematis. He tossed the bines and tendrils back into Rosemary's yard. *Effing mess - lazy bitch - ruddy tart - full of weeds.*

'Oh!' Georgie said.
'Do what?' Trevor asked. 'What did you say?'
'Nothing.'
It was safer to be silent.


Gil is fifteen. Moonlight falls through the gap in the drapes on this hot June night. *Betty, oh Betty, oh Betty, my love* is the first line of his first poem, for he has fallen in love with Farmer Luckin's milkmaid, and the line is stuck in his head, as irritating as a tick beneath the skin. Like any luckless swain, he cannot sleep. Outrageously, animals and birds sleep outside, the rabbit in his warren and the swallow on the wing. He watches fish when he wades upstream, feet pained by sharp stones. The fishes cannot close their eyes, but they pause and float in a kind of sleep under the bridge, knowing they are hidden. If fish can sleep, can they not love? *Betty, oh Betty...* He must escape his own maddening words.

He climbs from his bed and creeps past his brothers, head to toe under their covers. In the next room, his sisters' faces are bleached by moonlight, for Molly cannot sleep with the shutters closed. Through the half-open door of his parents' room, he sees his mother, her long hair in a grey pigtail, her mouth open, a girl and an old lady all at once.

Downstairs in the little parlour his father sits at his desk. In the sconces, two candles flicker their light over the paper, where his father draws plans for the garden, a glass of brandy beside him. Tomorrow his father's sleeplessness will throw him down into the pit and his sadness will seep into the very mortar.

Gil opens the yard-door, steps out, his feet bare on the brick path. The moon shines above the hanger, a perfect disc. An owl calls to its mate. To wit. To woo. Gil throws himself on the damp grass, lets the dew seep into his night shirt as he watches the worm casts rise on the lawn. The huge effort of worms, he thinks. He throws a stone into the cedar tree hoping to disrupt a roost. But there is no chittering reply.

The house slumbers, its limestone brightened by moonlight. Gil stares at the night till the dawn chorus begins its notations, and bands of mist over the field line up like ghosts of hedges. *Betty, oh Betty, oh Betty my love,* the birds call out of time. Last year, Betty was a sensible girl, her head resting against a cow's warm flank, squirting the teats with methodical hands, saying, 'You could never marry me, Master Gil, even if I let you have your way, so please sir, keep your distance.'

Now, a year later, gossip whispers that Betty is with child by Farmer Luckin. Thoughts of Betty's child won't leave Gil, whether he is eating his porridge, learning his Greek and Latin or kicking a ball with Thomas. His mother bans all mention of Farmer Luckin. Thomas lets him win at everything.

Betty is sent away and her child with her. His feelings subside over time. His first lesson in love. Thank you, Betty. You were wise to reject me. No one told him where Betty went.


Gil is forty-three. The old sleeplessness has returned. It is three weeks since the day of Mary's wedding. There were only a few in the congregation. The bride herself was not one of them. She sent Goody Newton to deliver the message that Eddy Kemp was not the father. It matters not, says Eddy, all that matters is Mary and the baby. He would marry her still if she would have him.

Since then, Mary has moved to Priory Farm under the protection of Farmer Luckin, who cares nothing for morality, so long as a girl works hard.

Mary's refusal to name her bastard's father ripples through the households of Hartisborne.

Women look askance at their husbands. Young men let it be known that Mary is nothing to them. They hint that Luckin's sheltering of Mary tells a story. Truly they suspect each other, but blaming Luckin clears them all.

All the gossip about Luckin reminds Gil of Betty and his youthful heart. He wonders what happened to her and Luckin's bastard child. Thoughts of old Luckin with Mary torment him. The farmer's grizzled face, his gnarled and seamy hands. Then also his mesmerising smile. His voice that, even now, can make maids preen and laugh.

Gil's stomach turns with such jealousy and disgust that he cannot put pen to paper. He prays for peace, for the power simply to watch a hedgehog and describe it. Oh Lord, is this too much to ask?

Is it his duty to persuade Luckin to marry Mary? Could God play such a terrible trick on him? For years, he has striven to overcome his revulsion, to work with Luckin in parish matters, to acknowledge their distant relationship. They are cousins, several times removed and not close family.

He must ask Luckin for the truth. He must be brave enough to face him, for Mary's sake. It is too late to help Betty. She must have died or settled afar for he never hears of her now. The women are tidied away, dismissed from service quickly when with child, passed to another parish and made invisible.

As a natural scientist, he knows his love for Betty was no more than the end of childhood, nature preparing him to father a new generation.

And yet, that old sadness grips him. The longing for children of his own. He wishes the wood pigeons would not flaunt their endless courtships. Such blatant creatures, with their bowing and nodding, billing and cooing. Why can't they be more discreet? When he was younger, he would have used them as target practice, but now he lets live, envying them their ungainly nests and acts of love.

To write of wood pigeons is a fine distraction from distress. He picks up his pen. A wood pigeon balances on a tree outside, carrying a stick in its beak. The bird stares at Gil as if to say, however make-shift, there is always a solution. Then the bird flies off to make its nest in a privet bush at eye level to passers-by. The nest won't last a moment when the homeward boys see it, but the wood pigeon builds on, proud of its clumsy weaving.

# CHAPTER 4

Her old terror of the dark returns as Georgie hurries through the slush under the dripping trees. There's a presence as if someone is watching her in the dusk. She looks around. The trees are just trees. The slush is slush. The glint of the stream below is comforting. It's only fear following her. Fear of Trevor, who is not here and who believes she is at Bracco & March.

She won't be home tonight. The second night she has stayed out without telling Trevor. She imagines him trying to heat the soup she's left him. Worrying perhaps. Working himself into a rage. Hammering on Rosemary's door to use her phone. Threatening to tell Celia about the last time Georgie stayed out. Will Rosemary give way and tell him where Georgie is?

A pheasant flickers clumsily up the bank. A blackbird sings. She is safe in Hartisborne with the descendants of the birds Gil knew. She's safer in this wood than she's ever been at home despite her mud-filled shoes rubbing at her chilblains.

The field gate swings open and bashes behind

her. Here is Priory Farmhouse. And here, at last, is Tom's barn-cum-studio in front of an arch of misty trees.

Georgie picks her away across the slurry. The cold rain plasters her hair. She unlatches the barn door without knocking and enters.

Georgie eases off the damp fur coat. She panics. It is too dark. She finds a light switch. A bulb hanging from the beam flares into life. She picks her way over the rough floor, jabbing her cold toes on discarded tools. She spots other lamps plugged into extension leads and switches them all on.

She has brought no fresh clothes with her. Celia's skirt is sodden with mud. The lining too. She fears Celia arriving home earlier than expected after her weeks away, wanting to wear her suit, rifling through the wardrobe at Marco's house, demanding to know whether they've been burgled. 'Absolutely done in. Frightful journey. Had any floozies back, Marco?' A joke of Celia's? Maybe Georgie is nothing special.

Georgie mutters on aloud now, unwillingly possessed by Celia. 'What does Titmouse have here? Trestle table, brushes bristle-side up, cartridge paper, bird books, Shell Guides, maps, oil paint, charcoal, pastels, rag, scissors, knife, crayons, pencil... ' Celia's voice itemises everything. Titmouse is her pet name for Tom.

Maybe if Georgie takes off Celia's suit, her voice will fade. She unzips the skirt, while Tom's painted blackbirds, owls and ducks flutter from the beams, watching with startled eyes.

Georgie lays the skirt across an old armchair. Her hair drips. Her legs shake with cold. She climbs a ladder to a hay loft, at the end of the barn. Here is Tom's bed, covered with a red and yellow Indian cloth. A fraying towel is folded on the pillow. Georgie smells the towel to check it's turps-free and wraps it around her hair. 'Typical Titmouse, using rags to dry himself.' She will not, she tells herself unconvincingly, have regrets about Marco or guilt about Celia. In two weeks, she'll be living here in Hartisborne. Celia will be free of Georgie.

Downstairs again, she attempts to fire up the Calor Gas stove, but the lighter won't work, and she can't find any matches.

There's a hammering on the barn door. Georgie freezes. A man's voice calls, 'Tom, Tom! Are you back? You've left all the lights on again, you old sod.' The door opens. 'Oh. Who are you?'

'A friend of Tom's?'

'You know his name because I called out *Tom*!'

'No. I really am a friend of Tom's.'

'He told me he was going to London.'

'Why call his name if you knew he wasn't here?'

'He doesn't always stick to a plan. I didn't want to barge in on a life model or – well, you never know exactly. You must be cold.'

'I walked from the village, and then the rain

set in.'

The man circles the trestle table suspiciously as if Georgie may have tampered with Tom's work.

'He said I could stay here.'

'Oh, did he?'

'Look, I can prove I know him.' Georgie fetches her handbag, conscious that she looks ridiculous wearing a slip and a jacket and with her head wrapped in Tom's ragged towel. She takes out the map's envelope. The name Georgie Gardner is framed by beak to tail swallows, Tom's visual signature.

'Yes. That's Tom's work. Sorry to doubt you, but last week someone disconnected the spark plugs in the tractor engine. Then some yobs messed around with the hay bales in the other barn. Probably to do with the street lighting business... oh never mind. I'm sorry if I was rude. We farmers are suspicious types.'

'You're Farmer Luckin from Gil's letters!'

He seems too young to be a farmer or to be Tom's landlord.

'I'm not quite two hundred years old. But his Farmer Luckin was my ancestor, yes. It's nothing to be proud of according to our local history fanatic, Mrs Camden. Come over to the house and get warm.'

Georgie drapes her wet coat around her, picks up her handbag and the muddy skirt and follows him out of the barn. She slips off her mud-caked shoes inside the farmhouse door.

'My cleaning lady left me a shepherd's pie for dinner. Are you hungry? I can put it in early.'

'I'm starving.'

'Hang on.' Nick rummages in the airing cupboard and hands her a fresh towel. 'Do you want to change? My mother's left some clothes upstairs. Or you could borrow one of my jumpers?'

'I'd love something dry.'

'Mum's room is upstairs second right– take what you like. The bathroom's next to Mum's room.'

'Thanks.'

The bathroom houses a vast stained bath, a cracked basin and a cranky cylinder that burns her hands with hot water. She unwraps her hair and plonks Tom's towel on the floor. She strips off Celia's jacket, her own slip and her stockings. She washes the mud from her legs and dries herself.

Freshened up and wrapped in the new towel, Georgie enters Nick's mother's room. From what Nick said, she'd expected drawerfuls of clothes but there is little to choose from.

In the wardrobe, there's a fifties dress with a nipped in waist and a full skirt. She loves its satiny green. She can't bring herself to wear another woman's underwear, so keeps on her damp knickers and bra, then manoeuvres into the green dress and zips it up the side. The hairdryer burns dust which makes her choke. She is still cold, so she puts on an angora bolero from the wardrobe and finds a new pack of stockings in the drawer. She blows the hairdryer up her skirt to dry out her suspender belt before rolling on the stockings.

If only Nick's mother had left some slacks and a jumper. An invisible hand on her back propels her downstairs with her armful of wet clothing.

'Oh!' Nick says. 'I thought you were my mother of about ten years ago for a moment.'

'Do I look like her?'

'No, thank God.'

'There wasn't much choice.'

'But wasn't there a whole heap of clothes on the bed?'

'There was only this in the wardrobe.'

'She must have been back without telling me again.'

'Will she mind me wearing this?'

'I don't care if she does. She hasn't lived here for years. Since Dad went, she's been popping in unannounced. Though she barely bothered to visit when I was a kid or when Dad was ill.' Nick slams a metal tray of shepherd's pie into the oven. 'Don't expect too much. Sylvia – she's my cleaning lady - isn't the world's best cook, I'm afraid.'

'Perhaps I should change?'

'You look great. Classy. Here, let me dry those.'

He takes the wet bundle from her and drapes

them on the clothes horse. It is odd to see him carefully arranging her stockings, slip, jumper and Celia's jacket. 'Smart clothes to wear in the mud!'

'I dressed for my interview.'

'So you're the mysterious outsider who somehow heard about the museum job? But now I get it – you heard about it from Tom. What happened?'

'I got the job!' Georgie blushes with the pleasure of telling someone.

Nick pauses. 'Ah! Poor Joan... and then there's Maisie... such a great kid... but anyway we should celebrate. Shall we have a drink? I'll get the fire going in the long hall. I keep it made up, in memory of Dad really. We used to have drinks' parties and carol singers in – that kind of thing. Dad was all for an open house. And he's always been a sucker for artists, like his musician pals and Tom. If it wasn't for the farm, he'd have travelled round in a band, I think. I'll smarten myself up. Shame Tom isn't back to join us.'

Georgie hears creaking above her head, the gurgle of the ancient pipes and some sloshing around. Nick returns in clean shirt, jeans and a jacket. 'Will this do?'

'Not up to my level of poshness,' Georgie says, swinging out her skirt.

'I defy anyone to match my mother's level of poshness. Shall I squeeze an orange and make you gin and orange? Or would you prefer gin and French, my mother's favourite tipple?' Nick fetches some glasses, a bottle of Noilly Prat and another of London Gin. He pours himself a whisky.

They move through to the long hall where the fire crackles and smokes. 'Let's have jazz.' He puts a Miles Davis LP on the record player.

Georgie sips her drink. 'I'm guessing your father has died? If you don't mind me asking?'

'A couple of weeks ago. I wouldn't be here at all if he hadn't got so ill. I'd just been given a job with the UN.'

'So grand!'

'Not as grand as it sounds. I studied Agricultural Economics at university and worked for the civil service. I was just about to move to Rome to work for the UN's Food and Agricultural Organisation. My mother was determined I shouldn't take over the farm. But then Dad got ill. So, I gave up the job in Rome before I even left London and came back to look after him. And now, I'm Farmer Luckin. They've made me a school governor and want me to stand for the Parish Council. The whole village is on the lookout for my ideal woman, preferably from farming stock, because we're supposed to marry each other. There's a conspiracy to make me stay, and the worst of it is, that sometimes I want to. But on bad days, when Wilf the cowman is barely speaking to me, then I regret my lost chance and imagine myself sitting by the Trevi fountain with a glass of wine.'

'So, your mother doesn't live here?'

'There's a superstition that no women can live here because of the Priory's past. That's my mother's excuse for leaving. The ghostly monks stalked her or some such nonsense. Let's eat in here by the fire. And let me get you another gin and French.'

He holds out his hand for her glass.

'Can I help in the kitchen?'

'Just relax or choose another record. Then, you can tell me how you know Tom.'

Georgie hopes she won't have to talk about the bookshop. She sifts through the LPs, wishing she hadn't thought of Marco. The fire exhales a billow of smoke. Sparks fly, dotting the green dress with tiny scorches. What will Nick's mother say? She puts on the latest Cliff Richard, blows fluff from the stylus and lowers the arm.

She sways to the music to warm herself. An invisible dancer – or is it the gin - dizzies her around, until the green dress flares out and the room whirls. When Nick opens the door, Georgie falls into an armchair, embarrassed.

'I'm sorry I talk about Dad so much,' Nick says, handing her a drink. 'What about your parents?'

'I'd love to have stories about my parents,' Georgie says, 'but I know so little.'

From upstairs in his study, Gil can hear Thomas scraping his boots by the garden door. The snow has melted, but not the discomfit of Mary's wedding day three weeks ago which still lingers in his mouth, a sour taste.

How much easier to be bird than human, unencumbered by social laws. He turns his mind to the mating of wrens and their nest-building. The song of generation is everywhere. All nature tunes up to the deed. Gil dips his pen. He ignores the creaking of the stairs and, instead, begins his description of nests woven by a male wren to court a female.

Thomas' feet approach. The steps of one with news to impart. *Which nest will the female choose?* Thomas is at the door. *The nests are low built.* A perfunctory knock. T*he wren hops and flutters, coaxing the female to select her new home.* Thomas bursts in.

Gil lays down his pen and blots his work, anticipating Thomas' words. 'Mr Gil, I think you should know… ' So many sentences begin this way. Everyone assumes the village is Gil's responsibility when he is merely the curate, standing in for a frequently absent vicar.

'Mr Gil, I think you should know that I spotted Mr Blundel walking past the pipe barrel, talking to himself loudly.'

When Blundel shouts at the breeze, vagabonds hide among bushes, fearful of being moved on.

'He'll be here in a moment. Shall I tell him you're out?'

Gil hesitates. How much more agreeable it would be to stay at his desk, weaving a wren's nest with his pen, than to listen to Blundel's thunder.

'It will be about Mary, Mr Gil,' Thomas says. 'If only she had married young Kemp.' The words 'if only she had married young Kemp' are Thomas' frequent refrain.

There is a great hammering on the front door. Gil rises from his desk.

'Can you show him into the little parlour? And furnish whatever refreshments you think best?' Blundel is known for gluttony.

Gil straightens his wig and brushes down his clothes. He is a short man whereas Blundel, the parish overseer of the poor, is a giant. Yet Gil is, after all, a Fellow of Oriel and of the Royal Society, whose motto 'nullius in verba', *believe nothing from words alone*, he must now employ against Blundel's flim-flam of self-righteousness. Gil rises to his full short height and assumes his gravest expression. He's always been secretly afraid of Blundel, a man too coarse to comprehend a woman like Mary.

Blundel stands in the little parlour, a fat black crow squinting at the portrait of Gil's brother.

'A great likeness to Mr Benjamin,' Blundel says, proud of his acumen.

'It is indeed.' Gil extends his hand. All

bonhomie.

The reality of his brother, the impatient publisher in St Paul's Churchyard waiting on Gil's *Natural History of Hartisborne*, nagging him for the pages, disconcerts him. Ben would not approve of this interruption, when Gil should be writing about wrens. Yet Blundel, though narrow in mind, is a conscientious man, going about his parish duty. And it is Gil's parish duty, as curate in charge, to listen to him. Ben's painted eyes rebuke him for wasting time, while other less talented curates churn out their inferior nature studies.

'And how are you keeping Mr Blundel?' Immediately, he regrets his courtesy. An open question flings the gate wide on Blundel's grievances.

'Ah Mr Gil, I carry a heavy load in ensuring parish funds are not worn down to a mere sixpence. I'm beset by ingrates who would drain our resources in a moment if they could. Petitioners I've refused send the fox in to plague my chickens. Some evenings my head aches so - and my knees! – I can scarcely move them for the weight of my conscience.'

Or the weight of your belly, Gil thinks. 'Will you try some ale? I don't think you've tasted it since we used the new hopping method. Thomas, could you fetch some refreshments?'

Gil sits, and Blundel sits which at least reduces his height.

'I know you keep out of village gossip, sir. So, I daresay you've heard nothing about Farmer Luckin and his abuse of me?'

In fact, Gil has heard several versions of Luckin chasing Blundel from the farm. In all the accounts, Luckin's weapon varies. There have been axes, pitchforks – the two most consistently mentioned items – but also a hatchet, a carpenter's sawtooth dog, a knotted rope, and a deer's skull used as a missile. But caution, caution. This is all hearsay. *Nullius in verba*. After all, here is the man himself.

'I heard some slight rumour?'

The hatchet and the deer's skull turn out to be Luckin's chosen weapons of threat.

Thomas brings in ale, a joint of cold pork, a crock of pickled apple and a hunk of bread. He serves Blundel an ample plateful. It is ten in the morning. Gil is not even hungry but not to eat with Blundel will smack of unfriendliness. He toys with a slice of pork and takes a sip of ale. Blundel talks on with his mouth full. Gil's stomach turns.

'You mention rumours, sir,' Blundel says. 'There are plenty of those.' He pulls the bread apart and stuffs it into his mouth.

'What kind of rumours?'

Gil nods at Thomas to stay in the room.

'Very fresh bread, sir. Fine baking. And the sage on the pork adds a piquancy – I must tell my wife. And the pickling of the apple… certainly a delicacy. The thing is the father of Trimmer's child…'

'Mistress Mary Trimmer,' Gil says, determined that Blundel should speak of her with respect.

'I believe she no longer works for you, sir?' Blundel holds Gil's eyes for a moment, while chewing on a piece of crackling.

'Mary is welcome to work here until her time comes,' Gil says. 'The village women carry on with their tasks until confinement and afterwards. They're not fine ladies. They bring their babies to the harvest fields and the orchards. But you know the ways of our people as well as I.'

'But is Trimmer one of our people? That is the question.'

Gil looks away. Through the window, a blackbird pecks at something on the outer sill. Gil wonders what the bird is eating. Not a length of greasy crackling at ten in the morning. He must write about the elegance of birds as opposed to men. Or would it make a sermon? A veiled attack on Blundel? The temptation shames him.

With a great crunching, Blundel finishes off the crackling and takes a draught of ale.

'I solicit your help, your reverend, to enforce parish law and persuade Trimmer to own the truth. You are known to have an uncommonly close relation to her. Otherwise, I will need to ask the justice to rule on this matter.'

'The law states that a woman cannot be interrogated while she is with child.'

'She cannot be interrogated as to the father, but a settlement case is different. And a bastardy examination can be held a month after the birth, sir, but, by then, with the fees to a midwife or a doctor - or that man midwife over Alton way who charges so much more than the women- she could have cost the parish a pretty penny. And if the birth goes badly, the cost is greater. Better to return her to Binford and let them pay.'

'Nature must take its course. Settlement can be settled later.'

'She should name the father lest she and her bastard become leeches on parish funds. If her child is born here, it will have seven years settlement which could cost a pretty penny if it turns out sickly.'

'Mary should not be coerced. There may be reasons for silence.'

Blundel sniffs, a beagle scenting the chase.

'If the father is violent or married, for example,' Gil says pointedly.

'Like the father of Annie Adkins' child,' Thomas offers.

'Exactly,' Gil says. 'Annie Adkins told you the father's name, under duress. Then, her lover beat her until she miscarried, which saved him and his wife the upkeep of a child and left Mistress Adkins bleeding and in long sorrow.'

'Annie Adkins is recovered well enough and

has married now.'

'She fears she cannot bear another child,' Gil says. 'She was married four months with no conception and her husband has turned her out.'

'I am not responsible for the evil deeds of her bastard's father. There is no likeness between the cases of Trimmer and Adkins. '

'And why not?' Gil asks.

'Well sir, since you ask, there are only three names mentioned as possible sires of Trimmer's child. Firstly, there is Edward Kemp, a man whose paternity Trimmer denies, even though, God bless him, he is still ready to marry her and act the part. That man is no woman beater.'

'No, he's a gentle soul,' Gil agrees. 'If only she had turned up. I had my wedding sermon ready days beforehand,' he lies, 'and all would have been well.'

'The second name is that of your cousin Farmer Luckin.'

'Farmer Luckin is a cousin so far removed that he is almost a stranger, and for pity's sake, man, he's old. He must be seventy or more.'

'Too old to sire a baby,' Thomas says. 'I doubt his organ would support the deed.'

'That's a tasteless speculation, Tom.'

'No one knows Luckin's age or what he is capable of. Though he chased me with a hatchet, I don't think Luckin would hurt Trimmer, but maybe you are right - she is frightened of him - and therefore refuses to name him.'

'And the third candidate?'

Thomas shakes his head at Gil.

'An awkward matter, sir. One I scarcely dare raise.' His mouth swells into a smile, revealing a bit of crackling caught between his wooden and his real tooth.

'Come to think of it, Mr Gil,' Thomas says hastily, 'Farmer Luckin may well be sturdy enough to sire. Why I saw him lift a stook that three younger men couldn't haul on to the cart.'

'Tom, please don't interrupt. Now Mr Blundel, be frank. Who is your third suspect?'

'They say that Kemp and Trimmer wanted to protect you by marrying but, at the last minute, Trimmer couldn't carry the lie through.'

'You have delayed Mr Gil for long enough,' Thomas says.

'No, Tom. I wish to understand Mr Blundel.'

'Well, sir, if you must have it in plain speech, you are the suspected father.'

Gil is nonplussed. If only he were an impulsive philanderer. Such a man could become a father. 'Your suspicion is nonsense.'

'Oh, it's not *my* suspicion. It's what the whole of Hartisborne is saying. Personally, I suspect Farmer Luckin. An old dog doesn't change. But the odds in The Compasses are on you, sir.'

'Mr Gil is a man of God,' Thomas says.

'Yes, and plenty of clergymen have ridden their maids. Some have married them, of course. But I mean no disrespect. My point is that if Trimmer could be persuaded to name the father, all suspicion would drop from you, sir. I come here in good faith for the sake of your reputation.'

'Is that so?'

'I thought it right to apprise you, and your man here, that such rumours flow along the street.'

'So that we can do what?'

'Why, defend yourselves vigorously!'

'Defensive talk implies guilt. What do you think, Thomas?'

'Never apologise, never explain – so my old mother taught me.'

'So, there is cause for apology?' Blundel's face sharpens. He's on the scent of a philandering curate, a pandering serving man.

Gil stands. Blundel remains sitting, which for once gives Gil the advantage of height.

'You have insulted me, as a man of God, as a gentleman and as a… ' what else could he add – a triplet is a forceful tool of rhetoric – 'and as a scientist.'

'A man of honour,' Thomas suggests too late.

'You eat my meat and drink my ale, and all the while, you judge me a rake.' He sounds like a character in a novel by the late Mr Richardson. How Miss Butter would laugh, were she here. But it is no laughing matter for Mary.

'Perhaps if the church, if you sir, advised Farmer Luckin of his duty, it would not only save parish funds but save your reputation too, sir.'

'Mr Blundel, you have excelled yourself.'

'Thank you, sir! I do my best.'

Thomas steps to the front door and opens it. 'Mr Gil has an urgent paper to complete. His publisher has made me answerable for his delays.'

Blundel feigns admiration. 'On what subject, sir?'

'The mating habits of wrens.'

Blundel's operatic laugh rises to the ceiling. He gathers up his heaviness. 'Well sir, we will talk again when you've finished such important business!'

Blundel leaves, chuckling about the fitness of a little man writing about little birds. Thomas slams the door behind him.

'Well, what do you think, Tom?'

'Better not to have mentioned the wrens.'

'I mean is it my duty to tell Mary to marry Farmer Luckin?'

'There is another solution, I believe.'

'Unless the real father comes forward, I can think of none.'

Thomas coughs and hacks. Gil would think it a swallowing of laughter if he weren't well acquainted with Thomas' throats.

'If you cannot see the answer, which, in my view, is somewhat before us, take comfort in this. Mr. Blundel's term of office ends in a fortnight. If John Carpenter is elected overseer, as we expect, he will find kinder ways to help Mary.' Thomas slides away down the hall before Gil can reply.

Through the window, a ray of sun floats a leafy pattern on the table. Blundel's greasy plate and knife rest in a shaft of light.

Winnie must have written the letter during the day, while Wilf was working at Priory Farm. Cheeseparing, Winnie used to call him. Yet, she'd still managed to save for postage stamps from the housekeeping.

Was she so scared of Wilf, her own loving husband, that she had to go out secretly at night? From inside the pub, enjoying their lock-in, their emergency oil-lamps, the roasting fire, the regulars had heard nothing, not even the screech of brakes. The car must have been coasting on ice, saving money. Or the battery was flat perhaps, and so the lights weren't working. Some tight bastard, saving on petrol. If the engine had been running, Winnie would have heard the car, even though she was a bit deaf. But a voice inside him says she did hear it, sensed its weighty shadow moving over the ice towards her. Maybe she stepped out because nothing mattered to her anymore.

If Wilf hadn't gone to the pub, Winnie would

have stayed home. His presence would have stopped her from posting the letter. She went to the post box that night because he was out, because he disapproved, because he had forced her to be secretive. Because she knew he was fed up with her writing to their son Arthur, who had disappeared in the war. But Winnie wrote to him daily, as if her letters would bring him back. *Eighteen years have gone by since the war ended, and Arthur is never coming back.* He'd wanted to scream that at her but hadn't. If she kept writing to Arthur, maybe in a way he still existed.

Had Wilf been at home, they would have listened to the play on the wireless, perhaps with a cup of Ovaltine and the letter nowhere to be seen. She would have darned his socks. He would have stoked the fire. When the power cut out, they would have lit candles. And later kissed each other goodnight, before turning their backs away in bed.

Hours after he'd left, she must have taken the letter from its hiding place. And then slipped on her coat, gloves and scarf. You wouldn't wear a coat out in the cold, if you didn't care what happened to you, would you? You'd dart out in your nightclothes or not bother to change from your slippers, but maybe the thought takes you at the last minute or maybe the thought was there, but you hadn't decided and that was why you'd left the torch on the door mat instead of taking it with you. But you couldn't know that a car with no lights was coasting down the hill over the ice? That it would slip as it rounded the corner and roar into life as it hit you and drove away?

At that moment, did she finally understand she'd never see their son again? Did she throw herself in front of the car? Perhaps she thought it the ghost of a car, as there was no sound beyond the creak of wheels and crack of ice. Ghosts are known here, but not the ghosts of cars.

Winnie's decision, if it was a decision, won't change the bitter taste in his mouth. He blames the darkness. Had there been streetlights, Winnie would never have walked in front of the car, and the driver would have seen her. If it wasn't for old Gil, the street wouldn't be dark. Reason says that other villages with streetlights went dark during the power cuts of the big freeze. But that doesn't change the fact that it's old Gil's fault that the driver didn't see Winnie, that no one realised she was gone until Wilf staggered home from the pub.

His wife's bloody body frozen on the street is what happens when there's no progress, when villages are mired in the past, fall into the pocket of museums and the like. Darkness, darkness, that's all they want and everyone in their place like before the war.

The unknown driver was a murderer but the anti-light contingent, sentimental fools worshipping old Gil, were also to blame. Reality.

That's what was needed. Living in the present, the modern world. Not denying death like Winnie or pretending the past hadn't passed.

Without Saint Gil, the village would have streetlights and new houses so that villagers could still live here. The museum would be a hotel offering the youngsters jobs. If people had grievous visions - old Sylvia comes to mind - then streetlights would banish them as they'd banish so many other goings-on.

The Colonel says, 'But you can't know whether Winnie would have had her accident even with street lighting?' What was he implying – that Winnie did herself in? That she was mad for writing to a dead son all these years? The Colonel raised his secret fear, and Wilf hates him for it.

The past shouldn't have such a hold on the future. Old ladies could walk the street again if the by-pass had been built across Wakeling park and under the hanger.

If he stands a few yards from Winnie's grave, where the earth is still fresh, the snow thinner, he can get a good aim at Gil's headstone. Bullseye.

# CHAPTER 5

Gil winds his watch with his swallow-shaped winder, a gift from his sister. His watch does not keep time, and neither does he. Water voles, his new subject, disappear into mud holes, evading his pen. His brother Ben worries that other natural scientists will steal his thunder. But thunder cannot be stolen. If he is a slow writer, if the garden rather than the page beckons, and the doings of villagers are thrust upon him, so be it. Ben must go on waiting till Gil has settled this business about Mary or till he is an old man fit for nothing but to sit and write. An old man with a wife is a bearable thought. An old man alone, with no one to call him from his desk, less so.

That Gil is still a bachelor is not for want of his friends' ingenuity. Now even Thomas has allied himself with Gil's aunts and gossiping nieces to become yet another matchmaker, hinting slyly at Gil's love for Mary.

These are the women whom friends and family have, at various times, designed for his heart: Miss Hecky, sister of his hypochondriac friend and herself no epistolary slouch in accounts of bloodletting, heartburn and ague; Miss Katy, the laughing London visitor of last summer; and Miss Butter, the vicar's younger cousin, a traveller to strange lands, and a friend who might promise much intelligence on exotic flora and fauna were she not fixed on being a character in a novel, with a string of foreign lovers. His own choices in love failed long ago.

Gil is twenty-seven. He enters a secret engagement, that no one is to uncover but a few of his close men, who, on the discovery, blab so much in their cups that Oxford soon knows all. His friends disapprove, he, being a gentleman, and Jinnie, hailing from trade. He lives for his visits to her mother's shop, the haberdashery where his grandmother's tenants deliver their rent and where he collects the moneys from Jinnie's hand.

Jinnie's mind is a quill sharpened on items, invoices and imports. Though his friends mock him with talk of measuring rods and shillings per yard, he minds none of that, for the young Gil likes to quantify and compute, just as he now likes to measure rainfall, weigh blossom and list the price of each barrow of dung. In numbers, as well as in wine, truth is to be found. An accounting woman, a woman of a mathematical bent, could add much to his enquiries into natural history. And if married to Jinnie, what linen and muslins he could bestow on his sisters, what drapes for the house. But beyond these considerations, he loves her face and her kisses, and she loves his face and his kisses. Reason and passion are in accord, and that, he knows, is a rare blessing.

On the journey to Oxford, despite his nausea and vomiting as the coach rocks him along the road, his mind flies to their nuptials. Soon he will be ordained and in two or three years a curacy may well arise and with it an income, and then he and Jinnie will be wed in Hartisborne Church, for he can picture their ceremony in no other place.

Yet, the fates will trip a Christian as much as an Ancient, and, while staying in college for a Fellows' meeting, the smallpox traps him in his rooms. The fever takes hold. His skin crawls with rounds of pus, till he becomes all toad and drinks himself senseless, taking any quack's suggested remedy to quell his fear of dying. Figs and tripe, washed down by Rhenish wine, and then by French, green tea, balm tea, and currants so dried and wrinkled, tart and dusty in the mouth, that he soaks them in brandy, sweet as fire. Then bohea, the finest, strongest black tea, burning his mouth, and more wine, three bottles more of Rhenish, two of claret and one apparently of piss-poor vinegar, unless that is the flavour of his stricken taste.

When he passes out, a vision of his childhood nurse, Goody Newton, sponges his face, takes away the pot from the close stool and billows the clean sheet like a shroud. The shroud should torment him. He is dying, isn't he? He must be dead? And Goody is here to lay him out? But Goody Newton's practised hands raise him from his bed and then slide the cool fresh sheet over the ticking. Do visions have scents? For on her, he smells the green leaves of Hartisborne, the wet beeches, the black marl. Can visions speak? For he hears her rural voice, saying, 'Promise me you'll be well somewhen soon, Mr Gil'. *Somewhen*, that beloved Hampshire word, trickles through his head, *some when*. Oh the vagueness of time. But *some* does not tell him *when* he will be recovered.

To bed again, while the bells of the colleges ring out their lack of synchronicity, as if Oxford changes time, repeats minutes, quarters, halves until the hours toll into an endless peal. Sundials and shadows, sand-timers and pendula. Time stalks his body marking out days in clocks of pus. In his sweating phantasy, his double takes him by the hand and leads him along Monksway to cool his feet in the village stream. The hallooing of a drunken student morphs Ovid-like into the lonely cry of an owl, flying low on a misty evening, threatening the ducks' eggs by the monks' ponds in Coombe Meadow.

In this delirium, the apparition Goody Newton

bathes him again, cools him with sponges and heats the green tea. When he wakes, it is no illusion. For here she is, wearing her homeliness like stained skirts, while urging him to drink her potions and telling how his father sent her.

He insists on a mirror. 'No, no, Mr Gil. Not yet,' says Goody, but she has always done what he asks, indulged him from a child, and finally she begs a mirror from that vain young gentleman on the neighbouring staircase. Gil observes himself, as precisely as if he were noting cabbage tops stuffed in the craw of a dead bird.

His skin is crusted like an old map. And he is but twenty-seven. He, who is known for his soft kisses, his handsome well-shaped face, who women turn to for embraces and sly smiles, laughing at his witty turns of phrase, he is nothing now but the roughest rind.

'It will fade, Mr Gil,' Goody says. 'Your father will know a balm, for sure.' She unlatches the window to listen to the bells, for Goody has lived a life of small compass and these bells playing games with time amuse her, but now her heaving shoulders betray her. She is a woman weeping out of a window to hide her tears.

'Yes, dear Goody,' he reassures her, 'we'll try balms and ointments. My father will find remedies in his herb garden, I'm sure.'

'A layer of cucumber is very soothing and fading to the scar,' Goody says, with her back to him still.

'Then I will cut as many cucumbers as necessary. I promise you I'll live under cucumber.'

'My sores were full as bad as yours, years ago, but look here.' She bares her arm again. 'Just the silvery traces, sir, and no harm done.'

Goody speaks true. Her scars are nothing but wavy lines. He recalls, though he was but a child, that it was a mild case, and Goody's pretty face, as it was then, barely touched, a fact much celebrated in the village.

Now, a scabrous poem about his current state goes the college rounds. He knows the author well and laughs, for it is the Oxford way to laugh at oneself. The poem takes a classical turn, conjuring a grower of melons who himself transmogrifies into a scarred and bumpy melon, like a creature from Ovid.

Did Jinnie hear this scabrous poem? Did some wag sing it under the windows of the haberdashery? She sends a message of worries about his suffering. She insists on meeting him, though Goody warns, 'You rest up, Mr Gil. Go home and use your father's balm before you meet any young ladies.'

But Gil is impatient to see her and takes Jinnie's impatience as love. Throughout his fever, not only has he fantasised the marriage ceremony in Hartisborne church, but the births of their seven children. In his mind, he has planned each child's inoculation. The nobility are infecting their young these days to save them later. No child of his is to suffer what he has suffered, and no child of his is to die of the smallpox, which swept away his three younger siblings, years before the other six were born. Everything can be turned to advantage and if his suffering resolves him to protect his own children, then he will thank God for it.

At last, and, without Goody's blessing - for he has returned her on the post chaise to Hartisborne with a pot of sodden fiery currants to chew on the way - he issues forth from college to meet Jinnie in the Botanical Gardens, his once fresh skin, as his rhymer friend has aptly quipped, like melon rind, and his head full of love and lore, children and science.

A grey day by the river. The clatter of small boats under the bridge. Jinnie standing in fine freshly sewn skirts. He would like to grab her by the waist and dance her down the garden paths, making her skirts fly along the flower beds.

He approaches. He watches her, as if through a telescope. His feet race forward. His heart too. Then, she sees him. She hesitates. He senses her mind computing, adding up the benefits of their marriage against this new repulsion. Reason says her love will overcome such a common disfigurement. Her reason would have triumphed, he is sure. But his pride cannot overcome her hesitation, the sums in her face, the forcing of a smile.

On the way back in the coach, he tortures himself with regrets. When the coach stops at The Compasses, he staggers out on to the village street, nauseous, and only just able to hurry the few yards to his home, tormented by thoughts of losing the woman he loves.

Now, in his agony, Gil tells his younger self that he should have waited till his pox rounds were healed, postponed his meeting with Jinnie and then met her in flattering candlelight. If the past exists elsewhere, as philosophers posit, then a younger Gil is still dulling his pox with wine, his thoughts, muzzy as clouds, yet beating in his skull like hammers. If only he could go back, entrust the wine to his friend the rhymer, swab the sores with Goody's ointment, mark off time in bells, clocks and sundial shadows, until his skin and his mind grew clear, then he would be married by now with children running around the garden and the finest discounted drapery adorning his home.

Is Jinnie really the woman he loves or another as yet unknown? A phantasy, someone he sees in his garden on his return to the village, a figment perhaps. He pictures this stranger as he saw her when he was twenty-seven, heart-broken and newly returned to Hartisborne. There she is, bundled in a fur of strange fashion, listening to a blackbird. He can feel her fascination with his observations. Perhaps she is the spirit of Hartisborne itself? Perhaps she is a muse?

A village dryad? More likely, he is still half-delirious from the pox, and yet this figment gives him a slither of hope.

Better to be alive than dead, better to be scarred than in a coffin like his friend, the gentleman-rhymer who died so quickly of the pox that the scabrous melon poem was still fresh in his friends' mouths.

Better to see the greening beech bring forth its lightness again under the sun, than never more to see it. Even if his heart hurts, his father needs comfort. Filial duties fall first to the eldest. Better to let Hartisborne enfold him, if the woman he loves cannot.

He puts his hands round Jinnie's waist and dances her back into the past.

And once Jinnie is safely fixed in the Botanical Gardens at Oxford, her skirts wistfully fluttering in the breeze, he allows himself to conjure the hope of another woman, the phantasy prompted in him, whenever he sees a blackbird darting and hopping across the meadow.

He imagines standing beside this woman, who is as observant as himself, which is why he loves Mary, of course. She looks at nature with a true naturalist's eye and she is a gardener through and through. If only it were as simple as Thomas suggests, that he could marry Mary and save her and so save himself. He could be her father's child and father his own children. He looks out of the window at the meadows of Wakeling Park and the hanger and the gardens. Even if all his obligations of property and his nephews' inheritance could be bypassed somehow to marry Mary, what if she says no?

At twenty-seven, he barely survived his broken heart, but he had youthful hope on his side. At forty-three, the body is less able, but the heart is even more tender. His vision is as open to nature's miracles as ever it was. He dips his pen and writes his garden journal.

How strange to start the day in Hartisborne and end it here in Trevor's house, hemmed in by the brown walls. The noise of Trevor throwing kitchen chairs and saucepans around the room forces her to close *The Natural History of Hartisborne*, leaving strings of dead bullfinches hanging from Farmer Luckin's orchard, a warning not to peck buds. Only this morning, though it seems a lifetime ago, she had walked with Nick Luckin over the grassy bumps of the Priory ruins past an orchard of gnarled trees, thankfully free of bullfinch corpses.

A sudden silence. Georgie freezes. The silence becomes eerier. Has Trevor harmed himself as he threatened? Has she caused Trevor's death as well as Aunty Connie's?

Now she creeps down to the kitchen. There's

a bread knife on the table and a loaf of bread on the board. Maybe the knife signals nothing more than an evening snack.

She mustn't let slip the reason for yesterday's absence, her interview and the new job. She mustn't tell about her night at Nick's farm. Trevor is not above writing to Colonel Camden to smear her character. He couldn't bear her leaving Palliser's to work in the bookshop and had sent Marco a peculiar letter, which Celia found hilarious and dubbed 'the anti-reference'.

'Where were you last night?' Trevor asks Georgie, as soon as she appears.

'I went to Tom Swallow's to find a book for Mrs Bracco.'

'Same excuse as last time?'

'I'm good at looking.'

'Did you find it?'

'Yes.'

'Why didn't you come home afterwards?'

'There was a power cut. It didn't feel safe to come home so late. Esme, Mrs Swallow, suggested I sleep on the couch.'

'So, no funny business?'

'I went to work early because Mrs Bracco needed the book.' Celia is still in Oxford, but Georgie implies she was waiting in the shop.

'And where did Bracco sleep?'

'He went home earlier.'

'And where did the effing Bohemian sleep?'

'If you mean Mr Swallow, he slept upstairs

in Esme's part of the house. Not that it's my business.'

Trevor feels the bread knife's serrated edges with his thumb.

'I don't want any little bastards running around because you can't keep your knickers on. Family habit, from what I've heard.'

'What do you mean?' Georgie asks.

'Don't,' Connie says in her head, pale as paper. She never would have said, 'Don't' to Trevor. She hardly ever stood up for Georgie, but now Connie is gone, Georgie endows her aunt with a smidgeon of courage.

Trevor smiles. 'Your own mother couldn't keep her knickers on. That's why we got landed with you. What book were you looking for?'

Georgie won't answer.

'There was no book, was there?'

Georgie puts the bread knife in the washing-up bowl and the loaf in the bread tin.

Trevor grabs her by the shoulders. 'No book, was there, you little bitch?'

Georgie pulls away. So many books have passed through her hands that she can't think of a single title. Then it comes to her. 'A French translation of Eugene Onegin by Pushkin.'

Trevor puts on a falsetto. 'Ooh, French translation. Ooh Mr Bracco, you're a clever git, aren't you? And you're getting up yourself, aren't you or is he getting up you?' He grabs Georgie by her sweater.

'Don't be so crude.'

'I know what you're up to.'

'What?' Georgie asks, jerking out of his grip.

'Covering up your whoring.' He lunges towards the bread board, but because Georgie's moved the knife, he veers away towards the cutlery drawer, rummaging for something sharp.

Georgie escapes and runs upstairs. She pulls her chest of drawers against the door again. She waits silently until Trevor gives up trying to force the door open.

She slips the photo out of *The Natural History*. Her mother's tiny grey and white face gives nothing away and neither does her cascade of roses and ferns. Was she already pregnant with Georgie? Perhaps, her mother and father had to get married. If so, she was there too, at the wedding, with both her parents. The thought gives her strength.

There's no Trevor in the picture as he didn't know Connie then. None of the women look like Connie. She must have become unrecognisable after years of living with Trevor.

He's rattling the door again. He can't shift it because of the weight of her chest of drawers.

'You effing little tart, effing slut, effing effer.'

It would be comical if it weren't so draining. Her body aches with fear. She's learnt to lie still, scared that if he hears her move, he'll start up again. She switches off her torch. And waits till she hears his bedroom door close. She'll do what she's done since a child. Dream of Hartisborne and follow the naturalist along its winding paths.

But Trevor returns, rattling the door and throwing himself against it. *Effing little tart*. Why is she the one in the wrong? He lives in hate, while she – the possibility turns into a certainty – is in love with Marco Bracco.

Now Trevor is trying to force his way in again. He's shouting, *effing whore, effing bitch effing with that Eyetie*. She wants to laugh but daren't.

She should confront Trevor with his own faults, but she is too cowardly to fight back. Let him rage and rant till he exhausts himself. She puts on some earmuffs, a recent buy because of the big freeze, and pulls *The Natural History* towards her again. She turns on her torch. She's always loved the story of the horse and the hen.

*Gentlemen,* Gil writes, *we notice that cooperation, loving care even, occurs between creatures of the same family. Horses stand head to tail, flicking flies from each other's faces. A bitch will lick her pups clean. A cow will nudge a calf to its feet. Moreover, affection between different species, for example between a man and his dog, is also observable. To illustrate my proposal that animals are as capable of friendship as mankind, I offer this anecdote.*

*On a frequent path* ~~to my weeding woman's~~

~~lodging at Goody Newton's cottage~~ he corrects his script to 'a parishioner's cottage', then he strikes out ~~parishioner's cottage~~. *On a path I frequent, I pass a meadow where dwell a solitary horse and a solitary hen.* ~~*Mary tells me*~~*...* no, ~~*my weeding woman tells me*~~*... I have heard that the hen, when released from its coop, rushes towards the horse and squawks a greeting, and that the horse whinnies at the hen. One hot afternoon, I observed the behaviour of this unlikely couple.*

*Both were sheltering in the shade of a great oak, the hen pecking around its comrade's hooves, the horse statue still. All was quiet, when of a sudden, the horse took fright, tossing its head and cantering skittishly from the tree's cavernous shade into the heat. Then the horse, seeing the hen still prospecting for food, ran around it, nudging and nosing, until it herded the bird from the shady spot. A moment later, a mighty branch shivered from the oak, landing exactly where hen and horse had stood. The horse had saved its friend's life, for its ears proved sharp enough to hear a tree's sinews cracking.*

*Gentlemen, we consider ourselves above the beasts, but the communications between species, even between plants and animals, may be superior to our human perceptions.* ~~*Mary*~~*...* no, ~~*my weeding woman avers*~~*... The hen and horse remain devoted companions, for in their loneliness, they have struck up a friendship beyond our quotidian understanding.*

Gil spatters the desk with ink from his

crossings-out. Really, he is too old for this game, tempted all the time like a young buck to mention Mary while trying for scientific objectivity. The anecdote will not suffice for a reading at the Royal Society or earn a place in his book.

Nevertheless, he will never forget his walk to Mary's lodging last summer, the fall of the branch in the thunderous heat, and the way the horse and hen stood tenderly side by side contemplating the gashed tree, as if the almost losing of their lives bound them together in a strange love.

Georgie takes off her earmuffs. Trevor has grown quiet. She hears him shuffle off to his bedroom. Can this go on for ever? Till she dies? Or till Trevor dies. After all, Auntie Connie was her blood relative, and Trevor isn't. She doesn't owe him anything except her keep when she was at school. Even a horse and hen had a better relationship than she has with Trevor.

Trevor knocks on her door. 'I was worried about you last night,' he says. 'It's only natural.'

A kind of apology? To deter him, she switches out her torch and lies in the terrifying dark.

In the morning, when Trevor has gone to work, Georgie packs the leather suitcase and a grip. She should write a note so that Trevor doesn't think she's gone missing.

'Dear Uncle Trevor... ' But he's not *dear* is he? And he isn't really her uncle. 'To Trevor, I have a new job and am moving away.' *Disloyal bitch after all I've done for you.* 'T̶h̶a̶n̶k̶ ̶y̶o̶u̶ ̶f̶o̶r̶ ̶e̶v̶e̶r̶y̶t̶h̶i̶n̶g̶. Don't try to find me.' She signs the note.

She knocks at Rosemary's door to say goodbye.

'You're doing the right thing,' Rosemary says, hugging her. 'I don't know how you've stuck it all these years. And you've always loved Hartisborne.'

'Don't tell him where I am. He must never know.'

Georgie is scared to walk up the road in case Trevor returns.

'I'll come with you,' Rosemary says.

She walks her to the bus stop and waits with her.

'If you need to,' Georgie says, 'you can write to me at the museum. I'm going to rent the farmer's flat in the village, but I don't know the address yet. I always dream some unknown relative might come looking for me. Or Morwenna and Uncle Tris might visit again.'

'I'll let you know if anyone comes.'

On the bus, Georgie touches her secret post office book. She'll have just enough for two weeks' keep even though the job doesn't start yet. Yesterday Nick said she could move into his flat across the road from the museum, whenever she likes.

She drops Celia's suit into the drycleaner's near

Bracco & March and pays ahead. She can leave the receipt for Celia. Her conscience, at least in that respect, will be clear.

She opens the bookshop door. Celia steps out of the back room. 'So, what happened? Did you get the job?' she asks excitedly. 'Marco told me about it.'

Marco, it turns out, has flu. *I may never see him again.* She hands Celia the dry-cleaner's ticket with a mumbled apology.

'I don't mind you borrowing the suit. I know how much you love Hartisborne. You've already packed,' Celia says, eying her bags.

'Now I've told my uncle, I can't go home,' Georgie says.

'Yes, safer to leave while you're ahead.' Celia opens the cash drawer. 'Here's your pay. Go right now.'

'Are you sure?'

'Best thing for everyone,' Celia says. There's an awkward pause. 'It's not your fault. Some people are like weather. And you will never change them.' She opens the door and, not unkindly, hurries Georgie out.

# CHAPTER 6

From Hartisborne High Street, Sylvia stares up at the window of The Granary Flat where Georgie is Nick's new tenant. Sylvia has just cleaned the church. The vicar no longer pays her because she does it as an antidote to sleeplessness rather than as a job. Last night she had wandered the village, trying to tire herself, and she'd noticed Georgie's light burning in the early hours.

Sylvia sees the light go out. Miss Gardner is an early riser. Sylvia approves. She heads away from the church, knowing the stone floor is gleaming with water, the mop is draining in its bucket in the belfry and the pews have been waxed to a shine. After she's been to Priory Farmhouse, she'll rest on her moth-eaten chaise longue, taking sleep by surprise rather than warning it ahead by going upstairs.

Miss Gardner knocks on the window and waves. Sylvia waves back. Nice girl. Mostly, the young don't bother with her anymore. Her mind leaps to the tea she's going to give Georgie. Jellies in glasses for starters, then fish paste sandwiches, sliced cucumber in vinegar. Scones. Her heart rises. Probably more than her scones will. Something to plan. Buy butter instead of margarine? She composes a shopping list in her head, as she rides her bike through Monkswood to Priory Farm.

Sylvia eyes the empty beer bottle, the open bottle of gin and the half empty whisky bottle. Not even a glass of sherry at Christmas touches her lips. At sixteen, she took the temperance pledge and has never wavered from teetotalism.

When she was growing up, her father had drunk all evening. And once when her sister arrived home later than she predicted from her job in Hanger House, their father had cornered Emma in the cottage's small kitchen, shouting and swearing.

Sylvia sat in the crook of the stairs, watching through the crack of the door. Her sister was crying. Her father pushed her against the cupboard, his hands round her neck. Sylvia was frozen. She knew she should act, but she couldn't. Emma managed to loosen his hands and screamed.

Their brother Ed rushed in and separated them. He punched his father in the face, He pulled open the stairs' door to usher Emma to safety and went white with anger when he saw Sylvia. 'What were you doing? Letting him kill her? How could you sit there? What's wrong with you?'

Sylvia was ashamed. Emma's neck was red. She was shaking. Would she have let her father kill her sister? She vowed then never to drink like her father did, never to touch a drop and she never has. But the inner reproaches never cease. Her sister could have died, been brain damaged. Maybe that's why she's haunted by time-slips. The women of the past, caught in the village's paths and pursued through tunnels of trees, can't hear her warnings. She can't enter their time to help them. But what's the point of her gift if all she can do is stand by?

Later when she was a suffragette, she had been bullied by the police. The feel of spittle on the skin, a knee in the backside. She saved herself but not others.

Once she consulted the vicar, hoping he could banish her visions, but he merely asked whether she'd been drinking when it happened. As if! she'd said proudly for she has never broken the pledge and never will, and she despises him for implying as much.

Should she talk to Nick about his drinking? Last week, she told him that, as a Church of England school governor, he should attend Sunday services. He'd laughed and said a farmer couldn't arrange his hours around church services.

Sylvia rinses the beer bottle and puts it in

the crate, forcing her gaze away to stop herself counting the empties. Nick has pulled himself together since she found him grief-stricken in the days after Richard's funeral. Nowadays she checks on him even when she's not working here.

In the long hall of Priory Farmhouse, the embers in the hearth are still warm. Wood ash rimes every surface. Nick has left another beer bottle on the coffee table with a candle stuffed in the top. A tumbler with lipstick round the rim reeks of gin. The record player lid is open. The red-light blinks. The case is hot to the touch. Fancy leaving it on all night without a thought for the wasted electric.

Sylvia lifts a rumpled blanket from the floor. A stocking slips from its crease. She feels down the side of the sofa where Nick often loses his change and retrieves instead a hair-slide, rather like the one she saw yesterday in Miss Clifford's thick bob of red-gold hair.

Now she understands. The school secretary must have been here on a date. Silvery powder rises from the overflowing ashtray to join the dust motes floating in the sunlight's shafts. Nick and Miss Clifford must have been smoking, drinking and who knows what else. A vision of Claire Clifford doing the twist in her navy-blue mini-skirt flits through Sylvia's mind. She guesses the monks egged Nick on last night.

Only the Norman church is older than Priory Farmhouse, the village's most ancient home.

Often, she'll clean the church for no pay, to inhale that odour of flowers and cold stone. Once she heard the naturalist's voice saying, 'We'll wait. We'll wait.' And glimpsed a wedding with no bride.

Here, the scenes of her life stretch back through two wars to her family's early troubles. Yes, trouble on trouble, and her son almost lost to the second war, and the church, like a brooch pinned to the grass. The church is benign, whereas at Priory Farmhouse, the monks are infecting Nick as they've infected every man who ever lived there.

Sylvia rolls the stocking and places it beside the hair-slide on the coffee table. As she pushes the carpet-sweeper over the rug, she feels the monks' breath on her skin.

She blames the monks for Nick's poor church attendance, for his drinking and the possibility he may turn out like his father. The monks didn't take religion seriously. They created their own permissive society, poached deer and fermented ale and wine. They were herbalists and medicine men, experimenting with concoctions, no better than these modern-day drug addicts with their psychedelia. When the village women grew bored of their hard-working husbands or wanted a simple to help them bear a child, they crept along Monksway to visit the priory at night. Some returned with a child in their belly, the problem solved.

When the bishop sent officials to excommunicate them, the monks armed themselves and frightened the bishop's men away. And when, at last, the monks were smoked out of the priory, their barns and haystacks burning, they left behind a spirit of anarchy and impiety, of lust and drunkenness. The presence of a woman always rouses them to their games. Mothers die young. Wives leave their husbands.

Sylvia feels sorry for Claire Clifford, a modern girl with a professional job and a smart Morris Minor, being corrupted, not by Nick. No, Sylvia doesn't blame him, but by seven centuries of untamed male spirit.

Sylvia sniffs. The yeasty smell of ale brewing is often a sign the monks are about, defying her with their drinking just like her father. The monks find ways to make her dizzy. She's sure they want to set off her angina, but Sylvia has lived so long that she doesn't fear death.

No one speaks of the advantages of being well past eighty, or even heading towards a hundred. She doesn't know her true age and is all the better for it. She could throw herself in front of an assassin. She could dive into a nuclear cloud, especially if her sacrifice would save her grandchild, her son or even her daughter-in-law. But she knows no individual act of bravery will protect her loved ones from nuclear fall-out.

Maybe she can't fight nuclear bombs, but she's certainly not afraid of ghosts. Sylvia strips Nick's mattress energetically as if to prove it. She beats the pillows into shape, then fetches clean sheets from the airing cupboard and tucks them in tightly, as if hospital corners will rid Nick's room of its sinful activities.

There is a shouted, 'Hello, Sylvia!' from the field below. The kitchen door opens. Water runs from a tap.

Sylvia picks up the laundry basket and goes downstairs. Nick is manhandling a tin from the oven. The yeasty smell is from his homemade loaf, made with treacle and stale milk. Her own recipe passed on to him. He loosens the loaf from the tin and tips it on to the trivet.

'Hello,' Nick says again. 'Like a cup of stir-up?'

Nick passes her a cup of instant coffee and gestures to a pack of chocolate biscuits. She sits at the kitchen table, trying to forget the hair-slide, stocking and empty bottles.

'How is Mr Swallow?' she asks, nodding her head in the barn's direction. She is fascinated by the artist. 'Have you seen his pictures lately?'

'He's gone all chary about showing me.'

Sylvia suspects she is the only Priory visitor who hasn't been invited into the barn to see his work. No one thinks her artistic, she supposes.

'Does he need any cleaning done?'

'I shouldn't offer, if I were you. I doubt he'd get round to paying you. He owes me quite a bit of rent. Don't tell Mum that. I've heard from the archaeologists again. They could start the dig in

Cloister Mead later this summer. Only I'd have to get Mum to agree.'

'You should leave it be.'

The excommunicated monks, banned from burial in consecrated ground, had made the farm their graveyard. Their bones and the bones of their women are wrapped in nettle cloth. Best to let the past lie, even if it grows as tall as the nettles in Cloister Mead.

'I'd be fascinated to see what they find.'

'Wine flagons and women, if the old stories are right.'

When she was younger, younger than Nick's girlfriend, she'd felt hands patting her hair, someone's breath in her ear and an invisible hand on her waist. 'Best to let sleeping dogs lie.' She brushes the biscuit crumbs from her dress. 'Perhaps I should look in Mr Swallow's barn? In case it needs a tidy-up.'

'I can't let just anyone into his studio,' Nick says.

Sylvia musters all her hurt pride and hoists herself onto her bunioned feet.

'Don't forget this.' Nick hands her an envelope of money.

Sylvia puts the envelope in her coat pocket.

'I'll ask Tom to show you his work another time. To go in without asking, makes it seem like I don't respect his privacy.'

The monks follow her along Cloister Mead, murmuring 'just anyone', laughing at her and spinning stones at her bike wheels.

When she leaves the farm and fastens the field gate, a weight falls away. At least Nick is recovering from Richard's death. She is even glad he has fun with Miss Clifford, dancing and what not. If indeed it was Miss Clifford? There are already rumours about Nick and the museum girl, his new tenant in The Granary Flat. 'Miss Gardner renting his flat doesn't mean anything,' she'd said to Miss Adkins in the village shop, outraged at Nick being pigeon-holed by his father's behaviour just because he put up a young woman on the night of her interview. She's certain that if the lane had been clear, he would have driven Miss Gardner into Hartisborne and asked Sylvia to put her up for the night.

After all, Nick is too young to be living alone in Priory Farmhouse, when other men his age are jiving to Elvis Presley and Cliff Richard. He should marry Claire Clifford, a farmer's daughter. Everyone thinks she's suitable. She might stick it out at Priory, whereas a stranger, a Londoner like Georgie Gardner, would never take to the farming life even without ghostly monks. Look what happened to Marilyn Luckin.

Tom Swallow cycles through the mud towards her, weighed down by heavy panniers. He often leaves his bike at the station, when he visits his two families in London. Sylvia disapproves of Tom's divorces though Tom in person is hard to dislike. She could have peeked into the barn after all. He would never have known.

Tom shouts out, 'Hello, Mrs Kemp. How are you?'

Sylvia waves in answer, but Tom has already ploughed on, mud spattering his suit trousers.

She wishes he would turn around. She would like an artist to see her swift movements. Draw her. Immortalise her. Not many women of her age can ride a bike uphill at this speed. She is as fast as the girl inside her, who, fifty or sixty or was it even seventy years ago, ran from Priory Farm Cottage screaming for help. She pedals away from the stinging stones, and into the sunshine, as she turns into the village street.

It is fully morning now, sunny even. Georgie need no longer fear the dark. It is a new freedom to keep the light on, something Trevor never allowed. But now she pays her own bills and leaves the standard lamp on all night, letting its glow shine through her open attic doorway.

She climbs carefully down the shaky ladder from her bedroom in the Granary Flat roof.

In London, Trevor will be making his breakfast, swearing at the kettle and leaving the toast to burn between the grille's clamp on the hot plate. No one will be there to tell him he has shaving cream under his ear or urge him to clean his teeth.

While she lived with Trevor, he was a force to

be avoided, a thunderous pressure, but now she is away, she blames herself too. Why didn't she break through his anger? Defy him? She wasn't always a child. She was fifteen when Tristram and Morwenna came to visit and should have had more gumption.

She was in her bedroom when she heard the doorknocker. She opened her bedroom door quietly. Down below, she heard familiar voices. She could scarcely believe her ears. It was Uncle Tris and Morwenna. Morwenna said they would come, but Georgie gave up hope ages ago. Cornwall was such a long way away, and they didn't write to her. Georgie ran down the stairs.

Morwenna was clutching a shopping bag of roses. She never went anywhere empty-handed. 'Now, what will I take them?' she used to say if they were visiting someone. She loved giving. She'd raid the garden for a cabbage, a bunch of dahlias or pick a bowl of blackcurrants. Now she put down the bag and caught Georgie in her arms and hugged her.

'You've grown, my lovely.' Morwenna wouldn't let go until Trevor stared her down.

Trevor ushered Morwenna and Tristram into the sitting room. 'Upstairs and brush your hair,' he said to Georgie. 'You're too untidy for visitors.'

'Alright,' she said. Let him bully her all her liked, so long as she could see Uncle Tris and

Morwenna.

Georgie stared at the mirror. Trevor was correct. Her hair was a mess. She brushed it carefully and pulled it back with a hair band. She straightened her skirt and her blouse, and then rubbed a scuff off her shoe. Her old clothes and uncut hair won't pass muster, but she's done her best. Not that Morwenna or Tris will care, but Trevor will care, though he won't pay for a trim at the hairdresser.

She walked rather than ran downstairs, stepping carefully to be a good girl, so that Trevor and Connie will be proud of her, rather than ashamed as usual. She opened the sitting room door. There was no one there.

She tiptoed into the hall, tense now, sensing an emptiness. She opened the dining-room door. Morwenna's offering, long stems of budding roses from the farm wrapped in newspaper, lay on the table, but there was no sign of Morwenna or Tris or Trevor. Had they all gone into the yard? Back in the kitchen, she saw Connie through the kitchen window, out in the back alley, peering at the house through the open gateway.

Connie came in, wiping her hands on a tea towel. She was usually rigid about washing-up and never brooked an interruption, but she must have abandoned the sink and gone outside.

'Where are they?' Georgie asked.

'Oh, they didn't want to stay.'

They couldn't have gone far. The front door

was slightly ajar. She pulled it open. Tris and Morwenna were standing on the pavement outside Rosemary's, arguing with Trevor.

'Wenna!' Georgie shouted. 'Wenna!'

Morwenna walked towards her. Tris too. Trevor grabbed his arm. There was a scuffle. Tris shook off Trevor's hand. Morwenna put her arm round Georgie. Tris joined her. He was wearing a black mourning band on his jacket sleeve that Georgie hadn't noticed in the dark hallway.

'Are you alright?' Morwenna asked her. 'Didn't you get my letters?'

'No. Did you get mine?' Georgie handed her letters to Aunty Connie for the stamps that she wasn't allowed to buy herself.

'My mother has passed away,' Morwenna said. 'You didn't write back when I sent the news. So, I knew something was wrong. I knew you'd have written, when you heard about Mum.'

Aunt Julia was dead. Georgie couldn't believe in death, though her own parents were dead. *I didn't know them at all.* She marvelled at this new thought for she had created her parents so often in her mind, as she also created the naturalist. *But I knew Aunt Julia.*

'Alright Trev?' It was Bill, their neighbour on the side that wasn't Rosemary's. He bustled up to Tris and Trevor.

Tris moved away from Trevor.

'He's bothering my niece.'

'That's baloney,' Tris said.

'Who are you?' Bill asked Tris.

'Georgie was our evacuee. She's fond of my daughter – they used to be like sisters.'

'I want to live with them again.' The words were out of Georgie's mouth before she knew it.

'Conditioning. Twisted her mind,' Trevor said.

'We'd like to invite you for a holiday,' Morwenna said.

'See? They don't want the likes of you to live with them. I'm her legal guardian, you know.'

'No, Aunty Connie is.'

'Same thing. I'm head of the household. What I say goes.'

'Where do you live?' Bill asked, still unsure who to back.

'Cornwall,' Morwenna said.

'Make a nice holiday for the girl,' Bill suggested. 'The seaside and all that.'

'She came to us in a terrible state– dirty suitcase – rough clothes – ringworm - lice – no manners. Don't trust them an inch.'

'We wanted to see Georgie because we didn't hear from her,' Tris explains. 'She didn't answer our letters.'

'I didn't get them,' She would have loved letters from Morwenna.

'My wife was ill and wanted her to be in touch,' Tris said. 'And now it's too late.'

'She didn't know, Dad.'

'I'm sorry.' People said that about death, but Georgie had never had to say that before. Poor

Auntie Julia. She saw a coffin in the darkened room where Auntie Julia used to sit with her migraines and grief, listening to the sea echoing in its deep pool under the cliff.

'Here we go. Waterworks again.' Trevor pushed at Georgie, adding, 'Such a little phoney. Doesn't give a damn about your wife.'

'I do!' Georgie screeched. 'I do.'

'Let her come to us for a break,' Morwenna said. 'Please Mr Cousins. It would do us all good.'

'Don't trust him an inch,' Trevor gestured at Tris, for Bill's benefit.

Bill shrugged. After all what was Tris to him? Trevor had been his neighbour for years.

*The Natural History of Hartisborne* was in the house, with the wedding photograph. If she could just run up and get it. Go with Morwenna but hold on to the last trace of her real parents. She paused.

'Come on, my lovely.' Morwenna took Georgie by the hand, breaking the spell. She and Georgie walked so quickly that they were almost running.

'See? They're abducting her!' Trevor shouted at Bill. 'Help me!'

'Where is Mrs Cousins?' Tris asked calmly, blocking Bill and Trevor from Morwenna and Georgie as they hurried along the street. 'We met Georgie's mother years ago and, after she died, we spoke to her sister, Mrs Cousins, on the phone.'

'Threatening my wife now!' Trevor said.

'Not at all. We could discuss the holiday...'

'You should go,' Bill said. After all, better the devil you know. 'Trev can't let you clear off with his niece. You got to watch out for young girls these days.'

Trevor dodged around Tris, ran up the road, grabbed Georgie's arm and pulled her from Morwenna. 'Call the police,' he shouted to Bill.

'Yes, go on,' Georgie called, 'Call the police. He's hurting me!'

Reluctantly, Trevor dropped her arm but pushed her along towards the house, his hand in the small of her back.

Bill wavered, hoping other neighbours might turn up to decide matters. But the street was stubbornly empty.

'I think we'd better go, lovely,' Tris said to Morwenna. Then, standing in Trevor's way, he said, 'I'm sorry you didn't take our visit in better part.'

Bill looked doubtful. It was hard not to like Uncle Tris. He peered at Tris' mourning band. His own wife died a few months ago. 'You've suffered a sad loss,' he said. Tris would understand what it was like to wake with the bed half-empty, to put out one cup and saucer, to listen to the wireless alone. 'How long is it since...' but Trevor interrupted him.

'Not at all convenient.' He marched Georgie away and pulled her up the steps and into the house. 'What would your aunt do if you went on holiday? You never stop to think about her, do you, you selfish little bitch?' He hissed the insult once the others were out of earshot.

Georgie wanted to scream and shout, but it was not in her nature. The force of Trevor's will was stronger than his hand gripping her arm. She didn't even struggle as he closed the door and shut her in.

One foot after the other, that's all it would have taken. Why didn't she run after them? Call them back? Why didn't she tell them what it was like to live with Trevor? But she froze. It was over so quickly. For years, they've been walking down that street away from her, looking back at her over their shoulders. Uneasy. Sad. Reproachful. She could have changed her own life, but she didn't because she wouldn't make a fuss.

Sometimes the could-have-been life floats before her, the train ride back to Cornwall with Morwenna and Tris, and then helping on the farm, the old stove open on a winter's evening, the logs spitting, or walking home on a June day, the hedge roses swaying against the stone wall, the cats basking on the steps, the scent of the sea breezing in from the echoing cove where seals turn their noses to the sun. There would have been no more Trevor. And she never would have met Marco or Celia. Never turned into a bad person and slept with a married man.

Now she is safely in Hartisborne, she could write to Tris and Morwenna, but her shame about their London visit weighs on her as if she is still a self-conscious teenager. She wasn't brave enough to defy Trevor. She is a letter-down of people, deceiving Celia, neglecting Morwenna and Tris, thinking only of being with Marco on the day her aunt died. The quiet leafy light of Hartisborne illuminates her faults and those of her upbringing, but that doesn't mean she can overcome them. She must hide from Connie's dying face. Block her ears to those last rattling breaths. Look away from the first desperate evenings spent with Trevor.

She pours herself some cornflakes, switches on the mock walnut wireless with its dials, marked frequencies and loose knobs. It once belonged to Nick's grandmother, another object anchoring him to Hartisborne. 'This is the Home Service…' She has a good job in a beautiful place. No one is going to shout at her. She will try to block out Trevor's voice.

The sycamore buds are bronzy-green A spotted woodpecker taps at the tree's bark, reverberating, as it did in Gil's time. *I have a key to your house*, she tells Gil, excited at the thought of her new job.

She waves at Sylvia. She is going to tea with Sylvia and is excited by that too. Nick told her ahead that she must accept the invitation. 'Of course, I want to go,' she'd said. 'It's not exactly a culinary delight,' he warned her, 'but you can still have a nice time with Sylvia.' 'What will we talk about?' Georgie asked. 'Ask her about her visions. And act as if you believe her.'


At church last week, Gil saw a wink pass between Blundel and the church warden. A new lack of respect. The baby isn't mine, Gil argues in his head. But such gossip delights the village.

According to Augustine, the past lives in memory, though the saint allows for the anticipation of the future, the planning mind. Gil should leave the past and instead pursue stratagems to discover the father of Mary's child. Even if Binford certificates her and vouchsafes to pay the child's expenses, there are few funds to be had there.

If this pain endures, he may be driven to act like the maidens who, when troubled by love, consult the echo by shouting at the hillside in the Echoing Field. He often laughs at these girls, but now he understands. When they hear the echo, they hear their own desires, voiced by the authority of nature, emboldening them to make their future wishes come true.

Consulting an echo will make him appear mad, but to have his hypochondriac friend M. on side might mitigate much harm to his reputation and curacy. Apart from the prudence of pre-empting gossip before it reaches the Bishop's palace, he needs to confide in a friend. He and M. were students together and have witnessed each other's follies, though M. was long engaged to Mrs M. and never wanted another.

He begins his letter.

My dear M.

*I was sorry to hear that you were troubled by the rheumatism this winter. You mentioned a fever too. For this, my friend Goody Newton recommends crushed dried lemon balm, the leaves torn into a cup of rum and hot water. The good woman claims her concoction is also a remedy for a broken heart, though I gladly aver that neither you nor the admirable Mrs M. will need drink it for such a reason* ~~while you are both living~~.

He shouldn't mention death to a man so fearful of mortality, so fearful of leaving his beloved wife alone. Instead, he will meander towards matters of the heart via his health, a subject sure to attract his friend's attention.

*You ask after my health, and I must admit I suffered from a rheum in February* – how tedious this kind of writing is – *and an aching hip. Consequently, I find myself thinking of old age and whether a companion might alleviate future sufferings as the joints stiffen and the memory declines.* M. enjoys this sort of talk while Gil abhors it. His memory is perfect. His body is agile from all his walking, riding and gardening.

Sitting and complaining is the harder thing for Gil, while M. scarcely moves from the hearth or desk and is becoming heavier by the day. But he must tread carefully, as if on stepping stones over a stream. M. is a man of great sympathy when his friends complain of illness or age. *In short, dear friend, ~~I am suffering fro~~m…no… I find myself - ~~overtaken by~~ - somewhat in that fever which the Romans considered a madness.*

The classical illusion sets his passion in context. He is Ovid, Propertius, Catullus, a poet lunatic with love. He must approach M. with both learning and common sense in order not to overwhelm him before he introduces the figure of a weeding woman. M. has always respected rank. His letters are a chessboard of bishops and knights, chequered with interest and patronage. Though Gil can't endure the manipulations of patronage, he knows M. is a good man, with a fine eye for those to help, the stirrup for many young clergymen needing preferment.

*My weeding woman is with child, the child of an unknown man. Yet I want to save her, to marry her, to father my own children with her.*

If only M. were here. So much easier to talk than to write about such awkward emotions.

*I know you will consider it a madness that my fancy lies this way. Let me put the case to you. She and I share an intelligence about natural lore, and she is a willing student. We have easy ways with one another. I am not suited to fine ladies or soirées in London, while nature calls me outside with such force. And Mary is just such another.* ~~She has such golden hair, such a gentle touch and a plan for scented plants to bloom in winter's dead season.~~

Will this persuade M. of Mary's worth? A man who cares but little for gardening or nature? M. would as lief sit by a fire on a hot June day, writing wheedling letters to the Bishop, as pick blackfly from the French beans under a glorious blue sky.

~~*Mary will make a magnificent housekeeper.*~~

Truth demands he strike this out. Mary trails dirt indoors and forgets meals when overtaken by the urge to dig, plant or prune. Her neglect of the domestic would be of no consequence in Gil's house with Thomas to look after the household. Now, ironically, Luckin employs her as his kitchen maid. How hateful to think of Mary, trapped in Priory Farm's dark kitchen, the flames tearing up the chimney, the smoke swirling into a semblance of monkish robes.

*Mary will be a kind and fruitful mother.*

His fantasy runs on children playing among the seven hedges, hiding behind his wooden statue or circling round inside the pipe barrel, dizzy with laughter, on summer days when Gil will no longer envy M. and Mrs. M. the happiness of their brood.

*Dear M., I want to marry Mary and offer her and her child a home. I love her and I wish, nay, long, to be a father to her child and our children. Please give me your blessing. Speak well of me to your uncle the Bishop, for I need my curacy, which is little enough to live on, even with the rents from the glebe. I must stay in Hartisborne to finish my life's work, as you have urged me to do. In short, I entreat you to visit, to learn to know my Mary and for your Elizabeth to do so too.*

Can he imagine Mary in conversation with Mrs M.? Well, perhaps. Mrs M. is a great reader. Mary is a great observer of nature.

*Many a man has married his maid*, as M. joked in his last letter, ribbing Gil about his single state with no knowledge or thought of Mary, with no idea that he was jabbing at Gil's dearest temptation. *And you Gil, will marry your maid at sixty and no one will care.* But if not reprehensible at sixty, then why so at forty-three? Perhaps by the age of sixty, gentility matters no longer. A man is justified in marrying anyone for the sake of his old age.

Saint Augustine says the past still exists. If only he could walk into that past before Mary succumbed to her lover. If only he could carry her away to future safety. But would his brothers, sisters, his nephews and nieces, all the future inheritors of this modest house and park, accept the union? Could they, for all their modern ideas, countenance being disinherited by the illegitimate offspring of a weeding woman?

Gil seals up the letter and addresses it. M. is staying in Winchester in rooms provided by his uncle, the Bishop. Gil walks to the post office full of fear, not wanting to be the butt of M.'s humour or the subject of gossip in the Bishop's palace, yet determined to prepare the ground for his offer to Mary.

His proposal will wait till the swallows appear again in case the father of Mary's child reveals himself. Then he will be forced to laugh off his love to M., naming it a momentary obsession. Between March and May, nature is beneficent. Snowdrops and crocuses blow. Seedlings appear in the glass house. The orchard blossoms. M. is his friend and will take his side in this. Surely?

# CHAPTER 7

Whenever David puts aside time to write, the Pearsons always disturb him. So today, he's donned his London suit and made a point of telling Nev and Romilly in front of Georgie that he's off to the British Museum. Georgie playacted a loud farewell at the front door and slammed it hard, while David hightailed it upstairs to his study and locked himself in. It's all ridiculous.

Georgie opens the museum's door to the garden and keeps it open despite the weather. If landscape has a voice, then this is the voice of Hartisborne, rustling trees, churring, twittering and a few dogs barking in the distance. The neighing of a pony. The patter of rain.

Georgie is typing labels to replace those ruined when the pipes burst. 'A giant dog's collar belonging to the vicar who had to defend himself against rioters in 1830'. So, not even fifty years after Gil died, the village's arrangements disintegrated. The vicar became frightened of his parishioners, and they presumably were frightened of his dog. She understands. Hasn't fear of Trevor spoilt her life?

Her fingers ache. She stands and shakes her hands out, as her typing tutor once taught her. David's pretence is affecting her, making her uneasy about lying to Nev and Romilly. She paces round the little parlour, discontented for all that she is in Hartisborne.

Georgie pushes a loose block of parquet with her foot. Up and down, click-clack. Three times she pushes it and wishes she could see the naturalist. A shadow falls in the hall, as if her wish has come true.

The shadow is Nev Pearson's. He is a heavily built man whose light footsteps don't match his appearance or his clumsiness.

'The window latch in David's study needs mending,' Nev says. 'I could do it while he's out today.'

The Pearsons are banned from the study, since Nev crumpled up some precious documents and threw them in the waste paper basket. Although David rescued the mystery note with the 'shape of my longing' written on it, and Georgie ironed it under brown paper, the note is more creased than it was when David found it. The last straw for David was Romilly knocking down bottles of ink with the curve of the Hoover tube and splattering the rug and his notebook.

After an awkward showdown, where David relied rather too much on Georgie for support – 'I'm sure Miss Gardner will agree with me' and

'Don't you think, Georgie?' - he declared that the study is always to be locked and only Georgie is allowed the spare key.

'I haven't got my key with me,' Georgie says.

'Nip across the road and get it,' Nev says, 'there's a good girl.'

'I can't leave reception.'

'There are no visitors,' Nev points out.

'I would feel unhappy, like it was a dereliction of duty.'

Nev blanches but holds his ground. Georgie shifts in her seat. The key in her pocket jabs into her thigh.

Georgie makes a counterattack. 'Have you seen how this block flips up? An old lady tripped yesterday. She fell over and hurt her back.'

Nev shrugs, as if this is no business of his.

'I was wondering whether you could mend it today, as there's going to be a school visiting tomorrow.'

'It's up to Mr Daunt, I suppose.' Pearson can't abide dealing with the lower ranks, like Georgie.

'I was talking to David about it this morning – before he left - and he's very keen that we fix it today. That old lady nearly hit her head on the contour map of the Weald and Downland. David asked me to ask you if you could put in a temporary measure. But if you can't do it, people say John Kemp is an excellent carpenter.'

'I suppose Sylvia suggested him? She *is* his mother, you know.'

'No, it wasn't Mrs Kemp. Several other people recommended him. Miss Russell, for example. And the vicar's wife.'

'John Kemp's a busy man. Won't give a small job the time of day.'

'I've checked the insurance documents. Now we've seen the problem, we have a legal obligation to ensure our guests don't trip.'

'I doubt the museum can afford Kemp. You'd need to ask Colonel Camden before proceeding.'

'I'm sure the Colonel will agree when he looks into our public liability terms.'

Pearson parries, 'Sometimes, you put me in mind of Clara Schumann.'

'Really?'

She has seen a sketch of Clara Schumann. Soulful eyes and a fine neck. More like Celia than Georgie. She fidgets at the loose wooden block with her feet. 'You see if this flips up, then before you know it, a pensioner trips and breaks their hip. Their leg needs amputating. Then, they get gangrene and die. Their family sues us. The museum is shut down. And we all lose our jobs.' Nev won't know she's recounting the fate of Rosemary's grandmother.

'Well,' he concedes grudgingly, 'you may have a point. Yes, you do remind me of Clara Schumann. Definitely, something about the eyes. And the concern for detail.'

'I'm going to phone John Kemp.'

'After Schumann's suicide, Brahms took up

with Clara. A marriage of true minds. With Schumann out of the way, who knows what happened between them?'

'Perhaps you do?' Georgie kicks irritably at the loose block.

'I can only guess, though Clara Schumann wasn't the sort to dally with a lot of different men.'

Last night, Nev had seen her in the pub with Nick and David. He'd tapped on the window and waved to let her know he was watching her. *Hanging around in pubs – flirting – drinking – living the bloody high life.* A vision of Trevor eating his lonely dinner flashes into her mind and won't leave. Why should she enjoy herself when he is so unhappy?

'I'll phone Mr Kemp for a quote,' Georgie says. 'Unless you can fix it?'

Pearson shrugs. 'Clara Schumann was about your height, I believe.' He moves closer. The warehouse flashes into her mind, but Nev merely bends down and pushes the block into place. 'Bit of glue might do it. No need to bother Kemp for a little job like this.'

The vicar, never one for confrontation, has gone to London, leaving Gil to officiate at the Easter service and the Easter Monday vestry meeting where new parish officials are to be elected.

Blundel's year over, he is obliged to cede his post to another man. If a candidate is proposed and appointed but refuses, he can be fined. Since no man wants to overload a neighbour with unpaid duties, it is Hartisborne's custom to nominate an unopposed and willing villager.

Gil is relieved that Mary's settlement status and the identity of her bastard's father will soon be matters for popular John Carpenter, carpenter and shopkeeper.

The vestry is more crowded than usual as this is an open meeting. Some suggest that the group reassemble in The Compasses, but Gil shakes his head at the verger, and mouths, 'the vicarage'. John Carpenter hasn't arrived, and the matter is not yet a settled thing. Mary's fate should not be in the hands of men in their cups.

'In his absence, the vicar has offered the vicarage's hall,' the verger announces.

The vicarage's old hall is dark for the room still has no glass. Gil unboards a window, letting in the spring sunshine. When his grandfather was the vicar here, the walls were knobbly plaster and the floor hardened earth. At the vicar's behest, John Carpenter recently laid floorboards and raised timber panels to hide the roughness. There are settles and benches on the new boards, and a small table where Widdowson, the parish clerk, can record the proceedings.

As the men grow quiet, Gil looks out through

the wooden bars down to the stream of fancy rills and little waterfalls, where a thick oak has fallen picturesquely in great curls and splinters. He has always loved this view. On his summer holidays as a child, he would roll down Church Meadow through the meadow flowers to paddle in the stream. In winter, he slid over the snowy bumps on a broken plank and trudged up the slippery slope, the plank bumping behind him on its rope. He had no thought then of meetings and accounts. Nothing but nature and sensation interested him.

Though it's a chilly April day, isn't that someone paddling in the stream? A woman, with her back bent over the bank. Could it be Mary? What is she studying? Water voles come to mind. Or a mallard's nest? He turns away reluctantly because the verger is calling the meeting to order.

The churchwardens and overseers present their accounts. Church repairs are approved, the wardens thanked, and the overseers praised for their thriftiness. This thriftiness is new. In a neighbouring parish, a magistrate recently reprimanded the overseer for not spending funds on helping vagrants or encouraging marriages. Gil told Blundel this story to give him the hint. Nevertheless, Blundel explains proudly how he has issued passes rather than money, and moved the homeless to another parish, rather than aiding them.

The new church wardens are duly elected. Mr Deadman is a mason and will help with the church's maintenance. Mr Tanner is a cabinet maker, who will ensure the church is well-furnished. Last year's church wardens are thanked, and they thankfully retire. Widdowson is to remain clerk for another year. Clerking is a paid post, and Widdowson does the work admirably. No one wants to see him go. The parish constable is to change from Mr Christmas to Mr Leather, a man too malleable for the task, but we are a small pool of fish after all.

The remaining post is that of overseer of the poor. As they are about to propose John Carpenter in his absence, Farmer Luckin enters, carrying the stench of Priory Farm on his boots. Behind him, Rosie Carpenter, Carpenter's eldest daughter rushes in.

'I'm sorry, sir,' she addresses herself to Gil though he is not in charge, 'but my father is passed out with the toothache. There's an abscess in his mouth as big as a pigeon's egg. The doctor fears blood poisoning and doesn't know when father will be better. He is very honoured, but his health is against being elected for this year.' Blushing Rosie imitates her mother's decisive tone as best she can.

No one will want to blame or fine John Carpenter, with his useful shop, tolerance of credit, his helpful apprentices and numerous children. If John says he has toothache, he has toothache, even though he seemed fit as a fiddle only yesterday.

'Who will be the overseer now?' the verger asks.

Parish clerk Widdowson holds his pen aloft to record their decision. He is left-handed, Gil notes. His quill has therefore been plucked from the right wing of a goose. The feather curves over the back of his hand just as it should. What power decides which hand we use? Do animals too have a preferred side? Has any scientist studied the left preference? Is it inherited or learnt? It seems a wonder that Widdowson is such a fine tailor and handyman in his everyday life. But he has had all his tools made for left-handed usage. Widdowson would be an ideal overseer himself, a quiet charitable man, whose tact and clear script are invaluable as parish clerk. He would make an exceptionally wise parish overseer, but it is an unpaid post and Widdowson has a large family.

In some parishes, women fill the role if their husbands are ill or die. So, Mrs John Carpenter, Daisy, as she was before marriage, could take up her husband's duty, but she has a deaf son she worries about. Sam does not speak because he cannot hear but has a gift for beekeeping. He walks the village covered in bees, can coax bees into a new hive and loves to eat honeycomb. He feels the bees' vibrations. And the bees trust him and rest on him. Mrs John Daisy, as she is now known, attends to him lovingly, training him in shop work as best she can, though beekeeping is surely Sam's destiny. Sometimes Gil suspects that Sam's life unmarred by silly conversations has given him an extra sense, which bees and animals understand. Sam's mother, Mrs John Daisy helps her husband with his business, tends to her elderly father and inducts her other five children into the trade. Is it fair to call on her, especially now Carpenter himself is ill?

Luckin says, 'We all agreed that Carpenter is the man we want. So - Mrs John Daisy can serve for him till his dratted tooth is taken out.'

People nod and concur, but Rosie calls out bravely. 'My mother says to say she cannot do it.' The meeting turns towards Gil as curate.

'Rosie,' he says, 'could you ask your mother to reconsider? Your father will be recovered soon, and your mother can then step down.' Mrs John Daisy is so capable that she would make a better job of parish overseer than Carpenter himself.

The rate-payers murmur assent and wait for Rosie's reply.

Rosie blushes, a shy girl forced to talk to a roomful of men. 'My mother says I must say no for all of us Carpenters and for the sake of Sam in particular.' She whispers to herself, 'There, I have said it.'

'Sam is away, isn't he? At some form of asylum, I've heard,' Mr Tanner says. 'He's no longer a burden to Mrs John Daisy. And I expect you are all grateful for that.'

'My parents have sent him north to a new school for the deaf,' Rosie says. 'And it is costly for my father.'

'Waste of money. Can't make a silk purse out of a sow's ear,' Blundel mutters.

'What does our new churchwarden, Mr Deadman, have to say on the matter?' Gil asks, inadvertently offending Mr Tanner, the other new churchwarden.

'Well,' Deadman says, 'in other years in such a case, the current officer has served again.'

'Indeed,' Tanner concurs.

'I pay the most, and I want Carpenter with Mrs John Daisy as temporary officer,' Luckin states.

Tanner, enjoying his power to aggravate Luckin, says, 'In other parishes, the overseer sometimes sees two or three years of service.'

'Let us stick to the rules,' Luckin says. 'Or release Widdowson from the clerk job and appoint him!'

'Mr Widdowson certainly has the qualities,' says the verger, 'but we need him as clerk.'

Widdowson nods gratefully. His numerous family needs the extra money from his clerking.

Blundel clears his throat. 'Gentlemen, though it would benefit my business greatly to give up overseeing, I offer to retain the post to help our friend Carpenter.'

There is a long silence. Rosie Carpenter shuffles uncomfortably. Then someone complains about the hard benches and suggests adjourning to The Compasses, as if they can drink the problem away.

Luckin says to Blundel, 'It is illegal to continue in office when there are other candidates.'

Tanner weighs in. 'Other parishes do reappoint when necessary.' He owes Blundel money but will not consider himself unduly influenced.

'Who has it in his heart to take on this duty?' the verger asks. There is a muttering of excuses for no one here wants to judge their neighbours, send vagrants away with passes or decide on dole money.

'Well, Farmer Luckin, perhaps you are fitted for the work?' Deadman says, irritated by his outbursts.

'No,' Luckin says, 'Every man must know himself. The office of overseer demands a man with patience, generosity and a love of service. As I'm sure you'll agree, I'm not that man. And neither are some others.' There's a burst of laughter and a solitary clap, as Luckin stares out Blundel. 'Self-love,' Luckin goes on, 'greed and pomposity are undesirable in an overseer.'

A silence follows, leavened by a few coughs.

Blundel stands and exclaims, 'I object to your inference, sir.'

'I spoke only of myself, but if the cap fits...'

'Anyone may see from my parish accounts that I am honest with the ratepayer's money and a fair man.'

'What about Annie Adkins?' Luckin asks.

'What should I have done?' Blundel asks the room. 'Left her to the expense of the parish when the man could pay?'

People look away. After all, that's what the parish is for, to step in when individuals fail of their duty, to cushion the blows of fortune.

'The cost of her sin would have fallen on the ratepayer,' Blundel says weightily.

'Wasn't it ever thus?' Luckin asks.

Widdowson murmurs. 'Should I be noting this discussion?' he asks Gil.

Gil shakes his head.

Tanner chirps up, 'When decisions are hard, Mr Blundel is not afraid to make them. We all benefit from his clarity.'

'Annie Adkins lost her child,' Luckin roars. 'And now she's in the poor house since she's lost her wits with grief. That was a saving of neither soul nor purse.'

'Are you saying I am not fit for office?' Blundel asks. He moves towards Luckin, until they are within spitting distance.

'You sup nowadays with the father of Adkins' child and his wife. He gives you the little paddock rent-free - and a strip of glebe - for calling off the constable.'

'Adkins couldn't prove he was the father.'

'Naming should be enough.'

'As you said, the woman has lost her wits.'

'She was a fine healthy girl before her bastard's father beat her almost to death.'

'Come, come, gentleman, this is Hartisborne,' Gil says, 'where we settle differences with a word and a smile.'

'I'm sorry my father is so ill with the toothache,' Rosie Carpenter mumbles.

'Carpenter's tooth is not the cause of this argument,' Luckin says.

'More like the expense of trying to educate a half-wit,' Blundel murmurs, master of the acid aside.

'Come, someone, offer your services. Or I will nominate one of you and you'll be fined if you refuse.' Luckin stares at each of them in turn.

'The Adkins story scares me. I couldn't deal with such situations,' says a man called Spriggs.

'Adkins has only herself to blame for giving in to a married man.'

'It's hardly Mr Blundel's fault she chose to encourage an adulterer.'

'But did she choose?' asks Mrs John, who has crept into the meeting and been masked by Luckin's bulk. 'We hear other stories in the shop.'

Luckin says, 'We were discussing your candidature, just until your husband is well enough to do the job.'

'I'm flattered, but it would be impossible with Sam and the other children.'

'It must be hard to bear an idiot child,' Blundel says.

'I'm sure your mother can vouch for that,' Mrs John parries, her eyes narrowed, her tone dangerously quiet.

Rosie is crying. 'Sam is no idiot!' she screeches. 'I hate you, sir.'

Mrs John Daisy takes a deep breath. 'Sam is not an idiot. He was born deaf, as you very well know. And he is learning his signs and doing well at it. When he returns, you'll see his true powers of mind. But there are fees to pay. We need to work hard, and now with my husband's tooth, we are even more hard pressed.'

'Entrusting Sam to a charlatan, I daresay,' Blundel mutters. 'when the faculties the good Lord gives can't be changed.'

Gil glances at the verger. It is a vestry meeting, and the verger should be keeping order. He takes the hint.

'Gentlemen, Rosie and Mrs John Daisy, I'm sure we all wish Sam well in his new endeavours, but now we must concentrate on parish business, if you please. Our business is to nominate and then elect a new parish overseer of the poor. And given – don't write this down – ,' the verger says to Widdowson hastily, 'given we prefer a volunteer – there is currently only one candidate. I move then that Mr Blundel be reappointed for a further year.'

There are sixteen people in the room. Gil cannot vote unless needed in the case of a tie. Mrs John and Rosie Carpenter cannot vote. Blundel may not vote for himself. Widdowson, as clerk, does not vote. Eleven others then. Six men led by Church Warden Tanner, raise their hands for Blundel.

'Shall I write it that Mr Blundel takes up the post again just until Carpenter is well?' Widdowson asks, his left-handed pen lingering unwillingly over the paper.

'No,' says Blundel. 'I will not be a filler-in in case the year's accounts take a muddling turn. I take the whole year or nothing, though it will be hard on me and mine. But at least our friend Carpenter can fully recover. And let it be recorded,' he says to Widdowson, 'that I do this for the sake of friendship and the benefit of the parish'.

Luckin lets out a loud sigh and turns to Gil. 'What are you thinking, man? You should exert your influence.'

'I cannot.'

'So, the church is happy to take our rates but won't step in to stop injustice.'

'The Vestry must represent the duties and wishes of the rate payers.'

'For God's sake, man!'

'The Vestry has voted.' Never has Gil's powerlessness in worldly matters irked him more.

Tanner, enjoying his new importance, announces, 'Then we elect Mr Blundel for a further year of service as parish overseer of the poor.'

The six people who voted for Blundel applaud. On his suggestion, the group adjourns to The Compasses to drink Blundel's health on parish expenses.

Before Gil blocks up the window, he observes the woman is still down by the stream, turning over stones as if looking for something. Has she seen a bullhead among the river's stones? Is the woman even Mary? Of all the young women of the village, only Mary would observe the stream so closely.

He replaces the board, clicking the wooden latches into place. He straightens the benches. His grandfather would have managed things better, found a way to persuade the Vestry to act more justly. But Gil is no politician.

Once the war was over, the child Nick enjoyed entering the village on a spring evening like this, when the air was scented by lilac, clematis and the woodiness of the hanger. He would drink a bottle of Tizer in the pub garden, while his father went inside for a pint or three. Unless The Pipe Barrel was playing, the publican refused to ignore his age. And so Nick spent long evenings on the bench by a sunken trough, counting tadpoles in the murky water, until Sylvia happened by and took him to her house to play cards beside her old-fashioned range.

Sometimes Sylvia put a blanket over him as he dozed on her mothy chaise longue. His father would collect him after closing time. And sometimes, if Richard had made a heavy night of it, Nick woke at Sylvia's and had breakfast with her. When his mother heard about this from Louise Camden, she insisted on boarding school. At thirteen, he left the village to board and never felt quite at home there again.

'We had fun, didn't we?' Dad was beset by doubts about his life as its end drew near.

'Yes, lots of fun,' Nick replied.

'We had a laugh, didn't we?' his father asked, clutching his hand.

When his mother had newly departed to London, everyone told Nick that London was far away, that his mother couldn't be blamed for not visiting him often and that his father, what with petrol still rationed, what with the farm, couldn't be blamed for not driving Nick to visit her. These days, Marilyn and Dick drive to Hartisborne regularly to inspect Marilyn's share of the inheritance.

This evening, they are going to be in The Compasses and have insisted he join them.

Nick never knows how to introduce Dick. *My mother's boyfriend*? Dick is too old for that. *My mother's …what? Lover? Paramour? The person who is screwing my mother…* Nick feels sick.

Now he dallies along the village street. If he arrives late, he needn't feel obliged to buy Dick a pint or a brandy or whatever the bastard drinks.

Perhaps it is unfair to dislike Dick so much when he played no part in his parents' separation. Most villagers judge Richard Luckin to blame. All that flirting. Fooling around with any woman new to the village. The long affair with Iris. Poor woman. Stopped her marrying, and now she has no children of her own. Wasted the best years of her life, but she's to blame too. A schoolteacher should set an example.

Anyone could see how close Richard and Iris were, on those nights when The Pipe Barrel played in The Compasses. When his father and Iris sang, the air vibrated with their harmonies. Stop it, Nick says to himself, as the village's whispering reaches a crescendo. The footpaths and woodland clearings tell tales of moonlit meetings. He pauses in the street to let the whispers subside.

A few budding bluebells, descendants of bulbs planted by Gil, blue the gravel under the museum wall. A nestbuilding jay flits onto a twig of lime in the pollarded row. Wallflowers sweeten the air outside the pub. Red letters spell out Courage above the door. That's what he needs. Pints of it.

Nick takes a deep breath and enters The Compasses. His mother is already in the saloon bar, boasting to Joan, Maisie's mother, and interrupting her glass-washing, by flashing her hand in front of her. Joan's face is averted. Why can't Mum take a hint?

'And this is Dick, my fiancé,' his mother says loudly.

So that's it. She can marry Dick now his father is dead.

'Hello Nick, what can I get you?' Dick asks, holding out his hand.

Nick ignores the gesture. He won't shake hands with the bastard. *Soak him for all he's worth*, his father whispers. 'I'll have a pint of Director's and a double whisky chaser,' Nick says. Dad laughs his approval.

Dick doesn't flicker an eyelid but pays for the drinks from a role of fivers held together with an elastic band.

Marilyn lurches forth to kiss him on the cheek, but Nick holds back, waving at her vaguely instead. 'A bit early in the day for whisky chasers?' she queries, wearing motherhood as a disguise. One of Dad's expressions.

Nick picks up his drinks and heads over to a window table, far from the bar and Joan's ears. Marilyn follows him.

'Now Nick, Dick and I need to talk to you.'

He hates the way Nick and Dick rhyme. His mother doesn't even ask how he is.

From his vantage point at the window, Nick can see Georgie walking towards the pub. She stops to talk to someone out of sight. Nick cranes his head to see more but without success.

David Daunt comes in, adding another witness to his mother's heartlessness.

'Don't go into a dream. Concentrate,' Marilyn snaps. 'As you can see,' she says, flaunting a knuckleduster of a ring, 'we are engaged. Dick asked me, as soon as he could.' She peters out, realising it's bad taste to celebrate his father's death by flaunting her new freedom. 'Do you like the ring? Twenty-two carat gold. The emerald is real! Dick bought it in Hatton Garden.'

Tiny white diamonds clutch at the large square emerald. At least they haven't stolen a Luckin heirloom.

Nick downs his whisky chaser. 'Thanks for letting me know before anyone else.' He nods sarcastically in Joan's direction.

Joan was his own first love, just a couple of years older than him. Puppy love. A crush. Who thought she would have a child so young? Maisie is nine now and a clever, sensitive child. Joan kindly brought her down to see Dad when he could no longer go into the village. Maisie, in a woolly hat, her face bright with cold, cheered them all up. Nick had shown her the well in the kitchen, and Maisie had clapped her hands. An unexpectedly happy day.

David Daunt checks the door frequently, looking out for Georgie.

'Nick, could you just concentrate?'

'On what?' Georgie will come in soon. She'll see him with his mother and this dickhead. He will be as embarrassed as a teenager. In fact, he already is.

'We want to involve you in our wedding.'

Nick finishes his pint. Dad with his laughing luminous eyes waits to hear what they propose.

'Can I get you another drink?' Dick asks.

'Surely, it's Nick's turn,' Marilyn objects.

'Special occasion.' At the bar, Dick orders another pint and another double whisky chaser.

Joan mouths, 'Don't get drunk' at Nick.

'Have you fixed the date for the happy day?'

'That's what we want to discuss.'

'Long story short,' Dick says, returning with Nick's drinks, 'your mother is attached to Hartisborne and wants us to be married in the church here.'

'It's such a pretty church… and… I'd like you to give me away,' Marilyn says. 'And organise everything. Be the host?'

Before Nick can refuse, Georgie walks in. She waves hello at Nick, who raises his hand as if casually. She joins David, who gestures at the bar, saying, 'Have anything you want.' David is usually tight with money. He must be out to impress. *You're jealous of David*, Dad teases him. Of course, I'm not, Nick answers. I'm with Claire. I'm not like you, Dad.

'Didn't you hear me?' Marilyn asks. 'What's wrong with you?'

This light-headedness must be hunger. Nick ate an early sandwich in the field with Wilf at eleven and has had nothing since. 'I need to order steak and chips.'

'Yes,' Dick says. 'Let's all eat something. Marilyn? What would you like?'

'I'll put it on your tab, shall I?' Nick asks.

'Splendid. I'll have steak and chips too.'

'Chicken salad,' Marilyn says sulkily. None of them look at the menu. Steak and chips or chicken salad is all the pub offers.

'Right you are.' Nick knocks over his chair, as he hurries to the bar.

'See? He's not taking it too badly,' Nick hears Dick whisper to Marilyn, as he rights the chair. In the bar mirror, he glimpses his mother rolling her eyes.

Nick nods at David and Georgie. 'How are you both?' He's made them sound like a couple.

'Not so bad. And yourself?' David asks.

'Meeting with my remaining parent,' Nick gestures to Marilyn. 'Come to announce her engagement. The king is dead. Long live the king.'

He's being embarrassing but can't stop himself. Georgie picks up a beer mat and inspects it.

Joan catches Nick's eye. 'Yes, Nick? Not another round?' She leans forward and whispers, 'It's too early to get drunk.'

'What are you having?' Nick asks Georgie and David.

'We can't let you pay,' Georgie says.

'Don't worry about it,' Nick says.

'Well, as you're offering, I'll have a gin and tonic,' David says. 'How about you Georgie?'

'I don't often drink.'

She had drunk plenty that night at Priory Farm. There had been a drunken kiss, and then she had pushed him away. To clear things up, he had offered her his mother's bed, saying he already intended to spend the night in Tom's barn, that he wanted to lay in wait in case hooligans damaged the tractor again. She'd believed him. Properness was preserved. Not that there was anyone to notice. They could have had an orgy with only ghosts as witnesses. And now he wishes they had.

'Two double gins and tonics,' Nick says. 'Put them on my mother's fiancé's tab, will you? And have one yourself, Joan.'

'But I don't even know your mother's fiancé,' Georgie whispers to Nick.

'He wants a party,' Nick says. 'You'll be doing them both a favour – and me. Come and have a look at my mother's engagement ring. She'd love you to admire it.'

'I'll bring the drinks over,' Joan says, organising a tray. 'And I'll take cash for mine.'

Nick fetches two extra chairs and ushers Georgie and David to their table.

'This is Marilyn, my mother, and this is Dick, her bloke.'

'Fiancé,' Marilyn hisses.

'How could I forget.' Nick downs the whisky chaser. 'These are my friends from the museum, David and Georgie.' Couple talk again.

He should introduce Georgie to his mother as their new tenant, but he doesn't want her to cross-question Georgie about her income or complain about Tom still owing arrears. He can't bear Georgie to witness the sharpening of his mother's eyes when money is in the air. She's been shirty about Dad's landlord abilities since discovering Joan pays a peppercorn rent for her one-bedroom cottage. 'Dad liked to help people out,' Nick explained. 'His thoughtless generosity affected me financially, while he loved to play Mr. Popular,' his mother had complained. She should be happy now with her fat emerald and her rich fiancé.

'We met at Richard's funeral actually,' David says, holding out his hand.

'Really? I expect I was too upset to notice,' Marilyn says. 'And the church was packed. Were you there too?' she asks Georgie, looking her up and down.

'No. I've only recently… ' Georgie breaks away to call out, 'Hi!' Then, she turns to David. 'I promised to give her a hand.'

Miss Bewley has come in and is talking in a low voice to Joan, while trying to be invisible.

'Iris!' Nick calls out. 'How the hell are you?'
'Hello, Nick. Hello, Mrs Luckin. How are you?'
'Mum's engaged! Isn't that grand news?'

'Oh, yes.' Miss Bewley looks quite relieved. 'Very good news. Congratulations Mrs Luckin and... sorry, I must just work this out. Two crates of lemonade. I can take them. I'm sure I can carry them down to the school.'

'I said I'd help you carry a crate,' Georgie says. 'I'm sorry David, but I volunteered you for the other crate.'

Nick jumps up. 'Oh, I can take the other crate and then you and Georgie needn't carry anything at all. David and I will manage.'

'Why is it,' Marilyn mutters to Dick, 'that when that woman appears, everyone falls over themselves to help her?'

'Don't you like me giving Iris a helping hand?' Nick realises he's shouting. Joan makes big disapproving eyes at him.

'Honestly there's no need to interrupt your time with your mother. I'm so sorry, Mrs Luckin.'

Joan leans across the bar and touches Miss Bewley's arm. 'No one need haul heavy stuff around. I'll ask Matt to run the crates round in the car.'

'As long as he's not too busy?'

'God forbid Iris should cause a problem,' Marilyn says loudly.

'Thank you so much, Joan, if you think Matt really won't mind? Goodbye Mrs Luckin. Good to meet you, Mr... er um... Goodbye Nick. Thanks for your kind offer, Miss Gardner. That was very good of you.' Miss Bewley shuts the pub door gently behind her.

'So bloody pious. And a luddite to boot. Wilf tells me she's part of the anti-streetlight faction. I can't think what your father saw in her. Not his type at all.'

'He loved her voice, I suppose,' Nick says. A shadow falls over his mother's face. Dad's friendship with Iris Bewley was always painful for her. He should be angry with Iris not his mother. Yet, however unfilial, it is his mother he resents.

When the meals arrive, Georgie and David escape to the next table to make room for the food. They lean their heads together, peering at a notebook. Perhaps it is a work meeting, after all.

Hungry and drunk, Nick eats his steak and chips too quickly, while his mother drones on about the farm.

Georgie is laughing. Her fingers are almost touching David's. Nick wishes he hadn't pushed those drinks on them.

' ... tarmac the lane,' Dick adds, 'proper half-rent to you, of course...'

What are they on about? Nick asks himself as he drains his pint and then swallows the chaser, before gesturing to Joan for another drink.

'Does it really say, 'my longing'? he hears Georgie ask David.

'Look, you can make out the word if you concentrate...'

Nick leans towards them. 'What are you two

talking about?'

'David found a mystery note in the naturalist's handwriting,' Georgie says, then reads out Gil's words. '*A figure in the lane, as if my longing had taken shape.* There's no record of it in any accounts. It was stuck behind the drawer of Gil's desk.'

'Will this make your name as a scholar?' Nick asks.

'It might if I could find a viable rationale for the reference.'

'In other words,' Georgie says, 'we have no idea what it means. Or if it means anything at all. It could be a rough draft of something Gil ditched, or it might be a note of what someone else said.'

'What was it again?' Nick asks.

David opens his notebook and reads out the words he's copied down.' *A figure in the lane, as if my longing had taken shape. At other times, in the street, in the garden, the seat by the wall? Was it a phantasy? Or my longing?*'

By chance, there is a lull in the conversations around them. Even Marilyn and Dick appear interested. Joan leans over the bar to hear more.

Dick says, 'Perhaps he was in love.'

'That's what I think,' Georgie says.

'But longing isn't love,' Marilyn says. 'It's only yearning.'

'Is it?' Georgie asks. 'Is longing always for someone in the past? Or can you long for someone in the present?'

'Longing can occur in the present,' Marilyn replies, 'but the object of your affection must be unobtainable.'

'You're the expert, I suppose?' Nick asks.

'No, your father was the expert,' Marilyn says. 'He was attracted to what he couldn't have. I asked for a divorce repeatedly. He always refused. So long as he was still married to me, he was in a state of bliss I expect, as he could yearn for something illicit. And staying married made him an object of longing for all his women. He remained unobtainable and therefore infinitely desirable to self-denying types like La Bewley - and others.' She gives Joan a discouraging glance. 'Earwigging, as usual,' she mutters to Dick.

'Do you live in Hartisborne?' Dick asks Georgie politely.

'Yes, I'm renting… ' Georgie trails off as Nick shakes his head at her.

'I suppose you're potty about the naturalist, as you work in the museum?' Marilyn breaks the silence.

'I'm in love with him, actually,' Georgie says. A whim of honesty and gin.

'There you are. She's in love with a man who's been dead for two hundred years! Impossible longing right on our doorstep. Do you moon about his grave talking to him?'

'I do!' Georgie says.

'Does he reply?' Nick asks.

'He seems to.'

'Maybe he puts the thoughts in your head?' Dick says.

'That's how it seems, yes.'

'So, when you're in the museum, are you thinking about him all the time?' David looks curious, envious even.

'I am!'

'I'm supposed to be his biographer. I read and re-read all his letters and the garden journal, yet I barely get a glimpse of him. To me, he's always a cypher,' David says.

Nick can't take his eyes off Georgie. Her face is filled with light. She really is in love with a man who has been dead for two centuries. What a weird thought.

Marco, Georgie thinks, you'd laugh if you were here. If only you were here. She glances at the pub door as if Marco might walk in. To her surprise, the door sways open, wavering back and forth in the draught.

'There. Look!' Georgie says, 'Gil just came in. Can't you see him?'

To her delight, they all look round.

'That ruddy latch,' Joan says under her breath, collecting the empty glasses. Distracted by the door, she knocks Marilyn's drink over her skirt.

'For Christ's sake!'

'So sorry.' Joan swipes half-heartedly at Marilyn's lap with a bar cloth.

'If that's really old Gil, why is he here?'

'He's come to celebrate a wedding.'

'Maybe it's ours,' Dick says, squeezing Marilyn's hand.

'No, no. It's the wedding of a *young* couple.'

Marilyn frowns, taking against Georgie properly now.

'There will be dancing,' Georgie says. 'And he won't go home till two in the morning.'

'And that will be the last time, he dances,' David says. 'It's in the letters, isn't it?'

'So, you're not in touch with the supernatural,' Marilyn says. 'You're just parroting your reading, aren't you?'

'Gil and I have such a strong connection,' Georgie says. 'No one really understood what a wonderful dancer he was because he gave it up. And I know why.'

'I should be taking notes,' David says uneasily.

*'Maybe you should, Mr Daunt. Notes are always advisable when one is investigating local history,'* Georgie says in Mrs Camden's voice. She takes a sip of her gin and tonic.

'You sounded exactly like Louise Camden,' Marilyn says.

'Can you do Mum?' Nick asks.

If Georgie was with Marco, she'd mimic all the voices she could, making him laugh so much that he couldn't resist her.

*'If only you'd taken that job in Rome, you'd be fixed up with a rich Italian woman by now instead*

*of wasting your life on the farm.'*

'That's amazing,' Nick says, but he's embarrassed. Mum will know he's been talking about her.

'I'm sure I don't sound a bit like that.' Marilyn grips Dick's hand.

'I'm a bit drunk. And then I get mimicky. It's a silly party trick. No offence meant, Mrs Luckin.'

'None taken,' Nick says to cover his mother's silence.

A hush falls in the pub, while two hundred years ago, young Gil whirls Betty round and round to the sound of the fiddle and the serpent.

Georgie asks Joan for a glass of water. Time to sober up or she'll be mimicking them all.

Nick catches Georgie's eye. He raises his glass in a private acknowledgement of their previous drunken evening.

'To the happy couple,' David says, misinterpreting Nick's gesture and toasting Dick and Marilyn in just the way Nick had feared all evening. 'Congratulations on your engagement!' The other customers cheer and clap. The public bar joins in too.

Nick orders another drink. Joan refuses to serve him. While they argue, the pub door shifts in the evening breeze. Someone must have left the room, but only Georgie notices.

# CHAPTER 8

This morning, Gil trips and slides along Monksway, barely noting the deer slots or the wagtails ticking up and down on a tree fallen over the stream. Farmer Luckin has summoned him to Priory Farmhouse and Gil's reward will be a glimpse of or hopefully a meeting with Mary. If he finds her alone, he intends to make his offer.

In Luckin's orchard, a string of dead bullfinches loops between trees, warning birds away from apple buds. Twenty-four dead bullfinches, all male, never to be fathers. Now Gil mourns two dozen songs that won't be sung, two dozen red flashes that won't be seen, two dozen nests never to be made. And a hundred eggs that will never crack, a hundred fledglings that will never fly. Luckin is no worse than any countryman. Nonetheless, the dead finches stoke Gil's disgust.

'How-di-do, young Gil,' Luckin says, when Gil arrives. He still addresses him as a boy though Gil is past forty. Luckin and Gil are distantly related through his grandmother. Like Gil, Luckin has a dimpled chin, angel without, devil within.

They sit in the long hall with tankards of spiced ale served by Mistress Barnes, the housekeeper. The monks' refectory table glows with beeswax.

Logs bubble and spark in the great hearth. Someone - surely Mary - has placed a jar of kingcups on the table. Only last spring they identified the habitats of kingcups in Hartisborne, enjoying the search together.

Though it is day, the room is gloomy. The tallow candles steam and drip. Gil holds a scented handkerchief to his nose. Dead cows float into his mind as the fat burns. He should be flattered at such parsimony. Wax candles would be a show of formality.

'Now young Gil, I promised your grandmother I would pass on the old family stories and indeed the Priory heirlooms.'

Gil sighs and feigns interest. Old men fall into monologues, and Gil must endure it. A chance to meet Mary must arise if he can make himself listen to Luckin for long enough. He peers at the open doorway, hoping to catch Mary in a shaft of sunlight, carrying a basket of bread, like some maid in paintings of a hundred years ago. He shakes away the vision. For under such a painterly ideal, lies the early morning labour, the grinding of corn, the harshness of exhausted lives.

'Pay attention, my boy,' Luckin says refilling

his tankard. 'As I told your father, you need to get your mind on practicalities.'

'Yes, indeed, sir,' Gil says, retreating to his younger self, who was not a gentleman or a curate, but a boy playing round Luckin's farmyard, his mind firmly on practicalities, as he dissected a dead sparrow or wiped the vernix from a lamb.

'Inheritance,' Luckin begins, 'is a tricky business.'

In the background, he can hear women talking of ovens, sugar and pressing primroses into layers before adding brandy. Mary and the housekeeper are evidently making primrose wine. Perhaps they went out early with a basket and gathered the primroses, their fingers on the hairy stems, their hands now blessed by the damp scent.

'Long ago, when villagers stole the cloister stones for their dwellings, my ancestors – some say they were the monks' bastard offspring – proclaimed themselves the owners of this land. And since then, we Luckins have been keepers of a secret legacy.'

A donkey brays outside. A cockerel doodle-doos. Cartwheels roll in the yard. Men's voices halloo. Gil strains to hear Mary as the housekeeper tells the visitors to scrape their boots.

Luckin stands up and goes to open a chest in the corner of the room. While he lifts out blankets, Gil listens to the rolling of a barrel on the flagstones, followed by a grinding bash and curses.

'No Farmer Luckin today?' one of the men asks the housekeeper.

'Entertaining a visitor,' she says.

'A young lady, I bet?'

'No. A parson.'

'How is Mary?' Gil asks Luckin's back.

Luckin turns back to him, a carved box in his hand. 'She advises me on plants.'

Gil feels a stab.

'And she goes animal watching with young Ollie Knight.'

Another stab.

'And does Eddy Kemp go animal-watching with them?'

Luckin puts the carved box on the table. 'No, Kemp isn't interested. The girl wants to tell you her observations, apparently. She watches water-voles in the mill ponds. Sometimes I fear for her mind.' Luckin's tone is tender.

Outside, the men are teasing Mary. 'Not seen such a pretty face, since? When was it Chris?'

'Oh, not since Billingsgate last Tuesday at ten in the morning.'

Gil hears Mary laugh.

'The prettiest girl in London sells samphire at the fish market. Well, I used to think her the prettiest girl, but she's not a patch on you, is she Chris?'

'No comparison. The samphire girl is coarse as a fisherman and salty with weather.'

'Whereas this one...'

'Plush as a rose... lovely as a cherry...'

'Ripe for the plucking.'

Gil senses the monks hovering, alive on his retina, and all of them bearing the lascivious expressions of the two men.

'Stop it, you two. She's already taken,' the housekeeper, Mistress Barnes, says.

Mary must have come to an agreement with Eddy. Why feel sad? The marriage to Eddy is what everyone desires. Then he hears Mary's murmur.

'Not really taken.'

'Your Eddy is round here all the time.'

'So, there's no hope for Chris here then?' the man asks.

Can't these men see she is pregnant? Gil strains his ears to hear her, but at that moment Luckin succeeds in extricating an object from the box with his stiff fingers. He approaches Gil eagerly.

'Thomas tells me you are translating the ecclesiastical accounts of the village?'

'Yes, I thought it might be a useful task.' But who cares about ecclesiastical accounts when strangers are flirting with Mary?

'There's a record of relics, is there not?' Luckin asks. 'Do you remember what they are?'

'A toe joint of St Richard and various scraps of

cloth. Oh, and an osculatory bearing a bone, said to be the little finger of St John the Baptist,' Gil says off-handedly.

Luckin shakes a small box in Gil's face. A fragment of bone, visible through the box's glass, rattles inside it. He puts the box, a frame of wood with a glass side, into Gil's hand.

'You think this is the osculatory? And the bone is John the Baptist's?' Gil asks. The relic has been missing for centuries

'We see what we want to see, whichever age we inhabit.'

'What will you do with it?'

'When I'm gone, the farm will go to my nephew. He dislikes anything that smacks of papacy and is a whig through and through. He's a man of science like yourself but without your sympathy for human folly. When I'm gone, he'll bring in new furniture and new-fangled farming. And then, when he's near destroyed our farm, he'll move back to London and put in a tenant. You are a relative, a scientist, an antiquarian and a cleric. If you say the osculatory should be returned to the Bishop, I will do so. If you say it's no more than a family joke, it's still part of our history, and I must pass it to someone who will value it. My nephew is a trampler. I don't trust him with the past.'

Should Gil, with his scientific reputation, argue for the keeping of a relic? Should he offer it up to his bishop? A monkey bone parlayed into importance in some Eastern market centuries after John the Baptist lived and sold to desperate souls till it fell into the hands of the dissolute monks.

'Who will you recommend as tenant?'

'Kemp is a hard worker. And if we can persuade Trimmer to marry him, even better. Kemp's cottage is too small for a family. Mary's child could enjoy the run of my land. I'd like to see them settled in this house.' Luckin's wrinkles transform into a map of liveliness.

Is this the hint? That Mary's child is Luckin's? Will the farmer be laughing at his nephew in the afterlife because his natural heir is in situ, while his legal heir lives elsewhere?

'What do you say young Gil? Will you be the keeper of our family relic?' Luckin holds the osculatory in the candle's light. 'Even if this is an animal bone, the lips of our ancestors touched it for centuries. I don't want my nephew throwing it in the privy.'

He hands the osculatory to Gil, who places it reluctantly in his pocket. He makes to leave, but Luckin holds his arm.

'This is not all I want to say to you.'

Here it comes. The terrible avowal that Luckin is the father of Mary's child.

'Use your influence with Mary. Persuade her to marry Kemp. Tell her my plan for the farm.'

The worst interpretation springs into Gil's head. Eddy and Mary will live here, while Mary is forced to be Luckin's mistress. The idea tortures him.

'Blundel never gives up. The man's a wasp, buzzing after her and frightening her. She should marry Kemp and put a stop to it. You say nothing. Do you know of another man in the case?'

Luckin's will radiates from those shining eyes and forces Gil to turn away. Maybe his talk of Kemp has been a game to uncover Gil's true feelings. He is tempted to confide in another man, even in Luckin.

'Mistress Mary, remember me. I'll be thinking of you all the way home.' The shout of the deliveryman breaks Luckin's stare.

Outside, Mary calls out, 'I won't be thinking of you.'

'That won't stop me dreaming of you, my lovely.'

The poor joke and flirt more easily than he ever could. Gil hears the pony and cart rumble out of the yard and then laughter, as Mary and the housekeeper hurry past the open doorway.

'Do you know of another man who should be with Mary?'

There is a long silence. 'Only Kemp,' Gil lies, not daring to confront the old man.

'Then, I will call in Mary and leave you to your persuasion.'

'Mary! Mary, quite contrary, bring us some more ale, girl,' Luckin thunders.

After a moment, Mary comes in with the jug.

Luckin asks her, 'Have you stowed the saltfish?'

'They brought in the barrel but forgot to take it down to the cellar. We can't roll it down the steps, sir.'

'You shouldn't even try,' Gil says quickly, fearing for her baby.

'I'll see what can be done.' Luckin leaves, with a pointed look at Gil.

'Good day to you Mr Gil,' Mary says.

'Good day to you, Mary,' Gil replies. 'Thomas is missing you in the glass house.'

Mary blushes. Her hand falters. Ale pools on the table. Gil mops it with his kerchief.

'He hopes you will return to us soon.'

'Mr Blundel told me it was unfitting, sir, now I'm in the present case, for me to work alone with a single man and a reverend.'

'But Ollie has passed on my messages?'

Mary nods agreement. 'I daren't come into the village for fear Mr Blundel will take me to the justice.'

'Farmer Luckin thinks Eddy would be a good match for you.'

'I know, sir.'

'He has requested me to persuade you, as your curate - and your friend – to marry Eddy and give your child a father.'

'I am waiting, sir.'

'Waiting for what?

'I am waiting for the swallows to arrive. If nothing happens then, I will wait for them to leave.'

It irks him that Mary believes swallows migrate.

'You'll be a mother before the swallows hibernate. You must act now. Why, I will marry you myself!'

There. He has said it, in exasperation, almost as a joke.

Mary smiles. 'Sir, I am honoured. It is generous of you to try to make things right. Of course, if I wed, I'd want your blessing.'

She thinks of him merely as a curate then. To save face, he changes tack. 'You could have the gardener's cottage in Wakeling Park. Old Dan is lonely there since his wife died. If I'm not mistaken, you and I have many common interests that promise happiness together.' But he should be talking of Eddy. What a muddle.

Is he offering her a job or his hand? He should have taken her in his arms, pursued the point more physically. He was known in Oxford as a good kisser. It was even his nickname. Kisser Gil. Jinnie loved his kisses. But he stands back. So much older than her, her employer. No, he will wait on her answer as if she is a gentlewoman.

'Your child could grow up as mine.'

'But this is not your child, sir. And though he or she grew up in the grounds of Wakeling House, it would not be their home.'

'It would be as if it were.'

'I have no dowry. No property. And there is my mother.'

She understands him then.

'My father too suffered from winter darkness. I'm not afraid of your mother.'

'I must wait until the swallows leave. And then I will know what to do.'

'But is Farmer Luckin a good employer?' Do you sleep in his bed with him, is what he really wants to know.

'It is not Farmer Luckin that makes me ill but the ghosts. Please don't smile so, sir. I feel them about me like so many Blundels.'

'A fancy of a woman with child?'

'It is always difficult to be believed by men. I know we are supposed to be scientists sir, but sometimes I wish I had a spell about me, some magic or holy protection.'

On an impulse, Gil draws the osculatory from his pocket. 'You see this bone? It is a relic and said to be St John the Baptist's little finger bone. The monks, the priests, sometimes the common people would kiss it when they prayed for health and protection.'

She is very close to him peering at the wooden box with its glass side and worn metal frame.

'Shake it,' he says, handing her the osculatory.

Mary takes it and shakes it. The section of bone rattles. 'They kissed this?'

'Well, the box anyway. Their lips touched this

glass. It was called an osculatory because it received oscula – the Latin for kisses.'

'Can I kiss it?'

'Yes, of course. And make a wish. Or say a prayer.'

Mary holds the container of bone to her lips for a long moment. 'There, I have made my wish. Or call it a prayer, if you want, sir.' She laughs. 'Now it's your turn, Mr Gil.'

His fingers touch hers as he takes the little box.

'That's where I kissed,' she says, pointing.

The glass is still misted with her breath. He presses his lips to the place her lips touched.

He understands why Luckin doesn't want the relic lost, for it carries the belief that one person's love, present or past, can still help another. He will keep the osculatory among his treasures, with his pressed butterflies and blown eggs.

Nev Pearson opens the squeaky door and startles Georgie from the window. 'I've taken Mr Daunt's post up to him in the study.'

'Anything from a journal or college?' Georgie can't resist asking, though she'd vowed not to alert Nev to David's dreams of publishing his speculations about Miss Butter and 'the shape of Gil's longing.'

'I don't nose into other people's correspondence.'

'No, of course not,' Georgie says, sorry to offend him.

Nev takes a letter from his jacket pocket and bangs it down on the table. 'This came for you,' he says. He whistles a few bars of Der Fledermaus under his breath. 'It's been forwarded from that bookshop you worked in.'

Georgie fidgets with the envelope, hardly daring to look at it while Nev is there.

'It's marked urgent.' Then instead of leaving, Nev stands in the doorway talking about Costanza and Mozart. Luckily, the impecunious pair distract him from her letter. After moving the door back and forth a few times to prove the hinges still squeak, Nev says, 'Aren't you going to open it? People don't write *urgent* for nothing.'

She's conscious of his curiosity, as she takes the paper knife and slices through the envelope's crease to slip out Rosemary's letter.

'Oh, it's nothing much. A letter from my neighbour in London.'

Apparently convinced, Nev leaves to fetch the Three-in-One oil.

In the letter, Rosemary says she is worried about Trevor. Guilt makes Georgie tap faster at the typewriter, pushing away the thought of Trevor's loneliness and her fear of phoning Rosemary.

Nev returns, with the Three-in-One, stretching out his oiling operation with a long speech about The Magic Flute. '... more or less a fringe production… followed his heart…no idea it would …never lived to see …'

Her hand reaches for the telephone on the museum's reception table. She dials Rosemary's number.

'Hello, Cathy? Is your mother there?'

'Making a personal call!' Nev snaps. 'Have you asked Mr Daunt whether you can use the telephone?'

Georgie puts the receiver down. Rosemary probably isn't even in. Maybe just as well. If Trevor somehow had the means to trace a call from Rosemary's phone, then he could discover the museum's number.

Nev circles her suspiciously, gesticulating with the oil can. Please not Beethoven and his nephew again. Georgie fetches a cloth and trails round after Nev mopping up spots of oil.

'How did you become so interested in music? Were you a musician?'

Nev closes his face and hurries out, muttering something about Romilly calling him for lunch. His hands are shaking so much, he can hardly open the squeaky door.

The naturalist's clock in the hall strikes one. Georgie checks her purse for change, slips on her coat, leaves the museum and hurries down the road to the phone box near the pub.

She pulls open the heavy door. She dials

the number and waits for Rosemary to answer. 'Hello, hello?' Georgie calls into the receiver. 'Are you there?'

'Hang on,' Rosemary says.

Georgie presses Button B and slots in her money.

A woman appears outside, gesturing at her watch, though Georgie has only just got through. Georgie mimes an apology through the glass.

'Hello, hello,' Rosemary says.

'Are you alright?' Georgie asks. But Rosemary can't hear her and keeps shouting, 'Are you there?'

The waiting woman taps on the glass.

'Look, I don't have much change. I only have a minute or two left.'

'You need to visit Trevor.'

'Why? What's the matter with him?'

The woman knocks more loudly.

Georgie's money runs out. She fumbles in her purse for more change. The woman knocks again. Georgie pulls open the door to explain she needs to make another call, when the phone rings. Rosemary must be phoning her back. 'Rosemary, is that you?'

'Is Audrey there?' a quavery voice asks.

'That'll be for me,' the woman says. Georgie has no choice but to cede Audrey the receiver and wait for her to finish. The minutes of Georgie's lunch hour tick by until she has to accept that Audrey's call will never end.

On her way back to Wakeling House, she passes Miss Bewley with a crocodile of children, scuffling towards the zigzag path. Miss Bewley forces a smile when she sees Georgie and says, 'Nature walk.' Miss Bewley can scarcely keep up with the chattering children, who ignore her instructions and rush on.

'You look well,' the butcher calls from his shop doorway, waving his hook at her.

'It's the Hartisborne air,' she says. 'So different to London.'

'Couldn't stand to live in the smoke myself. This is the place to be.'

He returned from the war without his hands, to the green embrace of Hartisborne. He learnt how to use custom-made fitments, the blade, the hook, the knife-sharpener, each one attached to a wide leather belt which he slides onto his stumps. The butcher is always smiling and laughing, flirting with women, turning the injury done him into a performance, a talent. Is it his brush with death that's made him appreciate life? His resilient nature? Or is it Hartisborne performing its magic?

But if Hartisborne saves people, why on earth is Georgie still scared of the dark, still scared of making a phone call? *Whatever happens to me will be your fault, you effing bitch.*

She unlocks the door and races up to David's study, hoping the Pearsons won't hear her unlock the door. A shadow jumps out at her. A man wearing a tricorne. It's David, fooling around.

'Did you think I was old Gil?' he asks.

'For a moment, I did,' she lies. She laughs because he expects it.

Marco would have noticed she was anxious. He would have put his arms around her and wheedled her fears out of her. 'Nev said you had a letter. Any news on your article?'

'It's from my college. Probably just Francis.'

Georgie can tell he's unnerved by the letter and too scared to open it. David reveres his former tutor, Professor Francis de la Salle and fears losing his goodwill through delaying his book. She leaves him to it.

As the lonely afternoon goes by, she would almost welcome Mozart's rehearsals to calm her worried mind, but Nev Pearson is absent, and David is still upstairs, making nothing of the shape of Gil's longing.

She opens *The Natural History of Hartisborne* and reads about a newt drawn up from the well. She goes into the garden and over to the stone well near the Pearsons' cottage. Two hundred years ago, someone, Thomas perhaps, drew up a pail of rollicking water and found the newt with its bright yellow splash and frilled head. Georgie sees the newt vividly. Writing and reading are such strange powers, a magic passing between minds over centuries.

No one has written about Trevor and Connie or ever looked at them with the loving curiosity with which Gil looked at the newt. No one has ever asked whether they were shaped by evolution, the need to survive or their habitat.

What if she wrote a natural history about Connie and Trevor? Their appearance, their environment, the way they spoke. Would this tell her anything that wasn't routine or habitual? To understand Connie and Trevor, she would need to know their history and her own, but they are more mysterious to her than even Gil and his friend Miss Butter are to David.

Once he has read past the happy news of another child safely delivered by Mrs M., Gil notices that M.'s letter hints at scandalous rumours reaching the bishop's ears. He should never have confided in M. who suggests he avoid scandal and flee Hartisborne, the very source and matter of his writing. The bishop hints at other livings, including benighted Binford. Has M, his bosom companion at Oriel, betrayed him by spreading rumours in the bishop's palace, jeopardising the small income that helps, along with his rents, to maintain Wakeling Park?

Gil dips his pen but, instead of writing to M., he describes the newt the gardener hauled from the well. That flaring yellow stripe, the dragon-like comb. When he has found both flow and precision, and thus avoided replying in anger, there is a knock on the door.

It is Ollie Knight garbling a message. 'Mary Trimmer says she seen the first swallow, Mr. Gil.'

Gil fixes his pen in its holder. He blots his words. The newt will have to wait, suspended in pouring water, as angry at being hauled from its habitat as he himself had been a moment ago at the prospect of such displacement.

Gil's thoughts leap ahead to meeting Mary, and yet he manages to give his instructions calmly as if there is no import in Mary's message beyond continuing their scientific enquiry into the hibernation of swallows.

The boy is to spread the word, hammer on doors, go to the baker's, the undertaker's, to the farms, find children, girls or women, anyone inclined to help. He must go to the workhouse and drum up those who are desperate for pennies and farthings. Each villager is to pass the word to the other that a swallow has been seen.

Thomas will furnish anyone who wants with an apple stick from last autumn's pruning, thin enough to insert into a chalk crack or a mouse's hole. Thomas carries the bundle to the yard's gate. At the school for a dozen boys opposite Wakeling House, the pupils race out to grab a stick.

Gil divides up the search parties, this one to go to the Punfle path, this to King's Field, this to the Echoing Field, this to the Common, this to the

Lythe, this to Noar Hill where the chalk diggings offer an ideal landskip.

'But what about Monkswood, Mr Gil?'

Gil calculates the time it will take Mary to walk there from Priory. No one is to go along Monksway but he. His heart beats like wings in his ears. 'I have designated the locations according to a specific method of scientific enquiry.'

Thomas shoots him a quizzical glance.

The boys will climb trees and peer into hollows. The women will peruse low house eaves, twisting thin twig ends under gutters and through gaps in tiles or thatch. Where they can't reach, they will ask the thatcher to bring his ladder and continue the inspection. They will investigate every hole drilled by a woodpecker, every chink in limestone.

Gil has heard an account he barely credits, but which must be tested, of a man pulling a stick from an April pond, whereon swallows clustered in a ball like frogs mating. Could they indeed spend winter underwater without drowning? He must send boys to Priory Ponds in case such a conglobulation can be found.

As Aristotle says, one swallow does not a summer make, but one swallow signals that more will follow, returning from wherever they disappear to in autumn. Perhaps now they wake from their sleep, now they ready themselves to fly from winter hidey-holes and if so, he and his motley observers will discover the secret of their awakening. Then at last, he can write to the Royal Society and counter hypotheses of migration with evidence of hibernation.

Some years ago, he observed sand martins flying in and out of a sand cliff in Suffolk. He sought them later in the local sand quarry, where they merrily entered the tiniest of cracks and brought forth their young. Surely then, as he said to Mary, the swallow and the swift too, their fellow hirundines, might find their way into earth or stone for winter, sculpting a tunnel with sharp beaks. But Mary, like many of his fellow scientists, believes hirundines fly across the globe to warmer climes.

'You need evidence, Mary,' he'd said. 'We'll never make a natural scientist of you if you don't support your ideas with evidence.'

'But I can never travel the world, Mr Gil, and so how will I ever know?'

Mary had been much taken by his father's map, that time he was poring over it in the garden. 'Just think Mr Gil, perhaps our swallows fly over the ocean, right over your brother, Mr Jack, on the Rock of Gibraltar, all the way to Africa.'

In shared silence, they saw his brother Jack staring into the sky, hot, homesick and debt-ridden, asking himself which swallows came from Hartisborne. In Spain too, his brother writes, the swallows disappear before winter.

In previous years, Gil's hunt for proof of hibernation thrilled and frustrated him. Yet now, behind the ambition to solve nature's puzzle, lie thoughts of Mary's promise to answer him as to the father of her child, 'when the swallows return or when they leave'.

'I have assigned myself Monkswood,' he tells Thomas. 'I fancy those tree roots and hollows may harbour hirundines.'

'Well, Mr. Gil,' Thomas begins, 'I could take a fancy to that myself,' but Thomas, seeing Gil's face fall, adds, 'if I weren't set on Coneycroft hanger as a likely spot. As long as that accords with your scientific plan?' He can read Gil like the weather and though he would enjoy the search more with Gil, Thomas nobly holds back. 'If you see Mary Trimmer, remember me to her.'

'I surely will, Tom,' Gil says. 'But I doubt Mary will have leisure for swallow hunting now she works for Farmer Luckin.'

Thomas whistles irritatingly under his breath.

Gil hurries across the street, past a hanging pig. Why they bleed the damned carcass right opposite his front door, he knows not. The stench of dead flesh and iron blood must nauseate any woman with child.

In Monksway, the bluebells cleanse his nose of butchery. The beechen trees set forth a little green now, so light and happy among the ancient hollow trees.

The advent of his favourite birds is even

more propitious than usual, heralding not just summer but the revelation of Mary's story and the fruitful summer of his life. He is determined now to make his offer, warmed by the memory of touching his lips to the osculatory, kissing Mary's kiss.

# CHAPTER 9

Sylvia's bramley is about to blossom in the hedge between her cottage and the Camdens' house. Come August, Mrs Camden will blame her for the wasps because the apples fall into her garden. The truth is Mrs Camden doesn't like Sylvia living next door.

From up here in her bedroom, Sylvia can see Mrs Camden opening the curtains of her casement windows. Tulips wave pink squares from a fancy urn on the Camdens' flag-stoned terrace.

Like Sylvia - in this they are equals - Colonel and Mrs Camden will both vote in the parish council election today, though husband and wife are on opposite sides. Mrs Camden will vote for herself. Her ticket is street lighting, a popular issue. Mrs Camden will set her hair in curlers, apply her make-up, and steam her dress so that it falls in flawless lines, then take out her curlers and tease her hair into shape to look the part of the ruling class.

Sylvia has never mastered a neat appearance despite all her cleaning jobs. She inspects her bedroom through Mrs Camden's eyes. The bedspread is faded, its once bright colours barely there. Jack brought it back from India where he was a soldier and where he had loved an Indian girl before his feet and lungs were damaged in the first war, before he met Sylvia. Mrs Camden wouldn't think much of the rag rug which Sylvia made on long evenings alone by the stove, cutting up Jack's shirts after he died. When she's weeding by the hedge, she'll hear Colonel Camden say, 'Poor old Sylvia! She needs more help with her garden.' That's who she is now. Poor old Sylvia.

She is not someone Mrs Camden would associate with jewellery, but Sylvia has her collection in an inlaid box on the chest of drawers. Her mother's broken string of jet beads. The brooch, given by an older cousin, when she recruited Sylvia. 'So, we shall know each other and preserve our femininity.'

Sylvia loves the purple and white violets, entwined with green leaves. Purple for dignity, white for purity and green for hope, the colours of the suffragettes. She wore it to her son's wedding to lend herself strength to let him go. She wore it to her grand-daughter's christening, and before that to Jack's funeral though it was too pretty for a funeral. She wears the brooch when she needs courage, but it never gives her enough. She remains the girl on the stairs watching her father shove her sister against the wall. A by-stander still.

Mrs Camden wouldn't be able to vote for herself, if Sylvia hadn't lain in the muddy road, heard mounted police clopping towards her while men gobbed spit on her face. Even after all this time, she's weighed down by guilt because she didn't challenge the policeman who dragged her friend away. And she didn't chain herself to any railings or go to prison or have a tube thrust down her throat.

These days there's the women's liberation movement, civil rights in America and ban the bomb. Because she goes to church, everyone assumes Sylvia is of the old guard, an aged cleaning lady, empty of ideals. She'd gladly explain her views, but no one wants to hear from an old woman.

Dressed and ready, Sylvia hops on her bike and rides to the village hall.

In the makeshift booth, the pencil on its string wavers in her hand. She would like Hartisborne to have street lighting, especially since Winnie's death, but that means voting for Mrs Camden. Can she forgive her for dissuading the Mothers' Union from helping Joan when she was pregnant? To vote for her would be disloyal to Joan and Maisie. Also, Mrs Camden is the chair of the school governors and makes life difficult for Iris Bewley. On the other hand, not to vote for street lighting is disloyal to her friend Winnie's memory and hard on Wilf.

Arthur Deadman and Miss Adkins are standing for the parish council too. Miss Adkins is against street lighting because of bats but really because there was no street lighting in the naturalist's day. She likes Miss Adkins, but aren't people more important than animals? Aren't living villagers more important than the dead? She should vote on principle not personality.

Lighting isn't the only issue. Miss Adkins wants more play equipment for the recreation ground, a new bus shelter and a lower speed limit. Arthur Deadman promises to keep footpaths open. Her pencil hovers. The lone swing on the rec, Maisie as a baby, the leaking bus shelter, the straggling street where Winnie died while the driver escaped. The village flashes round Sylvia as if she's rotating in the pipe barrel. It all matters but choosing one issue denies the solving of another.

Finally, she draws her cross.


Gil reaches the bank where beech roots bend outwards over chalk as if beckoning a hand to grasp them. He lays down the spare stick and pokes his own stick into chalk cracks, but half-heartedly, often breaking off to look for Mary.

The school-boys halloo from the Lythe across the stream. A meadow of marram and squelch separates the two paths to Priory. Mary will walk this way surely, on his side of the stream, drawn to hollows under roots, where swallows may flitter into limestone chasms.

He hurries down a bank of leaf mould, crushing bluebells, his feet cracking last year's beechnuts. Here comes a distant figure in a red cloak. It is Mary. She has no stick. Clearly, she trusts him to provide one. She pauses, looking about her, not yet aware of him. She fences at something invisible and then runs towards him. She cries out, 'Mr. Gil, Mr Gil! Something's been at my hair like fingers.'

'Come here, Mary,' he calls. Come here, my darling, he calls in his head. The ghosts can't get you here once you're over the priory boundary. 'I've brought you a stick, my dear.'

Mary is puffed, her eyes ringed by tiredness. She laughs when she takes the stick. 'Oh Mr Gil, I was searching all along the way for the right stick.'

Science not superstition is his metier. Yet his mind cannot rest on swallows, though Mary is full of the year's first sighting, and did she do right to alert him, she asks again and again, for she feels she does nothing right now. There is an atmosphere, a strangeness at the farm.

'I cannot sleep there, Mr Gil,' she says.

'It's your condition. Many women find it so, I've heard.'

'I went to my mother's for a night, walked all the way to Binford, and I slept like the dead. But then in the morning, we argued. She didn't want me to return here. And when I got back to Hartisborne, Mr Blundel swore at me for a whore and told me to go back to Binford. But oh Mr Gil, I want my child to grow up here.'

'It's natural that you sleep better at your mother's,' he says. 'She must miss you.'

'I can only stand to live with her in winter when she needs me most. I'm like the swallows. I must return to Hartisborne in the spring. Mr Blundel pursued me down the street and threatened to take me to the Justice.'

'Blundel knows it is illegal to give a woman a bastardy examination while she is with child.'

'But his issue is settlement, and there is no law against a settlement examination, with or without an unborn child. Now I'm caught between millstones like an ear of grain. Last night I dreamt my head was on an anvil. Before I could rise, a carpenter drilled a hole in my skull.'

'You dreamt of trepanation?' How curious. Amongst the family relics, Farmer Luckin had shown him a round of bone on a string thought to be from a woman's trepanned skull.

'You should change your situation. You could marry Eddy and, when Dan Rushmore moves, my gardener's cottage will be empty. Your child could play in the park.'

He disappoints himself. He could have proposed. He could have swept away her troubles and raised her up. He could have offered to be the child's father. Instead, he offers her the gardener's cottage on condition of marrying Eddy. Why can't he speak of love? Why so circumspect when she trusted him with her very nightmares?

'I have to wait Mr Gil before I can answer Eddy. Or anyone.'

'You said you were waiting for the swallows' return.'

An image of Mary holding her new-born in his house, takes hold of his fancy. In the birthing chamber, Goody Newton passes the caudle cup to local women. Thomas would make the caudle good and strong for Mary and all her visitors, with the best wine and oats. What a happy vision.

'I cannot decide on anything. My head is a fog. I would sleep anywhere, in the haybarn if necessary, if only I could sleep without dreams,' Mary says. She puts her hand on Gil's arm.

'Insomnia is a sapping ill, but it will pass soon enough, and then you will be your old self again. Let us concentrate on our search. And our conundrum - do the swallows stay or do they go? Are they native or migrants? Here is your stick and here is mine.'

'Thank you, Mr Gil.' Mary dries her eyes.

'Now where shall we begin?'

'Last year I saw the swallows swoop over the mudbanks by the stream,'

'They swoop for the gnats, do they not?' He knows the answer, but it is his practice to build

Mary's confidence in observing.

'We could step on to the stone islands and poke our sticks into the bank opposite?'

'You base your plan on previous observation like a true scientist.'

How pompous he sounds, but his pomposity works. Mary is reviving. She has always loved the swallow search.

They scramble down to the stream, where the water ripples around a shale island. 'I don't think we can reach', he says. 'In drier years, we'd hop from island to island.'

Mary unbuckles her shoes and kicks them off, lifts her skirts, unties her garters, pulls down her woollen stockings and hangs them on a hazel bush. Gil turns his head away and then can't help but look, when he hears her gasp. 'T'is cold. Pass me the stick, if you please, Mr Gil.'

Mary paddles out to the island. She's tied her skirts up high without a thought for what Gil might see, the shapeliness of her legs, taut from working and walking. She has no fear of him. His curacy makes him a eunuch to her, rather than a flesh and blood man. He passes her the stick. She pokes it into the bank.

'Beware of the water rats,' he calls. 'In case you disturb their nest.'

Her downturned face hovers above the water, investigating. The sun casts leaf light on her skin. There are moments you hold in your heart's memory forever. Mary's concentration, her bending and looking, her curiosity. The stream dazzling its water over her feet. Her unruly hair lit by the April sun. The new curve of her belly. He will throw off his shoes and join her. Maybe he will tell his love after all, standing beside her, their feet bare in the water like Adam and Eve.

Damn it. A sudden hullabaloo. The schoolboys have abandoned the long Lythe, and here they come along Monksway, playing at sword fights with the apple sticks. They jostle and shout. Mary drops her skirts and sloshes back to the land, a band of water soaking her hems. Gil averts his gaze, then runs up the bank to the track.

'Is that the best you can do?' He roars at the boys, jumping out at them as if he's a lion, thrilling them with his mock anger, making them laugh. He martials them up the banks to the fox holes and a place where he says he'd once seen sand martins. He makes it a game. Who can get there first, who can be distracted from Mary and her bare legs.

When he looks down, Mary is sitting by the stream, drying her feet on her skirt and then easing on her stockings under cover of her petticoat. Gil sends the boys up to the top field. Mary buckles up her woodland shoes. Her hair catches on a twig. She rises, climbs up the bank. Gil can see her looking around for him. He steps out from behind the vast trunk of an ancient beech.

'There you are, Mr Gil.' she says. 'I have found you.' She smiles.

'Well, Mistress Trimmer. All this fresh air! You will sleep well tonight, I'm sure.' His voice is falsely avuncular.

'I hope so,' she says, 'or I think I will go mad.' She throws down the stick. 'I must off back to Priory. I wish you well of the search. Will we ever discover the mystery of the swallows, do you think, sir?'

'If we don't, other scientists will.'

'I want us to be the first.'

'It's not important to be the first, only to find the truth and share it.'

'Yes, truth is the object,' she says, frowning.

If truth is the object, then why not speak? 'Do you remember our talk at Priory? I ask you again whether you wish me to marry you or not.'

She scuffs the leaf mould with her shoe and watches a wagtail by the stream.

'Nothing has changed, and so I must wait now till the swallows leave.' She walks on, looking about her, as if truth can be found in the leaf mould, bluebell drifts, in the clumps of yellow kingcups that mark the path to Priory and in the cling of the black marl that clogs the feet of the villagers planting them in their ways.

A wagtail dips over the water, and is joined, in a flash of yellow, by another wagtail. Why can't human courtship be as simple? He watches the birds, until the boys return.

'We've not seen one swallow, Mr Gil,' a boy informs him.

'No swallows do not a summer make,' he quips half-heartedly. Yet Mary saw one.

Nick sits in the cowshed with a sick calf. Through the open side of the shed, he can see swallows swooping over the farmyard. He's waiting for the vet. The calf is slowly dying, its tongue dry, its eyes dulling. Nick strokes it gently. Does it understand what is happening? If only the vet would come soon.

Nick says aloud, 'Dad how can I save this calf?' Dad was good on diseases, gentle with animals, often knew what to do without the expense of calling the vet. Wilf could help but he hasn't turned up at work today.

Nick doesn't know how to manage Wilf. Should he tell him off? Give him notice? He's taken to being late or bunking off or swearing at Nick under his breath.

Dad, how can I be Wilf's boss when he's so much older than me? He talks to Dad when there's no one here, confides in him as he never did in real life. If he were to leave Priory, he fears Dad would go silent or fade away. He counts the weeks since he's seen him, as if he's just gone on a trip, like he did once with a woman friend who wasn't even Iris, leaving Nick to caretake the farm, when he was only fifteen. His mother was supposed to stay with him, but she couldn't face sleeping at Priory again, she said. So Nick was left alone.

Wilf had kept an eye on him. Winnie made extra sandwiches so that Nick had some lunch. Wilf kept him beside him on the farm, grudgingly advising him. Perhaps his father told Wilf to look out for him. With his son lost in the war, a fact that Wilf accepted but Winnie wouldn't, perhaps Wilf resented looking after Nick, a spoilt boy back from boarding school. Maybe Wilf couldn't sympathise with Nick's loneliness because Wilf had gone to work at fourteen and thought nothing of Nick being alone at fifteen.

Nick hears the vet's van arriving. He brushes straw from his overalls. 'It'll be alright now,' he tells the calf. True or not, that's what you say to children.

And it isn't true. The vet confirms there is no hope.

The vet has put the calf out of its misery, and Nick is making himself a late lunch though he hardly feels like eating, when Claire phones him. She sounds urgent and direct like she used to before she suspected him of liking Georgie.

'I need you to come to the school,' she says. 'Miss Finch is on a nature walk with the infants. There's no one to help me. And I don't want to phone Mrs Camden or the vicar.'

'Why not?' Why me is what he really meant.

'The juniors have trapped Miss Bewley in her classroom and bolted the door on the assembly hall. I can't get in to help her. I keep telling them to unbolt the door, but they can't shift it now. So now the children are trapped too. The new girl is crying her eyes out. It's mayhem. Miss Finch might not be back for ages.'

Nick jumps into the Land Rover, glad to leave the scene of the calf's death. His mother's words echo in his head. *You'll never run the farm as a business if you're always wasting time on village demands.*

As he rattles down the village street, he sees Georgie outside the museum talking to some tourists. She waves. He glances away guiltily, haunted by the gentle long-lashed eyes of the calf.

Claire shows him what has happened. Through the wired glass panes in the assembly hall door, he can see one end of a skipping rope tied to the classroom's doorhandle and the other to the piano. The rope's tension holds the classroom door shut. In the assembly hall, a kind of antechamber to the classroom, the boys are throwing bean bags at the girls, while one boy rips the sash from a new girl's dress. Nick hammers on the door, scaring them into silence. The new girl is crying into the gauzy material of her dress.

Claire whispers, 'See.'

'Listen,' Nick shouts through the door, 'One of

you, get a stool and unbolt this door.'

'We've tried,' Maisie calls, 'But the bolt won't move.'

'You bolted it! So you must able to unbolt it!' Nick shouts. He glimpses Iris's pale face through the distorted glass of the two doors as she tugs at the door handle in vain. The heavy piano won't shift at all. Iris has always been slight. Since Dad died, she has shrunk even more and lost her resonant authoritative voice.

'Untie the piano and let Miss Bewley out. Then she can unbolt the door.'

'We can't get the knots undone,' Maisie calls. 'It was Danny,' she adds and starts to cry.

'Are there any scissors in there?'

Maisie goes on a search, but there are only gym mats, skipping ropes and hymn books. He spots the pole used for opening the high windows. He could ask Maisie to open the window and then he could climb up a ladder and drop through a pair of scissors.

Claire worries this is unsafe. Supposing the children attacked someone with the scissors? One boy cut another boy's ear only the other day. And since then, scissors of all kinds have been locked in Miss Bewley's desk after use. Nick says he's surprised that no governors were informed about this. Claire ducks the question by offering him the caretaker's toolbox.

Nick finds a chisel and a hammer. Then he climbs on a stepladder and chips away at the top of the door until the bolt becomes visible. 'Pliers,' he calls to Claire. He works at the bolt until it pulls back a little, then chips more away from the bolthole. Eventually, he uses the chisel to force the end of the bolt back. He climbs down and opens the damaged door.

When Nick enters the hall, the children go silent, expecting him to bawl them out. Several children raise their hands and ask, 'Can I go to the toilet?'

Nick moves away from the stampede. Behind the glass, Iris is ashen, scarcely holding back tears. He can't bear to leave her imprisoned any longer. He fiddles with the knot impatiently, wishing his fingers weren't so covered in hard skin. He can't get a purchase on the skipping rope at all.

'Here,' Claire says, offering some large scissors from the office.

Nick hacks through the rope. It slackens and falls loose. Iris opens the door.

'Okay Iris?' Nick asks gently. 'Claire will make you a cup of tea in the office.'

Iris nods. Like a sleepwalker, she follows Claire out.

Through the hall window, Nick is relieved to see Miss Finch and her class crocodiling up the path past the weigela. He outlines the situation to her.

The children tell Miss Finch different versions of what happened. They are terrified by their ability to overturn authority. Nick hears her saying, 'Maisie, I thought better of you.'

'Danny wouldn't listen to me!' Maisie says. 'He just wouldn't.' She bursts into tears.

Nick wants to defend her but pulls himself away. Miss Finch is calling all the children into the assembly hall to read them the riot act. They don't need him now. But in case they think they do, he waves at Claire and Iris through the office window, runs to the Land Rover and drives home.

He would like to tell Georgie the whole episode, but it was Claire who called him. Claire is his girlfriend, isn't she? The truth is he thinks of Georgie more often. He must never treat anyone the way Dad treated women. He should tell Claire it's over. But he's scared of having nothing except the farm and long days with Wilf. Anyway, Georgie is in love with old Gil, isn't she? You can't fight the competition if they're dead.

Nick leans his arms on the table in his garden and wonders why his mother left the ruddy thing here. Its pedestal leg of mock walnut is peeling. Its round drawer has warped and stuck. He wants to talk to his mother. He wants to ask her about ghosts, about his father, about Iris Bewley even. Just as he considers driving to London to interrogate her - why shouldn't he surprise her for a change - the phone starts ringing inside. If that's Mum, then he'll make her answer his questions right now.

'What do you want?' he asks tersely.

It is Mrs Camden interrogating him about the lock-in incident. Why didn't he call on *her* for help? Indeed, Miss Clifford should have telephoned *her*. Miss Finch should have reported the event immediately to *all* the governors, not just Nick. Mrs Camden has been telling Nick and the vicar for months now that something must be done about Miss Bewley. And this humiliating event, Nick can tell she enjoys the words - *this humiliating event* - is the last straw. She will call a village meeting to discuss the matter of Miss Bewley's incompetence. She hopes for Nick's support. There is also the issue of suitable visitors to the school. Miss Bewley's plans with that artist Mr Swallow are most unfortunate.

'I think the lock-in and Tom's art visit are completely separate issues, aren't they?' Nick asks.

'It's all part of a picture of incompetence and decadence,' Mrs Camden snaps.

The receiver drops from Nick's hand involuntarily, as if some other hand slammed it down. No one ever puts the phone down on Mrs Camden.

# CHAPTER 10

Gil has arranged to send sticklebacks to an engraver in Fleet Street, with the fish to be drawn from life. The Thames is full of sticklebacks, and the engraver could send his own boy for a London catch, but these must be Hartisborne fish and not imposters. The fish must be packed for the journey before the morning post chaise leaves at seven.

So, he's up at dawn and off to Monkswood with nets and jugs and his nephew Ben. Ollie Knight will meet them in the wood. He is a great stalker of fish, sometimes catching a wriggling lamprey in his bare hands before it slips away to die.

Fish listen, notice shadows and the movement of water. They know the places where boys dip nets or scoop them up in crocks. However rivalrous they are, this knowledge must be passed from fish to fish, but Gil knows not how. Do fish speak? Is there room in their heads for dreams? Their existence seems a mere flicker of nest building, courting, fertilising, then death, yet they live their lives vividly in ripples of sun, sudden warmth, deep cold, flittering shadows.

Clouds catch in the hook of the bend, the darkest water trapping light. Gil sits on a log, alert to any bubbling eddy. The boys are quiet too. A flush of red imbues a silvery fish. Scraps of water buttercup, grass, stems, leaves, caught on the stream's stony bed tell of the fish's nest-making. The stickleback, rosy with lust, zigzags up and down. A female must be nearby. And a rival. Ollie plunges in his crock. Ben scoops water in a jug. The three of them lean over the catch. Sticklebacks no longer than a boy's finger shimmer in the jug. Some eggs will remain unfertilised now, nesting grounds will go unprotected, as these would-be fathers travel to London, slopping inside their vessels.

When Ben and Ollie have dug out clumps of moss, Gil packs the moss into the basket around the crock and jug, hoping its green dampness will last until London.

On the way home, Gil tells the boys of tiny dragons who live in moss. If the moss dries out, they dry too and rehydrate when the moss dampens. Gil promises to show them the dragons through his microscope. He once showed Mary, her eye close against the eyepiece, the dragons wriggling in her magnified vision. 'More like bears,' said she who had never seen a bear. He checks his watch. He had not thought of Mary for four minutes, until these dragons ruined his resolve.

Moments ago, this poor stickleback was

swimming in the sunny stream, merging with the stones and shale, hiding in the shadow of the wooden bridge, revealing its gleams changing from brown to silver to red, twisting and turning under the pussy pads of fallen willow seed. Now a milk jug circumscribes its life. The engraver in London will scratch the fish's likeness into the plate, no less a miracle, he sometimes thinks, than the huge sundials he's heard of in India, commemorating their maker, boasting of time passing, while the limner is a time-fixer.

Engaged in such musings, Gil carries the basket carefully towards the post chaise waiting at The Compasses. He senses a shadow behind him. Blundel overtakes him and blocks his way. The post chaise is about to leave.

'One moment, Mr Blundel,' Gil says, pointing to the chaise.

'When your business is done, your reverend, I beg the courtesy of your attention.'

Endeavouring to ignore Blundel, he explains the delicacy of his commission to the driver, who, for his part, boasts of delivering eggs without cracking them and puddings of spun sugar without damage. Gil dallies over the discussion, hoping Blundel will weary of waiting. The driver and the post-boy assure him that the boy will deliver the sticklebacks safely to the limner's person in London without one drop of stream water being spilt.

Now as his fishy cargo rattles off, with, Gil

suspects, nary a chance of arriving alive or wet, he tries to slip away as if forgetting Blundel's presence.

'Sir, I need to consult you on matters of parish funds.'

Funds, of course.

'To make matters short, sir …'

When did Blundel ever make matters short? Wakeling House, a breakfast of chops and the pleasure of showing the boys the moss under the microscope all beckon.

'When you visited Farmer Luckin, as I heard you did lately, did he give you assurance of maintaining Trimmer's child once born? Or will he rather throw Trimmer onto the parish?'

'There was no hint of her being expelled from his care,' Gil says. His stomach rumbles.

'I am heartened to hear that, sir.' Blundel's sour face belies his words. Luckin, a villain, and Mary, starving and then ejected, is a story he would prefer.

'But have you had an actual assurance that Luckin will provide for the child?'

'Not an actual assurance.' One cannot lie to an overseer, more's the pity. 'Is not the father to bear the responsibility of paternity?'

'Precisely my point,' Blundel says. 'She knows who the father is and should make him bear the cost. She has brought this expulsion on herself.'

'But has she?' Gil asks. Strange that until the hint from Mrs John Daisy at the Vestry meeting, he had never considered Mary's silence as hiding a ravishing. 'I will speak to her again, urge her to confide in us, her neighbours and well-wishers.'

'I hope you will, sir, since I've heard from Mrs Blundel's cousin who supplies the kitchen at Winchester that certain rumours have now reached the Bishop and are causing concern in the palace.'

'Good day to you, sir.' Gil walks off sharply. He will not be blackmailed. He had trusted his friend M. when he confided in him. He never once thought he would spread rumours about him. Even the prospect of the boys' wonder at the tiny dragons does not soothe him. There can be no natural history of Hartisborne if the bishop moves him on.

It is days since Georgie opened the letter. She puts off her trip to the phone box, never has the right change, never gives herself time. One evening, she forces herself to make the call, wishing she didn't have to know about Trevor.

Often, Rosemary hears Trevor shouting through the wall. In the evenings, from her bedroom window, Rosemary sees Trevor burning things in a dustbin in his yard.

'What sort of things?'

'Exercise books? That's what Cathy thinks.

Yesterday, I took my courage in my hands and complained about it. Trevor says I haven't got a leg to stand on because of Cathy's transistor radio.'

'Maybe I shouldn't have left.'

'You couldn't have gone on as you were. I'm not saying you should come back to live here. But maybe you could drop in to see how he is.' Rosemary says. 'Best take him by surprise.'

The money runs out. Georgie replaces the receiver. She sinks against the side of the phone box, unable to summon strength to open the door. The strange woman with the pramful of sticks bangs on the phone box door. Reluctantly, Georgie stands and pushes it open.

'So sorry,' she says. 'Are you waiting for a call?'

'No,' the woman says – she always wears a slash of red lipstick for her wood collecting. 'I was worried about you. Hope you haven't had bad news?'

'Just a bit tired,' Georgie says. 'But thanks for asking.' The hanger looms over the village. She could go for a walk in the woods, as Gil did, as the stick woman does every evening. She doesn't have the courage. She is afraid of being out in the dark, just as she's afraid of Trevor.

If she visits Trevor, she could visit Marco in the shop afterwards. How quickly she falls into an old groove, as if Marco is a match flaring against the darkness. In fact, he is a man who doesn't write to her, whose marriage she may have damaged, who is probably glad to be rid of her. Nevertheless, the thought of seeing him warms her and makes the trip to London more attractive.

She takes out a scrap of paper with John Kemp's number on it. She has been practising Romilly Pearson's voice for the last few days. Georgie dials. A woman answers. Georgie inserts her change.

'Hello,' she says. 'It's Romilly,' then adds, unsure of the level of formality needed, 'Romilly Pearson.'

'Hello,' young Mrs Kemp says warily, 'are you alright? You don't sound quite yourself.'

'I've had a bit of a throat that's all.' Would Romilly say that? It is more of a Celia expression. 'The thing is Captain Pearson is overwhelmed with work and that new girl keeps on about the loose parquet block in the little parlour. I was wondering if your husband could fix it?'

'He doesn't like to tread on the Captain's toes,' young Mrs Kemp says hesitantly. 'And the museum takes a long time to pay. I keep John's books, and I've been quite shocked. Everyone else pays by the end of the month.'

'The new girl deals with invoices now, so it should be quicker,' Georgie says. She'd found a shoebox full of unpaid invoices. When she'd checked with David, he confessed he worried about asking the Colonel to countersign cheques because Mrs Camden makes a huge fuss, when he delivers the paperwork. She demands he justify every item, even though museum expenses are none of her business. Bruised by these encounters, David avoids approaching the Colonel and has taken to stuffing bills into the shoe box and conveniently forgetting to pass them on. 'Is that fair on tradesmen?' Georgie asked. 'They have to feed their families.'

'I hadn't thought of it like that,' David admitted. In fact, he still hadn't paid the plumber after he fixed the burst pipes back in January. 'My stepfather always delays payment – he says they expect that.'

Young Mrs Kemp hesitates. 'Isn't maintenance Nev's job? John won't like to take other people's work.'

'But this time,' Georgie-Romilly says, 'the Captain would welcome the help.' She'd almost slipped out of Romilly's voice, almost said 'Nev' instead of 'the Captain.'

'If John were to come, and I'm not saying he can, what would be a good time?'

'Thursday afternoons work well,' Georgie-Romilly says eagerly. The Pearsons have Thursday afternoons off and go to Winchester on the bus.

Young Mrs Kemp sounds relieved. 'So Nev won't be there? Okay then, I'll see if John can pop round and take a look.'

'I hope he'll be able to do it straightaway. I'll tell the new girl to expect him and to put his bill through quickly.'

'Oh, can you thank Nev for that record he brought round? We tried it on the new record player – John's bought us a portable – and it's very beautiful. A lovely tune.'

'I'll tell him. What was it now?' Georgie asks. She hadn't seen Nev as a giver of gifts or a friend of the Kemps.

'A Little Night Music, I think. My mother-in-law enjoyed it too.'

'The Captain will be so pleased,' Georgie says in Romilly's most pompous tone, and as if as an afterthought, 'Perhaps you could ask John not to mention the parquet block to the Captain. You know how down he gets if he can't manage everything. As we'll be out on Thursday, he doesn't really have to know.'

'I see.' A pause. 'Yes, of course.' Mrs Kemp says, as if she does know this. 'But won't it seem as if the floor's been mended by magic?'

'Sometimes problems do just go away,' Georgie-Romilly states.

'Oh, yes, I see,' Mrs Kemp says emphatically. What does she see, Georgie wonders. Does she think Romilly is operating behind the scenes all the time? It would certainly explain how Nev hangs on to the job.

Georgie had vowed to drop her voices once in Hartisborne. Yet she feels exhilarated as she hangs up the phone, both true and untrue to herself. Young Mrs Kemp and Romilly are bound to talk soon, but hopefully the block will be fixed on Thursday afternoon, and even if they have a conversation of misunderstandings, it won't really matter. However uncomfortable Georgie feels, hasn't she saved a visitor from tripping? And removed a worry for David? The mimicking of Romilly is a small deception for the sake of the greater good. But do ends justify means? Years of Trevor's commentary have convinced her that she is useless, yet she has this gift for voices, and there's nothing wrong with using it for the greater good. She walks home down the dark village street, a solver of problems, a boon to society, at least here in Hartisborne, though her visit to London looms ominously.

Gil lingers on questions of love, physical, divine, affectionate, familial, as his mare clops her way through the wet May lanes. Are swallows in love when they make mud nests? Should he use the exempla of nests in his new sermon? Should he talk of how a blackbird hollows a woven ball with its body, how woodpigeons pile up clumsy twigs or how a coot amasses a pond's debris into a messy heap?

He doesn't yet know what moral point these exempla make, but, when reading the Bible, he seeks out the natural world, rather than hellfire and brimstone. The fall of a sparrow, the lilies of the field, people seen as walking trees, little foxes, the vixen, the gazelle, the grapes, the crops, the gleanings. After all, the ancients were peoples of the outdoors, and surely these glimmering moments, cooking fish on the fire by the sea of Galilee, show them as creatures who are a part of nature. There must be matter for a sermon here, but is there any morality? Unless to understand the science of bodies, plants and birds is moral? He'd like to think that investigating a natural history is morally good. But sometimes he fears he is just passing time in a country parish, despite his brother's thorough belief in the book.

Gil is riding to Binford, where he will stand in for the vicar, a bon-vivant, who barely sets foot in his own living. When word came that a curate was needed to cover, the usual man being sequestered with smallpox, Gil volunteered. It will stand him in good stead with the bishop, who need never know his motive, which is to remove himself from Mary after their ambiguous words during the swallow hunt. And he has another motive too.

If Mary's settlement in Hartisborne is denied, Mary will be passed back to Binford. He is curious to see her home parish, perhaps to meet her mother. All he knows about the woman is that she is a plantswoman, who suffers from winter darkness. Moreover, the bishop's hints communicated in M.'s letters about accepting the living of Binford have grown louder. The bonvivant incumbent has married well, holds two other livings and prefers to spend his time in London. He would like nothing better than to give up this woeful place, where there are few of his rank, and the rate revenue is low. M. points out that in Binford, Gil would be a vicar rather than a curate. And, as Binford is only ten miles from Hartisborne, he might return regularly to Wakeling House, his garden and the landscape of his natural history. If Gil were vicar of Binford, and Mary were removed thither to live with her mother, maybe he could help them both? See Mary every day? For instance, she and her mother could work for him in Binford Rectory garden. But to lose Hartisborne would be to lose his book, his daily observations, everything he holds dear.

This short break from Hartisborne could be a relief, wearied as he is by Blundel's obsession and his hatred for those who resist him. In truth, Gil wants to think about Mary but not think about her. See her but not see her. Binford, for all its disadvantages, is somewhere different, even if it is Mary's legal home.

Fortunately, Miss Butter will be visiting Hartisborne on his return. She provides distraction with her tales of Turkish markets, wild pomegranates and with her talk of golden mosques and blue lupins growing among ancient sarcophagi beside a turquoise sea. On her last visit, she scared Gil's nieces and nephews with tales of giant bats and had them laughing at her account of tortoises mating, their shells clacking against each other on the steps of an old temple, a cacophony of generation as she described it, expounding at length on their long necks and gasping orgasmic faces, for Miss Butter can be as blunt as any man in a tavern, though always more fluent.

What can Gil offer her in return? Only the news that the cowslips fared well and filled the Ewell with low yellow light. That the house martins have returned. She will judge him a dull man indeed, not knowing that his passion is as fierce and slow as any tortoise's or that Hartisborne is as exotic to him as Turkey is to her.

Stories and travel are good bedfellows. 'What news from the Rialto?' his father used to say, after he ceased to go out. Gil entertained him with stories of the harvest mouse or hedgehog. His father had the same keen interest in rustic creatures and local matters. Swifts glimpsed over the stream, arcing and dipping or John Carpenter advertising his shop with a card saying 'John Carpenter, Carpenter' were stories to amuse them both.

In the last days with his father, Gil would repeat rumours of the Binford woman, a toad doctoress of natural lore or, as some would call her, a witch. The doctoress strokes her toads and wipes their secretions onto cancerous tumours. He and his father used to talk into the night about the old cures, superstitions and the need for science. As his father weakened, Gil wished he had tried toad sweat to heal his father's tumour. He will call on the toad doctoress for science's sake, but there will be no father to report to on his return. And no father with whom to laugh about Blundel's absurdity. His father had the melancholic's cutting wit and would have diminished Blundel's pomposity in a moment – giving Gil more confidence to fight him. Yet this rapier-like ability receded when faced with less local issues.

'What news on the Rialto, Gil?' A man known from boyhood press-ganged into the navy, the selling of human souls in Bristol where Gil once took the baths at the Hot Wells. The sulphur still on his skin, Gil went aboard a slaver and shocked himself at the sight of tight berths, chains and bloodstains. And the church itself, he guessed, invested in such business. Now he had proof of man's inhumanity to man, but couldn't recount it to his father, in his last days, who only wanted to know of the swallows' return. Gil does not consider this ripping of African child from African parent or any child from any parent a part of God's plan. And as for Europe's travellers to the South Seas and beyond, they only allow a native to pass without murdering him if he isn't wearing gold or silver, booty that can be ripped more easily from the dead than the living. But Gil has trained his mind not to dwell on these affairs because his old Pa in his sad last days could only be cheered by charms of goldfinches or a nest of owlets. No slavery, no plundering, no murder of tribesmen could be mentioned to a man who fell into the abyss so swiftly, dropping into the mind's hell, at any word of the world's evils. And so, we look away from the wide world, Gil thinks guiltily, and comfort ourselves with local noticings.

Now he finds his father's phrases on his own tongue. Whenever he sees Ollie Knight, he says to him 'What news on the Rialto, Master Oliver?' And Ollie, all desire for knowledge but with little chance of it, wants to know about the Rialto, and then Gil fetches his father's big Atlas. They examine Venice huge upon the page, enlarged by its own power, and there, in the engravings, the famous bridge.

Gil, trotting on, considers the places he has never visited except in books, unlike the fine young gentlemen who can afford the grand tour or who rush off to explore the Americas or Africa. Quite apart from finance, family and duty and the fact that he is no longer young, Gil's travel sickness restricts his journeys. He can ride a horse in the fresh air or walk, but travel by carriage wracks his body, though he occasionally undergoes a trip to London or Oxford.

Now his mare clip-clopping through a ford, splashes mud on his britches. Water runs from the corners of his tricorne on to her mane. From a high bank, a fox watches man and pony pass, noting them, Gil guesses, in its animal memory.

Miss Butter, her head full of Musulmen, caiques and golden domes sparkling in sun, will be arriving soon in Hartisborne, stepping out of her carriage with that bewitching face, her talisman of safe travel, hidden under a veil.

Mary will be serving Farmer Luckin his supper of mutton and ale. Perhaps the farmer has settled her in the late afternoon by the fire, with the light flickering on her face and hair. Perhaps he has asked her to stay for company while he unfolds one of his ghostly stories, for Richard Luckin knows how to spin a tale. What if Luckin, old as he is, can still tantalise a pretty girl albeit one with child? Would they go to the act confident there could be no conception while Mary is pregnant? But Gil must not picture it, or he will become as prurient as Blundel. His pony bucks and naysays him loudly in remonstrance. Concentrate, his little mare tells him. Escape your thoughts.

Just in time, for that way lies the hell of his father's over-sensibility, Gil arrives at a set of hovels, heaped around the vicarage, a dank place, overgrown and neglected. He wonders where Mary's mother lives. He dismounts in a driving rain, his cape heavy with water, while the thorny may by the door salvages its blossom from the gale. The air is full of sour hogwash, the stench carrying into the vicarage garden. Hey ho, his life of travel. Yet, he's heard the canals of Venice stink and not every palazzo is lined with marble.

Hey nonny-no. He walks into the vicarage. No maid or manservant greets him. 'My people will look after you,' the bon-vivant had written him.

Eventually he finds a scruffy youth slumped at the kitchen table in a drunken snore. Gil drops his saddle bag loudly. His exotic life. And the youth, half-asleep, murmurs, 'Mary, Mary…'

A coincidence, he tells himself. So many women are called Mary, after all.


After a session in the pub with Nick and The Pipe Barrel, David, fortified by beer, rushed home to explain his new suppositions to his former tutor, Professor Francis de la Salle. He transcribed Gil's unfinished note just as the words appeared on the page, and then on a fresh sheet, painfully typed out his one-fingered thoughts identifying the object of Gil's longing. In his drunken state, he considered himself a retrospective matchmaker, crossing off the romantic candidates in Gil's life. Time and time again, he returns to Miss Butter, unable to strike her name through, and in his letter to Francis, he has elucidated his reasons.

Of course, it's a hunch, a guess, a feeling, not a proven thing, but one has to start somewhere. Miss Butter certainly exerts a pull. She didn't stay in one village all her life but took carriages across Europe, walked in the mountains, camped in the desert with wandering tribes in North Africa, stayed in rooms carved of rock in Turkey, reached Mongolia and saw corpses picked clean by vultures. Her diaries are fascinating if a little overblown. Now and again, David wonders whether he is being taken in, whether the lady protests too much but then he shouldn't doubt her accounts because she is a woman. And her ebullient style is refreshing.

When he wakes in the morning, he dutifully puts aside a couple of hours to type a section of his book on Gil, knowing he is going to reward himself later by reading Miss Butter's letters. He must go to the British Museum and read her diaries in her own hand, find out about her correspondents and see her embroidery, a fragment of which exists in the Victoria and Albert Museum, its pattern devised from an ancient Turkish tile.

He would like to visit the Butters' country house in Kent, where Miss Butter stayed when she wasn't visiting famous scientists and travellers like herself. He may find a clue there, if only Francis will vouch for him to the current owners, the descendants of her family line. He longs to see her portrait which has always hung in their dining room, but of which there is no reproduction. He'd like to search every book in the Butters' old library, looking for billets-doux, clues, inscriptions.

On the other hand, the current owner, Viscount Alexander Butter, is a drug-addled playboy who may well have ripped out the library as soon as he inherited the house. Living beyond convention evidently runs in the family. For all David knows, the young viscount may have thrown darts at Miss Butter's portrait or graffitied a moustache on her comely face.

Maybe Marco Bracco, Georgie's former employer and expert on antiquarian books, could ask to see the library? And David could go with him incognito so that the family aren't alerted to David's suspicions? Last week, he mooted this idea to Georgie, but she wasn't keen to be the conduit to Mr Bracco. 'They'll think he's just a book dealer – which he is – whereas you are doing proper research. Ask them yourselves and tell them your theory.'

David is frightened of the druggy viscount and the psychedelic shirts he's seen him wearing in a Sunday supplement. He'd be safe with Marco even though he doesn't know him. Or Tom? There's an idea. Tom Swallow can handle anything. Or Nick? Maybe the three of them could go together? And maybe the viscount would like the idea of Tom, an artist, an exciting person? Unlike David. Of course, he could take Georgie? But supposing she fell for the viscount? A tremendous womaniser according to the gossip columns. 'Blue-blood Butter in the gutter with drunken model' had been a recent headline in The Sun. Or maybe the unknown Marco could join Nick, Tom and David to shore up the troops. Nick's Land Rover (another reason for inviting Nick) will make an impression on blue-blooded Butter, however alternative he claims to be.

Of course, Gil would fall for glamourous Miss Butter. But would she fall for Gil? Wouldn't he seem dull and conventional in comparison to her adventures? Would she want to be trapped in Hartisborne? Carriage-sickness was a mundane excuse for their lack of coupling but could well be the truth, though David would have preferred a more romantic reason. Doubtless it's true that Gil wouldn't be able to accompany her to Turkey or anywhere further than his little mare could take him. And as Marilyn had said in the pub, longing was all about the attraction of the unobtainable - so Gil probably pined for Miss Butter all his life.

No other woman outside of his relatives is mentioned so consistently. Unless one were to count the weeding woman? David quickly discounts her. She was of a different class and barely fleshed out at all. It's highly unlikely that someone as sophisticated as Gil would ever long for a weeding woman. The very alliteration is embarrassing and cheap.

Every day, David waits for Francis' reply and the written recommendation which will take him inside Miss Butter's ancestral home. Finally, when pretending to be in London, he sees an envelope pushed under the locked study door, presumably by Georgie, though he'd heard no one on the stairs. At last! Francis has replied! He tears open the letter.

*My dear David,*

*I hope you are well and your new assistant (I heard about her from Everard and Louise Camden) is aiding your research.*

*I cannot categorically say whether 'the shape of Gil's longing' is or is not Miss Evangelina Butter. But I think it unlikely. The page is undated and apparently unconnected to any particulars from his history. The letters suggest Gil entertained only an amused tolerance for the vicar's niece, while – you are quite correct on this - he found an anthropological interest in her travel tales (which some think vastly exaggerated by her voracious novel-reading). This scrap may simply be an ephemeron. If you were to excavate my desk drawer – God forbid – you would find many a drivelling fragment the purpose of which even I, its author, can't remember.*

*Do beware of the dangers of a cul-de-sac. The naturalist's life offers so many other paths to explore. Young scholars are often attracted to romance. Forgive me if I venture to suggest they find it in their own lives and not impose it on the dead.*

*Meanwhile the move to Burford has gone reasonably well, and we are settled. At least until the next crisis. (My life perhaps biases me towards Gil being happy in his batchelor state.) Yet it is my cross and I must bear it.*

*I'm looking forward to reading your manuscript, but better to steer clear of the siren Butter. Please give my best to Everard and Louise.*
    *With fond regards,*
        *Francis.*

David shakes the envelope to make sure it's empty, then tears it inside out to make double sure. There is no letter of introduction to the contemporary Butters enclosed. For the first time ever, Francis has declined to support David. It is a blow.

# CHAPTER 11

'Our congregation has dwindled,' an old lady wheezes as she opens the creaking door to her box pew.

The wooden shingles on the roof of Binford church let in water and birds, so much so that, when he investigated the church on the Friday evening, Gil had found the chalice grimed with tarnish and full of bird dung, a foul thing. Only with much bribery had Gil persuaded the shabby youth to wash the chalice and then polish it. He discovered the altar cloth was the farmer's tablecloth, spotted with goose grease and sauce, stinking and foul to the touch. The farmer is churchwarden and should provide something better.

On Saturday, after sleeping in damp sheets of dubious cleanliness, Gil parcelled up the altar cloth himself and rode to the farm, where he affronted the farmer's wife by requesting a fresh cloth. During his ride, he saw few women. None of them struck him as a candidate for Mary's mother. He could have enquired about her from any passer-by on the pretext of a message from

Mary, but he shirked the challenge. Now, before the service begins, his eyes search the scant gathering for anyone resembling Mary.

Gil pours the sour wine (the bon-vivant spends little on communion wine), into the now clean chalice which he sets on the threadbare, almost clean cloth, with a bunch of pinks he picked from the vicarage garden to freshen the air.

He will make Miss Butter laugh later by describing the tall box pews, all different heights, higgledy-piggledy and everyone bringing in their dogs, and the congregation small in all senses, a very short breed of people so that he, short himself, can barely see more than a bonnet-top while he expounds his sermon. Invisible and few the congregation may be, but they make their presence felt. Marbles and cards spill out from one box. Tooth-marked apple cores spin into the aisle during the responses. Children stifle giggles and coughs. A man sings out of tune and la-las through the words of a psalm he has never really known. The dogs growl at each other, snuffling at cracks in the pew timbers and howling if anyone manages a high note. Few parishioners take the eucharist, perhaps fearing to drink from a bird-splattered chalice, though today's service is a rare chance to add to the necessary minimum of three communions a year.

Gil preaches to his invisible audience,

frustrated at wasting his carefully composed sermon on spiritual travel. He speaks faster, keen for the moment when he will see the parishioners as they leave.

Two bent old ladies shuffle out leaning on sticks, with no bone power to look beyond the floor or acknowledge him. A vagrant, he of the vibrant la-la-ing, lingers by the near-empty collection bag, which Gil thinks best to hide under his cassock. Twelve children tumble from the last pew with their mongrel dog and a one-eyed cat called Pirate on a lead. He asks them their names and is amused to find they will be at evensong too.

'Our mother is hard-pressed,' a boy with an incipient moustache tells him. 'She sends us to every service - when there is one. So, we will be here this evening too, your lordship, Sir Reverend.'

This eldest child palms some playing cards into his pocket as he speaks, while a girl of about six crawls around on the pew floor picking up marbles. Two pigeons ,trapped inside the church, panic and leave white traces. The toad woman, for it must be she, crosses herself as if a papist and waits to speak to Gil.

The toad woman, a fellow natural scientist in a way, seems his nearest ally. The sick come to her in the absence of a real doctor, and so he asks if any in Binford need comfort.

They walk together to a mud-filled farmyard.

Gil marks every hovel, wondering which is Mary's mother's dwelling.

The toad woman suggests they visit Arthie, a farm boy. He lives in a loft above the cattle he serves. His feet are rotten because no one gives him dry stockings. Gil watches the toad woman fill a bowl with comfrey and water to soak Arthie's red feet with their foul flaking nails and terrible smell. Gil is forced to hide his nose in a lavender scented handkerchief. Binford! What a place! Would he want this as his parish? He would not.

What does Binford's vicar care for his parishioners? Ensconced in his London house, recounting poems at soirées in an affectedly rhythmic voice, he gives them never a thought. A tremendous flirt, he promotes himself to the ladies with false piety and to the men with his fine cellar.

Gil prays with Arthie and blesses him. Yet, he knows the toad woman's calendula ointment will be more soothing to the boy's sores than prayer. Suppose Mary's child ends up like this? In that sense, Gil agrees with Blundel. Marriage would give Mary and her child a better life than Binford ever could.

Though Nick would like to be early to The Compasses, so he can have a drink with Georgie before Claire arrives, he must wait for his mother and Dick to visit.

They have chosen today to organise their wedding with the vicar and are dropping in on him first to discuss his role as host of the ghastly event. The list of wedding guests nags at his brain, and yet he's asked no one, at least not formally. Claire tells him that wedding invitations should go out months ahead, but as he couldn't face sending them, the invitations will arrive only a month beforehand.

The choice of wording is delaying him.

*Nicholas Luckin invites you to celebrate the marriage of his mother Marilyn Elspeth Luckin to Richard John Congreve Ellingham at St. Mary's Church, Hartisborne, on Saturday 28th June 1963 at 11.30 a.m and afterwards to the wedding breakfast at The Compasses.*

Was that the correct wording? Should he put 'warmly invites' when he feels no warmth about it?

Marilyn and Dick are late, though Nick impressed on them in the phone call that he must be at the pub by six.

At quarter past six, Dick's Hillman pulls into the farmyard. Stones flare up from the tires as Dick parks. Marilyn opens the car door and gets out. She wears a twinset and tight skirt, with her hair teased up. She must have dressed up for the vicar. Dick is in a light summer suit, looking every inch the spiv he is.

Nick kisses his mother, shakes hands with

Dick and invites them both into the kitchen. 'I'll have to leave soon. Claire will be disappointed if I'm not there.' No need to mention Georgie.

Dad, for all his faults, was never a strategist. He blurted out opinions, held women in thrall almost involuntarily, never wanting to say no to anyone, but his mother always has an agenda, whether it's manipulating Nick into wearing clothes she approves of or hinting he should marry soon or angling for an heirloom brooch that belonged to the Luckin family. It's ridiculous that a son should host his mother's wedding, but she's made him feel it is his duty.

After a walk around the garden, Nick makes a pot of tea reluctantly, while the evening ticks away.

'Isn't it about six months since Richard passed on?'

How can she not know? 'It's barely four months.'

'And I think the estate is still being valued?'

'It takes a while. I've been working through Dad's documents with the solicitor.'

Dick stares at the dresser, pretending disinterest.

'I thought it best to speak about this in person,' Marilyn says. 'It's so difficult on the telephone. You know how they listen in from the exchange.'

Nick often interprets the crackles and crossed lines as the monks protecting him from his mothers' demands. Of course, it must be the women at the exchange, crowding round each other's headphones to eavesdrop. He shudders to think what they know about his father's affairs.

'Darling, I may as well come out with it. I have written to your father's solicitor to challenge the will. As his wife, I was expecting to inherit. I've waited half a year, to allow you to adjust emotionally, but legally, as Richard's wife, I believe the estate should pass to me now, and only later to you, rather than us being joint owners. Of course, you'll get it in the end.'

'Dad changed his will after you chose to leave. It's perfectly legal and was properly witnessed.'

'By Miss Bewley, who is also a beneficiary.'

'He left her a small personal item in a letter not in the will. He left you all his savings as well as joint ownership of the land and the farm business, and I must say it's very difficult without the capital behind me, but I understand that he wanted to provide for you.'

'Actually, it's very *unfair* in comparison to the usual arrangements between a husband and wife. So, I'm making a formal challenge. It's nothing against you, Nick.'

'But you still want to disinherit me?'

'Don't say it like that. I put up with years of bad behaviour. The time I wasted with Richard, when I could have had another child or got a job. I don't want to take anything from you, but I do want recompense from him.'

'Taking my business and my home is harming

me not Dad.'

'You could have had that job in Rome.'

'You know why I didn't take it.'

'You're still young. You don't want the farm to be your only life. I had an idea which will suit us both. You have your freedom for a few years, while Dick and I run the farm.'

'But you hated living here, and neither of you are farmers.'

Dick fidgets with the windmill sugar spoon, bending the sails out of shape. Nick moves the sugar bowl away.

'Quite right. We're not farmers. And I didn't like living here because it's lonely. And then there's the strange atmosphere, like pipe smoke everywhere.'

'So why is it desirable now?'

'Because we will run Priory House...'

'Priory Farmhouse,' Nick interrupts.

' ...as a hotel.' His mother speaks over him as usual. 'We'll have visitors and staff. And we'll be offering the locals jobs. You know how disappointed everyone was that Wakeling House didn't become a hotel. You could try life outside of the farm. And if our venture didn't work, you could have the farm back. But at least you'd have travelled, met people, lived! Then farming would be a choice. I hate to think of you shut away down here at your age. I loved the idea of you in Rome.'

'I bet you did! And farming won't be my choice,

if I'm just the fallback for when your business fails.'

'It won't fail,' Dick says sharply.

Nick ignores him. 'A farm needs year on year care. The fields, the boundaries. The herd. The coppicing. You can't just let it all go on a whim.'

'You're twenty-six, Nick. It's exciting out there. Swinging London, and you're not part of it.'

'I need to lock up before you go.' Nick never locks the house usually, but he won't leave them to search for Granny Luckin's jewellery again. Then he remembers he'd promised to take the pub landlord Matt some cream. Nick fetches the enamel jug from the fridge. He covers with it a saucer and puts it on the doorstep. He pulls the door shut and manages to lock it with the ancient key that reminds him of a fairy tale. But how to organise the cream without spilling it in his car?

'We're late for the vicar,' Dick says. 'Do you want a lift?'

'Thanks,' Nick climbs carefully into the back of the Hillman, feeling like a child, with the adults in front. He balances the awkward jug and saucer, so the cream won't spill. The rusty old key digs into his thigh from his trouser pocket. Now he'll have to walk home through the woods, but he intends to get blindingly drunk, so maybe it's as well.

'You haven't said no,' his mother says.

'No,' Nick says. 'I mean I am saying no. I don't

see Priory Farm as a hotel. No one would come here.'

'Fans of the naturalist. People who adore the very thought of this village,' Marilyn enthuses, although she'd never loved the village herself. 'We could be a field work centre or something like that, while we rent out the actual fields to another farmer.'

'Even if I said yes, the monks would see your visitors off. You'd never make a profit from a bunch of spooked tourists, running out without paying.'

'Your father manipulated Marilyn with that rubbish,' Dick snaps. 'Everyone knows ghosts don't exist.'

'Mum thought they did. She wanted the vicar to do an exorcism.'

'Richard brainwashed me,' Marilyn says testily.

'Can you drop me at The Compasses?'

'Will you at least consider our proposal?'

'Why don't you think about getting a job, Mum? You've never worked. What do you do, Dick?'

'Dick's an entrepreneur.'

Dick leaps out and opens the door for Nick, hampered as he is by the cream. The jug and saucer quaver in Nick's angry hands. It would be childish to throw the cream at Dick.

'What was your last venture?'

'Stocks and shares,' Marilyn says quickly.

'Profit or loss?' Nick asks, his fingers

tightening on the jug's handle.

'A little of each. One must spread the risk,' Dick says evasively.

'Loss then,' Nick says. 'Watch out, Mum. And by the way, an entrepreneur runs a business, making and selling, rather than dealing in shares. You don't even know the vocabulary of business, Mum, so you can hardly expect me to trust you with a hotel.'

'Dick's plug business was very successful. I expect you're using his plugs all the time. And then he branched out into sockets. He knows what people need, you see. He's only gone into stocks and shares recently.'

'Must go. I've got a pleasant evening ahead with interesting people in the famous, delightful village I grew up in, where my dad left me a farm, and where I'm a school governor, on the cricket team and have a girlfriend. Why would I want to give all that up?' Nick slams the door.

His mother gets out of the car and straightens herself up for the vicar. Her emerald glints in the evening sun. 'Just the one girlfriend, is it? Louise Camden tells me all the gossip you know. You're turning into your father and you don't even realise it. That's why you should leave.'

Dick gets out and slams the car door.

'By the way, Dick, you've got a snick in the windscreen. Looks like a piece of gravel hit it on the way up the lane. The whole lot could shatter at any moment.'

Dick ignores him and takes Marilyn's hand. 'Have you got the list of music?' he asks her.

'It's in my handbag,' she says.

'Let's have fun with the vicar then,' Dick says. He nods rather coolly at Nick and follows Marilyn towards the vicarage.

'Break a leg,' Nick shouts at their retreating backs. Then, he sees Claire walking up the High Street. His mother's voice carries. He hopes she didn't hear Mum asking about just the one girlfriend.

'Are they going to be in a show?' Claire asks.

'In a manner of speaking,' Nick says.

Claire kisses Nick and puts her arm through his.

'Watch out!' He steadies the jug.

'Oh yes, we don't want the cat to get the cream.'

No, we don't, Nick thinks, watching Dick and Marilyn walk through the vicarage's wide gateway and trample over the grassy turning circle to reach the front door. Typical of them to disregard the rules of property.

'I suppose Marilyn wanted to discuss the wedding arrangements?'

'Not exactly.'

Maisie skips down the road, her eyes bright.

'Hello, Nick,' she calls.

'Hello,' Nick says. 'Shouldn't you be at home by now?' He tries to lose his bad temper. It's hardly Maisie's fault that his mother is a property-grabbing bitch.

'We were fishing for minnows in the stream in School Lane. Miss Bewley said we could.' She holds out a jam-jar with a little fish in it. 'I want to draw him, but I don't want him to die.'

'You can tip him back into the stream when you've drawn him.'

'Yes. Perhaps I should put him back in now?'

'You should go home. It's getting late.'

'But what if he dies? I'll be a murderer.'

'It's not murder when it's minnows,' Claire says.

'Don't think about that,' Nick says. 'Think about this. Would you like to sing a solo at my mother's wedding?'

'Yes, yes, yes, yes!' Maisie jumps up and down, nearly throwing the minnow out of his jar.

'I'll have to ask your mum, of course.' At last, his mother's wedding was making someone happy.

'Mummy would love me to do it, because I've been really sad about not being a bridesmaid and I've never been to a wedding.'

'I suppose you could be a bridesmaid too.'

'You'll need to ask Marilyn about that,' Claire says quickly. 'She'll be choosing the bridesmaids.'

'She told me to organise things.' While trying to turn him out of the farm.

'The bridesmaids are chosen by the bride.'

Claire is so conventional. She doesn't own him or his decisions. And after all, he's known Joan and Maisie all their lives. He turns to Maisie, determined not to give in to Claire.

'We'll have fun at the wedding, won't we? You'll make a lovely bridesmaid.'

Claire tugs his arm. 'Come on. Let's not be late for Georgie and David.'

Maisie walks on holding the jar tightly and turning to wave at them.

'You should have asked Joan first. She might not want Maisie to sing. And Marilyn might not want her to be a bridesmaid. And if she does agree, Joan will have to buy her a special dress. I'm not supposed to say but Maisie has free school dinners, so I don't suppose Joan can afford it.'

'I can pay for the dress.'

'You should definitely check these things with parents first, you know,' Claire says in her school secretary voice.

'I don't see as I've done any harm.'

'I'm not saying you have, though you probably have.'

Nick manages not to hold her hand, gesturing at the jug of cream.

'Don't be cross. It's my job to know about these things.' She pushes open the pub door.

Claire tries to link arms with Nick, but he shies away.

They join Georgie and David. David is down in the dumps, which cheers Nick up a little anyway. Georgie smiles at him and hands him her rent book. She's a better tenant than Tom and enjoys paying on time.

'Thanks,' Nick says as his hand touches hers briefly.

Gil gives the toad woman of Binford sixpence for her troubles. Later, in her kitchen, he is pleased to stroke a toad himself and feel the glands excrete their fabled sweat, while she boils him up some lime-flower tea.

'Do you know a Mrs Trimmer? Her daughter is called Mary,' he asks.

'Best not to worry her at the moment, sir,' is all the toad woman says.

'So, you know Mary?' he asks.

'I seldom see her,' the toad woman says, scattering more dried lime-flowers into a pot.

The toad woman isn't a gossip, more's the pity, but she is a find. Her lore fascinates him, and, he suspects, is not without foundation. For the sake of her conversation, he may well be persuaded to fill the bon-vivant's shoes again. Moreover, he admires the way the toad woman treated Arthie. His sisters will be interested in Arthie's story and will knit him some socks. The next time Gil is persuaded to preach in this benighted place, he will bring Arthie new warm footwear. He even thinks more fondly of Luckin, who would never allow Mary or any of his workers to be footrotted or hungry.

Before he leaves, Gil bribes the shabby youth to place pails to catch drips from the church's leaking roof.

He's surprised to find that concerns for Arthie and Binford church roof have diverted him from his worries. But, as he nears Hartisborne, Mary obsesses him again. Why didn't he ask the toad woman more about her mother? Why is he always so polite? So genteel? Such a sober curate while inwardly he's a wild lover? Luckin would have brooked no refusal of information.

Gil meditates on Mary as he trots on, breathing in the damp verdure. In the rain, he guides his pony towards those misty circles of light tantalisingly present at the end of lanes but never quite reached.

Often Sylvia glimpses him walking along the Ewell, head to toe in bees, or sees him watching David, who has taken to bee keeping under Colonel Camden's guidance. The white veiled hats, the loose white suits and gauntlets make the men look like astronauts on the green field.

Sylvia watches the bee boy watching the two men, laughing at them. He can move a swarm by holding out his arms, shift a bee cloud from trees in Gil's garden to an empty hive. The bee boy needs no jugs of smoke. Replete and happy, the bees trust him and so he transports them on his skin, his chest bare, to the hives by the gate in the seventh meadow. And sometimes he is older, a calm, tall man wearing bees as his shirt. 'Goodlooking too,' Sylvia adds, with a laugh.

Georgie says, 'So you really had a vision of Sam Carpenter, the beeboy in *The Natural History*? How exciting! You tell it so vividly.'

Georgie doesn't humour Sylvia as others do. Even Nick will turn away and smile to himself if Sylvia starts this story. She fears she is getting repetitive and should count how many times she tells the story so as not to irritate her son and his wife. Unlike them, Georgie is interested, because the story is new to her.

'Sometimes I see him with a girl in a red coat.'

'What does she look like?'

'I think she's pregnant, but it's hard to tell with all those layers of skirts they wore then.'

'Do you ever see the baby?'

'I hear sounds. I don't know what they are.'

'This is fascinating,' Georgie says.

'Is it?' Sylvia asks, moving Georgie's stemmed pudding glass, the tinned tangerines suspended in jelly, almost transparent in the window's light. She suspects Georgie of making fun after all. Although perhaps Sylvia is not used to words like 'fascinating' and 'vivid'. Her father, all those years ago, had no use for encouraging words.

And her son and his wife are wary of her visions.

'Do you think Hartisborne has trapped ghosts in its dips and paths?'

'I have thought that sometimes,' Sylvia admits.

'But don't you ever see your own family?'

'In my mind. But not in the way I see the pregnant woman or the bee boy,' Sylvia says.

Georgie is tempted to tell her about Gil, all her imaginings, about Marco, about the way when she wakes, he seems to lie on her like an incubus and then is gone. But Sylvia won't approve. 'That was a lovely tea,' Georgie says untruthfully, fidgeting a dried crust of sliced bread to the edge of her plate.

Sylvia keenly unpacks a Battenburg cake that got squashed in her bag. She gives them each a broken rhomboid with the marzipan breaking off. She never buys cake for herself, but Miss Gardner needs fattening up.

'What about your family?' Sylvia asks.

Georgie sighs. And offers up the little there is to say – Cornwall, the blitz, her father dead in Burma, the return to London, to Connie and Trevor. Always this lack and emptiness, and the distasteful thought that Trevor is the only person left who knows anything about her blood family.

# CHAPTER 12

Georgie dawdles down the street. The dustbins are on the pavement, glinting in the early summer sunlight and stinking of rotten vegetables. It used to be her job to fill the dustbin and drag it out for collection. When she knocks at Trevor's door, Rosemary lets her in.

In the kitchen, Georgie begins to clear up. It's habit, and she can avoid Trevor for longer. Rosemary says he's in the sitting room. No need to see him yet. There are greasy pans from the night before, dirty plates on the table, an overflowing ash can. Rosemary goes outside and shovels up some coke to bring in. It's summer now but she says Trevor should keep warm. She wipes her hands and dries up for Georgie.

'I do my best to help him out,' Rosemary says defensively.

'I appreciate it, and it shouldn't be up to you. You have your job and Cathy and your mother to look after.'

'Maybe - I know it's difficult - but maybe you and he should organise some help.'

'How long has he been like this?

'It's got worse and worse.'

'You didn't say it was this bad.'

'I thought he'd pick up again once he got used to you being gone.'

'So, it's my fault?'

'Maybe there's some way you could visit him more often?'

The doorknocker rat-tats.

'I'll get it,' Rosemary says.

She ushers the doctor in and asks him if he would like a cup of tea. 'Mrs Cousins' niece is visiting.' Rosemary gestures to Georgie, who nods at the doctor.

'Good morning,' the doctor says. 'I thought you lived here?'

'I've moved.'

'So, I see.' The doctor looks pointedly at the unkempt state of the house. He'd be even more shocked if he knew she hadn't even said hello to Trevor yet, that she'd do anything to avoid him altogether. She'd like to avoid the doctor too but instead opens the door to the sitting-room, lets him in and closes it again without even looking at Trevor.

When she'd asked for contraception, the doctor had examined her internally and roughly with his gloved hand. With his fingers inside her, he'd lectured her on morality and her reputation. He'd questioned her about her lover and made her argue for what she needed. She hasn't signed up with the Hartisborne doctor, who holds his surgery in the village hall, because she fears him seeing her medical notes.

In the kitchen, Georgie hears murmured talk leaking into the hallway. Then the doctor pops his head round the door. 'We need a powwow,' the doctor says.

Georgie, Rosemary and the doctor sit on the scratchy armchairs while Trevor has his feet up on the sofa. Tea spills into his saucer. *Didn't even come in to say hello to him - no effing respect. Wouldn't even speak to him if the doctor hadn't forced her.* Georgie knows what he's thinking. He looks terrible, unshaven, pale, his hair greasy.

'Well, I hear that you've moved away,' the doctor says. 'And that your uncle has found things difficult since then. The empty nest, you know.' He flashes his handsome eyes at her.

'The dog's dinner,' Trevor says. 'Who let that in?'

The doctor grimaces. 'Now, now. That sort of talk helps no one. I think it would be a good idea to see you alone... Miss?'

'Gardner.'

The doctor has an officer's voice. Uncompromising. Authoritative.

'I won't be talked about behind my back,' Trevor warns.

'Sometimes hearing from relatives helps with the whole picture. So, if you wouldn't mind stepping outside, Mr Cousins. I won't be long with Miss Gardner and will call you in a moment.'

The doctor stares out Trevor until he gives in and leaves.

'So, can you tell me about your uncle?'

Once, Georgie would have liked to tell someone about Trevor. Now an expert is waiting expectantly, it's difficult to explain. She notices the doctor glancing at her legs.

'Is your uncle a risk to himself?' he asks finally.

'I don't think so,' Georgie says. 'Not physically. He's sort of…' What is it about Trevor that makes her feel like she's being suffocated?

'He's a very critical person. Nothing is good enough.' She speaks softly hoping Trevor can't hear from the kitchen. The sitting room door is half-glazed. She'd see him if he were listening outside.

'Do you have a close relationship with your uncle?'

'He doesn't see me as a real person.'

'So, your uncle doesn't confide in you about his state of mind?'

'No, he doesn't. I don't really know him beyond the rules of the household.'

'Would you say the situation has deteriorated since you moved away?'

'Our neighbour Rosemary thinks so.'

The doctor gestures round the room. 'Look at the dust.'

'I used to do the housework. But I don't live here anymore.'

'Of course, I remember.' He pauses. 'You're a woman's libber.' The doctor licks his lip in a slightly suggestive way, sighs and puts down his pen. He looks more blatantly at Georgie's legs.

'Housework isn't the be-all and end-all,' Georgie says.

'To each sex, their duty,' he says. 'Your uncle isn't coping. Couldn't you help out?'

'Trevor's housework is not my business anymore. Anyway, I live somewhere else.'

'So, by moving away, pursuing,' he sniffs, 'your own career, you may have jeopardised your uncle's health? Women working has severe implications for the family.'

'Trevor wanted me to work. He needed the money,' Georgie says.

'Is there a man in the case?' Of course, he knew a man had been in the case when he'd stuck his fingers roughly inside her.

'What do you mean?'

'I mean if you're about to be married, to set up your own home, then naturally you cannot look after your uncle.' And the diaphragm will be forgiven.

'Yes, in fact, I am getting married soon,' Georgie lies, sensing a way out.

'And what line of work is your intended in?' the doctor asks.

'He's a farmer.'

'I grew up in the country myself, you know. As a farmer's wife, you will be too busy to look after

Mr Cousins. I completely understand. I'll call in your uncle and Miss Morton. No, do stay.'

Trevor comes in first. Rosemary stands awkwardly in the doorway.

'Mr Cousins, I've had a word with your niece. Bearing in mind your niece's news, it seems she can't return as your housekeeper, as we'd hoped. Maybe a cleaning woman would help?'

Trevor snorts with disgust. 'Thought I was ill. That's why Miss Nosy called in the doctor,' he says pointing at Rosemary.

'Anxiety,' the doctor says. 'And grief for your wife. This will help.' He passes the prescription to Trevor.

'Shouldn't you find out why he's anxious?'

'He may well be anxious about you, Miss Gardner. A young woman away from home, pursuing her own career and about to be married out of the blue.'

'No one's asked me if they can marry her.' A flicker passes over Trevor's face.

'I'm over twenty-one. And you're not my father.'

'But I am your stepfather,' Trevor says.

'You're not my stepfather.'

'As good a father as you'll ever get, Miss Snob.'

'You're my uncle-by-marriage.'

'It's much the same relationship though, isn't it?' the doctor says, looking at his watch.

'Not really.'

'You see - she denies what we've done for her.

Took her in and brought her up,' Trevor says. 'Why are you getting married? Are you up the duff? Who is it?'

'No one you know,' Georgie answers.

'Maybe you can be happy?' Rosemary whispers.

Georgie nods uncertainly.

'She's been nothing but a worry,' Trevor says.

'A source of anxiety,' the doctor says sympathetically.

'Permissive society,' Trevor says.

'Quite,' the doctor says. 'So many parents come to me in distress now. All these musicians and their noise. And the skirts!'

'She broke her aunt's heart. That's why she died,' Trevor says. 'Walked out for a bunch of bloody bohemians!'

'I work in a museum. I don't see what's bohemian about that!'

'Anyway, you'll be giving that up when you're married,' the doctor says. 'I think tranquillisers in the first instance,' the doctor says. 'Low spirits are so often a sign of abandonment.'

'I don't know how I'll cope,' Trevor says in a self-pitying voice.

'Man up, Mr Cousins. Worse things happened in the war.'

And with a wave of the prescription pad, the doctor leaves.

Rosemary takes out the tea things.

'That one's in and out too often,' Trevor says.

'Effing bitch. Thinks she's the bees' knees.'

Rosemary pops her head back in. 'I'm off now then,' she says.

'I'll come with you,' Georgie says, not wanting to be left alone with Trevor.

In the hallway, Rosemary whispers anxiously, 'You get back to Hartisborne. Get back to your life. I don't think Trevor's as bad as I thought. I'm sorry I called you in.'

Trevor comes into the hallway. 'Still meddling, are we?' he says to Rosemary. Then he shuffles into the kitchen.

Rosemary hands Georgie her coat. 'At least the doctor knows about the state of him now. I feel better for that. I hope you're inviting me and Cathy to the wedding. Congratulations! Who is it? Send us all the details!'

Georgie can't think what to say about her supposed wedding and mutters something about a farmer she's met. She hurries off, worried that Trevor knows she works in a museum now. If only she hadn't risen to the bohemian bate. But he doesn't know where the museum is. And he'll think there's a fiancé in the background to protect her.


Gil rides home in a heavy May rain, through a wind which shakes the beeches so violently that the stony lanes are scattered with torn-off leaves, lightening the puddles with green. Campions shake along the banks, their pink more vivid in the rain light.

As he nears Hartisborne, he looks out for Mary – he can't help himself – though she would hardly be wandering through such an unseasonal tempest unless she knew - through the mysterious transmission of thoughts perhaps - that he was passing. Mary, Mary, he thinks, I'm missing you. Come forth and see me. Every shape is Mary's shadow, a sudden shaft of light, an elbowing branch, a shower shaking from a tree, a rounded curve of chalk.


Georgie walks along the south bank, grey with building work. She crosses Waterloo Bridge. All is grey. The river laps the stony shore in afternoon mood. She tells herself she is merely walking to work off her fear of Trevor. She wanders up The Strand, turns past St Martin's Church and reaches Charing Cross Road.

It's three o'clock now. Marco should be in the shop.

Through the window, she can see Celia shelving books. Marco pats her arm, gesticulates and pulls faces. Celia laughs. Marco says something in her ear. She throws her hands in the air. Then Celia fidgets some fluff from his jacket. Georgie watches the Braccos floating in her glassy reflected face. Celia hands Marco a mug of tea. Georgie turns away from the shop and walks to Waterloo Station.

When she arrives at the town station, there is no bus for another hour. She decides to walk the four miles back to Hartisborne via the footpath over the fields. Maybe the walk will calm her mind though the clouds look black. And wasn't a May downpour forecast on the wireless this morning. But what does anything matter now? There's nothing to distract her from Trevor. *Married man – foolish bitch.* Georgie begins to sob. Trevor was right. Her shoulders shake. Her grief pours out in the rain.

A songbird makes her pause. Such a beautiful song, such a tiny bird.

Suddenly, here is a woman, strangely attired and wet through, peering into the bank. Gil's cape is drenched, his boots let in the water, and he can't quite shake Arthie's feet from his mind's eye, but still this woman watching and listening catches his attention, though she is nothing like Mary. He slows with interest. His pony shudders uneasily.

The woman is picking campions. In such a rain as this! She pulls at the plants untidily, breaking off wet stems with one hand and clutching her growing bunch in the other. He calms his pony. He sees what the woman sees, two golden wrens flitting, then one pausing to sing, its volume far greater than anyone could expect from that tiny chest. The song of a golden wren in rain is so full-hearted.

The woman pulls aside her wet hair from her ear, determined to listen. To speak with her would break the moment. What strange shoes she has, but he knows her as one of his own, as Mary is one of his own. An observer, a searcher after truth. And after yesterday's dismal Sunday dinner at the farm in Binford, the greasy tablecloth, the tittering children and more especially the haunting image of Arthie's blue and red feet with their white unhealthy nails, he is glad to find a kindred spirit. He waits till the golden wrens have flown and then approaches her, handling his little mare with care so as not to frighten her from her reverie or splash her.

'Good afternoon, madam,' he says.

She looks right through him. Not everyone likes a curate. She may suppose he will reproach her for being out alone or some such nonsense. 'I see you take an interest in our ornithology,' he says. She says nothing, though she looks at him or rather through him. Her skin is freckled, healthy and her eyes full of sharp intelligence. And some sadness. Some hidden hurt. The rain drips on them both. The broken chalk boulders that have fallen into the lane, obstruct them both. They breathe the wet garlic scent of Jack-in-the hedge and the headiness of hawthorn blossom. He waits. Still nothing. 'Well good day, madam,' he says, disappointed at her lack of response.

Her head turns sharply towards him. She must have heard him. Or could she be deaf? But no, wasn't she just now listening to birdsong? Then she walks quickly towards the village. Queen Anne's Lace ruffles and flies among the campions. Suddenly, there's a downpour of hailstones

The young woman begins to run. He trots slowly after her, the hailstones stinging his hands on the reins. To his mare's consternation, he rides past his own house to watch her hurry across the Plestor and up the steps to the granary loft, clutching her bunch of wet campions. Is she the baker's new girl perhaps? He had addressed her as a gentlewoman.

To the relief of his mare, he turns back to Wakeling House. She has endured much indignity already, liveried these past days with an incompetent stranger. Now she whinnies with delight, when Jonathan, Thomas' younger brother, opens the stable yard gate.

'Thought you'd forgotten where you lived, Mr Gil,' Jonathan says.

Gil forces a laugh to please Jonathan. 'I almost forgot myself in a dream.'

Hartisborne enjoys seeing him as eccentric and sometimes he humours them with the act.

In truth, he had almost forgotten his nagging

yearning after Mary in his curiosity about the oddly dressed woman. He must distract himself more often, serve others and not think of Mary at all. But how is she, he wonders, banishing the thought of Luckin caressing her pregnant belly.

He dries off, drinks his tea and resists being drawn into gossip about Binford by Thomas. He will save his stories for Miss Butter.

There is time for a little writing. Upstairs at his desk, he notes the movements of the golden wren and the loudness of the song. The green light of the lane falls on the young woman's face. He could record their meeting. People are part of natural history too. Yet, maybe she is no more than a vision. He dashes down a remembrancer of this and the other times that he has seen her that only he will ever understand.

Thomas interrupts. Time has flown. The fire is ready, the card table laid. Miss Butter is about to arrive with news of abroad. How woeful Gil's stories seem. A dirty chalice, a gaggle of children, Arthie's rotting toes. She would rather hear about Blundel, Mary and Luckin, but he will not oblige with stories closer to home. He blots his scrawl and straightens his wig. In the great parlour, mating tortoises, blue lupins and the joys of Turkey await him.

Thomas meets him at the foot of the stairs.

'I wonder - does the baker have a new woman working for him?'

'Not as far as I know, sir,' Thomas murmurs,

brushing Gil's jacket with a deft hand.

'Miss Butter there?'

'Fanning herself by the fire. The vicar is poorly and has not come.' Thomas winks. He suspects the vicar of match making.

'I hope you won't mind staying to pour the wine.'

'The entire evening?'

'Yes, that would be best. I know it's a bore to hear all her stories.'

'I will endeavour to bear it, sir.'

Thomas loves stories and wine. He loves to hear Miss Butter. And if Tom is right in his suspicions, Gil needs protection from that throaty sensuous voice and wild cleavage shifting beneath some spangled Eastern shawl.

'Good man. Let us go in. We'll take some glasses of my father's best white port.'

Good evening, my dear madame, he is about to proclaim as he throws open the parlour door. But first he calls Thomas back from his port-fetching. 'By the way, have you seen Mary Trimmer? How is she?'

'Poorly, sir. Poor Mary. There is talk of her losing her wits. And now Farmer Luckin is away, Mistress Barnes fears Mr Blundel will take her from Priory Farm. He came to the farm three times yesterday, but Mary hid.'

His heart beats with fear as he kisses Miss Butter's hand. He is deaf now to mosques and Eastern butterflies, blind to Miss Butter's gauzy bosoms, thinking only of the dangers of childbearing.

# CHAPTER 13

Nick has laboured over the invitations despite his hatred of the task. He was true to his father. Now he will give his mother what she wants, a large wedding with every pew filled. He will do all this, despite her stated intention of disinheriting him. 'You must be a bloody saint,' John Kemp had said when he'd confided in him the other night in the pub. 'Yes, she's taking you for a fool,' Wilf had muttered, 'but she is your mother after all.'

His mother plays on his guilt about his father's behaviour, though Nick shouldn't be held responsible for Dad. He shouldn't be made to feel guilty for his loyalty to Dad. Dad didn't leave after all. Or criticise his competence.

He'd like to prove to his doubting mother that he has an orderly mind by providing her with a typed alphabetical list of invitees, but it seems wrong to ask Claire to type it. And he can't ask Georgie, because Claire wouldn't like that. His mother questions him about the list so often that it's become a point of honour to copy it out neatly, even though his hands ache from hooking down the nettles and brambles in Cloisters Field. And his mind aches with worry about whether he should let Marilyn and Dick have the farm. If he is to keep the place, he should show he can manage any situation and create the wedding they want.

Now, his mother sits at the kitchen table, pen in hand, eying the list cantankerously.

'Who is Georgie Gardner?' she asks.

'You know – you met her in the pub,' he says, 'David Daunt's assistant.'

'Didn't take to her. More or less said I was too old to get married.' Marilyn strikes out Georgie's name.

Nick had imagined chatting to Georgie at the reception. She was the one person he was excited to ask.

'I've already invited her,' Nick says.

'Tell her it was a mistake. She hardly knows me anyway. And whatshisname – the wet curator - can represent the museum.'

So, this is the lofty way his mother sees the wedding, like a state occasion. The vicar will represent the church. Matt the publican will represent the pub. The butcher will represent the butcher's shop, and Wilf will represent the village cows.

'Iris Bewley?' His mother's pen hovers dangerously.

'I thought you'd like the school to be represented.'

'You must be mad.' Marilyn scores out Iris' name with thick Biro strokes.

'She wouldn't have come anyway,' Nick says. 'But it's only right to invite her as she's coaching the choir for the big day.'

'Louise Camden can represent the school. She's the chair of governors,' Marilyn says, missing Nick's irony.

'Joan Hill?' Only his mother can inflect a name with so much scorn.

'I've been friends with Joan since school.'

'She'll be needed in the pub for the reception.'

'Yes, I thought of that. So I asked Matt and he can spare her beforehand as long as she's there to serve the guests afterwards.'

'I'm not having Joan Hill at my wedding or her little bastard child.'

'Don't talk about Maisie like that! I've already asked her to be a bridesmaid.'

'You have not?'

'I have. You said you wanted lovely music. I thought it would be a nice touch for the youngest bridesmaid to sing a solo. And she's really excited about it.'

'Maisie can't be a bridesmaid at my wedding. She cannot sing in the choir, solo or otherwise. She mustn't be there at all. It's much more advisable – especially now - for us to keep them both at arm's length.'

'Us? You mean you?'

'No, 'us'. It's not in your interest to cultivate

this obsession with Joan and Maisie.'

'It's not an obsession. I grew up with Joan. And Maisie is a great kid.'

'You can have all these other people, Alf, Eddy, Wilf, and whatshisname - the wet curator - but I draw the line at Maisie and Joan.'

All very well for her to say 'you can have' all these people. He hadn't wanted to ask anyone and was only doing it for her.

'Joan's already said she'd rather earn money at the pub, but I thought I'd send her a formal invitation anyway in case she has second thoughts. But now she'll have to look after Maisie.'

'How terrible that she can't use my wedding as a baby-sitter.'

'You've put me in a very awkward position.'

'You shouldn't have blabbed before I checked the list,' Marilyn says.

'At this rate, I won't be showing up myself.'

He grabs the list, writes his own name, Nick Luckin, and crosses it out.

'Don't be like that.'

'It's weird for me to have to walk you up the aisle.'

'Sons often do that for widowed mothers.'

'Merry widow!'

'Oh, come on. Honestly, have whoever you like to my wedding except Joan, Maisie or Iris Bewley. And I'm not keen on that Georgie – and neither is Louise Camden. She suspects her of cosying up to those two hags, Sylvia and Iris. Otherwise come and come all. Dick can afford it.'

So far, Nick has paid for everything, not knowing how to ask Dick for the money. 'Who is Dick inviting?'

'He hasn't got round to a list.'

'How many people?'

'I'm not sure.'

'Dick hasn't got any friends, has he?'

'He's always worked so hard, never really had time for socialising.'

'But he must have relatives? Has he been married before?'

'Of course not. If either of us was divorced, the vicar wouldn't marry us in church.'

'Dick could be a widower.'

'He could be. I'm not entirely sure.' Marilyn looks uneasy.

'You haven't asked him.'

'He's never mentioned anyone.'

'Do you know anything about him at all?'

'Everyone knows his plug business.'

'For god's sake, mother, show some curiosity about the man you're marrying. What about our property? If you die and haven't made a will, he'll inherit from you. I don't want to share the farm with him!'

'All you can think about is the property. Just like your father.'

'If Dick has nothing to hide, then why doesn't he invite friends and relatives?'

'He has a sister. I didn't take to her. So, we haven't met up since.'

'How do you even know she was his sister? It could be a kind of plot like in that novel - The Wings of the Dove.' He'd laboured through the book at school, hating every minute. His English teacher said it might come in useful and now at last it has.

'Dick is a good person. Quiet, hardworking. He doesn't mess around like your father.'

'Dad was hard-working.'

'True. But he wasn't a good person.'

'Depends how you define a good person.'

'He wasn't good to me. This is a chance for happiness. You should be glad I'm not going into old age alone.'

So, the evening winds on with them snapping at one another and drinking too much of Wilf's home-made cider. Nick's head throbs. How will he tell Maisie she can't be a bridesmaid after all? For some reason, this question obsesses him more than the money Dick owes him. More than the incomplete arrangements and unsent invitations. He must disappoint a child and upset his old friend Joan. He hates himself. He hates his mother. And there's that strange smoke in the house, getting in his eyes, as if Dad is still here smoking a cheroot.

When Gil arrives at Priory Farmhouse on his mare, Mistress Barnes is crying, worrying about Mary, saying she's missing, though she slept in her bed last night. She blames herself for not paying attention, for trusting Mary. She so often slips out in the early morning to count the swallows' nests. But now it is eleven, and there is no sign of her.

'She was counting swallows' nests?' Gil asks. Doing it for me, a voice whispers.

'Look,' Mistress Barnes says.

She gestures him into the barn, where Mary has tied small platforms of woven willow under the beams and rafters to support a village of mud nests. The swallows swoop in on scimitar wings carrying insects for their chicks.

The earthy floor is dashed with white mess. Mistress Barnes tut tuts at the sight of it.

'When I found she was not at breakfast, I thought to seek her here. She watches the swallows as if learning them by heart. Why would she wander off so near to her time? Mr Blundel must have taken her!'

'Calm yourself.'

'*Make sure you look after Mary* were Mr Luckin's last words as he got in the chaise. We've checked the coppice, sir. And all the fields. We thought she might be with you. Perhaps she felt the cramps and is with Goody Newton.'

'Goody is to act the midwife then?' Gil asks.

'Yes, yes, it was settled weeks ago. The women are ready,' Mistress Barnes says, 'for the birthing. Some are helpful. Some just after the caudle cup, but no matter, we would have made Mary safe and now you men have pulled her this way and that with your arguments. She could be anywhere.'

'Mistress Barnes,' Gil says, suddenly taking both her hands. 'Tell me what I must do.'

'Try Sally Newton first. Supposing Mary has gone there in labour? What a fool I was not to think of that straightway.'

Occam's razor comes to mind. The simplest option must be considered first.

He trots away, his eyes searching the stream, the beech trees, the muddy hollows along Monksway, calling out *Mary, Mary*, not caring whether he draws attention to his distress. He sees another woman, not Mary at all, for this woman has heavy hair and wears strange clothes. She is the same woman he'd seen in the rain. Today, she is watching fish in the stream.

'Mistress,' he says, 'have you seen a young woman with child walk this way?' She finds him impertinent perhaps and whispers under her breath. 'No, it can't be true.' He looks away, looks back and she is gone. He has no time to wonder about the mysterious stranger and trots to Goody Newton's cottage, dismounts and ties up his mare at her gate.

When she won't answer her door, he walks

in. Her living room is curtained by drapes. The daybed is a straw mattress, spread with a leather sheet, on which lie bolsters and woven blankets. Here is the birthing stool. Here the ingredients for the caudle, kept close to her fireplace, and here the wicker cradle.

Goody has been readying for the occasion. Ship's biscuits, griddle cakes, a jug of brandy and of ale, a knife, a hook and a net. The scissor blades ready to cut the cord. All the tools are here but mother and baby are there none – and no Sally Newton either. No gentleman, unless he is a man-midwife or a husband called in after the event, ever goes to the birthing chamber. Bunches of mint, rosemary and lavender have been placed round the room to quell the stench of blood.

But no Mary, no Mary, no Mary. And more surprisingly no Goody.

He sees the hook and knife and feels faint. He opens the windows. The sweet scent of roses flows into the room. He wonders about a newborn baby's sense of smell. But there is no baby yet. And no Mary either.

The next likelihood is that Mary is in Binford with her mother. The next – and least palatable – is that Blundel has taken her to the justice.

What if she chased after a swallow, ran under its flight to discover its secret life, and got caught in brambles or fell in the stream? The poor sometimes disappear and are found later, half-eaten in a wood, or as a body fished from a well. Or never found. Or found half-dead, beaten like Annie Adkins by her lover.

Mary and her child must be protected, given the best chance. It doesn't matter about marriage, he realises. Only Mary's life matters. And her baby's life. And their health. He leaves through Goody's front door, giving Mrs John Daisy a shock, for she is standing on the step clutching her skirts, as if in pain.

'I've heard you're looking for Mary Trimmer,' Mrs John Daisy says. Her face is furrowed and her tone sharp.

'Yes, I am. Do you know where she is?'

'Mr Blundel forced her on a donkey and took her to the magistrate,' Daisy says.

'But the bench doesn't sit today?'

'They have taken her to the Justice, to Mr Fitz-Scott in Hartley Plaisir.'

In truth, there is nothing unusual in this. Why should they all travel to town when they can ride or walk the three miles to Fitz-Scott's house where his drawing room doubles as an impromptu court.

'We tried to reason with Mr Blundel, sir, when we saw him riding with her past the shop. Rosie went out and shouted at him. John ran after them, quoting the law. But Churchwarden Tanner was riding with them. They said they were on parish business and that as John hadn't wanted the job, he should leave those who did to get on with it. We lent Clerk Widdowson our pony so that he could catch up in the hope of making a fair record of proceedings.'

'They should have consulted me.'

'They said they tried but you were out, sir.'

'I went to Priory to enquire after Mary.'

'It's bad luck. A tangled net.'

'Yes, it is. But I will go after them. Can you send Ollie Knight to Priory? And let Mistress Barnes know what's happened?'

Mrs John Daisy nods.

'Mr Fitz-Scott, the justice, is a good man.'

'Mary should not be riding a donkey so near her time. Women have miscarried for less.'

'I'm surprised Mary allowed them to persuade her.'

'They must have man-handled her. Since Farmer Luckin has been away, Blundel has followed and harried her, and set his men on her too. I said to John- why would he do it? And neither of us knows.'

'Duties can often be misinterpreted,' Gil says, getting impatient to leave. Why stay so even toned? So cautious? Such a diplomat? He hates Blundel as much as Daisy Carpenter does.

Daisy narrows her eyes at his falseness and scuffs the dirt with her shoe, then says quietly, 'Please find her. Tell her from me that the Carpenters will always be her friends. Indeed sir, we are as good as family to her. She will understand my meaning.'

'God bless you,' Gil says. 'I'll send a message if we need Goody.'

'Yes, please do, Mr Gil. I'll find Goody now and tell her what's happened.'

# CHAPTER 14

Sylvia turns right under the hanger on to the lower path that trails along Park meadow behind the Museum's garden. She can see the naturalist's house. From this side, the ha-ha offers no illusions.

Mr Daunt is setting up a trestle table on the grass. Miss Gardner flaps a long white cloth over the table. David catches the other end and smooths it down. Then Georgie places a jug of flowers on the table. They lay the table, passing each other the cutlery. Probably enjoying themselves.

Sylvia feels a pang for those midsummer meals of old when the former owners invited everyone to gather in the naturalist's garden. When she was a girl, people played fiddles and danced. At least five men worked in the garden then and they'd be at the party now with their wives, and so would the rest of the village. Music and laughter would echo off the hanger.

No locals will be asked tonight. It's all cliques and groups now. She wonders what they will talk about. Something rarefied. The life of the naturalist. Art and politics. If she were there, she could fascinate them by describing her time-slips. Her journeys into the past would make good dinner-party stories, though no one really believes them, even though Georgie had humoured her.

Evening sun glows through downy clocks in the meadow. The grass is pink and golden. She'll cut some twigs of beech and some campions and put them on her husband's grave and on Richard Luckin's grave too.

When Richard held a party on his birthday down at Priory, he always drank too much and flirted with some girl, while Iris looked on. Sylvia considered that cruel. Miss Bewley couldn't say anything as she had no official relationship with Richard. A few summers ago he'd twirled young Joan Hill round and round till she fell down giddy with laughter. Joan's dancing must have unwound the past, for Sylvia saw another woman dancing, a pregnant woman spinning round and round alone, her skirts flaring out. She was singing something, but Sylvia couldn't catch the words or the tune.

It is David Daunt's birthday, which is also Nick's father's birthday or was. His father always held a party at Priory. The guests walked through the woods from the village. His band The Pipe Barrel performed. Last year, when Nick visited from

London to celebrate, Dad had told him about his cancer while that dreadful hurdy-gurdy played on in the long hall.

Nick hardly knew Claire, but in his shocked state, she insisted on comforting him. Driven by his father's illness, he made quick decisions. He'd given up the job in Rome, moved away from his friends in London and back to the farm, leant on Claire and grown angrier with his mother.

And now his mother is marrying a stranger.

Nick fears being unfaithful to Claire. He wants to be honest with women, something his father never achieved. After the meal tonight when he takes Claire home, he'll break up with her, if he can face it.

He walks to Hartisborne through the woods along Monksway, taking his time, so that he can think out what to say. He doesn't want to hurt anyone. Neither did Dad, but he hurt people anyway.

He likes Georgie, not even sure why. She went to London a couple of weeks ago and wouldn't say why. Supposing there's a boyfriend there? Jealousy is such a terrible feeling.

Nick shouldn't be afraid to be alone. He shouldn't think, *better Claire than no one*. There are few people his age in Hartisborne and he'd needed Claire during his father's illness. What a terrible way to think of her. He must break up with her. Tonight? And spoil the evening? Or wait till tomorrow? Or next week? He wanders along disconsolately, no longer looking forward to the meal, unless it is to see Georgie and not be alone on his father's birthday.

Wilf watches Nick walk away through the woods. He slips round to the farmhouse's back door. He tries the handle. Nick never locks the door, but today he has. Wilf can see the pottery bowl on the dresser in the kitchen where Nick slings the Land Rover keys. He climbs onto the low windowsill and peers in. He rattles the frame but the inside catch, though always ropey, won't give.

'Hello. Is Nick about?' Tom Swallow asks, making him start away from the sill. 'He was supposed to give me a lift.'

Wilf climbs down as if nothing is wrong and says, 'Think he's gone to the village. Saw him walking off through the woods.'

'Would he mind if I borrowed the Land Rover then?' Tom asks.

'That's what I was after, but he's locked the house. I was looking for a way to get the key.'

'The key's in the ignition. I just had a look.'

Of course. Damn it. He could have been on his way by now without having Tom on his case.

'Where do you want to go?' Wilf asks. 'I'm insured to drive it and you're not. I can drop you off somewhere if you like.'

They walk towards the farm's courtyard,

where the Land Rover is parked at a sharp angle.

'I need to get a few things first,' Wilf says. Might as well brazen it out.

'Need any help?' Tom asks.

Well, why not? Wilf is almost laughing inside. He dislikes Tom because people say women pose naked for him in the barn. Fly-by-night type with two marriages behind him. And he's not so clever after all.

'I need a couple of spades and some rope,' Wilf says.

'Not burying someone, I hope?' Tom jokes.

'Just the opposite,' Wilf says. Then adds, 'Helping Fred with a bit of digging work under Coneycroft hanger.'

'Righto,' Tom says. He follows Wilf to the garden shed, takes a spade from him and slings a proferred coil of rope over his arm. Wilf takes another spade and mallet – you never knew what you'd hit. Ground that hasn't been dug for years can be hard. They stow the tools in the back of the Land Rover. Wilf tosses in an empty cardboard grocery box.

It's a dry warm evening. Dust is flying over Priory Farmhouse, creating a misty cloud. A grouse screams in the field, throwing its head back in horror.

'Oops,' Tom says. 'I've forgotten the vino. Just a mo.'

Wilf slows at the barn-studio. Tom shoots out of the Land Rover and comes back a moment later with two fat raffia covered bottles.

'I've got some more of these,' Tom says conversationally. 'If you ever want to stop by for a glass of bottled sunshine.'

'More of a beer drinker,' Wilf murmurs. He imagines them sitting outside the barn-studio on the bench, drinking in the evening light, chewing the cud, man to man. 'Where are you off to?' he asks.

'It's David Daunt's birthday. They've invited me to the museum for a celebratory meal.'

Oh, I see. The museum people. The worshippers of Saint Gil who are blocking the safety of the villagers with their Luddite ideas. His heart hardens towards Tom. He banishes thoughts of comradely wine drinking. 'Is that where Nick was going?' he asks.

'Yes, he forgot to take me.'

So, Nick would be out late carousing with the curator and his assistant again. Fraternising with the enemy. He'll walk home drunk along Monksway and won't notice the Land Rover's gone. All Wilf needs to do is park it somewhere discreet where it can't be seen from the museum or the church. But what about the tools? He stops at the top of Gracious Street to let Tom out. After all, he said he was off to Coneycroft hanger. He drives on round the corner and waits until Tom will have gone inside Wakeling House. Then he reverses in a gateway and drives back to the Plestor.

No one is around. He takes the tools and stows them under the cave of the second yew tree in the churchyard. If anyone sees him, they'll think he's going to tidy up Winnie's grave.

Then he slips into the Land Rover and drives off down Gracious Street again. He pulls into the gap in Coneycroft meadow and walks back up the lane, taking his time. He'll go to The Compasses first and have a drink. He'll be pleasant and chatty. He'll be giving himself an alibi. No one will suspect. The museum lot will be busy with their snobbish meal. He will wait till it's too late for anyone to be awake.

He composes his face. Everyone will say later that he was cheery, somewhat better than he had been. He knows the nature of village conversations, the putting to bed of a tragedy with some accepting phrases. He imagines the sentimental conversations about Winnie. How would they go? 'Out of her misery, reunited with her son, freed from her delusions, not a bad way to go, worse for Wilf.' People always tried to make something good out of something bad. But he'd show them the error of their ways.

'Pint of Best, Joan,' he says with a smile as he leans against the bar. The taps and bottles are lit by a dusty shaft of light. A sour hoppy smell fills the bar, as Matt tries a new barrel. Joan pauses from cleaning out an ashtray with a paint brush, wipes her hands and draws him a pint. 'How's your girl?' he asks. And he and Joan chat as if nothing is wrong, as if Hartisborne is not about to change for ever.

Nick returns to the little parlour, trying his damnedest not to worry about how he will break up with Claire. He ducks through the arched open doorway into the garden and bangs his head. He has loved this doorway since childhood. The magic door into the garden, a door that suggests people of olden times were as short as gnomes. Of course, Gil never hit his head on the door. He could walk through without even bending his neck.

Georgie fetches him a glass of wine. The prospect of breaking up with Claire – and the worry over his mother's wedding – recede somewhat, as he gulps it down.

'Where's Tom? I thought you'd bring him.'

'Oh drat, I forgot to tell him we were leaving. Have you been raiding my mother's wardrobe again?'

Georgie is wearing an outrageous fifties' skirt and a stole that glimmers when the light catches it. 'School jumble sale,' she says.

'Definitely not my mother's then. She ostracises the school jumble-sale.' He tries not to think about his mother, but she wheedles her way into everything.

Claire wears a slender shift dress. Her hair is bobbed like Mary Quant's. Claire is smart and up to the minute. Some people might say Georgie looks a mess, but he would never say that, though his mother definitely would.

The museum bell jangles. Georgie lets Tom in. He waggles two raffia covered bottles of Chianti as a greeting.

'Smells good. Sorry I'm late. You went without me, Nick!'

The five of them gather round the table outside, while David carves the chicken and Georgie hands round a bowl of new potatoes with mint from the garden. Tom fills everyone's glasses with David's Muscadet, saving the Chianti for later, and the atmosphere warms, though the damp is rolling in across the meadow from the woods.

'There's a sixth place,' Tom observes.

'I invited Iris Bewley,' David says, 'but I don't think she'll come. I've laid a place though, because if she does come, I want her to feel welcome.'

'So thoughtful,' Claire says warmly.

'It was Georgie's idea,' David admits.

'Love this summer savoury,' Georgie says to David, changing the subject. 'I've never tasted it before.'

'Gil used to grow it -so we do too,' David says. 'It's rather stronger than thyme.'

They're drinking the last of the Muscadet

when the museum bell tolls again. David leaps to his feet.

'Iris must have turned up after all,' Tom says, as he opens the Chianti. 'She'd better have a glass of this.' Tom sets a full glass by the empty place.

Through the garden door, they hear voices in the hall. A woman's voice. Claire and Georgie roll their eyes at each other and groan.

David's words filter back to them, '… a few guests for supper … not really a good evening to discuss it … not quite the right … well, of course, if it's urgent …no, of course not, do join us …'

Georgie bangs her head on the table in mock despair. Why can't David be firmer? He lets everyone walk over him.

As David ushers the visitor forward, they hear the now unmistakeable tones of Mrs Camden.

'I thought it better to tackle this immediately than let it run on.'

Nick and Tom rise politely as Mrs Camden enters the garden.

'Oh, Mr Swallow. I didn't expect to see you here.'

'Isn't the world just full of surprises?' Tom says. '*We* thought *you* were Iris.'

Mrs Camden looks past him to David. 'I'm afraid Miss Bewley would rather sit with the dead than join you for supper. I saw her in the churchyard again. Such a gothic addiction to gloom and hardly a good example for her pupils. You've wasted your invitation, Mr Daunt.'

'It was my invitation actually,' Georgie lies so that Mrs Camden can blame her rather than David for not being invited. 'I organised this for David's birthday.'

'Really?' Tom says. 'I thought David was the mastermind.'

Georgie shakes her head at him.

Nick tries to help by saying, 'How is Colonel Camden?'

'Oh, what a beautiful table. Such a fine candle in the lantern. And the hanger, so… so resonant… in the evening air.' Mrs Camden sits down to rhapsodise in Iris Bewley's place. She notices the wine, sips it, and says, 'Such a *gener*ous glassful. I had no idea Miss Bewley was such a drinker.'

'Tell you what,' Tom says. 'Why don't the rest of us have a stroll and an intercourse fag while you two talk business?'

'Thank you. It's confidential school business, so I need to talk to Mr Luckin too,' Mrs Camden says. 'Perhaps you could stay, Miss Clifford, and take some notes?'

'I'm sorry but I'm not at work right now,' Claire says rising to go with Tom.

Tom and Claire duck under the topiary yew arch and hurry into the walled garden.

'Come on Georgie,' Tom shouts when safely out of sight. 'Come and show us your melons.'

Georgie stubbornly remains. It's David's birthday after all and she can't let him be eaten alive by Mrs Camden. Besides melons grow on the other side of the garden.

It is three miles to the justice's house, a manor next to a pond and church in a hamlet, which was once a prosperous village that all but died out in the plague years. The inhabitants of Hartley Plaisir isolated themselves to save their neighbours in Hartisborne. They wanted other's lives to continue even if their own could not.

Cornflowers and golden corncockles nod along the way. Chalk daisies fill the lane and wave their white heads. Heat ripples over the fields. Gil's heart lifts with the beauty of it all, giving him hope for Mary.

He passes the spot in the lane where he'd seen the strange woman on his return from Binford in May. She is a momentary thought. Mary fills his heart. It is a hot day, a sweet day, and yet uncomfortable for a woman near her time to be bounced along on a donkey. Gil feels anger rising in his throat. Damn Blundel! Damn him. His little mare starts. She doesn't like him shouting. Like his parishioners, she expects him to act the diplomat.

Truly, Mr Fitz-Scott, the justice of peace, has created an enviable green bower with the effects of a surrounding wilderness. He fancies himself a great gardener and is also writing a natural history which he likes to read to Gil for praise not comment. Fitz-Scott gardens well, writes badly and is a good man.

As he dismounts, Gil notices two ponies and a donkey tied to the fence on the meadow side of the garden. He hurries along the path, flanked by bourbon roses with the petals drying on the deep crimson blooms, the scent tangible. Honeysuckle creeps round the windows. Mary would love this garden, but that is no consolation for her illegal interrogation. He knocks. Fitz-Scott's man takes him through. All the men are seated. Mary is standing. She is hot, sweating and holding her hands to her back, as if in pain.

'Ah, Gil!' Fitz-Scott says. 'Have you come at last about my chapter on hirundines? I sent it weeks ago and have been eagerly awaiting your commentary. And now you must wait a little longer yourself. We have just concluded our business, and I must hear Mr Widdowson's account of proceedings. You are welcome to stay as the settlement issue concerns your parish.'

Gil sighs. He is too late. Why can't a man as well-meaning as Fitz-Scott, a fellow natural historian, see why this proceeding is all wrong? Why has he allowed it to go ahead at all?

'If I may interject,' Gil says, 'it is a hot day for Mistress Trimmer to be standing so near to her time. She is perhaps thirsty or hungry. May she not be offered a seat and refreshments?'

'You are quite correct,' Fitz-Scott says. 'I

forgot my duties. Mistress Trimmer, please go to the bower seat in the garden. There is no need for you to hear the record of proceedings. My housekeeper will bring you some ale and nuncheon.'

Fitz-Scott calls his housekeeper. She takes Mary's arm and whispers the location of the little house. They walk away. Mary turns her head away from Gil. Is she disappointed in him?

Mr Blundel whispers something to Fitz-Scott.

'Of course, the girl won't go anywhere,' Fitz-Scott says with irritation. 'She's about to give birth. I've heard this examination because you insisted, but there is no need to treat the girl like a criminal, whether she is a migrant or not. And that case is not closed.'

Fitz-Scott gestures to Widdowson to read out his notes.

'The examination of Trimmer, Mary, a single woman, 27 years of age, was taken on this day the thirtieth of June, 1763. For the last six years, she has worked in service in the parishes of Binford and Hartisborne. She has not completed a twelvemonth of service in either of these parishes. She now lives in Hartisborne, which she claims is her birthplace. Trimmer claims a simpler and sometime midwife, one Sally Newton, known also as Goody Newton, delivered Trimmer as a baby in her cottage in Gracious Street, Hartisborne.'

Blundel interrupts. 'The record suggests

Newton has given a statement and yet she is not present as a witness here. Widdowson, you're including village hearsay with no evidence.'

Fitz-Scott sighs. 'Mr Widdowson, though we did discuss the hearsay about Newton, please strike that out and include an account only of what is proven, not of our informal discussion.'

Widdowson draws a line through his writing with his left-handed quill.

'Shall I continue?'

'Yes, please do.'

'The parish overseer says there is no evidence for this claim beyond Newton's say-so.'

'You should scratch that out too,' Fitz-Scott says, 'as it now won't make sense.'

'True, your honour,' Widdowson says. Then he continues, 'Trimmer knows not the identity of her father or whether he is or was a settled Hartisborne man. For the last six years, the examinant has received part wages of £3 per annum for her work as a weeding woman for the curate at Wakeling House in Hartisborne and paid some 3s a week to board with the simpler Newton. In the winter, the examinant worked at The Hoe and Shield inn in Binford, returning from thence in the spring to Wakeling House where she regularly continued in service till Advent as a weeding woman.' Widdowson consults the room. 'Any corrections?'

Widdowson looks at Gil, but there is little he can add.

'Trimmer is with child and likely to become a burden on the parish. After a short engagement to one Edward Kemp, a settled parishioner, she declined to wed him, denying his carnal knowledge on her body. She has since left Wakeling House and entered the service of Mr Luckin of Priory Farm also in Hartisborne Parish. She has worked there for nearly four months on a wage of £3 per annum and provisions And this examinant on her oath further says that she was never married, that Kemp is not the father of her bastard, that she never rented any house or dwelling of £10 per annum or ever paid parochial taxes, and that, since quitting Wakeling House and her other places of service, she has not done any act to gain a settlement in Hartisborne or elsewhere, though she says that both she and her mother were born in Hartisborne but there is no witness or proof in either case beyond the simpler Newton, who is not present.'

'Ah, stop there,' Blundel says. 'You struck out the rumour of her birth in Hartisborne earlier and, to refer to it here, introduces the idea again.'

'May I offer a further thought?' Gil asks. 'If Sally Newton says Mistress Trimmer and her mother were born in Hartisborne, then I would believe her. She is a truthful woman. Her testimony should be heard.'

'Mr Gil has a point,' Fitz-Scott says. 'We say there is no evidence for the girl's birth in Hartisborne, but there is some evidence in a possible eye-witness. Therefore, the issue of settlement cannot be concluded. Thank you for your clarity, sir.' He nods at Gil. 'Please record this, Widdowson.' Fitz-Scott painstakingly dictates, 'On the advice of the curate of Hartisborne, we will call in further evidence of Trimmer's birthplace. For now, she may stay in Hartisborne. If, after the birth of her child, she cannot give proof of settlement, she will be passed to Binford for certification there. Sworn before me on the day and year above written. Henry Fitz-Scott Esquire, justice of the peace, witnessed by Jonah Blundel, parish overseer and Peter Deadman, church warden.' Did you get that all down, Widdowson?'

Widdowson blots his copy and reads the record back to the JP.

'This is a sudden change from what we discussed,' Mr Blundel argues. 'By the time of her certification, she will have cost the parish a pretty penny. We all agreed that Trimmer be passed to Binford.' He looks angrily at Gil.

My presence turned the conclusion, Gil thinks with astonishment.

'We should still require her to name her bastard's father.' Blundel says, going as if to fetch Mary.

Gil could object on a legal basis. But if Blundel breaks the law, he could be prosecuted. Gil holds his counsel and his breath, hoping Blundel will walk into the trap.

'As you know Mr Blundel,' Fitz-Scott says heavily, 'it is against the law to question a woman as to paternity within a month of her confinement. We are here to uphold the law, not break it.'

If only Fitz-Scott had let Blundel cook his own goose. But he is even less of a strategist than Gil.

Blundel and Tanner mutter insolently.

Fitz-Scott turns a deaf ear. The chatter of parish officials is beneath him.

Blundel tries again.

Yes, go on, Gil thinks. Put yourself in the wrong. Widdowson's eyes meet Gil's. Widdowson raises his quill. Let us record your law-breaking.

'As you know, sir, if the child is born in Hartisborne without proof of paternity, it becomes a charge to the parish, for seven years. This could be avoided if we discovered the father's name.'

'Trimmer is a hard-working woman, by all accounts and has the patronage of Farmer Luckin. Except for help for her confinement, I don't think she will bother the parish funds too much.'

'Though a month after the birth, we have every right to bring a bastardy case, do we not, your honour?' Blundel manages to sound both threatening and obsequious.

'Rights and moral behaviour are not always identical,' Fitz-Scott says. 'Harassing a young woman does not become parish officers. Let me not see you back here too early.'

Fitz-Scott dismisses the Hartisborne party. Blundel and Deadman step outside. Fitz-Scott gestures for Gil to stay, while Widdowson slowly packs his writing implements into a leather roll, delaying procedures to avoid riding home with the parish officers.

Gil overhears Blundel through the window, shouting. 'I can't abide a woman who deceives.'

For courtesy's sake, Gil lends his attention to the JP who asks him to investigate the father's identity without harm to the girl.

Fitz-Scott is hard of hearing. Gil is forced to repeat his remarks, while his own ears only want to hear what's going on outside where voices are raised in anger. A donkey brays. His own little mare whinnies in distress. And one of Fitz-Scott's geese sets off its honking warning. Is Mary sobbing? 'Sir, I should attend to Mistress Trimmer. The parish overseer berates her.'

'These petty enmities, Mr Gil, do ill become your parish,' Fitz-Scott says as if the petty enmities are Gil's fault.

'I've got her,' He hears Tanner shout. 'Up you get, Missy.'

'Trimmer seems a docile woman.'

'Yes, I think so.'

'Hands off me, you rat-faced pimp.' Very docile.

'Though one can never assume to know

someone on a slight acquaintance,' Fitz-Scott muses.

'She kicked me,' Tanner calls out in disbelief.

'Feel that?' Blundel shouts. 'Wild little whore. Stop your scratching, missy.'

'Shall I secure her on the donkey?' Deadman asks.

Gil can't hear Blundel's answer. It seems inconceivable that Justice Fitz-Scott cannot hear the fracas outside. But his deafness is a blessing. To hear Mary cursing would lower her in the justice's opinion. There is a sudden silence.

'I must go, sir,' Gil says to Henry Fitz-Scott, 'and pour oil on troubled waters.'

'Well, that is a great disappointment. I hoped to share some refreshment with you and hear your comments on my hirundine study. Also, I have had a hopeful response to my paper on the coot, which I wanted to read to you.

'My regrets. Another time perhaps.' Gil hurries from the house, furious with himself for falling into such a time-wasting courteous exchange when Mary is being forced through the woodland on the donkey like a common criminal. They may try to divert her so that her baby is born out of the parish. He must catch up with them.

He mounts his pony and rides back the way he came. But of Blundel, Tanner and Mary, there is no sign, though he soon finds Widdowson waiting for him in the lane.

'Perhaps they went the other way?'

'Up over the hanger? In Mary's condition? Would Blundel try to make her miscarry?'

'It's odd that we see neither hair nor hide of them, sir.'

They ride back together staring into every bush and ditch, calling out, 'Blundel, Tanner, Mary' but no one answers.

# CHAPTER 15

'Take care,' Matt says, as Wilf teeters out of the pub. Wilf lingers under the open window, listening in.

'He'll be alright,' Joan says. 'It's not like he has to drive.'

'But I saw him driving Nick's Land Rover.'

'Maybe he brought it to the village for Nick then? I mean he's hardly going to drive the two hundred yards home, is he?'

'I don't like the look of him,' Matt says.

'It's not late. He'll sleep it off,' Joan says.

Wilf wants to laugh. They'd like the look of him even less if they saw what he was about to do. True enough – he's drunk - but he can hold his drink.

The moon is visible now even on this light evening. On a night such as this, no one would bother to argue for street lighting. He steadies himself on the wall along the edge of Wakeling House and then crosses the road. In the churchyard, Wilf ducks down and crawls under the second yew tree, where the evening light barely penetrates. He leans against the trunk next to his tools and rope, lies down on the yew needles in the dark green cave and falls asleep.

'I wouldn't have burst in on you like this,' Mrs Camden begins. 'But I've heard you are going ahead with the exhibition of the children's work – in collaboration with Mr Swallow.'

David catches Georgie's eye. She expects him to be brave. Nick taps his fingers on the table irritably.

'Well, it's not an absolutely fixed thing,' David murmurs.

'I thought it was,' Georgie says sharply.

'Surely it's up to Iris?' Nick says. 'She knows what she's doing.'

'But does she?' Mrs Camden asks. 'Her own pupils trapped her in her classroom and tormented her. She's obviously lost control of the school.'

'Tom and Iris' project is a lovely idea,' Georgie says. 'The children are really excited by it.'

'It's not up to us school governors to tell the head teacher what she can or cannot teach,' Nick adds.

'But it's not her doing the teaching is it? It will be Mr Swallow.'

'Tom's way of seeing…' Georgie begins.

'I'm not interested in his way of seeing.'

'But the children are,' Nick says.

'They love his work,' Georgie adds, though she has no idea whether they do.

'And it would look terrific hung around the museum. The naturalist's writing is so alive, and then the children would have a real connection with the past and take more interest in this special place where they live,' David says.

'You seem determined to carry this through despite Mr Swallow's divorces,' Mrs Camden says.

'Divorce can be a good thing. Wish my parents had done it. And divorce has nothing to do with this project. Anyway, it's up to Iris,' Nick says. 'She has the final say.'

'The parents are most concerned about the locking-in incident. Someone has suggested that we hold a village meeting to discuss whether Miss Bewley should remain head teacher.'

'Who made the suggestion?' Georgie asks, suspiciously.

'That's confidential,' Mrs Camden replies. 'Let's just say there is a general concern about the discipline at the school and a desire to discuss it.'

'Would you invite Iris to the meeting?' Nick asks.

'Details can be ironed out later. But as a fellow school governor, would you agree that a village meeting might be a good thing?'

'No, because it would humiliate Iris.' Nick drains his second glass of wine with a flourish.

'Children's education is more important than the sensitivity of teachers. We'll need to discuss this further with the vicar and parents. Let's speak again when we have a fuller consensus.' Mrs Camden mimes a line in the air suggestive of throat-cutting to end the subject. 'There's another matter which concerns only Miss Gardner and Mr Daunt.' She nods at Nick, as if to dismiss him but he ignores her and pours himself another glass of wine.

'What is it?' David asks. She is not the Colonel and is not on the board of trustees, he reminds himself.

'Romilly Pearson came to me the other day in a great state of upset - well I can only say - you hurt her feelings. It seems you gave the Pearsons a warning?'

'The museum collections need sensitive treatment.' Last week, David saw Romilly run the hoover tube over a stuffed dodo in the front parlour. A section of wing was sucked down the tube. She wasn't going to retrieve it till David insisted they empty the dustbag. Nev Pearson used Vim on the glass case of stuffed birds, leaving unsightly scratches. Romilly touches everything roughly. She tore the lining of Gil's replica bed-curtains made after his death by his great nieces. In the library, she creates unsightly spots on rare books by spraying them with a Daz solution. She grazes the pewter with a scourer.

David was quite right to give her a warning. But if he wasn't such a ninny, as his stepfather always says, the Pearsons would listen when he explains, as he frequently does, about the need for tender care of exhibits.

'This is a place of preservation. I know the Pearsons mean well. They want everything clean, spit and polish and all that, but they don't know how to deal with old things. They don't understand the patina of age, the respect for the past, the fact that the naturalist handled some of these objects and that there are hardly any stuffed dodos in the world and only the remains of one in Oxford.' As he talks on, a semblance of strength returns to him. He does have a vocation after all. He cares about these artefacts. He is a curator who preserves important histories. 'And at the annual washing of the china by the volunteers, Captain Pearson set down the box of porcelain with such force that several bowls cracked, and one of them was a butter dish Gil used himself. In fact, it was a gift from Miss Butter.' David laughs awkwardly.

He has been tracing every mention of Miss Butter to illuminate the love affair he imagines she was having with Gil. Miss Butter was a trailblazer, a modern woman before her time, and her journals are much more exciting than Gil's. His heart warms when he thinks about her which is why Pearson's rough handling of an item associated with her riled him so much.

Mrs Camden winces. Georgie nods encouragingly at David. Nick downs his third glass of wine and pours himself another.

'I'm sure poor Captain and Mrs Pearson could be trained up…'

'I don't think the situation would change,' David says bravely. 'The parquet block is never fixed and it's in danger of causing accidents.'

'Everyone is teachable…'

'I've tried explaining our work to Nev and Romilly, and, quite frankly, they don't get it. Nev told me himself that he only believes in the here and now.'

'That's odd when you think how obsessed he is with the lives of the composers,' Georgie murmurs, hoping to divert from the parquet block. John Kemp fixed it a week ago, and neither David nor Nev has noticed.

'Yes, you have a point Miss Gardner,' Mrs Camden unwilling concedes. 'My husband says Captain Pearson cares almost too much for the past, and of course the Colonel has known him for so much longer.'

'None of us is consistent, I suppose,' Nick says, topping up her glass.

'Nev put weedkiller on the flower beds because he saw a single groundsel plant. All the flowers wilted. The dianthus was done for. He's not even supposed to work in the garden. We use natural methods like the naturalist did.'

'My husband thinks highly of the Pearsons, as I'm sure you know. They feel dishonoured by the way you spoke to them. The fact that you didn't invite them this evening has also hurt their feelings.'

'I did the inviting,' Georgie lies. 'It was to be a surprise party for David's birthday, but Romilly got wind of it.'

'Their emotions aren't my business,' David says, buoyed by Georgie's support. 'My business is to preserve the museum collection. People who work here need an affection for the past, for objects and for histories.'

'Maybe I could help? I've trained many staff in my time. The issues you mention are not insurmountable with the right training.'

'Look, I just want them to take more care around the museum. I'm not going to sack the bloody Pearsons and make them homeless'

The bell clangs at the door. 'Excuse me,' Georgie says. 'I'll get it.'

'You don't have the power to sack them anyway. That would be a matter for the trustees, and my husband would never allow it. I find your swearing about our friends disrespectful.'

'Sorry,' David mumbles.

'This is David's birthday meal,' Nick says. 'We shouldn't be discussing his work now.'

Voices float through from the hall.

'I was on my way back from the churchyard and thought perhaps I would pop in, because I know Nick is here and it's Richard's birthday as well as David's, of course.'

'Oh, perfect timing. Just in time for dessert,' Georgie says from the hall.

Miss Bewley ducks through the arched door into the garden. Nick kisses her on the cheek. Tom and Claire stub out their cigarettes and leave the safety of the topiary hedge to approach the table once more. Mrs Camden rises and nods stiffly to Iris.

'Well, I've had my word, so I'll say goodnight. I do think it would be a mistake to fall out with the Pearsons, Mr Daunt. And I'm sorry, Nick, that we disagree on –,' she cocks her head at Iris ' - the other matter. I won't be giving way on that, just so that you know.'

Once she is out of the door. Georgie and Claire collapse into giggles.

'Was she threatening you, Dave?' Claire asks.

Georgie copies Mrs Camden's cut-glass voice, '*So sorry that we disagree.* David was magnificent. He stood up for the ethos of the museum.'

'Yes, I did, didn't I? Though the truth is I'm terrified of the bloody Pearsons. I was trembling when I had that conversation with them. And when it was over, I downed a glass of whisky and invoked the ghost of the naturalist to protect me. Since then, I've seen Nev following the tortoise round the garden. He spends hours watching poor old Timothy. And sometimes he seems to be humming or murmuring to him. Last night I dreamt he strangled him.'

'Is it possible to strangle a tortoise?' Tom asks. 'Wouldn't he retreat into his shell at the scent of malignant intentions?'

'I don't think we should speak ill of anyone,' Iris Bewley suggests warily. 'Captain Pearson had a difficult war.'

'Oh, come on Iris, you know Mrs C. is an old busybody and she's only backing the Pearsons to be annoying.'

'I won't say I haven't experienced a touch of her - I can't think of the right word - ?' Iris falters.

'Resentment?'

'I can't think why she would resent me. She sees me as an opponent. I don't know why.'

Louise Camden and his father flirting in the saloon bar flashes into Nick's memory. What a weird idea. Could it be true? It would certainly account for Louise's dislike of Iris.

'It's getting chilly out here,' David says. 'Let's move into the back parlour and pretend we're Gil's friends from the eighteenth century.'

They light candles despite the uncanny light of midsummer. David opens another bottle of wine.

'Dad would have loved this,' Nick says.

'You grieve for your father. But can you grieve for dead people you've never known?' Georgie asks.

'Still obsessed with the naturalist?' Nick asks. He never thought he'd be jealous of a man who's been dead for two hundred years.

'I was thinking of my parents and how I miss them, though I didn't know them. And all I know about them is that *The Natural History* was important to them.'

'That tells you they were admirable people. *The Natural History* is a bigger story than ours but told in little moments, the valuing of the merest ant or bee or flower,' Iris says, 'in the pattern of a whole connected environment.'

They hear the nightjars through the windows and their drunken talk travels through time, death and nature until the evening ends with Iris reciting Kipling's, 'The Way Through the Woods' in her rippling voice. 'I always think of Monksway when I read that poem. You know – that feeling of other lives from other times present but just out of sight. And I often feel metaphorically – at the moment- that there is no way through the woods.'

Gil's clock strikes in the little parlour.

'Goodness it's gone two. It's Midsummer Day already, and I have to teach tomorrow. Thank you, I'm glad I came,' Iris says to David.

'We'll walk you back Iris,' Nick says. 'I know it's a bad night for you.'

'And for you.'

'Let's all walk her back,' Tom says. They set off towards the schoolhouse, laughing, talking and smoking, while David who intended to stay and clear the table, suddenly runs after them, scared of missing out.

The moon casts a white light. Nick takes Miss Bewley's arm. 'I've been meaning to tell you how I miss you and Dad singing together.'

'That's sweet of you. I only sing in assembly now and that's a disheartening business. I think I've lost my singing voice.'

'You could sing now– in remembrance of Dad.'

'I'd wake people. They'd think I'd gone completely mad.'

'Go on, Iris,' Tom says. 'We'll join in.'

'What kind of thing did you sing?' Georgie asks.

'Folk songs. Richard had a wide repertoire.'

'Yes, Dad was a great collector of songs,' Nick says.

'What was his favourite?' David doesn't want to be left out of the conversation, though he's worrying about rats, bats and the leftovers on the table. Slugs will start on the remaining salad which he was saving for the tortoise.

'He liked *Early One Morning*,' Iris says.

'Let's go and sing it to Dad,' Nick says suddenly.

'In the churchyard?' Claire asks. 'I don't think you should, Iris.'

Miss Bewley murmurs. 'It's a whole year since Richard's birthday party, when he told us all he was dying. A year is nothing really, is it? I can see his face so clearly. I haven't forgotten him.'

'Sometimes I don't believe he's dead,' Nick says.

'I feel the same,' Iris says.

'So do I,' David adds, conjuring his few happy evenings with The Pipe Barrel.

'Go on sing him *Early One Morning*,' Tom urges.

'Tom, you shouldn't push people,' Georgie says.

'I only encourage people to do what they want anyway. Like with you and Marco.'

'What happened between you and Marco?' Nick asks too quickly.

Georgie pulls at Tom's sleeve, imploring him to be silent.

'In vino veritas,' Tom says, leaning on her drunkenly for balance.

They meander up the lane to the churchyard. Claire breaks away at the last moment.

'No, I'm sorry. I'm done in. I'm going home. Iris, why don't I walk you home?'

'I'm going to the churchyard with Nick.'

'What if Mrs Camden gets wind of it? Are you sure? You're already in her bad books.' Claire shakes her head at Iris.

'Quite sure,' Iris says in a firmer teacher's voice.

'Well, you're all crazy. Goodnight then everyone.' She walks away, glancing back now and again. Nick is ashamed to feel so relieved she's gone.

Iris Bewley admires the bunch of beech and campion on Richard's grave. 'It must have been Sylvia. I saw her here earlier.'

'What's that purring sound?' Georgie asks.

'It's the nightjars readying themselves to fly. They aren't purring. Their wings are vibrating.'

'The naturalist was obsessed with fern-owls,

which is what he called nightjars, and I think he believed the old stories about them sucking goats for their milk,' David adds. 'If we stay very still and quiet, we might see them rise.'

They wait a moment. The fern-owls don't rise.

Then, Nick says. 'Come on Iris, we're here now. And I'd like you to sing for Dad.'

Iris nods.

'On two?' Nick asks. Iris nods. 'One two, one two.'

'*Early one morning just as the mist was rising, I saw a young maid in the valley below. Oh don't deceive me, oh never leave me. How can you use a poor maiden so?*' Iris's tones are clear and tragic.

'That is so beautiful,' Georgie says.

Iris clears her throat again. David. Tom and Nick join in, and as they do, the vibration of the fern-owls increases. The birds fly up in the moonlight, circling round to catch moths. After each catch, they issue a single note, a tick, that drops like a feather.

'One more time. Just Iris,' Nick whispers.

Mrs Camden hears their voices outside her house, rising above the snoring of her husband. Mr Swallow has left his wife and children and has another family too. He has no right to be carousing in the early hours as if he has no care in the world. A failure, a fallen woman like Miss Bewley, should not be singing drunkenly in the churchyard, and she should not be teaching the village's children.

But it is not the immorality of the people in the lane that cause her to shed tears into her pillow.

David Daunt didn't invite her to the meal, but he invited Iris. It reminds her of her all-girls school where no one wanted to be her friend. She isn't a popular person.

Hardly anyone voted for her at the parish council elections despite so many wanting streetlights.

Miss Adkins hadn't helped by giving a nature talk in the village hall where she had explained, with slides to illustrate, how streetlights affected the mating of glow worms, distorted the activity of moths and insects and so damaged the habits of bats. Flying, feeding and sex would all be affected. And birds would take to singing in the middle of night, not that that seemed too terrible to Mrs Camden, who often lay awake cogitating on why her father disinherited her even though he'd promised not to if she gave up her place at Oxford. Miss Adkins too had behaved dishonourably towards her by using the Natural History Society of Hartisborne as a kind of husting, a week before the election. Even as she listened, Mrs Camden knew she had lost.

The villagers preferred the dark. That's all there was to it, the Colonel said. And nothing to do with her as a person. The Colonel says she wouldn't feel these things so sharply if she had children, but she hates him saying that.

This evening, before she'd knocked on the museum door, she'd wanted to be part of the cakes and ale. If only she had laughed and joked with them instead of complaining about Iris and her dreadful project with Tom Swallow, they would have invited her to stay and eat with them, perhaps in memory of Richard Luckin, who had stroked her hand so provocatively at his party last year.

She creeps to the window and listens. She slips on her slippers and goes downstairs. She knows the vicar's phone number by heart.

'Hartisborne 210.' Once she's announced herself, he snaps, 'I've got an early morning service at the hospital tomorrow. Really, Louise, I think you could leave well alone.'

'But shouldn't you check? You never know what profane things a man like Tom Swallow might get up into the churchyard.'

The vicar rings off, after sullying Mrs Camden's sensitivities with a disgusted sigh.

'Let be, let be,' the colonel murmurs in his sleep.

Wilf wakes in the cave of the yew tree. He sniffs the damp, woody air. He feels as heavy as a log. He puts his hand out to steady himself and pushes it right onto a bramble, but he mustn't squeal or give himself away.

Someone is singing. Beautiful, unearthly singing. Iris Bewley's voice singing that folk song which the school children had sung at last summer's church fete, when Winnie was still alive. Old Bewley's got the words wrong. Why sing 'mist' instead of 'sun'? Why would anyone 'tell the roses'? What a load of bunkum. Last summer, Winnie thought the song too corrupt for children – all about a man doing a woman ill. She had sudden moral flashes. But then women did.

Suddenly the song falls silent. A few hands clap. The little group laughs and then grows quiet. Like them, Wilf listens to the purring of the nightjars' wings, the vibrations and then the uptick sound when a bird catches a moth. He peers between the low yew branches. The midsummer moon lights the graveyard. The group is standing around Richard Luckin's grave, only a row away from Gil's grave. He waits, though his hands are itching to use the spade.

Finally, Nick takes Miss Bewley's arm and walks her out of the graveyard, over the Plestor and turns the corner towards the schoolhouse. Miss Gardner waves them goodbye and runs up the steps to the granary flat. David trots back to the museum. Tom Swallow lights a cheroot and saunters off along the straggling street, a thin trail of smoke rising above his head.

When there is no sign of Nick returning along the street – maybe he's having a nightcap with the teacher or gone off to share the school secretary's bed – behaving just like his father – Wilf eases himself and his tools out from the yew's low canopy and heads towards Gil's grave. Despite the superficial dew of night, the ground is hard. His shovel makes little impact in the grass.

Wilf digs a line around the grave to loosen the turf. The nightjars, his only witnesses, continue to rise, snapping up the moths, keeping up the low vibrato of their wings.

Wilf's hands shake. He is frightened of what Winnie would think and what the village will make of him afterwards. And curious too. Will the skeleton still be there? Will the coffin have disintegrated? Will he be able to leave the bones while he runs down Gracious Street to fetch the Land Rover? His arrangements are flawed. He should have driven the Land Rover back here, but just as well he didn't, or Nick would have seen it.

He visualises the rest of his plan to encourage himself. He will pack the bones into the Co-op box and drive to the coast. To Langston Harbour, Hayling Island or Southsea? He hasn't decided. He'll know when he starts the engine. And then before the sun rises, he'll throw the bones into the sea and drive back to Priory, arriving there before Nick or Tom are awake. He's banking on Tom telling Nick he borrowed the Land Rover to explain its absence when or if Nick goes home. He's on early morning milking duty tomorrow.

Nick won't be surprised to see him. And it'll be some sort of alibi.

Hartisborne will wake and find the naturalist is no more than a hole in the ground. And Wilf will express as much surprise as everyone else. The scenes flit by him as if he is in the cinema, though the reel always breaks in their local fleapit and sometimes the top half of the picture disappears and only legs walk around.

He slices a wedge out of the grass with the spade's tip. He'd started out as a gravedigger, so he knows what to do. It was the wrong job for a fourteen-year-old and a blessed relief when Richard Luckin's father asked for his help on the farm. When the old man died and Richard took over, Wilf stayed on, though they'd never taken to each other. Richard was a fly-by-night, a chancer, a charmer. Not Wilf's type at all.

The moonlight, the nightjars, the moths. The naturalist had described this scene. Wilf read extracts of his work long ago at the village school. He remembers the little black wood engraving of the nightjar that punctuated the pages. His teacher was strict, unlike Miss Bewley. None of them dared play up. The swish of the cane did not endear him to reading or to Gil.

'I'm doing this for you,' he says to Winnie's grave defensively. 'Without bloody tourists coming on bloody pilgrimages to Saint bloody Gil, we can have streetlights, the hotel we wanted, the new houses for locals. There could have been a job for Arthur if he'd come back.' He murmurs on to himself to justify his actions, keeping himself company. 'This is not helping anyone,' Winnie says. Another of her moral flashes. 'A bad deed earns a bad deed,' she used to say.

He has dug a shallow outline round the grave. He leans on the spade and listens to the nightjars. How shocked his old teacher would be if he could see him now. He jabs in the spade and feels the bite of earth. He pushes in harder, concentrating now, trying to get the words of Miss Bewley's song out of his head. He's going to carry this through and forces the spade into the ground, but a hand pats him on the back. 'Wilf, is that you?' He swings around in shock, dropping the spade hard on someone's foot.

# CHAPTER 16

At Wakeling House, Jonathan rubs down the mare and gives her water and hay. Gil takes some refreshment. Men arrive with sticks to beat the undergrowth. Women arrive with blankets and sugary treats for a birthing woman to suck on and aloes to sooth her pain. They run through tracks and dells, meadows and paths, calling, calling, shaking the undergrowth. Gil searches long into the evening. It is just a day after midsummer. The daylight lasts, but there is no Mary.

Next day, Gil sets off to Binford. Mary must be at her mother's.

All along the way he searches for her. Mary is on foot. She left the donkey with Blundel and Deadman. Has she dropped down in exhaustion? Can she even be alive?

In Binford, the philandering vicar is all bonhomie. He doesn't invite Gil in but walks him to the stables, where he asks the shabby youth to see to the mare. 'I know no one by the name of

Trimmer. Are you sure she lives in Binford?'

The shabby youth coughs, startling the tired mare.

'With respect sir, there *is* a Mistress Trimmer.'

'She is not a church goer then or I would have known her.'

Yet, you rarely linger in the parish long enough to give a sermon, Gil thinks.

'She lives in Raven Lane, near the hovels.'

'Oh, with that ungodly lot.'

You should be visiting the hovels, if that's where the poor live. The philanderer doesn't even know his own parishioners. Gil's heart quickens at the chance of Mary's nearness.

'Could you show me the way to Raven's Lane?' Gil asks the youth. 'We'll bring the mare along with us.'

As they walk, Gil questions the youth about Mary. Has she visited lately? Has he seen her? The youth mutters inaudible answers.

Gil forces himself to envisage Mary as an outcast, Mary being hounded across the village bounds to give birth in a ditch, so long as she costs the parish nothing. Mary's baby. Dead or alive? Another idea tortures him. Did she get back from Hartley Plaisir last night and find Luckin at home? Has she fled with a man old enough to be her grandfather? Is it suspicious that they are both absent?

Then Gil is tortured by Arthie's feet again and the toad woman's gentle hands washing them.

For all that the child would be better off in Hartisborne, maybe kindness can be found in Binford too. But birth in Binford will inscribe a life of poverty, vagrancy or migrancy. For what is there here? Mary's baby may turn into another Arthie, exploited and neglected. Maybe it would be better if Luckin were the father after all, if she could just stay in Hartisborne.

And so, Gil forces himself to wish for an answer which wracks him with jealousy and despair.

Barefoot children shout at them as they pass the hovels, until they reach a cottage in good repair. The cottage has a small orchard to one side where chickens peck at the grass. The front garden brims with flowers. Fruiting pears are espaliered low along the path. A hop vine runs over the porch. Neat strips of beds show a variety of vegetables, a frame of cucumbers, a flowering patch of potatoes, rows of lettuce, and at the back bee hives, a compost heap steaming and one melon spreading its tough bending stalk and blooming with orange flowers. Mary must have taken the seeds he gave her and tried out a melon bed here. His lessons have gone home. Mary is right to call her mother a plantswoman. New bean plants twist up sticks. Mary would be safe here with her mother. She would never starve. A great relief descends on him because he had imagined Mary's mother as a ghoul or demon, tormenting her child. And he is ashamed of harbouring this dislike simply because he knew of Mary's mother's hatred of Hartisborne.

'This is Mary's home, is it not?' Gil asks the youth.

'Yes, it is, sir,' he replies.

Even in Binford, a cottager can live a well-nourished life if they have but the lore.

After tying up the mare, the youth knocks on Mary's mother's door. 'Mistress Trimmer,' he calls when there is no answer, 'It's me, Adam.' He turns to Gil. 'Often Mistress Trimmer is stricken and takes to her bed, but not usually in the summer.'

'I can see she is full of industry,' Gil observes.

'Yes,' Adam replies. 'My family would not survive without her. She speaks harsh words, but she would never turn a hungry child away.' Adam shouts at the door, 'Mistress Trimmer, you have a gentleman visitor!'

A woman opens the door. Her hair is in a brown scarf. Her face is weatherbeaten, mapped by lines from working outside. Her hands are leathery and reddened with dirt around the nails. Her sleeves are pushed up. Gil sees the trail of a bramble scratch, the scabs tracing a line along her skin.

'What do you want, Adam?' She asks gruffly. She retreats into the doorway's shadow. He can scarcely see her face. 'I gave your mother a sack of vegetables yesterday. You can't want more already. Get more meat from the vicar's kitchen and give the children that!'

Adam kicks at the path with his head down. For a moment, Gil is shocked. So, Adam steals food from the vicar, and Mary's mother condones this.

'I'm not here on family business,' Adam says, embarrassed. 'This is the vicar of Hartisborne.'

'No, I'm the curate,' Gil corrects him.

'This is the curate of Hartisborne come to see you about Mary.' Adam backs away fearfully.

Mistress Trimmer retires further indoors. 'I've no business with that foul place. Good day to both of you.' She goes to close the door, but Adam rouses himself to block the threshold with his foot.

'Mistress Elizabeth,' he says timidly, 'the reverend gentleman has come about Mary and you should hear him out.'

'Is she here?' Gil asks. 'In her employer's absence, she was wrongly taken to the justice for a settlement examination. She escaped. She is near her time. She is missing. And all of Hartisborne is concerned for her.'

'Is that right?' Mary's mother asks suspiciously.

'She has been wandering around the fishponds, walking the hanger at night, standing for hours to watch the evening swallows. When I saw her yesterday, she had her wits about her, but villagers talk of her as if she has lost them.'

'No doubt they do!' Mary's mother speaks

bitterly. 'Spit gossip at her! I expect no less from Hartisborne.'

Her voice is familiar to Gil. Mary's voice, but older.

'Did you know she is lodging at Priory Farm and working there?' Gil asks her.

'No. I did not know that, sir.' She says it quietly, as if shocked by the news. 'So the employer who has gone away is Farmer Luckin?'

'Yes. He is suspected… ' How to put it? 'The overseer of the poor suspects him of being her child's father.'

'No. No. That cannot be,' she gasps. 'Foolish girl. She only went back to Hartisborne because I would not house her unless she told me the father's name. I would have done of course. It was a moment of anger. The gossip that reached us, sir, suggested you were the father, but I never believed it.'

'Thank you.' What else could he say? He is disappointed. He had felt sure that Mary's mother would know the father's identity. 'In Hartisborne,' he may as well tell her, 'the two candidates for paternity,' - how pompous he sounds – 'are Farmer Luckin and Eddy Kemp.'

'She didn't tell me that.'

'And since Farmer Luckin has protected her, opinion veers towards him.'

'It is foul, disgusting. I told her over and over that it's dangerous to give your heart to a place. But she would keep going back and back, obsessed with your garden, in love with the village. And now he has caught her, defiled her. The very worst and most unnatural thing that could occur. But sir, I fear she has discovered the truth and harmed herself.'

'We are searching for her everywhere. I hoped she was here.'

'I must return with you to find her. There are crannies, roots, dens we knew as children. Don't you remember them, Mr Gil? When we played together? Don't you remember me?'

'You are familiar. I recognise your voice.' And the eyes in the old face seem like the eyes of someone he once knew.

'*Betty, oh Betty, oh Betty, my love*,' she says bitterly.

'You are Betty Hambrook?'

'I married Steven Trimmer, but he died shortly after Mary was born.'

He recoils. Not because she is Betty, his first love. Not because she has aged like a gnarled thorn tree beset by wind on the downs. But because if Mary's child is Luckin's, the child is both Luckin's child and grandchild. If Mary's child is Luckin's, then Luckin has known his own daughter. Luckin would never knowingly commit the sin of incest, would he? Perhaps Mary has discovered the identity of her father and means to do herself harm?

Betty is choking with anger. 'I am full of fear,' she says. 'If I see Farmer Luckin, I will kill him.'

'We must find her.'

'Will your mare take two?' Betty asks.

'The vicar's gelding will bear two,' Adam says. 'I will be back with it in a moment.'

'But will he let you take it?' Gil asks not wanting to waste time.

'I won't ask him,' Adam says. 'He has a London lady staying and will be busy, I expect.'

Within half an hour, Betty is behind Adam on the gelding, and Gil is trotting ahead. There is so much he wants to ask Betty. But when he lists the questions in his head, horror at Mary's plight drives them out. He tells himself and he tells Betty, 'The child may be Eddy Kemp's or that of another man. We have no evidence Luckin is the father.'

Betty doesn't reply. She turns her weatherbeaten face away from him and will speak no more. Just once, she says, when the horses stop to drink from a stream, 'I thought you would have remembered me.'


Nick dallies at Joan's gate, knowing she's due at the pub, timing his visit to cut short reproaches. A strategy worthy of his father.

Joan's terraced cottage is a two-up two-down affair, with an outside toilet next to the woodshed. The cottages share a septic tank, emptied by the council's lavender wagon. He can't be blamed for there being no mains drainage in Hartisborne. Besides, he only charges Joan the same peppercorn rent as his father charged. Eventually, he intends to patch on a bathroom behind Joan's kitchen, but he will need his mother's agreement. It won't be easy. She doesn't like Joan. He hadn't expected his mother to become his business partner and he hates having to vie with her about repairs.

Nick practises a few carefully prepared words before he knocks on Joan's door.

'Hello,' Joan says. 'I'm just off to work, when Sylvia gets here.'

'There's something we need to discuss.'

A look of fear crosses Joan's face. She's almost shaking. 'I don't have time now.' She pulls him into the tiny sitting room. 'How is Wilf doing?'

'Recovering. Please you promised – don't tell anyone what he was going to do. He was in a strange state. The trouble is he can't get over Winnie's death.'

'Of course, I wouldn't tell anyone. You did well by him, by the way.'

'The vicar was surprisingly great-hearted. He agreed to the story about re-turfing and he actually helped me do it. Where's Maisie?' he asks.

'She's down at the church rehearsing her solo with Iris.'

'Oh, good.' Not the right thing to say, but at least she won't hear this. 'Look, I'm sorry to say Mum isn't happy about Maisie's solo.'

'I'm not happy about it either but I don't want to snatch it from her now.'

'I've made a mess of this. Iris said Maisie has a lovely voice.'

'She has,' Joan concedes with a half-smile.

'I was touched by you two visiting Dad before he went. I wanted to include Maisie.'

'I knew your mother would object and if you'd asked me ahead, instead of asking Maisie, I would never have let you invite her to sing. Now she'll be devastated.'

'I know. I'm sorry. I'll tell her if you like. I'll say Mum has changed her mind about the music.'

'But is anyone else singing a solo?'

'Yes, there is someone, but it's not a child.'

'We can say that then. She wanted a grown-up to sing solo. The music is too difficult for a child – something like that. Who is it anyway?'

Better not to say. 'Will she be very upset?

'What do you think? She's told all her friends at school.  Now they're going to say she was lying. Anyway, she'll be excited about being a bridesmaid.'

'Mum doesn't want her to be a bridesmaid or to come to the wedding.'

'She's going to be devastated. And it's all your fault.'

'Everything about this wedding is going wrong,' Nick says. 'It's right against nature for me to be organising it.'

'Oh, poor you! Think of Maisie. Everyone will

go past our house in their wedding clothes. It's going to be horrible for her. And then she'll see the reception across the road. And other children prancing about, having a lovely time.'

'What if I give you a tenner to take her out somewhere?'

Joan's eyes are blazing. 'There's no need to insult me.'

'Trying to make up for my mistake,' Nick says desperately. 'I don't want Maisie to be unhappy.'

'I'll cancel my shift at the pub and take her on a picnic. Just the two of us left out as usual.'

'Georgie's not going either,' Nick says.

'Maybe she can come with us? Make it a bit more interesting? And then Maisie will know other people were left out too.'

'I'll mention it to Georgie, if you like.'

There's a knock at the door.

'Come in, Sylvia, it's open,' Joan calls.

Sylvia steps in.

'Nick's really ruined things for Maisie,' she tells Sylvia immediately. 'She's going to be so disappointed.'

'I knew this singing a solo malarkey was a bad idea,' Sylvia mutters.

'I wish you'd told me that,' Nick says.

'When your dad died, I thought you'd see what's what.'

Even Sylvia is turning against him.

'I've got to go to work,' Joan says hastily. 'Goodbye Nick.' She pushes him out in front of her. Then turns to Sylvia. 'Maisie will be home soon. Please don't say anything until I've thought how to break it to her.'

Nick crosses the road with her, unwilling to part on bad terms. 'This bloody wedding isn't easy for me either, you know.'

'Oh, poor little Nick. Take the blindfold off.'

Joan opens the pub door with such force that it swings back and forth, as if the ghosts of Hartisborne are following her in one by one, crowding the bar and taking her part.

Maisie is skipping towards Nick along the cobbles. He bolts into the Land Rover and drives off before she can say hello. He can see her in the rear-view mirror, happy and important, bouncing up the steps to the cottage. The thought of hurting her is awful. He can't understand why he's so upset about it. But it's the most terrible thing. Tears prick his eyes all the way back to the farm.

Fortunately, he won't have to face Wilf, as he is off sick for a few days suffering the aftermath of his attempted grave robbery. If someone hadn't tipped off the vicar – the vicar won't tell him who – if Nick hadn't been walking back late from Iris's, Wilf would have committed a crime.

Once home, Nick opens a bottle of beer and sits at his mother's flaking table. He wants to tell someone about the whole Maisie business. He could tell Claire, but he wants to tell Georgie. Is this what Joan meant about him being like his father? Weighing up relationships with two different women?

The quacking of ducks on the pond fills his head like the monks' crazy laughter. After the wedding, he'll make it up to Maisie somehow, if Joan will let him.

# CHAPTER 17

Sylvia tries her suffragette brooch on her summer coat. The coat is new. Her daughter-in-law made it from a Vogue pattern. It was nice she was invited and only right, her daughter-in-law said, considering all the years Sylvia looked after Nick. For once, her daughter-in-law is on her side. She and Sylvia went to the haberdashers and chose the purple, white and green fabric. The brooch looks well on it. The coat hangs beautifully and has a swing. Her daughter-in-law is a good needlewoman. 'It's perfect for you, Mother,' she'd said in a moment of warmth, 'because it's timeless. And you can carry it off with your height. It's perfect for a wedding.'

Sylvia uncovers the mirror and looks at herself in its dusty length. The coat is more distinctive than anything Mrs Camden wears. She tuts at herself for vanity, persuading herself that she's wearing the coat for Nick. He needs his people there, she thinks. The village is divided between him and Marilyn, as it is divided between those who want the street lighting and those who prefer the straggling street to stay dark. Traitors, Wilf would say, traitors, stuck in the past, people like herself, who didn't vote Mrs Camden onto the parish council.

Marilyn Luckin has latterly become a streetlight supporter. She never liked Wilf in the past, but Sylvia observes Marilyn playing him along. Sylvia is suspicious of Marilyn and even more so of the silent Dick. Yet she will go to their wedding, for Nick's sake, of course.

She works at her long white hair and manages a heavy French pleat. In the mirror, she looks like someone who counts, a glamourous older woman wedding guest. She laughs aloud at her own pretensions.

With Colonel Camden's consent, the museum garden has supplied all the flowers for Marilyn Luckin's wedding. Yesterday, Miss Adkins, the retired florist, picked the carnations and took them to her cold pantry to form into Marilyn's bouquet. Georgie resents the depleted beds. She is sure Marilyn and certainly Dick can afford florist's flowers. A bare garden will be of no appeal to the museum's visitors. Yesterday, after Miss Adkins' visit, the flower arranging ladies picked all the sweet peas, stocks and peonies for the windowsills, the pews, the arch of the church porch.

Everyone is busy putting on glad rags and wrapping wedding presents, everyone except Iris Bewley, Joan, Maisie and Georgie. Nick came round last week, drunk and sullen, to regale her with the story of Maisie's disappointment and to tell her she was disinvited too. Georgie hadn't even wanted to go but being disinvited reminded her of forbidden pleasures, like Marco's fortieth birthday party, when Trevor wouldn't let her leave the house. And she'd feared having to stay in with Trevor forever.

She'd imagined dancing with Nick at the reception, but she shouldn't because of Claire. She doesn't want to be a shallow person without clear feelings and loyalties. Maybe it is better she isn't going to the wedding. She likes Claire and doesn't want to hurt her, just as she had liked Celia. So, what had she been doing with Marco? She doesn't know. She doesn't know herself at all. Sometimes she thinks her only authentic identity is as a reader of *The Natural History of Hartisborne*.

Georgie savours the cool air in the little parlour, the scent of last week's stocks, fading in their jug. If it's a quiet day in the museum, she will catch up on her reading. Weeks ago, Marco sent her a book via Tom. It was the first she'd heard from him, though Tom lets slip hints of gossip. She touches the parcel sometimes. And now she opens it. It is *Silent Spring* by Rachel

Carson, a good choice. She reads all sorts of messages into the title as if Marco is explaining his silence. But she knows the book is bigger than that and she's going to read it today while the village celebrates without her.

She can't resist watching Wilf driving the wedding party to the church in the Luckins' old-fashioned cart. From the upstairs landing window, she sees the bridesmaids piled on the back, and once everyone is in the church, she will go downstairs and open the book. She hopes there will be a note inside with a few warm words, 'with love from Bracco & March' or 'all my love, M.' or 'missing you, M'. Her mind leaps ahead to how she will respond.

She puts the book on the desk. Someone is rattling the door handle even though the museum isn't open yet. She unbolts the door. It's Tom looking skew-whiff in his suit, a few paint splatters on his roll-ups, his tie awry and his glasses blurred with fingerprints. He has evidently tried to brush his hair, because it's bristling up from one side of a make-shift parting. 'Got a carnation?' he asks.

They go into the garden.

'Hey!' David shouts from the upstairs window – 'that's my carnation.'

'Would a rose do?' Georgie asks Tom.

'A rose by any other name would smell as sweet,' he says. 'But you only have pink ones?'

'There are some crimson damask roses

through the archway,' she says, leading the way to the beds of the six quarters.

She catches up with David in the kitchen. Nev Pearson is there in his suit and medals, looking quite handsome. Romilly is wearing a twin set and pearls with a wide headband over her perm. David gives up his carnation to Nev.

'I can get you a rose like Tom's,' Georgie says.

'Well, Nev is going to be in the spotlight after all,' David says. David is being nice, pandering to Nev's damaged ego, Georgie thinks.

'Now Captain Pearson,' Romilly says, as she puts the carnation in his lapel, 'you stay calm and take deep breaths. Do you understand?'

Nev nods, looking glassy.

'Time to go,' David says. As usher, he must be there an hour early.

'Yes, come along Captain Pearson,' Romilly says. 'You'll feel better when you get there.' And the three of them leave Georgie in the kitchen to make a lonely cup of stir-up before opening the museum.

She can hear the bell captain ringing the bells up ready for the peal. The wedding is at twelve and whether anyone likes it or not, she's going to close the museum sharply at one and go on the picnic with Joan and Maisie, even though the museum should be open in the afternoon. Visitors will have to lump it.

The stuffed blackbird looks alert. She takes her copy of *Hartisborne* and slips out the wedding photograph. As usual, she can't find anyone resembling Connie. The wedding in the photo looks rather grand with so many bridesmaids, bouquets and suits. She has never considered the organisation involved until now. Nick has been weighed down by arrangements, constantly complaining and in a panic. Someone organised this wedding too. Someone knew all the guests, addressed invitations, paid for dresses, provided flowers. The bride and groom spoke to a vicar, chose hymns, argued about who to invite and somewhere some of these people must still exist and know Georgie's history.

She studies the photograph again and sighs. 'Gil, I know you better than these people,' she tells the shadow in the little parlour. 'I don't even know who they are.' Even this dead stuffed blackbird, eternally keen-eyed and ready to pounce, knows his part in the world better than she does.

Sylvia is early to the church. David gives her a prayer book and order of service and steers her towards the groom's side. 'The groom isn't bringing many friends, so we've been asked to divide Marilyn's guests on both sides.'

The window ledges spill with flowers. The pillars are wound with ivy and new green hops. A branch of wisteria trails under the stained-glass bird window, commemorating Gil. The scent of summer pervades the cold stone.

From here, Sylvia will have a good view of Nick once he's walked his mother down the aisle. Dick whatshisname is already here, waiting for his bride in his morning suit, his top hat resting on the pew. The members of The Pipe Barrel are here in their best gear. As she cranes round, Sylvia glimpses their instrument cases stowed under pews. They were friends with Marilyn in the old days, though they had taken Richard's side in the split. Sylvia darts them a challenging glance – *you'd better behave*. Lou and Eddy wink back at her.

She sits two pews back next to Miss Clifford and Miss Finch. Sylvia's brooch catches the light as it did on that walk home with mud splattered down her white dress, and her father shouting at her, as he forced her into Priory Farm cottage.

'Mum is not lesser than you,' she yells at her drunken dad. 'Leave her alone.' And when the punch comes for her instead of her mother, right into her gut, she is winded and sick, but something grows within, like the violets on the brooch, gleaming, separate, refusing to be beaten. And when he'd come in for a second punch, he'd hurt his knuckle on the brooch.

'Nick's so glad you agreed to come,' Claire Clifford whispers, squeezing her arm. Her eyes flick over Sylvia's clothes. 'What a lovely coat.'

'That's an interesting brooch,' Miss Finch adds.

'Yes, it's a…'

To Sylvia's disappointment, the two young women look away and scan the church for people who interest them more. It's what happens as you age, Sylvia tells herself.

There are raised voices by the door. She turns and sees David arguing with a stranger. The man wants to come in and is muttering about his *effing niece, right to be there, bloody, pardon my language, realises he's in church, bloody cheek, give her away, should have been asked.*

'This is the wedding of Mrs Marilyn Luckin to Mr Richard Ellingham. Georgie isn't even invited,' David murmurs as quietly and firmly as he can.

The guests rustle excitedly, peering round at the altercation. David's efforts to make the stranger leave are useless until Eddy and Lou of The Pipe Barrel grab him and march him out, telling him not to swear in church. Pot and kettle comes to mind.

Louise Camden has enjoyed dressing up. As a friend of Marilyn's, she has a pew near the front and for once is proud of Colonel Camden and his medals. To her surprise – it is a rare thing - she realises she is happy – and all because of Wilf and what happened after his attempt to dig up the naturalist's bones.

Thanks to you, the vicar said, I was able to avert a major tragedy. He'd said this at three in the morning, when he hammered on Mrs Camden's door and asked her if she could make Wilf some cocoa and help him sober up.

The vicar was limping when he and Nick walked Wilf round to her house. Both men came in and laid him on her sofa. Nick stunk of wine. Wilf stunk of beer. The vicar simply had bad breath from being woken in the early hours.

Mrs Camden – do call me Louise she'd said – made them all cocoa and gave them each a slice of cake. Of course, if she had won the parish council election back in May, Wilf wouldn't have been driven to such extremes. Part of her admired him. Such passion and determination. Such love and grief.

So dramatic too. To be called on secretly. To be useful. To be trusted.

'I know I can trust you, Louise. None of us must breathe a word of this,' the vicar said.

So that's why he hadn't woken his own wife, Mrs Camden realised. Susie is such a gossip.

'Yes,' Nick had added. 'Wilf mustn't be blamed. It's just grief playing tricks on him.'

'Quite,' the vicar said. 'And it's not like he'd ever do anything like this again.'

'I'm going back to the naturalist's grave to rough up the grass,' Nick said. 'I'll make it look like badgers.'

They agreed that this was for the best. The Colonel woke and came downstairs. He poured them all a brandy and they sat like friends around Mrs Camden's coffee table, forgiving in their conspiracy.

Afterwards, when Nick had taken Wilf home and the vicar had gone too, the colonel said to Mrs Camden, 'What a marvellous woman you are. You did all the right things, you know. And if you hadn't phoned the vicar, Wilf would be in terrible trouble now. He'd be ostracised by all the neighbours. And quite apart from breaking the law, he'd never really recover inside himself from behaving against nature.'

They stayed up till dawn and ate breakfast in the garden early, each remembering why they married the other.

Mrs Camden secretly thought, 'And if Iris Bewley hadn't been singing in the churchyard, Wilf would never have been discovered.' Perhaps a wrong thing could lead to a right thing. Perhaps she had been too hard on Iris, even on Tom. This thought didn't last long.

But it flashes up now and again, like here in the congregation, where they are waiting for Wilf to deliver Marilyn in the pony cart and then take his place at the back of the church. She turns to see the bride balancing on sling-back stilettoes as she advances up the aisle in her white suit, with its frankly too short skirt and too modern hat, a pill box of petals with a white net veil pulled over her eyes. Wilf slips into the back pew, and Mrs Camden half raises her hand in a wave.

Nev Pearson is to sing a solo. The vicar advised him to see sense, but Nick, wanting to make his lie true for Maisie's sake, insisted Marilyn agree to Nev's solo. Now Romilly and Colonel Camden smile at him encouragingly. Louise Camden grips her hymn book. She hopes the Captain won't let the Colonel down. He really is her husband's cross. Yet they both have to bear it.

Nev climbs onto the step below the altar rail. He faces the congregation. It isn't just me, Mrs Camden thinks. They're all holding their breath, expecting him to mess up. The younger Kemps nudge each other, whether in support or critique, she's not sure. David Daunt had a valid point. Nev never does anything right.

The organist begins. Nev coughs, gasps and dries up. The organist stops playing. There is an awkward pause. 'Could you play me in again?' Nev says calmly.

Louise has never heard him sing before. Ave Maria, pure, deep, powerful. No one moves.

No wonder Nev likes Schubert, David thinks.

Trust Mum to get so much more than she deserves, Nick thinks. Maisie wasn't up to this. But he feels a horrible pang for her.

*There is a heaven in us all, however flawed we are.* Inspired by Nev and his singing, the vicar surreptitiously notes this idea for a sermon with a stub of pencil he keeps in his cassock.

Apart from the organist who had rehearsed privately with Nev, only Colonel Camden is unsurprised. He knew this voice in the desert, at the unit's chapel in the camp near Tunis, at the impromptu funerals of their men. The dead come back to him, their young faces dirtied by sand, their bodies thin from dysentery, or yellow from jaundice. He takes out his handkerchief and mops his eyes surreptitiously.

Here he is, at home in peaceful Hartisborne, a place he once thought he would never see again, and where Nev, with all his passionate musical being apparently lost in anecdotes, has found his voice at last. The stained-glass birds in the window seem to sing too as they hop around on St Francis of Assisi's arm.

The young, he thinks, one must be on the side of the young, even muddlers like David and Nick. The young must have the chance which so many of his men never had. And even the middle-aged, he thinks, eying Marilyn's get-up and her impassive groom, are young inside and must have their second chance. He remembers when he and Nev were young, and what they'd felt for each other, but that is quite another story and something they both put aside long ago. All that is left is this, the music of suffering in praise of survival.

# CHAPTER 18

Gil and Betty say nothing on the journey. Gil leads the way, and Adam and Betty follow on the gelding. He takes the woodland route as shorter and, after a few fields, they see Hartisborne below them, almost hidden in the crease of its valley, with only the square church tower and a few roofs from the taller houses visible. Tired though the poor creature is, his mare shows excitement at nearing home. They pause on the ridge, looking around them, as if Mary may appear at any moment.

Then Betty speaks, 'I have not been here since soon after Mary's birth. I'd forgotten how Hartisborne casts its spell, making you want to stay forever, however people behave. It's as dangerous to fall in love with a place as with a person.'

'You speak true, Mistress Trimmer,' Gil says. He no longer has the right to call her Betty.

They take the short cut across the Ewell field, up Gracious Street, down the High Street and arrive at his stables. Thomas and young Jonathan come out to meet them.

'Good afternoon, Betty. It is many years since I saw you,' Thomas says.

'Good afternoon, Tom,' Betty says. 'What news of my girl?'

'On the way back from Hartley Plaisir, she told Mr Blundel she needed to do her business. They let her down from the donkey. And she wandered further and further into the bushes looking for a private place. She did not return.'

'She gave them the slip?' Betty says proudly.

'She did. And now there's no sign of her. Blundel's man took the dogs up there, but they didn't find a scent.'

'We will see Mr Blundel now,' Gil says. 'Is he at home?'

'I believe he returned a little while ago. Ollie was spying and heard all that I have reported to you.'

Blundel is in his yard, surrounded by skins of half-tanned leather. Gil plucks a sprig of mint on his way in and holds it to his nose. The ripe smell of untanned hides revolts him. But his current nausea has deeper reasons.

'Good day, Mr Blundel.'

Blundel nods. He is as sour as his hides. 'I am busy, your Reverend,' he says.

'I hear that you harassed Mistress Mary Trimmer all the way home from Hartley Plaisir and then you lost her.'

'I did nothing illegal. '

'You know the groaning is due.'

'And there was no need for all your force,' Betty says. 'She was born here, and you very well know it. You must remember her birth.'

'You have no proof, woman.'

'I am her mother and gave birth to her here in Hartisborne. What better witness could you have?' Betty says.

'I would not have recognised you, Betty Hambrook. Age changes a woman so.'

Betty does not flinch. 'What have you done with my girl? If you have interfered with her, I will kill you.'

'She's the one putting her own child in danger. I hope she will not do away with it. There are laws against that.'

'Why would she harm her child? Mary loves all living and natural things,' Gil says. 'We must bring her safely to the birthing chamber.'

'You speak as if she were a fine lady with a birthing chamber, no less.'

'A birthing chamber has been got ready,' Gil says. 'And once there, she will be in safe hands. But where exactly did you lose her? What was her physical state? Was she in labour?'

'I lost her at the turning towards Binford.'

'I understand you, sir. I see your plan. You were taking her to Binford? To give birth there? Knowing she was so close to the groaning? And then her child would be born in Binford with no cost to Hartisborne.'

'I knew not if she was in labour, but she was mightily puffed and breathing with little moans.'

'The groaning has started then,' Betty says. 'Stay away from my girl, or I will take you to the magistrate for your ill-treatment.' She shakes her strong fist at Blundel.

'Come, we must find Mary and leave Mr Blundel to his conscience,' Gil says. 'And later to the law.'

A cloud of dislike crosses Blundel's face. 'I'm surprised you care so much about Mary Trimmer when all your study is of birds and bees,' he says. 'I might think the rumours true about a certain curate and his weeding woman if I didn't know the more monstrous truth, that her own father has been busy on her body. And her child, if it survives – let's hope it does not - will be made from an incestuous seed. An abomination.'

'Did you tell her that?' Betty asks.

'I may have,' Blundel replies.

Blundel must have taunted Mary with this all the way back from the JP and the pointless interrogation, pushing her to abandon Hartisborne, maybe to abandon the child.

'Only Mary knows who the father of her child is,' Betty says but the hope in her voice is faint.

They start away. Gil turns back and shouts, 'You sir are not fit for your post. Your actions are unlawful. It is I who will be taking you to the justice next time.'

'Oh, I'm not concerned. When your fire dies, you'll be happier watching ants than prosecuting me. Do your worst. Stamp your little foot, sir. I'm not afraid of idlers, who produce nothing.'

Blundel knows where to aim the barb. All the years Gil has been writing his book and yet there is no book. To the Hartisborne villagers with their hard physical lives, he must appear a daydreamer, a slowcoach propped up by rents and his curacy. A small man busy doing nothing.

Betty and Gil take the bostal path, puffing up the hill both calling Mary's name. Now they will have to follow the path back to Binford, where there is no doctor, no mid-wife and only the toad doctoress to help her through her pain. But surely Mary can't have gone far? And she knows the secret paths and shortcuts back to Hartisborne. Gil sends Adam to Wakeling House to tell Thomas to put out a new alarum. And gradually the denizens of Hartisborne join them, till the hill is echoing with their shouts and the understory is alive with their sticks.

When Betty and Gil reach the top of the hill, they lean for a moment on the wishing stone. From the top of the zigzag, they see Goody Sally Newton, climbing as fast as she can to meet them, but it will be impossible for Goody to arrive in Binford in time to help Mary.

The wedding is over. Georgie can see the guests

coming along the street now, and there's Wilf driving the cart to take Marilyn and Dick the short distance to The Compasses. Confetti catches in Marilyn's spotty veil and Dick's top hat. She can see Sylvia on the Plestor talking to neighbours.

Sylvia looks distinguished, her white hair up in a stylish pleat, her Vogue coat flaring out and a brooch catching the light. Georgie shuts the museum early. But she waits till most of the wedding guests are safely in The Compasses. Only Sylvia is lingering, perhaps reluctant to go into the pub when she doesn't drink. Sylvia's son tries to persuade her, but she shakes her head and points up to the hanger.

They stay chatting as Georgie locks the museum door, hangs up the sign and heads out with the box of chocolates for Maisie in her bag, walking towards the path up to the hanger. She waves at John Kemp and Sylvia and hurries along, as if to say *I don't care about being left out*.

Joan and Maisie will be at the wood pond in the clearing. Georgie takes the zigzag path at a pace. She's walked it so often now that her legs are stronger, her body knows the way. Half-way up by the metal strutted bench she pauses to look at the famous view of the village.

Nick and David are down there in the pub. Better to think of Gil, walking up here too. She'll pretend he is with her pointing out flowers and animals in a calm gentle voice, just-as she'd imagined him as a child, when she felt excluded. To walk herself into a better state of mind, she'll take the longer route through the Echoing Field to the Clearing and try to blot out the sounds of The Pipe Barrel tuning up and the hectic chatter of villagers enjoying themselves.

The scowling man who interrupted the service is knocking on the museum door. 'It's closed,' Sylvia calls out. He nods curtly. Then he spots something and hurries on. Sylvia follows at a discreet distance. She's going up the hanger anyway and, so it seems, is he. Ahead she can just see Georgie's head.

When Georgie pauses to look at the view, the man slows and moves out of sight behind the bushes. Sylvia pauses too. He must be following Georgie. He's a mutterer and a huffer, breathing words she can't quite hear. He hasn't noticed Sylvia because he looks up not down, urging himself on as if he's chasing Georgie but hiding from her. Sylvia can hear his heavy, laboured breathing.

From below in the village, there's a round of applause, the sound of a drum and fiddle, and a dog yowling in protest. For a moment, Sylvia has a pang. She could be sitting at a table chatting to her neighbours with a glass of lemonade. Joan's brother is in The Pipe Barrel and Maisie's cousins are no doubt running around, eating up the sausage rolls and cake, while Maisie is left out. Loyalty to Joan and Maisie spurs her on. They will be waiting for her by the pond with rugs spread on the grass.

Sylvia looks up. Unexpectedly, Georgie turns left instead of taking the track on the right towards the clearing. The man turns left too, not pausing to look at the view of the South Downs but huffing on after Georgie towards the Echoing Field.

Goody Newton catches up with them. She leans on the wishing stone. The woods halloo with Mary's name.

'Oh Sally, Mr Blundel has upset my girl with a terrible tale,' Betty tells her.

Goody hugs Betty. 'It's alright Betty, we'll find her. Did she tell you the father's name?'

'No, she wouldn't. I thought she was protecting some weakly youth but maybe she couldn't bear to tell me such a terrible truth?'

A small blue butterfly alights on the bramble flower. Gil dislikes himself for noticing, living up to Blundel's disdainful view of him. Goody must have always known that Betty is Mary's mother. Why didn't she tell him?

Before they can make further plans, Goody says, 'Who is that strange woman along the path? I see her oftentimes, but she never answers to my greeting.'

'I see her too,' Gil says. The young lady of the campions is looking at him, through him.

'She wants us to follow,' Goody says.

'Hark,' Betty says.

They all listen.

'Can you hear it?' Betty asks.

'It's the groaning,' Goody says. 'Mary must be in the Echoing Field.'

She is not in Binford then but has outwitted Blundel. Her child will be born in Hartisborne. The groans echo over the view. The searchers pause in their hallooing to hear the screams of a woman.

Betty, Gil and Goody start to run. The village searchers begin to run too. They squeeze through the nettled gap into the Echoing Field.

Of course, he has no responsibility for her now, fucking bitch. She'll be sponging off another fool now, with a big house and land, a farmer, bob's your uncle, that's what she went away for to feather her nest, to marry money. If Connie was alive, she'd be excited about the wedding, but she'd be worried about the birth certificate, and he knows really it's his own fault. He wouldn't let up about Connie being a bit of whore before he knew her. And now she's dead. Fucking fool.

For years, she'd wanted Georgie back from Cornwall and he'd stopped her. For what though? The reasons are hazy now. Affording a child. Fear of himself. Fear that people would think she was his little bastard. And then, when he agreed, on condition Georgie was never to know who her mother was, he was surprised by the power of a child's presence, the questions she asked, the way she watched them. And the bloody mess. 'Children aren't born tidy,' Connie would say to him. And he wishes she were here to say it to him now. The house is so empty. Cooking doesn't do it itself. Thought the little bitch would look after him after all he'd done for her. But she was never grateful. Leaving the warehouse. Defying him. Staying out nights.

And there she is, her hair bouncing round these bloody zigzag bends – what idiot thought up this fucking path  - no idea who she is, a little bastard, thinks she's the bees' knees and that those stiffs in the wedding photograph are her relatives. She always thought she was above him and Connie because of that. He'd waited for this moment to have the last laugh. But now it doesn't seem so funny.

Anytime she could go to Somerset House and find out who she really is. So, he may as well give it to her. He'd thought she'd need a birth certificate to register the banns. But now he sees she was lying. The wedding was someone else's, an old bint by the look of her, mutton dressed as lamb, and a sap of a bloke he wouldn't trust with ninepence.

And she wasn't there. They didn't want her.

Maybe they found out she was a bastard or didn't like her as he'd never liked her, had he? He thinks of the panic of her getting away, when the Cornish lot came for her and a great fear came over him of losing her, though he would never admit it to anyone.

Farmer Luckin on his horse, pauses at the field's edge. Yes, those are his daughter's cries. She is in labour. A strange fearful joy possesses him as he urges his horse on. Two old women are crouching beside Mary. Goody, and another he doesn't recognise. They are pulling the girl to her knees and hooking up her skirts. He rides nearer.

'Get away with you, Mr Luckin - and you, Mr Gil,' Goody says. 'This is women's business. Tell them all to go home.'

Gil hurries away as Mary's groaning echoes down to the village. He urges the villagers to turn back and thanks them for their efforts.

What is the echo saying? 'One two, one two,' Mary must be counting her pangs as birthing women do. Or is it 'Wonder, Wonder'? Some villagers hear the word as 'wonder' and some as 'monster' depending on their views. Or is she saying, Songster, songster. Youngster, youngster. Or yonder? The echo goes on, guessing at her words and the hill rings with 'songster, youngster, wonder' according to the ears of each listener.

As Gil hurries to turn away the searchers, he sees the strange woman watching some dragonflies. They are dancing, mating, their turquoise lines shifting and floating between him and her. 'How are you, madam?' he asks. But she doesn't answer. She never does. Today though, she looks him straight in the eyes and murmurs something he can't quite hear before she moves on. He can't stop for her because he sees Luckin on his horse on the ridge. He trots after him calling his name. The reprobate will not escape him this time.

'I have a question for you,' Gil shouts.

The farmer slows his horse.

'What is it about?'

'Your daughter,' Gil says. 'I know Mary is your daughter. What on earth have you done?'

# CHAPTER 19

Georgie has imagined him so strongly that she can hear the swish of his body against the grasses, the soft pull as he detaches his clothes from a bramble, even his breathing heaving after her. She assumed he would be light of foot, soft of breath or trotting on his mare, as she'd envisaged him on that wet day a few weeks ago. Instead, there's all this heaviness, effort and huffing moving up behind her.

She decides not to look round and spoil her illusion. She knows how they will meet each other's gaze – over a butterfly or a bird or an adder flitting through the grass or a dragonfly, a thin turquoise line tracing curves over a pond. Only when they are both observing nature, do their gazes meet. She will wait for that sense of recognition. She won't spoil it by hurrying or turning or nipping her own vision in the bud.

When she has experienced Gil's presence, she'll hasten along to Maisie and Joan and share her cake with them. Suddenly the mood takes her to shout out to the naturalist now for she is at the base of the Echoing Field. She calls, 'Gil, are you here?' 'You here?' the echo replies. 'Where are you?' she calls. 'Are you?' the echo asks. The echo goes on echoing. 'Are you here? Are you here?' There are sounds like foxes mating, breathing, agonies of pain, a cat fight perhaps. Has her shouting disturbed a wounded animal?

She hurries on towards the top of the field and looks down. There's a man at the bottom. Not Gil. 'Come here now,' he shouts. 'Here now,' the echo calls. 'Now'. Georgie starts to run. And the man, huffing hard, runs after her as she takes a short cut to the clearing through a tunnel of hawthorn and hazel, slipping along in the mud, but still hearing that rasping breath. And that voice of nightmares returns, a voice she can never escape, here it is, 'you effing little bitch, you effing little tart.'


Sylvia is caught by a bramble. She doesn't want to spoil the Vogue coat and so pauses to unpick the thorns carefully. A couple of pulled threads. She should never have worn it here. Her daughter-in-law will be disappointed in her.

She loses sight of Georgie and the man. Oh, why did she put her coat first? Vanity, vanity. All is vanity. She hurries on to the Echoing Field, where she hears soft thuds like a pony cantering on muddy grass, and then voices. 'She must be here, I'm sure,' a woman says.

Up ahead, Sylvia sees a girl lying on the grass, groaning with pain, her golden hair matted with sweat. It is the girl Sylvia often sees in the woods, flitting between the trees or walking with the bee-boy. 'Hold on. I'll be with you in a second,' Sylvia calls. 'In a second' the echo says, as Sylvia runs uphill to the girl.

'Mother,' the girl calls. 'I am to be moved on, but I cannot move. I must stay here forever.'

'Forever?' the echo calls. A man and woman walk towards the girl.

'I see her now, Betty,' he says.

'Yes,' the woman says. 'I see her too.'

Before they reach her, the huffing man runs past them muttering. Then they vanish as if he has erased them. Sylvia scans the field, but they are gone. And the man, who reminds her of her father, has got away and is chasing after Georgie. The past has distracted her and left Georgie vulnerable.

A breeze blows through the trees, a great breath among the green beeches, creating a shower of beech nuts which sting Sylvia as she runs after Georgie.

Ahead in the clearing, Georgie can see Joan's red tartan rug and Maisie laying out food. 'I'm here,' she calls to Maisie and Joan, waving and running along the uneven ground made muddy by horses' hooves. Bees buzz in the bramble flowers. A wild honeysuckle emits its sweet scent along the dappled sunny walk. Maisie and Joan wave back. Then, Maisie comes running to meet her. Such a relief.

Georgie puts her bag down and opens her arms wide for Maisie to run into. She swings her round and round. They're both laughing and dizzy. Joan is arranging food on the rug. Georgie dares to glance back at the path. He's gone then. It must be her imagination playing tricks, just like it does when she imagines Gil. Her fear following her. Of course, it wasn't Trevor. He doesn't even know where she is. And of course, it wasn't Gil. How could it be?

Georgie takes the chocolate box from her bag and puts it on the rug, made lumpy by low thistles.

'Should we wait for Sylvia?' she asks Joan and Maisie.

'Yes, let's,' Maisie says.

'Have some lemonade,' Joan says. 'You look hot.'

'I came via the Echoing Field. It's crazy but I felt like someone was following me.'

'It can happen up here,' she says. Then, looking at her daughter, she adds, 'Maybe we shouldn't speak about it.'

'I know about the Echoing Field,' Maisie says. 'We talk about it at school.'

'It's just an echo,' Georgie says.

'Angela and Jenny say it's the ghost of a

woman having a baby,' Maisie says matter of factly.

'Perhaps we shouldn't go into it,' Joan says, looking uneasily at Georgie, who is sorting through her bag for the pack of cards. She leans over and whispers, 'Haven't told her the facts of life yet.'

'Everyone knows about that,' Maisie says. 'Anyway, I've seen a cow calving at Nick's.'

Before Georgie can deal the cards, the man comes into sight.

'Getting married to a farmer Rosemary says, without telling me, asking me, what would your aunt, not really that, thought you should know, you might have children, you might need – information – but not true - was it, you little liar?'

'Nick? You're going to marry Nick?'

'No, no. I didn't say Nick, actually.'

'Bleeding little liar.'

'Don't talk to Georgie like that and don't talk like that in front of my daughter,' Joan says.

'Georgie's a bleeding little liar, and I'll say so if I want,' Trevor says.

Maisie repeats 'little liar' in a sing-song voice.

Trevor glares at her. 'Can't you keep your brat quiet?'

Joan steps in front of Maisie. 'Get lost,' she tells Trevor.

Sylvia hears their voices from along the path. She's taken a shortcut through the brambles despite her coat. She sees the huffing man now. She knows his type.

'Hey, you,' she calls out to Trevor. 'You leave these girls alone.'

'Come on, Georgie, on your feet. I'm taking you home,' Trevor says.

'I'm not coming.'

'Yes, you are, you selfish bitch. I came along in good faith to give you what you needed but I see you're the same old liar you ever were. You're not getting married, are you? So, you're coming home with me, you effing little bitch.'

He has her by the shoulders, his forehead almost banging against Georgie's head. She is frozen like she was in the old days. *An effing little coward.*

'No!' Sylvia says. She runs at him, her white hair flying out of its pleat, the Vogue coat flapping. She pulls his hands off Georgie. His face is like the monks' faces, the faces of the men in her time-slip visions. His face is Sylvia's father's face. His eyes have that same grainy look.

Then she shakes him. She will shake the hate out of him. She is stronger than she thought. 'Don't touch her,' she says. 'You must never ever hurt her.' She shakes him with a rage that has brewed for decades. She doesn't know whether she's talking about Georgie, her mother or her sister. He tries to fight back, but his breathing is too fast. He is sweating. His grip is weak.

Joan shouts, 'Stop it, Sylvia. Stop it.'

She tries to pull Sylvia away and as Sylvia lets go, the man falls to the ground.

'Is he dead?' Maisie asks. 'Have you killed him? He looks dead.'

Georgie leans down and loosens his tie, strips off his jacket and starts to pump at his heart.

'Trevor,' she calls, 'come on, think of Connie.' She is crying though she never loved him. His groans seem magnified, caught in the echoing field before they float down to the village with her sobs.

'What have I done?' Sylvia asks. 'What have I done?

At the reception, Nick steps into the pub garden. A big table has been laid under a canopy, the top table where he will sit with Marilyn and Dick. He will have to make a speech, the last thing he wants to do.

Eddy, The Pipe Barrel's fiddle player, winks at him. Well, his mother wanted country dancing and she's going to get it but not before he's made his ruddy speech.

The caller arrives and sets up in the shade of the sycamore tree, while village children, all except Maisie, Nick thinks bitterly, dart under the tunnel of low-hanging tablecloths.

He hopes Joan and Maisie are well out of earshot, though sound travels up the zigzag when the village rings with music. Oh dear, poor Maisie, and it's all his fault. Why does his mother have to victimise people so.

Nick unfolds his speech. He had difficulty writing it and stayed up late in the farmhouse kitchen with a bottle of whisky as companion. Last night, gleeful monks had urged him on. He'd thought of writing something sarcastic like, 'though I hardly know my mother because of her infrequent visits when I was a child, it seems only right that I celebrate her freedom to marry because my dear dad, who so many of you loved, is no more.' He stares gloomily at Dick, a cypher who rarely speaks, and yet has maintained a successful plug business and made a fortune out of it or so Mum says.

So far Dick has contributed little to the wedding bar the rings. Dick has brought with him only his business partner as best man and an aunt and a cousin who barely seem to know him.

Lou from The Pipe Barrel tattoos a rhythm on his tabor to hush the assembled company.

His mother smiles at Nick, expecting something fluent. He can't ruin her wedding for her. After all, Dad hurt her, and isn't it right that she should find some happiness now? His speech with its harsh witticisms and loaded phrases is too unkind. He crumples it in his pocket, cursing the spirit of Priory Farm which had urged him on.

'Well,' he begins, lost, 'let's be honest,' – Marilyn tenses beside him – 'it's unusual for a son to take the place of his grandfather in giving his mother away.' What a complex mix of family generations he's brought in! And does it even make sense? 'But I am sure my grandfather would have liked to see his daughter take a second chance of happiness after her difficult separation from my father.' It seems wrong to deny Richard's part in the story.

Tom is nodding and smiling. As a twice divorced man, he approves of Marilyn's second chance.

'But I'm forgetting my duties,' Nick says, postponing more mention of Mum and Dick. 'I would like to thank the vicar, the choir, the bellringers, Captain Nev Pearson for his fine operatic solo (applause), The Pipe Barrel who will be entertaining us this afternoon and Matt and his staff here at The Compasses for the generous spread they've laid on.' There are enthusiastic cheers and whoops. 'Most of all, I want to thank all of you guests for making my mother's wedding such a celebratory …er…celebration. I hope it is everything she wished for.'

He wants to wrap up, but his audience expects more. Ed from The Pipe Barrel nods at him encouragingly and then at Dick, as if to say, 'go on'. So, he is expected to say something about

Dick. 'I don't know Dick very well, to be honest, but I look forward to getting to know him better, now our family relationship is a legal thing. So, here's a toast to my mother Marilyn and her new husband Dick. May they be happy together. Health and happiness to Marilyn and Dick!'

It has been such an effort, that he's almost relieved when Maisie runs into the garden just as the assembled guests are raising their glasses, 'To Marilyn and Dick'

'She's not supposed to be here,' Marilyn whispers to Nick.

'We need an ambulance up in the clearing,' Maisie gasps. She's muddy and sweating.

'Why? What is it?' Nick asks. 'Is it Georgie?' He doesn't know why he says that. More likely to be Sylvia and her angina. Maisie's bright eyes remind him of his father. Ridiculous. She's been running, that's all.

'He's dying,' Maisie shouts. 'Georgie says he's dying. She's thumping his chest to save him.'

'Who is it?' Colonel Camden says, taking charge.

'A man. He grabbed Georgie. Then Sylvia pushed him. And he collapsed.'

'Where are they?'

'Beside the wood pond,' Maisie says. 'Sylvia saved Georgie's life, but she thinks she's killed the man.' She adds as an afterthought. 'Mummy is crying.'

'I'll ring 999,' Matt says.

'Pearson, you and I need to get up there,' the Colonel says. 'And you'd better come too,' he says to the vicar. 'In case he needs the last rites. Someone fetch the stretcher from the village hall. An ambulance might not get through from Valence Lane.'

'I'll get the stretcher,' John Kemp offers.

'I'll run up the zigzag to help Sylvia,' his wife says.

'I'm so sorry Mum,' Nick says.

'I hope you didn't do this on purpose,' his mother hisses at Maisie.

'It's not my fault he's dying.' Maisie says vehemently and then starts to cry with the shock of it all.

'Go down to Miss Bewley's house,' Nick says. 'Stay with her, till your mum comes to get you. And,' he piles some sandwiches and cakes on a plate – 'take that with you. You must be hungry.'

'I don't see why that woman should eat my wedding food,' Marilyn says.

'It's for Maisie,' Nick says.

'It's a good idea,' says young Mrs Kemp, 'I always say food is good for a shock, and your sister must be hungry.'

Nick's head buzzes. He goes with John Kemp. 'Why did she call Maisie my sister?' he asks John, as they manhandle the stretcher out of the dusty cupboard and find the first aid kit.

'What the eye doesn't see, the heart doesn't grieve over,' John mutters.

# CHAPTER 20

Richard can't sleep. Even with the bed by the Rayburn, he tosses and turns and can't get warm. He doesn't like to call Nick. He knows his son is tired out and wants him to sleep this one night through. He takes the morphine pill the doctor gave him.

A strange happiness enters through lack of pain. All the past of Priory Farmhouse rises around him. Carrying Marilyn over the threshold in her wedding clothes, meeting Iris in the wood. And there's someone else he tries to picture but can't. His mother and father standing on the grassed over Cloisters, arguing on a sunny summer's day.

He'd tried to make Priory a happy place, hadn't he? Brought in music and friends. Cakes and ale. Wine, women and song. You could choose to live in a kind of hedonism instead of in the lonely beauty of the place, instead of with the ghosts.

He gets out of bed. Takes his heavy jumper from the chair and pulls it over his pyjama shirt, then pulls his trousers over his pyjama trousers. He's so much thinner now, the extra layers go on easily. He eases on his thick walking socks and pushes his feet into his work boots, his arms into the sleeves of his winter coat. He even remembers his cap and his driving gloves. It's cold out there. That's what everyone is saying. Even the stream has iced over.

He tries to remember who it is he wants to see. But it isn't a person. It is Hartisborne itself. To see the village one more time before he goes. One last look at his birthplace.

He shuts the kitchen door quietly. He climbs into the Land Rover.

Richard pulls out the choke, tries two or three times. He half expects Nick to wake and run out to stop him, but Nick sleeps through the noise. Perhaps he'll need the crank handle to get her going, but suddenly the Land Rover starts, and Richard – good to have his hands on the wheel again – glides over the ice and out of the farmyard. He roars up the hill in first gear and then turns into Honey Lane.

If he skids, if he dies, it doesn't really matter. He'll be dead soon anyway. With this thought and the morphine making him happy and reckless, he careers down the winding lane, almost bouncing off the deep hedgerows solidified by snow. In the village, he switches off the car lights. If anyone sees him, they'll hurry him back to his sickbed.

As it happens, no one is around. He slows down before he reaches Joan and Maisie's cottage. There's plenty of wood stacked by the front door, cut to fit their fire basket. He'd asked Nick to drive it over a few weeks ago. He pauses by the house but it's slippery, so he glides on down Gracious Street and manages to reverse in the Ewell's icy gateway. Up the hill again with the engine on and then back through the straggling high street, where he cuts the engine so no one will notice him. The soft slope of the street, the ice, the snow, let him glide through his birthplace like magic.

He looks up at the moon as he passes the post office. A strange watery halo that he may never see again. Then there's a thump near the post box. A deer no doubt, though there were no lights to dazzle a deer. He glides on, not strong enough to investigate or risk the cold. The handbrake has iced up and he can't use it. It was only a deer, he tells himself, or perhaps a badger. At the turning to Honey Lane, he starts the engine again. He steers gently, delicately, back down the lane to Priory, taking the deep curves more slowly. He pulls up in the farmyard and switches off the ignition.

In bed later, he re-visits the lovely drive, a last freedom, the church, the sycamore tree, the sleeping cottages, Wakeling House – all under snow - and his secret daughter asleep. And no one saw him, though he wishes Maisie had seen him, imagines her opening her curtains and thinking, 'That's my dad, come to check on me in the cold.'

The thump disturbs him a little. The deer will have died or limped off, He gets back into bed with his clothes over his pyjamas, something Nick will wonder about in the morning, but Richard is tired now, hallucinating monks – must be the morphine - and the faces of his own father and some old Luckin staring down at him.

He'll phone the pub and ask Joan to bring Maisie to visit him. Marilyn isn't here to disapprove. I'm grateful for a few things, he remarks to his ghostly ancestor. For my children, both a credit to me. For Iris. Even for Marilyn. And that Maisie is doing well at school despite everything.

The morphine takes him to the harvest field long ago when he sat on the back of the harvester and the square of wheat grew smaller and smaller, and rabbits, rats and mice ran out looking for cover. Then he was a giant, up on his high seat looking down. Now he is a mouse running between corn stems, sharp on his skin. He marvels at a poppy up-close, glowing with the sunlight shining through. The past comes for him now in glimpses. Sandwiches wrapped in waxed paper, made by his mother. All the women running out of the corn and over the new stubble to make a fuss of him.

Soon Nick will wake him with bacon, eggs and coffee and try to make him eat.

He falls into a sleep so deep that, at first, he

doesn't hear the telephone ring in the morning. Nick is talking somewhere, murmuring. He catches a few words.

'I don't think I'll tell Dad,' Nick is saying. 'He's suffering so much as it is. And I know he'd be devastated. He was always so fond of Winnie. He only has a few days left. He need never know.'

Richard returns to the drive through the freezing village, the cottages sleeping under the hazy moon. A last little adventure in Hartisborne, his beloved home, and the last time he'll ever leave the farm.

The deer, fox, badger whatever it was he hit goes out of his mind. He's shot enough of them in his time. No need to worry Nick or anyone else about it. A secret is always easier.

Outside, snow keeps falling, layering the Land Rover, covering its mud and stains with a new coat of white.

Colonel Camden has driven Georgie to the hospital. She would have preferred to go with Nick, but he had to salvage the wedding reception.

Georgie hurries down the cream-coloured corridors, breathing the smell of disinfectant.

This is the end of her little bit of independence. She will have to leave Hartisborne and nurse Trevor because there is no one else. She tries to think of kindnesses from him. Maybe a gruff pride in her secretarial qualifications? Maybe he'd cared when he'd prevented her going to Cornwall with the Nances? Maybe he was grateful for the way she'd looked after Connie? But only his criticisms stay in her mind. It shouldn't matter, she tells herself. Everybody's life is worth something. Everyone's life exists in a stream of nature. She shouldn't justify his existence by looking for some virtue in it or by measuring his treatment of her. Maybe there were reasons, experiences, some strange inheritance that had made his behaviour harsh, a force beyond himself.

But her understanding isn't necessary in the end. Trevor dies soon after she arrives at his bed.

His last words surprise her. He's always wanted to take the rug from under her feet and now he has.

After identifying him, she collects his belongings from the admissions office. A packet of senior service containing four cigarettes and a half-smoked one, a lighter, some change, his train ticket from London, his return bus ticket to the station, a grubby handkerchief with a fancy embroidered T on it that not long ago she had boiled on the stove with his others, picking them out with wooden tongs to rinse in the bowl before pegging them on the line. There is an envelope with her name on it in Connie's handwriting and some loose change.

Colonel Camden is waiting for her in the entrance hall. 'It's always a shock, isn't it?' the Colonel says, 'when someone leaves the world.' He invites her to his cottage for a drink with his wife, but Georgie declines. 'Nick and the younger folk are having a party down at Priory Farm. And we mustn't blame them for letting their hair down. I saw it in the war – it's the natural corollary to death,' the colonel says. 'I don't suppose you feel like celebrating, but I could drive you there if you want to go to it. You might like the company.'

'No, it's ok,' Georgie says, 'I'll go back to the flat.'

The Colonel drops her on the Plestor. 'Just knock whenever you need us,' the Colonel says.

Once in the flat, Georgie sits alone staring out of the window. A big moon lingers behind the trees on the hanger and lights the village with its glow.

She pours herself a glass of water. She gathers up Trevor's change. She doesn't want to own anything of Trevor's, so she will use his cash to telephone Marco. She leaves the flat and walks to the phone box. All is quiet. The pub is closed. In London, Marco may have gone to bed.

Boldly, she telephones his house. The phone rings on but Marco doesn't answer. She will try the shop. He sometimes stays late, stock-taking or repairing books. She imagines him, alone among the shelves, perhaps down in the bindery, his fingers working under the lamplight.

The telephone rings in Bracco & March. Someone picks up the phone. It's a man's voice Georgie has never heard before.

'Is Marco there?' Georgie says. In her nervousness, she mimics Celia.

'It's Celia for you,' the man says.

'Hello?' Marco says.

'It's me, Georgie.'

'Rob said it was Celia. Did you get the book I sent you?' He sounds wary.

'I recognised your handwriting on the parcel. For a long time, I couldn't open it, but I finished it today.'

'People say Rachel Carson brings the naturalist's work into the twentieth century. Thought it would be right up your street. Are you alright?'

'My uncle died this evening.'

Georgie slumps against the phone box door, pouring in Trevor's change.

'I'm sorry. At least you're free now.'

'There must have been something in Trevor's history that I didn't know, that made him how he was. I wrote him off. That's what I feel sad about.'

'You need to take hold of your life, like you did when you took the job in Hartisborne.'

'I can't exactly be glad he's dead.'

'Celia says I always say the wrong thing.'

'You're happy with her, aren't you?'

'I never said I was unhappy with her.'

'That's true. You didn't ever say that.'

There's a silence.

'Anyway, I didn't stand much of a chance – what with you being so keen on the naturalist,' Marco jokes awkwardly.

'I'll always love him,' Georgie says, 'but now I've met someone real. And even though I was one of your floozies,' she says *floozies* in Celia's voice, 'I thought I should tell you.'

'I didn't not care about you.'

'No, you just didn't really care.'

'I hope your new bloke works out. I do miss you, you know.'

'I was just an interlude.'

'I wouldn't put it like that.'

Trevor's change runs out. 'Goodbye,' Georgie says as the phone cuts.

Georgie wanders through the moonlight to the turning which will lead her to Monksway and Priory Farm.

Gil came on night walks and never feared the dark. He would stand still in the wood watching the night creatures come out, mice, deer, voles. He would listen for the skitter of a shrew. Tonight, she sees a lumbering badger and two badger cubs playing at the entrance to their sett.

She tells herself she is not afraid of the dark, of the owl hooting, the shifting leaves, the deer lolloping on the wooded bank. She keeps walking on over the marl, fingering Trevor's envelope pushed into her pocket, unopened.

Here is the place where Gil hunted for swallows. Here is where his weeding woman stood in the stream poking the bank with a stick. In the white light, she sees a girl in a cloak walking. Whether it's her imagination or a ghost, she feels no fear.

*Effing fool.* Trevor's voice mutters but his voice is weaker.

When she reaches Priory Farm, the doors are open to the warm evening, the windows are lit. She can hear The Pipe Barrel playing in the long hall. Light spills on to the priory ruins rucking the surface of Cloister Mead. She opens the field gate and sits on a grassy wall.

Outside the kitchen door, Nick is putting empties in the crate. He plonks down the bottles hastily, comes over and hitches himself up to sit next to her.

Nick says. 'Are you alright? How was it at the hospital?'

'Trevor died just after I got there,' Georgie says.

'Actually, I knew that. Colonel Camden phoned me. He says you're in shock. I'm so sorry.'

'How is Sylvia?'

'She's worrying that she killed your uncle. I told her he must have had a condition already.'

'Yes, the doctor said his heart had been dodgy for some time. And he probably had lung cancer.'

'Can I tell Sylvia that?'

'Yes, of course. It would have happened

anyway. I'm touched she tried to protect me – it's what my aunt should have done and never did.'

'Apparently, he asked several people about a farm wedding, which is why he came to the church. I wonder why he was interested in Mum and Dick? Did he know Dick, do you think?'

'He wanted to give me this.' Georgie pulls the envelope from her pocket, guiltily sinking her lie to Trevor about marrying Nick. 'I can't bear to open it in case it's full of abuse. I don't want that to be the last thing between us.'

'Shall I read it for you? I'll get a torch, and I'll get you some food. Matt bought the leftovers from the reception.'

Nick dashes off. Priory Farm roars with music. Couples come out and dance on the lawn. Nick appears again with a glass of champagne and a plate of sandwiches, a torch tucked under his arm.

He hands Georgie the food and drink. 'Might be an idea to fortify yourself.'

Georgie drinks the whole glassful and eats a sandwich. *Effing drunken bitch*. She tears open the envelope. Nick holds the torch's beam over her hands as she draws out a certificate.

'What is it?' he asks.

Georgie unfolds it. 'Mother: Constance Edith Gardner, shop assistant, and Father: unknown,' she reads. 'It's my birth certificate. Connie was my mother. That's what he came to tell me.' So that was why she was an *effing little bastard*. 'My mother pretended to be my aunt.'

'But why tell you now?' Nick asks.

Perhaps because he thought I was about to be married and would need the birth certificate, Georgie thinks but can't say. 'Maybe it was a peace offering. So, it must have been Connie who took me to Cornwall and who gave me *The Natural History of Hartisborne,*' Georgie says. 'That's why she hid in the back alley when the Nances came to visit. They'd have realised she was my mother pretending to be my aunt.'

'Did you never want to go to Somerset House and find out about your parents?'

'I must have been too scared. I'll have to get used to the idea,' she says to Nick. She can't tell him yet about Trevor's last words to her. 'What about your mother? Did she manage to enjoy the rest of the reception?'

'The boys in The Pipe Barrel saved the day,' Nick says nodding towards the house. 'They got us all country dancing, made a fuss of Mum and got Dick drunk. Then Wilf drove them to Newhaven and put them on the ferry. You know Mum and Dick are moving in here after the honeymoon? This is the last party I'll have at Priory unless I have a leaving party.'

'So, you're really going?'

'Yes. I rang the department in Rome. They were sympathetic about me staying to care for Dad. They're giving me another chance.'

'But can you ever leave Hartisborne? Even

Marilyn has come back.'

'Well, it is the parish of everyman's soul, so we carry it within us – all the arguments, rivalries, vanities, stories, seeds, nests, bees, histories, births, deaths. We can't ever leave it entirely.'

'I've just read *Silent Spring*. I know what I want to do now. I'm going to retrain as an ecologist. I'll learn about nature properly. Sounds mad but I feel as if that's what my love for Gil was leading to all along.' And Trevor's revelation, even if it's true, can't sweep that away.

'If you need a holiday, you could come to Rome?'

# CHAPTER 21

In the end, Colonel Camden writes to Viscount Butter vouching for David's professionalism as a researcher. Active research - talking to people and handling real situations - has never been David's forte, and the Colonel's unnecessary endorsement boosts his confidence.

Now David sways beside Nick in the Land Rover through an avenue of trees rising darkly from bleached grass along the drive. They advance towards a small mansion, Butterfield House, growing larger in David's sight and mind.

Miss Butter grew up here and died here. In old age, she became a pesky dependent relative. As a child, she rode a donkey through this meadow and wrote her first secret journal behind a haystack. Whatever foreign place she lodged in, she pined for this English scene but never stayed long when she returned. Her relatives mocked her for visiting a harem and called her the 'sultana'. No wonder she preferred broad-minded Gil.

Losing control of the farm has made Nick a little aimless. Why not have a day out with David instead of cutting the hay? Though, as they arrive at the Butters' estate, the hayfield hangs heavily on his conscience. He must not abandon the farm in a poor state. He is leaving for Rome soon, excited to go but sad too.

Last week, he and Claire walked the hanger to talk about their breakup. Claire despises him for his lack of honesty. Claire noticed the way he was around Georgie. 'You could have told me sooner,' she said. She says it's not his business to protect her or anyone else from emotions or to make Maisie feel special, or pander to his mother's every whim. Hartisborne lay below them, listening, witnessing, hearing their words float down, an audience to Nick's guilt and weaknesses, making him glad to be away today.

Various people in odd clothing and flowers in their hair rise out of the grass and watch them arrive. Nick is aware of his shirt, tie and short back and sides, his callused farmer's hands and methodical brain.

Alexander Butter, known as Sandy, waves at them and comes over. He wears a silky purple shirt open to the waist. His feet are bare, his hair is beyond his collar, his eyes are dilated.

Sandy offers them both a joint. Nick shakes his head. David takes a puff.

'I can't stay for long,' Nick says.

Sandy invites them in. Nick says he'll stay in the garden. 'Stuffed shirt,' Sandy mutters as he guides David away, leaving Nick to examine some broken glass houses.

After a while David finds him again. 'Sandy says he'll give me a lift to the station later, if you want to go home.'

'Are you alright?' Nick asks. 'You look a bit wobbly.'

'Just need more time to find what I want.'

'Are you quite sure?' Nick asks again.

'Sandy's sorting me out. It's a marvellous house, much larger than Wakeling House. I've got the run of the library and of the boxes stored in the loft. I'll need a few days here. Can you ask Georgie to take over for a while? And explain to Colonel Camden?'

'Well, I should really be cutting Combe Meadow,' Nick says. 'I would've done it by now if it hadn't been for the wedding.'

David is relieved when Nick drives off. The Land Rover, the dusty gates, the ominous trees strike David as very funny, as he stands giggling beside the cracked dried-up fountain.

Gil has never mentioned a visit to the Butter mansion, but David is sure that he'll find a billet-doux, an avowal or a diary entry, proving Miss Butter is the shape of Gil's longing.

Sandy loves David's theory. 'Hey, we could make a film about them. You've given me an idea for the title – *The Shape of their Longing*. I need some bread to run this place if I'm gonna keep it. Death duties and so on. I may even have to work.'

'Actually, I'm hungry,' David says, thinking of bread.

David watches the Land Rover out of sight, as do the meadow people before they flop into the long grass again. Then, David staggers into the kitchen to tear up someone else's loaf and eat it greedily, while his head spins with visions of Miss Butter.

'May I visit every room?' David asks Sandy.

Sandy shrugs his assent and rolls another joint. 'Give us a shout if you find anything.' He wanders off, already losing interest in the detail. The sun catches his shirt's purple as he stands in the garden doorway, surveying his property, blissfully ignorant of how the Butters gained their wealth but with an urge to hang on to it growing in his fuddled brain.

David grabs the rest of the loaf and hurries upstairs. He flings open doors, chests, cupboards, takes books from shelves and shakes them out. It's just a question of persevering. No one, not Francis nor Georgie, with their unfortunate scepticism towards his beloved Miss Butter, will stop him now. He has found his life's work.

Nick drives on uneasily. Is it wrong to leave David with Sandy Butter and that bunch of poseurs? He looks in his rear mirror. There's no sign of David anymore. The house and grounds have sucked him in.

Claire says he tries to protect people too much. His father, his mother, her, Joan, Maisie, Iris, and even David. He needs to let go.

Living in Italy should help, Nick thinks, pain washing over him at the prospect of leaving Hartisborne and Georgie. But there's also a pleasurable anticipation of the offices in Rome, new colleagues and helping the world to eat, to prosper, real work, nothing fanciful and pointless like inventing stories about long dead Miss Butter, and much better than staying at the farm, resenting Dick and listening to the murmuring monks. He accelerates, foot on the pedal, speeding towards the future.


On the train, Georgina murmurs in her sleep and reaches out her small pudgy hand for her mother. Georgina is too young to travel to Cornwall alone like the other children. Once she is settled, her mother picks up the book an old man has left on the seat. He got off at St Erth and must have forgotten it. The words look dull, but there is a wedding photograph slipped inside which interests her. If things had been different, if George hadn't been married with two children already, if he had not signed up again, she could be in a wedding photo like this with a spray of asparagus fern and roses, and she would still be part of her family who had disowned her since Georgina's birth.

Her mother fingers the torn pages. George had told her about a friend whose life was saved when a book in his pocket stopped a bullet. Now, dozing and dreaming on the hot train, Connie casts George as the owner of a bullet-torn book which saved his life in the trenches. She creates a memory so real that she eventually forgets it is fiction.

Connie intends to take this book, *The Natural History of Hartisborne*, to the lost property office. But when they alight at Penzance, they are hurried away with the evacuee children to a Methodist Hall near the sea, where the Nances take an interest in Georgie and invite them both to the farm.

It's only later after the awkward dinner where Connie couldn't think what to say or how to explain Georgie's father, that she finds the book in her bag.

From the open door across the landing, she hears Georgie murmuring. Absently, she takes the book with her across the upstairs passageway and into Georgie's room. Her little girl is asleep under a flowery eiderdown. Connie puts down the book on the bed and sits beside her daughter. 'I'll send for you when Daddy comes back. One day, when I'm fixed up, we'll be together again,' she whispers.

She hears Mr Nance, Tristram as he's asked her to call him, moving along the passageway. She hears his wife, Julia, laughing about something. She doesn't want them to think she is soft, so she tiptoes back to her room, forgetting to pick up *The Natural History of Hartisborne*. She'll catch the early bus to Penzance. Tomorrow night she'll be in London, waiting for bombs to fall. And Georgie will be safe here.

On the train, she remembers the book the old gentleman left on the seat. Ah well, he couldn't have really cared about it, as he left it behind.

Later, when she realises Georgie has assumed a family relationship with the people in the photograph, she doesn't have the heart to disabuse her. Children need a comfort object, don't they? No proper mother would take that away. Besides the book has made Georgie a good reader.

Trevor was always threatening to tell Georgie the truth. But for once, Connie prevailed. It was the only thing she was strong about, but at least it was something.

And then, at the hospital, Trevor did tell Georgie the truth, gasping out the words. 'That effing book you was so keen on – your mother found it on an effing train. It had nothing to do with you or Connie.'

Yet her love for the book and Gil was a real thing, guiding her life.

# CHAPTER 22

If Gil rotates anticlockwise in the pipe barrel, time unwinds, and he is back in his childhood. If he rotates clockwise, he swings towards the future. As Hartisborne spins round, he wonders whether he can wind time forward beyond his century to when men will fly, atoms will give up their secrets and the tiny dragons seen in moss through a microscope will rehydrate, grow big again and walk the earth. He does not believe in magic. He is rational. But consider the breaking of an egg, the emergence of a bud. Nature is a kind of magic, shape-shifting caterpillars into butterflies. He lowers the stick to the earth, slows the barrel and gets out.

He walks across the meadow and climbs up over the ha-ha. He can see the gardener's cottage and hear Mary's baby crying. He can see the many beehives Mary's husband has placed in a row near the vines.

Sam Carpenter is heaving a bucket of water from the well. Gil must leave them alone and let their family grow here in his garden. When the baby was born, Sam came back from the community where Mrs John Daisy had sent him, the place where they teach the deaf to speak with their hands. Sam can make his thoughts known now that Mary, Betty and Mrs John Daisy are all learning to sign too.

And Gil has no doubt Sam is the true father. When he writes up his observations of nature for his book, he lifts scenes from the storehouse of his perceptions and holds them up to the light to observe anew. And now he remembers the times when he's seen Sam with Mary. Sam and Mary wandering in Park Meadow. Mary shouting at bees through Sam's ear trumpet to discover whether they could hear. Mary sowing pollen-rich flowers. Sam opening his shirt for the bees while Mary watched. Mary flinging open each of the seven gates and dancing through them to chase Sam round the barrel's mound. Mrs John Daisy's tears as her son set off north and Mary waving to him from the straggling street, not yet knowing she was with child.

Betty will return to Binford when Mary no longer needs help. Gil keeps away. His heart must change, become numb. He must learn to see Mary as Mrs Sam Carpenter, his weeding woman and nothing more.

Luckin tells him he knew all along Mary was his daughter and was trying to protect her. The horror of incest has receded, and Blundel's assumption has been soundly refuted, though

Blundel still slanders Sam and Mary's marriage as a put-up job, hiding something worse.

Cobwebs glisten among the salvias. 'A little bit of bread and cheese', the chaffinch sings. Or sometimes just 'cheese, cheese, cheese,' almost monotonously. The house martins swoop for gnats circling in the sunlight. Dianthus sends a clovy scent along the paths. Syringa and philadelphus perfume the walls.

Georgie, standing between the beds, allows herself to think of Trevor. She makes a rule not to let him into her mind when she is indoors. And if she does, she must go outside, walk it off. Indoors is not safe but outside she is protected by trees, by birds singing, myriad nests and the beds which the naturalist had once dug.

Here, she imagines Gil bending to his plants, taking the early morning air. A figure in an old shirt, unshaven, no wig on his head, early and private like her, planning the day, the sweet day and what is to be done with it.

Strengthened by the naturalist's presence, she allows herself ten minutes of Trevor. Who was he? Why was he like he was? She, who wants to be a naturalist, an ecologist, has hardly looked at the people in her life, preferring to live in a fantasy. She should have asked Trevor about his family, his habitat. How did he become so bitter and small-minded? What happened to him? At the funeral, Mr Palliser had managed to summon a few words of praise. Trevor was always punctual, kept note of the stock accurately and had worked at Palliser's since the war. He liked a joke with the other men and had been badly affected by the death of his dear wife, Connie. That was all any of them knew.

Tom came to the funeral, so did Rosemary, Cathy, Trevor's neighbour Bill, and Nick. Colonel Camden came with Nev Pearson. They had tried to save Trevor and felt they owed him this respect. Nev offered to sing a solo, and she'd agreed. She didn't know what Trevor would like. 'Something manly and conventional', she suggested to Nev when he asked her. He sang 'To be a pilgrim' which didn't seem quite right for Trevor but was a favourite of Winston Churchill's and honoured a certain perseverance. Two of the ogling warehousemen from Pallisers attended and wouldn't meet her eye. Trevor must have told them she was marrying a farmer. They offered their condolences to Nick, assuming he was her fiancé, and avoided her.

Tired of Trevor, she sits on the seat under the clematis massed on the wall. A buff-tailed bumblebee buzzes among the stamens of the purple flowers.

The seat under the wall has always been a favourite place of Gil's, a warm place of comfort, of small natural miracles. A spider throws out a gossamer thread and walks on air between one bed and another. The buff-tailed bumble bees gather nectar in the clematis.

It is a sweet day, but his thoughts are not sweet, despite his interest in insects. He wonders what do to about the osculatory upstairs in his study? What if the bishop discovers he hasn't returned it to the church? And should he have responded to Miss Butter's undoubted advances? Should he indulge in some happiness of the flesh before it is too late? He would like to talk to a woman about his fancies, his love even, but his sisters would worry and disapprove. And he is now wary of confiding in his hypochondriac friend.

His sister-in-law has often been his confidante, but she is far away in Gibraltar and writes only of swallows. How can he conjure a woman who will understand and not judge? Not advise? But share his interests?

Miss Butter would cast no stone but then he would be in her debt. She would know him too well, throw him significant looks when Mary's name was mentioned. To be alone with the secret of his love is his fate, he decides, throwing a shell-less snail over the garden wall, then worrying about the whirling pain he may have caused the snail or whether its sticky mass hit a passer-by. It is so early still. Who will be abroad? Many folk. Labourers, woodsmen and farm women hurrying to their tasks. Last year in the early mornings he had anticipated Mary's arrival, planning her workday. His heart still leaps when he sees her.

*Betty, oh Betty, oh Betty my love.* The line of his young poem floats into Gil's mind as if the ghost of his fifteen-year-old self still walks between the flower beds of the six quarters.

There's a shadow on the bench beside him. The clematis casts a pattern of shade that almost resembles the shape of a woman tossing her hair in the wind. 'Betty, oh Betty, oh Betty, my love,' he says aloud and laughs at himself. The clematis' shadow stirs as if to touch him.

If she wanted to go back in time, it would be to see her unknown father and Connie, to find out what he loved about Connie before she changed, when Connie was still herself, how they met, what happened. But as she can't go back in time, she'll go where time is held. She'll go to nature, examine what grows, the cowslip seeds in their caskets ripening in the Ewell for next year. She'll go to the songbirds, the sticklebacks in the river, the swallows returning. The stream of nature exists and continues, despite humans, and existed and continued before Georgie was thought of, before Gil wrote his book.

Without *The Natural History of Hartisborne*, Georgie would have disappeared. The book still brings her pleasure, gives her strength, makes her look. Georgie is not proud of her longing. Even now, Marco might be a shadow between her and Nick, but the shadow is fading. She speaks her thoughts aloud quickly under her breath, telling her grief to the garden.

There is no one she can confide in about Marco or Nick. But without Marco, she wouldn't have known Tom, wouldn't have seen the advert in the parish magazine, wouldn't have escaped Trevor and come to live in Hartisborne. 'I am here where I always wanted to be,' she says aloud. 'And I must let go of Marco.'

And without Marco, she wouldn't have rethought her future. She wouldn't have read *Silent Spring* by Rachel Carson. So powerful, so ominous, so resonant. Maybe the consolations of nature would not continue, after all. And now she knows what she was born to do and why it is urgent.


'I am here where I've always wanted to be,' Gil says to the roses, wishing again there was a woman to talk with. 'I must let go of Mary.' He rouses himself. He'll shave, wash and then eat breakfast with Thomas. Afterwards, he'll check on the house martins nesting in the tower. He will pay Ollie Knight to pick off the shell-less snails and take them into the Ewell for the birds and hedgehogs to eat. Let nature deal with nature. He will send some cheeses and ale to the gardener's cottage for Mary, Sam and their baby girl. Maybe he will write to his bishop about the little finger bone of St John the Baptist and tell the whole unlikely tale. Or maybe he will hide the osculatory under the new floorboards that John Carpenter's man is laying in the little parlour. A holy relic of his love, carrying his kiss and Mary's kiss and the faith of centuries. It is a sweet day. He repeats this to himself, until he believes it.

A mottled stone lumbers from under the laurel hedge. Timothy the tortoise has roused himself and comes towards him eager for food. 'Hello, old friend,' Gil says, offering the tortoise a leaf from a bolting lettuce. Then he sits on the damp grass, unfolding leaf after leaf, and tells Timothy everything. Betty, Jinnie, Mary. Afterwards, his confessor obligingly retreats into his shell, taking Gil's secrets with him.


Georgie strokes the tortoise's shell, but Timothy won't move her head from its shelter. She has heard too much of humans now and is wary. Besides they misunderstand her, misinterpret her search for a mate, her seasonal longing to lay eggs. They mistake her sex and misread her movements. They watch her not knowing that she watches them and has a long, long memory. They live such short lives in such confusion. And long ago, one of them stole her from her habitat, bundled her on a ship to be sold by first this one and then another, until she arrived here, a grassy, lettuce-laden place but lonely without a mate.

Gil stretches out his hand and strokes Timothy's shell. It is warm and dry and ridged. Momentarily, he senses the touch of another hand.

Georgie starts away. A charge. Like touching Marco. That first time. She stares around her. There are rose petals on the grass but no roses nearby. A torn lupin leaf. A sprig of purple loosestrife. 'Who's been cutting flowers?' she asks Timothy.

The tortoise stays in her shell.

Such longing in the air. Such curiosity. Such sadness. Gil thinks of the eyes of the woman who was picking campions in the rain. He looks back beyond the tortoise. Surely that's her? Lifting a sprig of loosestrife? The hanger is singing. The last choruses of mating, territories and lovers' rivalries before August's quietness. Birdsong distracts him. When he looks again, the woman has gone.

'Worms busy?' Thomas asks, as Gil carries the flowers into the kitchen and piles them on the table.

'The birds were busy,' Gil replies. He mimics with his hand the small dips of the bluetit, the bigger curves of the yaffle's flight, the loops of the robin, the arrowed flight of the swallow.

'Bluetits, yaffle, robin, swallow?' Thomas asks.

Gil nods.

They eat their porridge and drink their ale. They have lived together long and barely need to explain themselves.

Afterwards Gil goes to his study and jots down a note about the shape in the garden, that sense of a visitation. He envisages the woman with the heavy hair, the way she looked closely at the golden wren. He will think of her when he's slow at writing, when his lonely life feels meaningless, or when he can't draw the words from his head. The ancients had their muses. All he needs is a reader who will look attentively at nature because of his words. One day she will open his book. He knows she is a phantasy. Nevertheless, he holds out his hand to her, and it seems to him that she takes it.

Georgie is in charge of the museum while David stays away on his wild goose chase. She loves Wakeling House but she knows she must make a plan for the future too. She rolls a sheet into the typewriter and begins to type. She will take science A Levels at evening classes. In three years, she could be at university studying ecology, botany or zoology. And if there are airmail letters to Rome and visits to Nick, that will be exciting. She has opened an interest-bearing post office account, her travel fund.

After typing her application, she paces round the little parlour, thinking through her plans. She trips on the parquet block which has risen once more. Even John Kemp couldn't fix it. She kneels down and pulls at the block. It comes right out. She puts her hand in the hole and feels the broken end of old timbers, the floor beneath the floor. Her fingers touch a tiny box. She wiggles it out, dusts it off with her skirt. Wooden sides and a glass front. And what looks like a small bone jiggling inside, when she shakes it. She knows what it is. She can't wait to show David, if only he would hurry back. He can write a fascinating article about finding the osculatory, recorded as missing in *The Antiquities of Hartisborne* which Gil translated from Latin. Yet it was here all along and not at Priory at all.

In the morning, Nev will be singing as he walks round Wakeling House, half-mending things and then abandoning them. He has found his voice again. Colonel Camden has confided in her the story of the bomb that killed Nev's choir in Tunisia. Nev is writing a requiem for them. She is authorised to employ John Kemp to maintain Wakeling house, while turning a blind eye to Nev's activities. People sometimes need a respite, the Colonel said, and Wakeling House is Nev's respite. It has been mine too, Georgie told him.

Georgie sits down at Gil's desk, where the osculatory now lives next to Gil's ink bottle and begins a letter. 'Dear Tristram and Morwenna, it has been a long time, but I have never forgotten you.' The ink flows freely. She reads the letter aloud in her own voice, before she signs it, 'your grateful friend, Georgie'. She slips it into an envelope. As she walks down the straggling street to post her letter, she passes the butcher who waves at her with his hook.

She walks into the churchyard. Someone has left a wreath of dog roses on Gil's grave and a many-sided flint. A woman and her child are walking away towards Church Meadow, having made their offering. Sparrows chatter over the stream.

After he has lodged the osculatory under the new floorboards and returned gladly, guiltily to the garden, Gil watches the hot air balloon floating low past the hanger and then rising up, becoming smaller and smaller, and travelling away. A man in the sky is as miraculous as a relic of human love. Goody Newton, Betty Hambrook, Farmer Luckin, Sam Carpenter, Mary Carpenter, even Jonah Blundel, can't take their eyes off the floating basket and the shots of gassy fire. Mary's children dance in the grass of the Ewell, excited and amazed.

What the swallows thought of the balloon and how this new form of flight affected their migration is not recorded.

So much to know, Georgie thinks. All assumptions must be questioned. So much to know if you look closely and curiously. If you keep walking down Church Meadow and through the Lythes and through the Candovers, or go the other way, over the hanger to the South Downs, you find paths that go on and on beyond Hartisborne. You find ports, harbours, boats and a wider world.

Maybe the swallows, swifts and house martins who take their own instinctive routes, wonder at our planes and buses, the lights that crowd out stars and confuse their journeys and their love, while we speed on, and only at the last, turn to look at other creatures and all the world that sustains them, discovering their lives and imperfectly glimpsing our own before they are gone.

# ACKNOWLEDGEMENTS

I am grateful to the British Library where I read numerous accounts of eighteenth-century settlement and bastardy cases and of parish law in action. Thanks to the late great Peter Scupham, who airily said, 'Have whatever you like from this bookshelf,' and therefore introduced me to *The Diary of a Village Shopkeeper 1754-1765* by Thomas Turner. And thank you Thomas Turner for your diligent recordings of daily life and the responsibilities of parish officers and villagers.

Thanks to many authors whose work I read including *Frostquake* by Juliet Nicholson, *Gilbert White, A Biography* by Richard Mabey, *When the Children Came Home* by Julie Summers. I intend to post my full bibliography and write about my research on Substack for anyone interested in the work behind this novel.

The greatest of thanks and respect to Gilbert White, father of ecology, naturalist, curate and author of *The Natural History of Selborne*. I have purloined and fictionalised moments from his life, journals and letters, for which I apologise. My Gil, of course, is not Gilbert White.

He employed a weeding-woman but certainly wasn't in love with her.

Hartisborne is not Selborne, but a fictitious place floating in time. However, if I hadn't, like White, been born in and grown up in Selborne, I never would have written this book or had the privilege of reading such evocative nature writing at such an early age. Without White, I may never have become a writer or been so absorbed in notebooks and journals – for he demonstrates the power of regular writing, of observation and of imagism.

Thank you to my parents, sister and my primary school friends. We were lucky enough to 'play out' in nature, a privilege few children now experience. I freely admit I have played fast and loose with the geography and place names of Selborne to create Hartisborne. Therefore, some field, lane and house names draw on their real models; others are invented or have been moved around.

I am immensely grateful to readers of early and later drafts: Vicki Feaver, Ben Mollett, Francesca Mollett, Stephen Mollett, Jane Rusbridge, Chloe Salaman, Jayne Sandys-Renton, Anna South, Margaret Steward, Gill Thompson and Juliet West. Thank you too to Bloodaxe Books, The Spring Poets and South Downs Poetry Festival for the essential companionship of poetry.

Thank you to the Royal Literary Fund for offering me work which has supported my writing. Thank you to former colleagues, friends and students at the University of Chichester for the creative atmosphere we shared.

Thanks to Giorgia Chiarion for the lovely cover design.

A special final thank-you to Jane and Gill for your generous wisdom and diligence in reading work-in-progress, and a loving thank-you to Stephen for a great deal of patience and for our writing lives, lived together.

# ABOUT THE AUTHOR

## Stephanie Norgate

Stephanie Norgate's plays have been broadcast on BBC Radio 4. Her three collections of poetry from Bloodaxe Books are: Hidden River (shortlisted for the Felix Dennis First Collection and Jerwood Aldeburgh awards), The Blue Den and The Conversation. She co-edited a book of essays, entitled Poetry and Voice (CSP). For many years, she taught on and ran the MA in Creative Writing at the University of Chichester, where she was Reader in Creative Writing. She has worked as a Royal Literary Fund Fellow at Southampton University and for the RLF's Bridge programme. She lives in West Sussex with her writer husband and has two adult children. Hartisborne is her first published novel.

Printed in Great Britain
by Amazon